THE MINORITY RULE

INTO
THE
FOG

BOOKS IN ORDER OF TRILOGY:

THE MINORITY RULE

THE MINORITY RULE:
BEYOND THE FENCE

THE MINORITY RULE:
INTO THE FOG

THE MINORITY RULE

INTO THE FOG

ALEXIA MUELLE-RUSHBROOK

First paperback edition 2023

Book design by Richellb

ISBNs:
Paperback: 978-1-7392662-2-6
ebook: 978-1-7392662-3-3

www.alexiamuellerushbrook.co.uk

For Sergio, my lighthouse in the fog

ONE

I have heard it said that it is always darkest before the dawn. But surely that is assuming tomorrow is going to be a bright day. What if the day is overcast with a fog that will not lift? A fog so dense you cannot see your way, and before you know it, you've been dragged into the dark of another night? Do you hope the sun breaks through tomorrow? Maybe you'll have mist, not fog – it's slightly clearer, marginally more optimistic, but ultimately, you're still walking with blurred vision. What does it take to see the next clear dawn? I'll tell you if I ever find out. Don't hold your breath though, for the fog has swallowed me and I have absolutely lost my way.

I have spent my life, or certainly the latter years of it, sure that there was more to life – more I could do with it, and for it. It turns out, in part at least, I was right.

The Powers That Be have more knowledge and power than imagined – more than even they imagine, as their head is unknown to even some of them. The Real Revolution hides and shines in equal measure. They are the iceberg dead ahead, yet you only see the tip: deep below those waters is a network, a root of life inconceivable to the average citizen.

And now I know?

I have but one choice. They call it two, but who, in their right mind, chooses imprisonment over knowledge? Imprisonment *for* knowledge? Not me, that is for sure.

1

My zest for knowledge has left me at the feet of my great grandmother, of Gee-Gee, whom I revered above all other family members, who I now see is the greatest deceiver of all. Her cause may be noble, but oh my, the means are hard to take!

Follow or die. Follow or be a chained breeding specimen. Follow and guard the Earth. Serve the Earth and be the Guardian. Be the Guardian, find your purpose – the purpose that I longed to find and now fear to be…but also fear to ignore.

So here I go, into the fog. Hopefully someone will hold my hand until I reach the light.

* * *

The sun is actually rising as I walk towards Aunt Dora's house, but it will take more than that to lighten my way today. I walk when I should run, but despite having three people whom I love waiting for me, I am in no hurry to arrive because that means talking. It means explaining all I have just learnt, as well as telling my husband his mother is dead – and why.

Gee-Gee instructed my Solarbug to drop me off along the river, the place I spend so much spare time, and which is normally a place of comfort and solace – but not today. Today, the water cannot flow fast enough to wash away or clear my thoughts.

Gee-Gee's parting instruction replays in my mind again: "Jog to Dora's, just like a normal day. You're out for exercise, enjoying the fresh morning air before breakfast. Once there you can talk, but you'll soon have a visitor. Follow their lead – it will not be hard."

"Who will it be?" I asked.

"You'll see."

With that she turned away. No further sentiment of remorse, no look of apology or attempt to hug or caress. She has confessed, I chose the path she wanted, now the new order begins.

The Director has spoken and I *will* do as I am told.

Despite my slow pace, I reach Aunt Dora's bungalow sooner than I want to. Her quiet little home sits on the edge of SubHub District 1 and coming from the nearby river at this time of day, I have seen precious few people. The majority of those I have seen are headed towards the Central Hub to work, not backwards out to SubHub Districts 2 or 3. A couple wave across the river as they survey the orchards. I don't know them, I've just seen them enough times to be on waving terms, friends by familiarity, not actual knowledge. Now they are witnesses to me being here, where I should be. Just as Gee-Gee planned.

"Maia! At last!" exclaims Aunt Dora as I scan the barcode on my left arm on the security scanner and open her front door. She must have been sitting in wait for me because the door has barely slid open when she pulls me inside.

She wraps me in her arms, simultaneously slipping my signal blocking bracelet onto my right wrist next to my watch – we all know the following conversation is not something we want heard by government algorithms.

I don't try to release myself – I badly need a hug after last night, but any comfort I feel is undone as I look over

Aunt Dora's shoulder and see Max waiting for me. He steps forward as I am released, snatching me into another hug and for a second, I want to recoil from him as guilt hits me like a wave, but instead I sink into his arms, hiding my face in his chest. He asks if I am okay, but I just hold him a little tighter in reply and shake my head.

"Hmmphh, are you comin' in here? You ain't gonna make an old woman come to you, surely?" calls Eve from the living room. She may be the oldest person in the Hub and suffering from dementia, yet when she calls, you can never ignore her. Despite the weight upon my shoulders, I cannot help chuckling at Eve's eternally forthright tone.

I follow the voice, gently guided by Max, who has taken my left hand and doesn't seem to want to let it go. I hope that remains the case when he hears all – otherwise our tender marriage could be about to hit a major wall. I can feel everyone's gaze, but no one speaks. I prepared and practiced what I would say on the way home, but now no words come. I stare at the cats, Smoggy and Squash, as they sit either side of Eve and envy their innocence – or rather, their lack of interest in the actions of society beyond their immediate needs.

"For someone who spent weeks telling me silence isn't golden, you are being annoyingly quiet now, Missy." Eve grins as she speaks, but as she pauses, she drops the hint of amusement and her face looks like stone: "You understand the darkness, don't you?"

"I do," I sigh. "For better or worse…I do." I am, as yet, undecided which I think it is.

"You found the AIP?" whispers Aunt Dora. "You found the Artificial Insemination Programme – did you find Lilith?"

"Yes and no." I shake my head. "I found the tramline underground, I took it as you directed, Eve. I found the headquarters of…well, let's say the AIP for a moment, but it is much, much more than that – the surface of which I have only scratched. I did not see or locate Lilith, I'm sorry, Eve, I know that is why you sent me…" I pause, waiting for Eve to react, but she doesn't. It is as though she is not in the least bit surprised and it suddenly dawns on me: "You weren't expecting me to find her, were you?"

"Maia? What do you mean?" asks Aunt Dora, confused. "Of course, we were – that was the whole point of your mission." She silently appeals to Eve for backup, but receives no reply.

"*You* were, *Eve* wasn't… Were you?" I turn from my aunt to Eve, hoping against all hope she isn't about to either lapse into one of her uncontrollable, unreachable fogs or clam up deliberately. Either would be incredibly frustrating at the moment.

"No," Eve whispers, staring down at Squash, stroking his vibrant ginger fur with a very shaky hand.

I feel Max's grip increase on my hand and I glance at him. He looks confused, but resolved. He wants answers and, being patient, he is going to wait until he gets them.

"What do you mean 'no'?" retorts Aunt Dora. "Eve, what have you done?"

"I started her on the path of enlightenment she asked for. I told you all you didn't really want to know…I told you if you are going to take them on, it has to be all or nothin'. That is not done in one go. It takes time…time to understand… then time to act." Eve pauses again and seems to be absolutely frozen, making me sigh in frustration. I was counting on her being lucid when I returned.

I want her to fill in the gaps, even if I don't know how to ask the questions. Her health has been declining so rapidly, I cannot begin to contemplate her not being able to finish what she has started. I am sure I cannot complete my mission without her – I do not even know what my mission *is* without her. I feel Max jump when she suddenly reanimates. I am so relieved I repress a smile, inappropriate as it may be.

"Hmmphh, you best tell me what happened then," Eve mutters as though she hadn't paused.

I start talking, letting my voice narrate the evening like it is reading the tale from a book. I feel myself shaking as I recall, but my tone stays steady.

I describe walking into the middle lift in the Central Hub Hospital, going down to a level I didn't know existed and exiting to a tramline that took me to a place beyond the entire Hub – a city I have lived in my whole life and never thought possible I would step outside of. I walked, unchallenged into a building – another hospital and laboratory – one I have grown up knowing only as the 'AIP.' The Artificial Insemination Programme. A research facility used in the battle against worldwide infertility – on the plus side, offering hope and help to couples who are unable to conceive naturally (even if it is regarded the lesser way to breed), and then on the negative side, it is a place of imprisonment for the fertile who disobey the law – a lifelong way to pay penance to society. I walked in there looking for information. For evidence of the place being 'more than.' What I found were rooms filled with SurrogacyPods, arranged like petals of flowers, all growing babies.

Some growing *my* babies.

I don't look at Max as I say this. I cannot. He knows I do not want children, and I know truthfully, he does. He knows I have spent six years avoiding the inevitable direction and dictation of the Powers That Be (PTB) to marry and be a mother. I am fertile – a rare, grade 3, prime Golden Goose. Spinsterhood and no family were never an option for me. I was always going to be matched and married and I will have to one day give birth, give up work, and be the housewife I have been prepared to be. I have 'donated' my eggs numerous times since I was eighteen and always wondered where those eggs went – how many were for research? How many went to lottery winning families? Would I ever see one?

Well, now I have seen six.

The image of my son, lying peacefully in his amniotic fluid in front of me will stay with me always. Beyond that, I cannot say how I feel about it. I simply do not know.

I move on with my story, telling Eve her phrase came in handy. "I have no idea how I remembered it, but it stopped the drone calling its alarm immediately."

Eve nods her head, the corners of her mouth pulling into the gentlest of a smile, but she does not answer. The nod is enough I suppose. She knew only too well that code would work, even if it made little sense to me at the time.

"'The road of real reckoning requires the revolution to reign'…you left that there, so you surely knew there was going to be a time when you wouldn't be on the same side of the Real Revolution?"

"Hmmphh, not exactly. I never designed anything without a second option…just seemed wise," Eve shrugs.

"What is the Real Revolution?" asks Max.

"The real government," I whisper.

"Of the AIP?"

"*Of everything.*" I pause, waiting to see if Max understands, he seems unsure, so I, unlike Eve, don't wait for him to ask again. "We have grown up thinking the PTB governs all the Hubs across the United New Earth. We have been well indoctrinated on how humanity epically failed and wars, nuclear wars, greed and gluttony polluted and destroyed Earth almost to the point of complete destruction – to the point that most people were killed, maimed, or left infertile and that the PTB united the embers, forming a global society focused on restoration of Earth and humankind." Pausing again, I observe my three companions, two of whom look afraid of what I might say next, the other is resigned – she already knows the truth. "Well, that is true, but what they fail to mention – largely because they do not all know – is that they are not the only *powers that be.* They are the frontmen, the ones that we, 'normal', dictated upon folk see and revere, but the true leaders are the R&R – the Real Revolution – the second *'they,'* you, Eve, were so reluctant to reveal. I doubly understand your reluctance now. I thought it was from a mixture of fear and respect for a cause, but it isn't just that. You are loyal because you are them…or were. I suppose I knew that to a degree at least, but you were not simply a part of the monster – *you founded it!*"

"What?" exclaims Aunt Dora. "You cannot be serious?!"

"You don't get to understand all I do without being involved. I told you…hmmphh, what does it matter?" Eve shakes her head and waves a hand. Suddenly, she cocks her head to one side looking at me. "No robot told you that, Missy… So, you were found?"

"As you intended."

"Hmmphh." I don't know why Eve is swearing – or at least her version of it. That sound is used in many ways, being neither true grunt nor word, just an expression of thought through a noise that I have never heard the like of from another human.

"So, you admit you wanted me to get caught?" I ask, holding Eve's gaze.

"Of course, she didn't – she gave you the code for the drone to get you out, right Eve?" Aunt Dora is almost pleading. I wish I thought it was that simple, but in the few months I have come to know, and indeed love, Eve Addams, I have also come to realise there is absolutely nothing simple about her.

"'Want' is the wrong word…but yes, I knew you'd learn more if you got caught," confesses Eve. "Did they find your button?"

"Yes, I think they destroyed it – or took it for testing first I suppose. I'm sorry—"

"Don't be, that was plan B anyway."

"Plan B was *not* getting caught??" spits Max. "Did you not think you should have mentioned that?"

"Of course not, she'd have been a nervous wreck," Eve retorts.

"I *was* a nervous wreck!" I still am.

"Exactly, and that was thinking you were just on a 'record and return' mission – best you knew a little, but trusted in my plan," Eve says without a hint of an apology.

"There is a key word there, Eve: *Trusted*. Maia trusted you—" Max sounds angry. I squeeze his hand and suck in my bottom lip, trying to calm myself down. My heart is racing, I don't think it has stopped racing since last night and I still haven't told him his mother is dead…

"I told you, more than once, I hoped Maia would go in and return intact…I included her continuing to have faith in me in that. I could have told you what you learnt without you seeing, but seeing *is* believing. A cowardly part of me didn't want to say it, I'll admit that, but it had to come from the Director – that is the only way you move forward. It *was* the Director that found you, wasn't it?" Eve narrows her eyes, staring through me. Her blue eyes are like piercing windows of knowledge that know and have seen so much – even now I understand but a fraction of her past. Do her actions need forgiveness? I am not sure it is for me to say.

"Yes, it was." I don't want to admit how badly I underestimated Gee-Gee. I thought she was just the Director of Fertility, which in itself is a role to be proud of. I have always been proud to be her great granddaughter…frustrated that she hasn't opened as many academic doors for me as I would like, but ultimately, she has always been my role model. The one whose footsteps I most want to walk in. Want or wanted? As always, the choice is not really mine. I am to become the next generation, just not quite like (or at all), how I thought.

"The Director of what?" asks Max.

"Fertility, as far as most know – but 'everything' is a better description, I think." Max's eyes boggle as I speak.

"Gee-Gee?" scoffs Aunt Dora. "You can't mean Gee-Gee? She has been the only voice of reason in our family – yourself excepted – no, I cannot—"

"Cannot or will not?" asks Eve. "Dora, think about it. She and George – why everyone old and outside your family called her Gee-Gee before they were ever great grandparents – George and Georgia Beaufort, husband and wife dream team of the future of agriculture and genetics. Tom and I may have led the engineering side, but we were far from alone… It was not just me who founded the R&R, there was a worldwide, select team who worked with hundreds of others, nay, thousands over the years, each playing a role, large and small – all essential in rebooting our dying population and world. It is no secret that the PTB rose when the world needed it most, you should be grateful they did. The R&R is just the necessary backbone to ensure the mission never fails. Even now, after what they did, how far they went…*too far*…I understand all that and don't consider my life wasted because you sit here today and others around live in peace."

"You sound like Gee-Gee," I say bitterly, suddenly questioning why I put myself in such danger if Eve is still going to defend the establishment. I wanted answers, I pushed for answers – but for what?

"Hmmphh, so I might, but they went too far, and she broke her promise to keep me family safe… I won't break mine to help you."

"Then do it – stop the riddles that you love so much and speak plainly. Why send me to be captured? You lost your button camera. Can you tap into what it recorded?"

"No, but I don't need it. Had you got out undetected, we could have shown the public the footage, but really, you were never going to capture enough to convince people of a second level of government or what goes on beyond the Hub fence. I needed to force Gee-Gee's hand into explaining everything to you herself, recruiting you herself. You'd be better protected that way and actually have a chance of finding my Lilith…" Eve's voice wobbles and tears flow as she pronounces her estranged great-great granddaughter's name. The innocent family member who fell in love with her infertile boyfriend and tried to marry him anyway. When I saw her outburst at the Matching Ceremony I thought of her as a cautionary tale and an enactment of what I wanted to do six years earlier with Theo. Thinking his name, I sigh, long and hard. I had been so happy to find closure when he returned, to find peace with our past, to be happy for his friendship – at work and socially – only to have his betrayal amplified when I understood all.

Max notices me deflate further and looks at me with concern. I promised that I would keep no secrets from him, that whatever we faced, it would be together. Our marriage may have been arranged, our families may be messed up, yet somehow, we found love anyway – proving the matching system works, the PTB might say. Maybe they are right, but it takes more than just science to make the magic of lasting love, and it is going to take a miracle to say what I need to.

I take a deep breath and say: "Theo is one of them… Gee-Gee recruited him to watch over Henry, your dad." I let that sink in a moment before continuing. "He has been monitoring my research in the lab, too, and altering results so I don't see the truth."

"What is the truth?" Max asks quietly, but his face has turned quite red.

"The R&R are actively testing epigenetics on the population – over the entire UNE."

"Epi-what?" asks Aunt Dora.

"They, like me and hundreds of other scientists, are studying varying effects on men and women's health, mapping what is continuing beyond decades-old nuclear radiation to cause infertility in humanity. The only difference is the R&R are deliberately causing, or rather, perpetuating infertility… testing different control substances in our food—"

"WHY?" exclaims Aunt Dora. "Why? When the population is decreasing so much, with so many infertile, why…just why?!"

"Because there are too many of us – or there were, and the Earth cannot cope with us. Earth needs to revive, nature needs to restore…for all of us to survive – and thrive."

Eve grunts softly. "You understand."

"We all understand that message, Eve," Aunt Dora chips in. "Every one of us has had that message imprinted on us from birth. I don't see what has changed in that…what justifies the deliberate poisoning of people…the denying our right to have children – *my* right to have children!" Aunt Dora holds her stomach. She is long past the age of bearing children now.

Although only forty-four, fit and healthy, no one has successfully given birth past thirty-three since the Fall of

What Was, and many hit menopause by the age of thirty. Grade 1 as she is, I honestly doubt she was ever really fertile anyway, but I hate seeing this window into her soul of regret. I suppose I knew she would have wanted children had fertility allowed – that, and if her first husband hadn't been a cheat, or second husband not died from radiation poisoning.

I have always thought of my aunt as a surrogate mother and have been eternally grateful for her. Mum is alive and well, but she's selfish and cold to put it mildly and understands me as little as I do her. She loves to boast of a large, fertile family regardless of any pain it might cause others and has made it plain she couldn't care less if I have aspirations beyond producing offspring. That is the goal, nothing else.

"Individual rights, self-importance, and greed beyond the greater good led to humanity's downfall, my dear," says Eve in a soft tone, although the words are anything but. "Hmmphh, I ain't no scientist, I left that to those who understood more – robotics, engineering, that's my field – but I know it ain't as simple as poison one, breed another. It is, or was, management and care thorough knowledge and progress."

"That is true from what I understand," I say, trying to soften the blow, "but it is beyond that. They are using golden eggs to pinpoint before birth who can breed. They want everyone's genetics and role mapped for decades ahead down to every detail, making a healthier, more sustainable, more predictable population."

"You sound fascinated," says Max disapprovingly.

"It is hard not to be," I admit. I am appalled by how far the R&R have gone – and plan to go with 'The Initiative' project – but at the same time, as a scientist, I'd be lying if I said I wasn't curious.

"So, you agree with what they are doing?" Max sounds uneasy.

"I don't know what to think."

"Have they truly recruited you?"

"In body, yes…but my choice was limited to be imprisoned in the AIP or join the cause. I didn't really see an option – my answer meant life, death, or imprisonment for you all, too. What was I supposed to do?" The tears I have been holding now flow. I can in part state what I have been told, reporting as matter-of-factly as I can, but when push comes to shove, how do I explain my choice was to hold my morals, deny the research and plan set before me, and be thrown into a life of egg donation and no freedom whatsoever – no husband, no family, no friends…no chance of seeking a better way – and subjecting my husband to the same fate elsewhere while my aunt and Eve would have been shot or poisoned for their part. Or I join the R&R.

I cannot beat them. I want knowledge. I hope to do better.

So, I join them.

I open my mouth to explain, but the security system rings out: "MARK JONES, HEAD OF SECURITY."

We all stare at each other. He has come too soon, my heart sinks: I haven't told all. I get up to answer the door, Aunt Dora grabs my right arm, removes my bracelet, collects all four and runs into her room to hide them in Eve's box. I nod once she is seated and walk to the door, sliding it open. My stomach knots as I look into Mark's eyes – my mind replaying the scene of death that played out only hours earlier, yet somehow feels like a lifetime ago. He rescued me: I know that. If it wasn't for him, I would be the one on the ground with blood trickling out of my head.

Mark stands with another officer, they greet me politely, but immediately look over my shoulder. I turn to see Max standing tall and handsome as ever behind me – his face is stern, his dark eyes almost speaking for him, anticipating bad news.

"Max Rivers?" Mark asks, although he obviously knows who Max is.

"Yes, how can I help you?" Max replies, putting a hand on my shoulder.

"I am sorry to have to inform you that your mother has passed away and your father is in the hospital," says Mark respectfully.

"What? I say before Max can reply. I feel his grip on my shoulder slacken and drop away. "What happened to Hen— *to them?*" I correct myself.

"I am afraid Mr and Mrs Rivers were the victims of a violent, jealous act of a colleague of mine. Peter Lloyd is a disgrace to the security services, and I am relieved to say has been eliminated. 'Though, sadly, not soon enough." Mark pauses. "We should perhaps continue this conversation inside. I will personally escort you to the hospital. Mr Rivers, your father is anxious to see you."

"Is–Is he okay?" stutters Max.

"He will be, he took a bullet to the chest, but it missed all the vitals, thankfully."

I stare at Mark, but he ignores me, and walks past following Max into the living room. His colleague hands me a bag but doesn't stop for a reaction. I glance inside and see the clothes I was wearing last night. Gee-Gee had made me change into 'more appropriate clothing for jogging' to complete my 'business as usual' appearance this morning. Something tells me my 'business as usual' exterior is going to be tested severely today.

No, not just today: my 'normal' just got rewritten and there is no going back.

I leave the bag in the hall and follow into the living room. Mark is repeating his tale to Aunt Dora and Eve while Max just stares. Within five minutes, Mark is escorting us to his Solarbug and driving Max and me to the Central Hub hospital. I haven't spoken for some time. I just sit, stunned, listening to Mary Rivers – cruel, cold, ambitious, murderous, Mary Rivers – being described by the younger officer as a wonderful, dedicated woman, a role model, and mother.

The tributes continue at the hospital as a doctor shakes Max's hand: "Such a tragic loss, she had such plans as Director of Agriculture…to be taken so young…out of a despicable fit of jealousy…" I look at Max's face, he isn't registering anything. I pull Max's arm away from the doctor's grasp, thank him, and ask Mark to direct us to Henry.

As we walk down the hall, Max turns to me, pale and quiet, whispering: "Peter killed her out of jealousy? A crime of passion? – Is that what they're saying?"

I open my mouth to speak, but the words catch in my throat. Am I supposed to join in this lie? Did I not promise to be open and honest always with him? Mark turns back, saving me from my dilemma. "It would seem he, Peter, was somewhat infatuated with your mother. He had been working alongside her since you all moved to this Hub, and took her friendship for more until he was rebuffed… He then cornered your parents last night in their home—"

"I was with them last night," Max says, looking at me. "They were not—"

"Never mind that now," Mark states authoritatively. "Let's get you to your father."

TWO

Henry is propped up in bed when we walk into his private room. He has monitors attached to him, and although my practical medical knowledge is limited, I can see his heartbeat is strong. Henry smiles warmly as his eyes focus on his son's face. He raises a hand which Max gladly takes and squeezes as he sits on the edge of the bed.

"What happened?" Max whispers. "I don't understand. I saw you both last night…you were both angry and tired, but Peter wasn't there – was he?"

"Son, oh, my boy, what can I say?" Henry is looking at his son, but I am sure he is talking to Mark Jones who is standing behind me.

I turn to Mark, but he makes no eye contact with me, instead focusing solely on Henry – speaking to him without saying a word. Although he has only been promoted to Head of Security Services by a matter of hours, Mark has long been thought of as the brains in the Force, always outranking his previous boss in wisdom and intelligence. Dad, as Governor of Defence, is his boss now, but even that isn't wholly true, because my father doesn't know the real hierarchy of government.

Confused and overwhelmed, I look back to Max, wondering if I should say anything or just watch. Father and son have always been clearly an older/younger version of one another, and even now I am struck by how similar they are. Both have olive brown skin, dark brown eyes, black hair, and matching kind, handsome, gentle expressions – when not overshadowed by Mary, who stifled the lightest of moments by her mere presence.

Not anymore.

No more will she dictate their choices, humble their mood, or squash their hopes…or will she? At the moment, even in death, she has managed to pale their skin and cloud their eyes.

Surely, that is normal? A wife and mother has just died.

I rebuke myself, of course, they are in shock – it is only right they mourn, regardless of what she was. Yet they don't know what she was. Not truly. They know she murdered Max's real mother. They know she blackmailed and bribed her way to wife and mother when she was infertile. They know she manipulated every and anyone to get what she wanted…

So, they *do* know…

But they don't know she tried to kill *me*.

Nor that, despite knowing that, *I* feel guilty for her death.

And her killer, her true killer, is standing centimetres from them right now. My saviour.

Henry is still looking for words. He is clearly very tired, I am not sure how long he has been out of surgery, but realistically, it cannot be long. Quite by whom or how he has been briefed, I have no idea, but Max is now looking to me for help with questioning. I sit on the opposite side of the bed to Max, take my father-in-law's other hand, and ask what happened. In truth, I am as curious as Max – for my version and Henry's cannot be the same.

"I–I hardly know," stammers Henry, closing his eyes. "Soon after you left last night, the door rang. Your mother let Peter in…he was angry… I think his advances had been rejected by Mary – they shouted, he pleaded… I told him to leave…he attacked me…we fought, he pulled his gun and shot her, then me…" Henry sounds like he is reading bullet points off a prompter ready for a speech. I've heard my dad in his study dictating notes to his autocue in the same way, except Henry hasn't prepared the intersecting lines. How can he? The story is fictitious and he is a geneticist, not an actor. "I woke up here, they tell me Peter shot himself afterwards…" A tear rolls down Henry's cheek and my heart aches for him. He isn't a bad man – naïve and cowardly maybe, but years of living under Mary's private dictatorship is more than most can take and still come out unscathed.

A doctor comes in, saving Henry from further questioning. She explains the surgery was straight forward and Henry is expected to make a full recovery given the proper rest and relaxation time to recoup. The doctor's exact words are: 'A little R&R and we'll have you back to normal, Dr Rivers.' The innocent reference to the Real Revolution makes my stomach churn. I have heard Gee-Gee use that acronym all my life. 'I just need a little R&R' being her go-to catchphrase whenever asked if she is tired or if there was a problem that she had to solve. I thought nothing of it, lots of people have catchphrases. Only most people are not hiding their secret organisation in their catchphrase, rubbing your ignorance in your face and making a mockery of your trust in them…

An unknown man pops his head around the door, nods at Mark, and they both leave the room. Max is still chatting to the doctor, but I honestly haven't registered many of the words. I look down at Henry as he struggles to keep his eyes open and ask if we had better let him rest.

"It would be wise to let him sleep undisturbed for a while. His body has had a massive shock – as has his mind," says the doctor. She reaches out and lays a sympathetic hand on Max's arm. "I am so sorry about your mother."

"If you're going to leave," says Mark re-entering the room, "you'll have to speak to the press. The vultures have smelled a story and you'll have to make a statement for your father."

Max looks shocked. "What? Why do I?"

"Because ten days ago the PTB made a big thing about the joy of joining two Hubs through your bloody wedding and your mother was the Director of Agriculture – a particularly vocal one. People *are* going to notice her disappearance from meetings, the news…you get my point. Best make a clear statement now and be done with it."

"I don't know what to say—"

"You don't need to," interrupts Mark, waving his right arm, pointing to his watch. "Check your watch. Your statement has just been emailed to you. Read that."

We don't have time to object. Mark, for the first time, stares at me, his eyes telling me to do my part – point Max in the right direction and hold him up if he crumbles. I would do the latter anyway, the former I would do if I knew what 'right' was anymore.

We are herded to the front of the hospital. Immediately outside the front doors are journalists and cameramen. News is limited in the UNE and news channels are sanctioned by the PTB, so any freestyle reporters are normally quashed before they ever press 'send' on their keypads.

Knowing this, I have no doubt these reporters know the line of questioning they are expected to go through now. I actually recognise a couple of them from our wedding – when I was made to memorise and repeat a speech so the whole UNE, in particular any potentially wayward youths, could see the wonder and efficiency of the matching system. Wayward youths like me, who once upon a time wanted to marry someone else, but now wouldn't want to be married to anyone else. The irony of the system working, even if I do not approve of it.

I sigh.

An action I have yet to be free of: even my happiest thoughts have weights to pull on my shoulders and push out air from my lungs.

I take Max's arm as we approach the bunch of microphones that have been left out for us. Max activates his watch and his speech flashes up, ready and waiting to scroll on as he speaks. His voice wobbles slightly as he begins, but he remains calm and collected, reading word for word the statement he has been given. All the while I stand solemnly by his side, keeping my face low and my grip on him reassuring. Outwardly showing nothing but support for my husband – and certainly no reaction to the fable that is being told.

* * *

Max and I arrive home in silence, both apparently unsure what to do or say. I had thought about returning to Aunt Dora's; however, our instructions were to go home and neither of us verbally suggested otherwise.

The front door slides closed and all is silent. I look around the room and feel lost and frustrated: this place was supposed to be a new start, a real home after 24 years of feeling like an extra, yet now I just feel numb. I look over to Max; he is staring at me, but I cannot read his emotion – possibly he doesn't know how to feel either. He hasn't cried yet and I am waiting for the floodgate to open so he can begin the long road to processing what has happened.

He walks upstairs without a word and I hear the bathroom door open and shut, then open again – it sounds like Max is pacing. I am not sure if I should follow him or give him space. While I am deciding he reappears, puts a finger to his lips and takes my hand, pulling me upstairs, into the bathroom. He switches on the shower and nods towards it, undressing himself simultaneously. Confused, I do as I am told, stepping into the shower and he shuts the door behind me.

"Right," he says sternly. "Are you going to tell me what the hell actually happened?"

"You mean—"

"I mean *actually,* not that cock-and-bull story we were just fed."

I close my eyes and tears roll down my face – not that you'd really notice as the shower has soaked us both through.

I take a deep breath. "Mary and Peter were waiting for me when I made my way back to you." I stop, waiting for Max's reaction. There isn't one. Unlike me who would jump in mid-sentence, he waits for the story to unfold, to hear it all, so I tell him: "They cornered me at gunpoint. Peter must have been monitoring me – or Mary, or both – either way, he knew I had used your mum's barcode to get to the tramline and they wanted to know how and why. I wouldn't say, so your mum threatened not only my life, but Eve and Aunt Dora's. I couldn't risk…I couldn't…" I sob, only just managing to control the urge to vomit as I recall what happened next. Max holds me, gently squeezing, whispering for me to carry on. I step back slightly so I can look into his eyes, tired, but resolved as they are. "We fought, Peter tried to shoot me… but Mark appeared—"

"Mark? New Head of Security Services, Mark?"

"Mmm-hmm, he shot them both in the head and led me through the trees to a car…where Gee-Gee was waiting for me. The rest you know."

Max rubs his face with his hand as he thinks. I begin to wonder if he is going to say anything, but I need to let him react in his own time. "And Dad?" he finally asks.

"I don't know. I knew nothing about that until you did."

"I thought so. Your shock seemed real, but not complete." Max seems distrusting – no, that is the wrong word…I'm not sure what is, maybe reproachful. "They were angry last night…both of them. Dad was weary of Mum's hatred and command. She was furious her control of us had been lost and her past exposed. I left them in anger myself, but not until I thought I had given you time to get in using her code undetected. I didn't think she would go out again…I didn't think it would be the last time I—" Finally the tears flow and I hold him. The floodgates, now open, cause his whole body to shake. I reach up and shut off the shower. If the R&R are bothering to try to hear our conversation or if the random algorithm wants to check on us, so be it. All they will hear is the mourning of a woman that, although deeply troubled, was all Max has known as a mother. Whether it is a release of sorrow, a relief of acknowledged pain, or a regret of all that will now never be, I let Max cry. He cannot bottle up his emotions, nor should he. For better or worse, in sickness and health – despite our families – we will prevail. *I hope.*

THREE

A message arrives on my watch just as Max and I return home from our second hospital visit to Henry. I have already heard from Aunt Dora, so I know it is unlikely to be from her and my father has sent a suitably politically correct message assuring us of my family's 'deepest sympathies and if there's anything we can do…' His messages, few and far between as they are, are always designed to appeal to the public as well as the recipient. One of his colleagues had his messages replayed to the entire Hub once as punishment for some 'personal indiscretion' – whatever that means – but as a result, Dad has taken great pains to make sure his texts and emails are as bland and on point as possible. No one is going to blackmail him. My mother has less sensibilities and left a gushing voicemail about how tragic 'it all is' and 'such a wasted opportunity to keep the title in the family – unless Max wants to put himself forward? Oh, but that is too soon…oh, what a shame… You'll have to make her proud and produce a grandchild as soon as possible – any luck there yet?' If there was more to her message, I couldn't say: I deleted it at that point. Thankfully, Max didn't hear.

Still reeling from previous messages, I open the latest with a degree of trepidation. To my surprise, it is from the Housing Association and simply says: 'Sorry you were not home when we called, we let ourselves in and repaired the network link to your study table. Our apologies for this oversight, we hope it caused no lasting inconvenience.'

"What the hell? Someone has been in our house while we were out!" I call to Max and reread him the message when he asks me to clarify my outburst. We stare at each other in confusion and walk silently into the study. Since moving in we haven't had a chance to do anything in or with this room – and certainly haven't detected or reported an issue with the network link to the study table. Max turns on the computer and everything seems normal. He looks up at me quizzically and I just shrug, I have no idea what we are supposed to find—

"*Shit!*"

"What?" Max asks, surprised by my sudden expletive.

"No…surely not…" I say walking around the table to where Max is sitting.

"What?" he asks impatiently as I run my hand along the underside of the table.

"No, sorry, I was going too far, there's no way—" *Click*. "Shit," I whisper as I feel something pop under my finger.

"What was tha—Whoaaa!" Max jumps up, staring at the wall to our left as a doorway appears from nowhere and opens into a lift. "What the…?"

I exhale. "The Director calls, I believe."

"You've seen this before?"

"I had no idea until yesterday, but Gee-Gee has a lift in her study. When I travelled the tramline, I realised there are little substations and routes from all over the Hub, but had no time to explore. It never occurred to me our house was linked to it…"

"Well, best we explore now together," Max says, gulping. "Shall we?" he says, extending his hand.

We step in and the door closes. The control panel has only one option. Down. I poke the arrow and the lift drops through the ground, opening to show the tip of an enormous network of tunnels and tramlines. Sat patiently waiting for us is a Solarbug, its destination – our destination – pre-programed. All we have to do is sit down and take in the scenery.

I find myself smiling as I watch Max examine the landscape. I can hardly claim to be well-versed with the layout; however, I do at least have a minor head start on him and I, in the most basic of forms, now understand Gee-Gee's amusement yesterday witnessing the wonder this place invokes when first seen.

I have the added joy of watching my husband though because I know the architecture and design will fascinate him even more than it does me. His passion for architecture flourishes despite his late mother's disapproval. She wanted a direct dynasty and Max to inherit her title. His fathers' love of science was okay as a backup to her status, but Mary Rivers' idea of true success was a family name that outshines and lasts. 'Doctor' was too lowly for her. As 'Director' she held true power and had every potential for more. This sentiment was absolutely music to my mother's ears.

I repress a chuckle. At least Mum will have to stop pushing that idea now. There is however nothing funny about the truth behind Mary Rivers – her life nor death – and thinking about it churns my stomach again. She was a manipulative, murderous, malicious person – happy to stomp on all dreams to achieve her own. Not that anyone will ever publicly know.

That is painfully clear from the statement poor Max read earlier: 'We are reeling from the tragic loss of my beloved mother, a dedicated, loyal, and loving wife, a true advocate of all the UNE holds dear…' In other words, they have made her a martyr to protect the R&R before (and beyond) anything else.

After all, they cannot possibly admit they were wrong about someone, can they?

The Solarbug stops by the main tramline and with no other options, we step out of the buggy and wait. I glance up and realise not only is our street marked on the wall, but there is also a digital timer counting down. Max follows my line of vision: "Huh, I suppose we have five minutes until our tram?"

"I guess so," I say, watching the numbers tick down.

Again, I am reminded of the SurrogacyPods – the ones growing my babies, incubating them with precision, their births mapped out to the second as the clock counts down on each pod. My eldest had three weeks to go…but he isn't my eldest, is he? I have six years of egg donations in the world. I could quite feasibly have five-year-old children. Children who are already being drilled that the PTB are the governors and saviours of humanity, that fertility is a gift they should aspire to obtain, but if graded 0-2, a vocation for the betterment of society and Earth are worthy and proper goals. Forget any thought of choice, of personal desire, conversation advocating change or challenging of 'the way.' Everything works for the greater good.

Would I teach my children differently?

Do I disagree with the grand plan?

Or just the method?

Or, as Gee-Gee so plainly put it, does the end justify the means?

Humanity did unquestionably fail in the past. Maybe choice – individual, selfish choice – was the cause of the Fall of What Was. Or is it just the excuse of those who seek to control all? They don't seek. They *do* control all...

"Maia?" I suddenly feel Max shake my arm, and I turn to him. "Good grief, I thought you'd frozen like Eve. Your face had completely glazed over!"

I smile, probably not as convincingly as I'd like. "Sorry, I was daydreaming."

Max puffs out his cheeks. "Pfft, you daydream a lot, but not like that!" Daydreaming and drowning out my surroundings has been a lifelong fault of mine. I try not to, but I lose myself in thought too easily. I apologise, making up a lame excuse for the numbers on the clock putting me into a trance, but I can see Max isn't convinced. I don't want to tell him I was thinking about babies.

The confusion I feel knowing I do not want them, yet have seen them and want them to have a better future, is indescribable. They would be exceptionally unlucky to wind up with a mother as extreme as mine – or come to think of it, as Max's. The vast majority are decent, caring people who want the best for their children – just within the confines of the given rule. My dilemma is not so much in regard to prospective families. It is the details of that rule...

"Maia!" groans Max. "You're doing it again! The tram is coming!"

Muttering an apology, I take Max's hand and we board the tram as soon as it stops. Neither of us verbally question the wisdom of our action, it is too late for that. There are three men at the front of the tram and a woman sitting at the back, none of whom pay us any attention whatsoever. Last night I felt physically ill at the thought of being seen or a scanner reading me. Wearing Eve's synthetic sleeve on my left arm, I had used Mary's barcode to open every door, tricking every AI system into believing I was someone else. Now I register as myself and nothing happens. The computer expects me, just as it expects Max.

I am still wearing the sleeve and the pearl necklace that activates it. I wasn't sure what to do with them…I didn't exactly get a chance to ask Eve this morning and I am suddenly anxious they will be detected. It wasn't earlier, but earlier I had the distraction of the button camera…

I unconsciously rub my left arm, only stopping when I see Max watching me, probably reading my code to see if I have the correct numbers displayed. I do. The synthetic sleeve is still tightly wrapped around my upper arm because pretending to be a dead person is not going to help right now. I know this, but I read my barcode anyway, just to reassure myself all is in order. I see my pedigree and for a second smile when I consider the recently added marital code. I look at Max's.

It is weird that our pedigrees are what put us on a shortlist to be matched – then our genes and health statistics were all set against each other in an algorithm that resulted in the

Genetics Committee agreeing to our match. How different life would be if the algorithm had stopped on another person.

For both of us.

The tram rises out of the ground and stops. We wait for the others to leave, then step out of the carriage onto the platform outside the R&R headquarters. I am yet to see this place in the daylight. I want to see what is beyond the fencing that surrounds us, as well as how the building truly looks. I suddenly consider exploring whatever is the next stop for the tram (assuming there is one) and wish I hadn't got off. But it is too late, the tram has retreated underground on its given path and Max and I are standing alone, hand in hand, both gently trembling.

A drone approaches us and I feel both our arms tense and hands simultaneously squeeze. It looks just like the one that caught me yesterday as it scanned my neck barcode instead of my counterfeit arm. Eve's secret phrase saved me then, but now, knowing we are expected, I do not think there is any point in repeating it now. The light on the front of the drone turns from green to amber as it spins to the back of us, scanning Max's neck, then mine. Apparently satisfied with our barcodes, the drone spins in front of us, returning to green. "Follow," it says, flying back towards the building.

We are led to a large conference room with an enormous oval table and glass walls. Standing inside I feel like a goldfish and wonder about the wisdom of a secret organisation having meetings with no privacy from passersby. I suppose everyone here is 'in the know,' but even so, it seems odd. No sooner have I finished thinking this, Gee-Gee appears, nods to us both, sits at the tip of the oval table and calls up the computer on the desk. The moment she does, the glass walls turn black and I roll my eyes – of course they have thought of everything.

Without speaking, she gestures for us to sit down. Lacking a better reason than wanting to defy her, I sit down without a word and Max sits next to me. Looking around the table, I count 25 projector points and although there are chairs at every position, something tells me these meetings are remotely attended more than they are physically.

"What is this?" asks Max, sounding frustrated at the silence.

Gee-Gee continues on her computer for a moment before she looks up and exhales before replying. "This is where we decide what is next…how we all proceed." She looks as tired as I feel.

"What does that mean?" Max retorts. "You make this sound like a new position, but you've clearly planned for it – otherwise why do we have a lift in our house? You aren't going to try and tell me there's one in every house?"

"No, indeed," Gee-Gee says as the corner of her mouth gives a slight inflection of amusement. "It has long been my hope that Maia joins the mission and placed you both in a house 'fitted' for her inclusion should the opportunity arise. Your late mother was also rather keen on your promotion, Max, although I am not sure where you stand on this issue – which is largely why you are both here now."

"Where I stand?" Max looks confused. "I have always wanted to be useful. I have many architectural and environmental design and development ideas, Mum has– *had*." He pauses, stumbling on the reality of the tenses.

"Mum always rejected my ideals for her own, hoping I would take interest in the agricultural sector…"

"I see." Gee-Gee smiles. "Then am I to understand that you, even with your newfound knowledge of our hierarchy, are willing to remain loyal to the cause at hand? That, if given a position of trust, you will not *disappoint*?" She pauses, narrowing her eyes. "Let me be clear – you would earn it, *nothing* here is gifted. All positions are earned, trust is proven…but *if* I explain the mandate of the R&R fully, *if* I show you beyond your current understanding, *will* you be the asset we want you to be?" Gee-Gee stops, studying Max's face. "Your mother lost her way quite spectacularly, the ripples and repercussions of which are a nuisance we did not need – a disappointment and embarrassment we did not need – and certainly will not repeat."

"I am not my—I *am not Mary Rivers*. She may have raised me, but my nature is not a result of her nurture. I am Maxwell Rivers, my own man." The determination on his face is impossible to miss. Only two days ago he learnt the truth of how his mother, his *real* mother died – how Mary took her place and the oppressive hold she has had on his father ever since. He cannot have dealt with that pain before she too was killed.

I know the need for closure, how badly that need hangs off your back and sways your thoughts. He might know the truth, but he needs time to process, to come to terms… But I don't think we have time to decide, our next move will be decided before we leave this room – particularly if we want to leave it with any notion of freedom. Looking at Max now, he has already realised this.

"Hmm," says Gee-Gee, weighing up the truth in Max's words. "Do you understand the mission? Do you know the motto by which all the R&R rest on?"

Max raises an eyebrow, unsure of the answer she is looking for. Of all the things I have told him about last night, I am not sure if I recounted the inscription on the painting in Gee-Gee's study. The one all directors have that depicts a half destroyed, half flourishing Earth – just the same as the monuments above this building and on the Central Hub Plaza. The only difference being there is no poem on the painting, no reminder for citizens of the past, and why a united, mindful future is the way forward. Instead, the painting has the motto, the mission reminder.

"Being Guardians of the Earth gives us no greater right to be here than any other species," I whisper.

"Precisely," says Gee-Gee. "Anyone, at whatever level of command in the Real Revolution, must understand and remember that simple, yet essential point. It is not an ideal to take or leave on a whim, it cannot be passed over for personal or family credit or betterment. Mary knew that, yet she chose to ignore it. Eve knows it – and largely lived by it more admirably than anyone—"

"Until she was betrayed for her loyalty," I spit.

Gee-Gee glares at me. "Lilith's situation is unfortunate. We agree on that. But truly, whether it justifies her 'relaxation' of tongue, is yet to be determined."

"What do you mean?" My heart races. "You wouldn't, not after everything she's—"

"Eve's service is beyond exceptional, but it does not give a free pass to—"

"What are you going to do?" I gulp down bile that suddenly rises in my throat. The image of Mary dropped to the ground flashes into my mind. The blood from the circular hole in her forehead will be eternally burnt into my memory.

"Well, that may depend on you both. We believe Eve's health is a factor in her revelations—" I open my mouth and Gee-Gee waves her hand, ordering me to let her finish as she impatiently answers my unspoken point. "Yes, yes, as well as Lilith's status." She pauses, staring into my eyes. Our eyes have always been a similar shade of brown, our features unquestionably cut from the same gene pool, yet in this moment, I have to question if I know her at all. "Your loyalty *could* be linked to her longevity."

I feel Max shift in his seat, but I do not take my eyes off my great grandmother. I look for a wince, a sign I may be misreading her.

Sadly, I am not.

Gee-Gee continues, "We want reassurances, commitment—"

"We? Who is this 'we' you keep mentioning?" I ask.

"The Board."

I cock my head to one side and pull a face, hoping she will explain. Instead, the projectors around the room all activate and the chairs are filled with people – holographic people. Max and I both gasp.

"Welcome to your first board meeting, Max and Maia. We sincerely hope it will not be your last, that would be most disappointing. However, life is full of disappointments and if that is the way you choose it to be today, we will clean up this mess and continue as before without you…or rather, without you *as you are*." The voice pauses and I am still trying to focus on the one who is speaking. He is the opposite end of the room to me, but I am sure I recognise his face…his voice… "You can, of course, still be useful to the Initiative and other fertility projects. If need be, you'd make excellent Ambassadors of Earth."

Ignoring the varying levels of threats for a moment, I ask: "Who are you?"

"Maia," says Gee-Gee softly, "you have met the Curator once before – you would be an asset on his team. Your research and his have long been aligned—"

"Professor Millar?"

Gee-Gee nods. A few years ago, the President General from United North America visited with a few of his officials. It caused a huge stir as movement between Hubs, let alone States, is almost unheard of. Professor Millar was in the travelling party and I had longed to sit in on his discussions with Gee-Gee and my (now late) Great Gramps. I had sat outside her study, desperate to hear their conversation, but heard nothing – of course not, they had whisked away through her private lift to here. The new levels of deceit just keep unfolding, don't they?

"What is an Ambassador of Earth?" asks Max, wisely considering the threats laid at our feet rather than who is doing the threatening.

"What all cadets of the FARM programme strive to be. The Fertility And Resource Management Programme is the more pointed name of the AIP – which is where you will go if you fail us here again. No ifs, buts, or maybes… you can find out more details later, but if you go, you go separately and eternally, make no mistake there."

"So, really, we have no choice. You must know we stay together or we—"

"*Die?*" Professor Millar chuckles coldly. "Don't be so dramatic, no Golden Goose is cracked so easily or without being properly collected. No rare jewel would be tossed aside, nor will you be."

"I think we have heard enough," says Gee-Gee forcefully.

"Indeed," says a female voice who doesn't identify herself. I follow the direction of sound and realise the voice came from an empty chair – or rather a blurred chair. All the other projectors have clear images of people – none, except Professor Millar, of whom I have seen before – but this one, on the opposite end of the table, parallel to Gee-Gee, is just a hazy blur. "We have heard your interview and should now convene without you and vote. Does the Board agree?"

In unison all the holograms grunt in affirmation.

"Then it is settled," says the blurred woman. "Please remove Max and Maia, Director, and we will come together in thirty minutes to finalise a vote."

The holograms shut off and the room falls silent. Holding Max's sweaty hand, I am not sure which one of us is shaking or sweating more. We turn to Gee-Gee as she stands up and opens the door. "Come, I'll show you to a room."

FOUR

Max and I are sitting on the edge of the bed and haven't yet spoken despite being left several minutes ago by Gee-Gee. She offered no encouragement, no words of wisdom. Nothing other than the slightest of nod as she shut the door, a nod accompanied by a look of regret – no, not regret, worry. Her face looked worried.

The room is, as always in the UNE, minimalist. There is a double bed and two bedside tables, plus one closet in the wall. No window, no computer, no adornment, although a door leads to a toilet and shower. How civilised. The walls are all white and bare with the exception of one painting. I silently shake my head. There it is again. The image that follows me everywhere. The Earth, half damaged – black, with burnt trees, rubble, pollution, and death depicted in intricate detail; half not – with flourishing green fields, woodland, and animals. This version is different to the one in the Hub though because the artist has painted Hubs amongst the life and death – providing a more precise vision of our place and our role in the state of the planet.

Max is studying the painting as keenly as I am and gets up to read the inscription underneath. The letters are plain enough that I can read them from here, yet I wait for him to say them aloud – and do my best to take in the words as I hear them ring through my ears:

"We are the Guardians of this land
No greater calling is at hand
The mistakes of the past, repeated will not be
Our mission will outlast the likes of you and me
There is no 'I,' 'maybe,' or 'just'
Our Guardianship is an absolute must
And so, we now place our hand on heart
Acknowledging this truth, from the very start
Though our service may bring trial and personal woe
Our mission, an honour, outshines any sorrow we might know
Our service is forever, lifelong, and without end
To Mother Nature, our hands, we lend."

"The R&R declaration, I suppose?" Max says after a moment's silence.

"One we're going to live by?" I ask cautiously. I feel like we are being swept along without actually stopping to ask if we agree.

"We have no choice," Max says flatly. "But yes, I agree, don't you? You already chose from what Gee-Gee implied…"

It is true, last night, I did choose the only option I could. I've been over that in my head a hundred or more times already. I don't know why I think it is any different now? Possibly just ignorant hope that I am not being swept along…that I choose this path. *You did choose this path – the moment you agreed to Eve sending you here.*

True.

I stepped into the dark looking for light and found this seemingly eternal grey.

I guess what I really mean is… "Yes, but are we united? Do you—" I cut myself off, unable to voice my self-doubting, self-loathing question.

"Of course," Max answers sitting down next to me. "Why do you doubt that? Surely, now more than ever we need each other? More than that, *want* to go forward together?" He sounds a little hurt.

"Yes, unquestionably, I do." I suck in my bottom lip, struggling to ask: "But you don't blame me for…for your mum's death?"

"What?" Max stares. "Why would I?"

"Had I not gone out, had I left things—"

"She would still have been controlling my father, still manipulating any and every one – scheming goodness knows what with Peter. She tried to *kill you*. Have you missed that fact in your mind? I haven't." His voice wobbles and a tear spills down his face as he pauses. Max wipes it away as he continues: "I–I'm not pretending to have taken in half of this yet, but one thing I do know is: no, I do not blame you."

Now is possibly not the time for this conversation, but if the vote goes against us and if what Professor Millar said is true, and we could be eternally separated, I want to say the things that should be said. The idea of losing him is too much and tears flood down my cheeks. Shaking, I reach out and hug him, muttering "I love you," into his shoulder.

He pulls me back and holds my face with both of his hands and says emphatically: "I love you too, but this is not goodbye. We will go forward as Guardians – of whatever the R&R want to call us – and we will do it together."

"We are very pleased to hear it," says a female voice – which I think belongs to the blurred woman. Where her voice is coming from, I cannot say. Honestly, it sounds like she is coming from everywhere. We sit facing the painting, the only real focal point in the room, hand in hand, and take in a deep breath as though the voice told us we are both about to be submerged in water. "Please wait while we vote."

We sit in absolute silence for what seems an eternity, but in truth it is probably no more than ten minutes. Knowing we are being listened to has stopped us from wanting to communicate, so we content ourselves with quiet reflection, mentally taking comfort from the other's presence – though if someone could tell our hearts, that would be wonderful, as I can feel and hear both of ours thumping through our chests.

"The Board has listened to what you have to say and has voted," the female voice eventually says. "I, the Arbitrator, have the pleasure of welcoming you into the R&R. If you, once and for all, agree to abide by our rules, our ethos, and declare you understand our declaration and mandate, as spelled out on the wall, please both raise your right hand and say, 'I do.' I will just remind you, this is a lifelong commitment, the path you are given is, and always will be, for the greater good. You may not like the path, but you will follow it. You will adhere, respect, and protect it. The Real Revolution is never, and shall never, to be mentioned whilst in a Hub. The use of the acronym 'R&R' is to be used, but sparingly – less is more. None is better for the majority. Once agreed, there are no other options, once details are laid out, the FARM is no longer an option. Should you betray us, only the grave awaits. Guardianship is forever. The privilege is there, should you accept it. What say you?"

Max and I look at each other, raise our eyebrows as well as our right hands and swallow the lumps in our throats:

"I do."

"I do."

"Then, it is my honour and duty to hereby declare you promoted to Guardians of the Earth. May you serve the UNE well."

FIVE

An unnamed man, probably in his thirties, leads us back into the conference room. Gee-Gee is sat for all to see as the glass is clear again, all the projectors are off and the room is silent. She gets up as we approach and smiles, perhaps a little cautiously, however she cannot disguise her genuine delight.

"I hope you one day share my joy for this moment. The future, I feel, is much brighter today," she says, hugging us. It is a rather awkward hug, but I do not rebuff her. Whatever now lies ahead, I need her. I longed for a family that would treat me as an equal, for genuine affection and a path that included knowledge, understanding, and a place I feel I belong. I hope now, in some weird, very unexpected and mentally, as well as morally challenging way, I have that. How much will I have to endure before I can make a difference? How much of the R&R research and practice will I find repugnant? I guess I am about to find out.

"What now?" I ask as Gee-Gee sits down.

"You carry on your current trajectory," Gee-Gee says without smiling. Why do I think I am not going to like the explanation? *That didn't take long, did it?* "You already have your designated path, Maia, as do you Max – for now at least. Your service will expand when your ability to continue as directed is proven."

"Meaning…?"

"Meaning, you will carry on in the lab with Dr Rivers. The research you have started, you'll continue—"

"The research that Theo sabotages you mean?"

"Precisely."

I feel sick…Never have I felt more pointless.

"That is important in itself," continues Gee-Gee after a short pause. "You are highlighting and collecting data we otherwise would not have. We still process and develop it— No, don't keep interrupting, listen." I close my mouth, just releasing an 'aah' sound as I was about to object. "You will carry on until pregnant and then, once the baby comes, you will fulfil the greatest honour of the UNE and raise your family."

I don't say anything, but I shake from head to toe. I rub my face with my left hand, the hand not being held by Max. I don't dare look at him. While he gets to go to work – to be listened to, to promote himself and his ideas – I get to pump out children. At best, I get to give my work to another… to my father-in-law or ex-boyfriend. The latter who lies and steals my findings, the former, knowingly, or not, lets him.

Oh! How I wish I were infertile!

Gee-Gee studies my face and sighs. "More will come, Maia, but we, *you*, must lead by example. To be a true, dedicated Guardian, you must sacrifice something, without sacrifice, you lack conviction and focus – which leaves your service flawed and weak and the cause suffers. That cannot be. We can and must always do better. We will not falter."

I wish this was an uplifting speech. I wish it didn't make me want to scream, but it does. I feel Max's grip tighten and I glance at him: he nods ever so slightly into the room. I look beyond him, but see nothing, then it dawns on me. That is what I am looking at – the empty room has ears. Play my part…learn something…anything that is useful or at the very least, distracting.

"So, I assume all those holograms are the Board?" I ask. "How many are on the Board?"

"Indeed. Twenty-five Trustees make up the Board, though they are just the Heads – the representatives of all in their State, if you will. The R&R Guardians are in any and every role across the UNE. There is no job too big or small, we are all essential parts that keep the wheel turning." Gee-Gee smiles with pride. This is a rare moment of seeing the sparkle in her eye that she used to have all the time – for the last year or so, since Great Gramps' death, that sparkle has been barely seen. That it should return now speaks of her passion, I know, but I cannot be wholly glad to see it.

"Why twenty-five? That seems an odd number?" says Max.

"Two per State," Gee-Gee replies.

"That makes twenty-four," Max replies slightly sarcastically.

"Indeed. The last vote is the decider, should the Three having a double vote not produce a decision."

"The Three?" Another new term for us to take in.

"The Director, the Curator, and the Architect have a double vote…the Arbitrator has the decider," Gee-Gee replies coolly.

I scoff. "So, you niggle at Eve's prior position, yet you yourself, *Director*, are now the Head!"

"It is an honour to be where I am. I will not apologise for it."

"Do we know the other members – will we be introduced properly?" Max asks, trying to alter the direction of conversation enough to prevent me from replying to that statement.

"No, you do not need to know them. Every hierarchy has levels—"

"And we're at the bottom," I grumble.

"Maia, will you quit sulking, it is unbecoming." I feel like I am talking to Mum.

"Where is Lilith?" I'll try a new topic. "Is the AIP here?"

"No, the FARM programme is not here. You're a long, long way off finding out about that."

"But it must be here, in this State?" I ask softly.

"Why?" Gee-Gee looks confused.

"Because you're here…?"

Gee-Gee chuckles. "I am not in charge of projects beyond the Hub – that is the Curator's domain. I oversee population and in-Hub life and projects." Shit, no wonder she thinks it an honour! It suddenly dawns on me the absolute level of power we're talking about and I shudder.

"And the Architect?" asks Max. Of course, that role is going to appeal to him more.

"They oversee design in Hubs and restoration beyond."

"*'They'*…you won't even give up gender?"

"Anonymity is a default safety net. That is enough for today – I'm afraid you have a funeral to prepare for. It goes without saying, I hope, these events are all classified. You leaving the Hub bounds is never to be mentioned. Tomorrow you are booked to go arrange the funeral, details are on your watches. After that, well you have a few days left of your honeymoon – try to use them wisely. To any news reporters you say you made all the comments that you are going to back at the hospital. We have released our report, everything is laid on Peter Lloyd's shoulders: your father will act as the doting, bereaved husband, as will you the mourning son and daughter in law. A tragic, unnecessary crime of passion – a waste of life." Gee-Gee scans the door and steps out into the hallway. She turns as she leaves and looks straight into Max's eyes. "I'm sorry what happened to your mother, your real mother."

Max swallows before giving a simple: "Thank you."

"We'll be in touch. Get some rest."

SIX

I was glad when the funeral was over. I hated the number of fake sorrys and even genuine displays of remorse I had to witness and thank. I hated having to participate in a voice call with Mary's family back in the Midlands Hub, pretending any of us thought she was an innocent, dedicated angel. She was dedicated, I'll grant you that, but the only genuine tears I have shed on account of that woman is when I wake up sweating from yet another dream of her final moments.

I resent what *not* regretting her death potentially makes me.

Max is just as torn.

Today he is angry at her: for her years of control, what she did and how, and at the fact her crimes are patched over as nothing – as though his real mother was nothing. In the next breath Max asked me if I thought it was okay for part of him to mourn and a part to be glad? Did that make him a monster? Of course, I told him he is no monster and it is understandable, right, and normal to feel this way…probably more normal than my cold response. She was, regardless of anything else that she was, his mother. The one who raised him, no amount of dwelling on what else she did is going to change that. She did want him to be elevated as much as herself and she did love him. Unhealthy and destructive as that love was.

I had to rebuke myself for questioning if the same can be said for my mother. She loves my siblings, she loves my grade 3 fertility status, she loves the fact I am now married – but can I honestly, hand on heart, say she loves me? Warts and all, me?

Potentially even worse, I questioned if I love her.

I suppose I do, I think it comes under the 'you do, despite yourself' category. To be fair to Mum, she is more in tune with the PTB rules than I am. She has embraced the family mandate so whole-heartedly, absolutely no one would ever suggest that she has missed the point or not done her bit towards society's ethos and ensuring future generations. Maybe I just have to accept we are two very different people and tell myself that is okay. We have our different corners of the world, of society, to adorn and cherish.

I do my utmost to repeat this to myself for the ten minutes Mum traps me on the phone this morning while I walk to work… 'It is okay, our priorities are different…it is okay, our priorities are different. Love manifests in different ways…it is okay – you no longer live with her…'

I glance at the people I walk past, wondering what drives their day – are they where they want them to be? Do they have mothers asking them cringe-worthy questions? Do they know about the R&R? Or are they blissfully unaware of anything other than what we are told? Do they rest easy at night believing the PTB, though strict, are transparent and work exactly as they think they do?

I envy their innocence.

But, my voice within, the one who will not let me rest – the one that pushed me to discovery in the first place – also tells me I am happy, intrigued, and excited to know more.

So really, I envy their *contentment*, because even now, my inner voice is pushing me, telling me my mission is only now beginning and I may be trapped in Eve's fog, but that doesn't mean I am going to sit still.

I walk into the laboratory for the first time since everything so spectacularly hit the fan. My mind replays scenes of anger and violence between Henry and Mary, of Henry on a pathetic camp bed covered in bottles, poorly trying to drown his sorrows…which led to revelations about which I hadn't even begun to theorise. I turn on my computer, logging in to see the results of my tests – all of which have been tampered with and my heart sinks. I want to be on the other side of this experiment. I want to be the tamperer, not the tampered-with.

I glance around the lab, checking for signs of Theo. Gee-Gee told me I was 'going to have to get over' my issues with him. Quite how I am supposed to do that when the very thought of him makes my stomach twist and heart thud, I have no idea. Once upon a time I had those reactions to him along with goosebumps of joy – every stolen look, touch or kiss producing electric pulses of happiness under my skin. And now? Now my skin recoils at the thought of him. I was so pleased to be in the halfway position – happy for our separate lives, yet content for work or even friendship to join us again. I struggle to imagine being able to build any kind of level of wall of trust between us again. I have no doubt for

Max's and my own sake I will have to pretend. Our very lives depend on it – as does Aunt Dora and Eve's.

Theo appears midmorning after everyone else has welcomed me back, expressed their condolences, wished Henry a speedy return to work, and filled me in on their progress. It is as though he knew all of that would be easier without his presence…which it probably was.

I am not sure what stance I expected him to take – the last time I saw him he seemed resolved, though I saw some distress at being exposed. I think I wanted him to beg for a pardon or at least express some further feeling of regret…that would have made me feel less used, even if I wouldn't have accepted his words. Maybe he knows that, maybe he doesn't see the need for further apology. Either way, he enters the lab, walks straight up to me, and talks about my work – the work I know he has thwarted and will not reap the results I expected at all. He continues speaking with ease and smiles as he talks like there is the possibility of a breakthrough… that I, Maia Rivers, might have actually just tracked a path to understanding the continued decline in human infertility.

Bizarrely, I laugh.

Not an all-out, gut wobbling, kind of laugh, just a gentle, 'what the hell world is this?' kind of laugh. A coping mechanism. A relief of tension. A 'I will not be beaten by your crap,' laugh.

Theo stares at me for a moment, his eternally dark, gorgeous eyes shining, even though they are undoubtedly confused. I just shrug and nod towards the charts he was pouring over, signalling my intention to carry on our ruse, not explain my mirth.

"Are you okay?" he whispers. It would seem my minor outburst has shaken his resolve.

"Quite," I softly taunt. "*I know what I need to, to serve* – as do you. Shall we continue?" I hold my tone as I mimic his words back to him. He doesn't miss my meaning as his cheeks flush. I am going to have to watch myself and not slide into a spiteful pit… I'll do that another day. Today, I am going to relish making him uncomfortable for a minute.

"I said that to you in earnest, Maia," he whispers, looking over his shoulder to see if anyone is listening to us. "I didn't know where I was going, nor what my service would entail. Information is dripped… I hoped – hope – you'll forgive—"

"Enough," I snap.

Understanding and forgiveness are two different things. One I cannot avoid, the other I cannot do. I'll not tell him this. I am bored to tears of feeling the victim of family and friends as well as of the government's ideals. No, not bored… I'll decide on a better word another day…but boredom is not possible for someone who jumps at every knock and now looks for extra meaning behind every simple word.

Saved by the bell – or more specifically, Ella, Theo's wife. She floats into the room smiling like she has just won the lottery. I don't think she has, she just has one of those (sometimes annoying) happy attitudes to every situation and wants to appease everyone. I cannot help liking her despite the obvious reasons not to…but I also struggle to trust her given her circumstances. I saw her at Mary's funeral; her smile was subdued then because, whether she liked her or not, Mary had been her boss, had been one of the driving reasons she moved to this Hub – and would have been her easy ticket to promotions.

She'll get there anyway, she is a genius and genuine child prodigy – and definitely wasted in mere tech support here. I refuse to feel sorry for her though. It is literally a matter of time before Gee-Gee or one of the other R&R Guardians or even Trustees welcomes her into the fold…by which point, she'll be further up the tree than me without an overpowering mother, great grandmother, ex-boyfriend, or goodness knows what to overshadow her path.

"Ah! Maia, how lovely to see you," beams Ella tossing her flowing red hair behind her shoulders. "I just bumped into Kate and arranged dinner for the six of us on Friday – I hope you don't mind us tagging along, but…"

"No, of course not," I fill in as prompted. I'm lying.

I haven't seen Kate since my wedding. She offered to come over after Mary died, but honestly, I didn't want to lie to her. I couldn't tell her the truth…and I didn't want to lie. Max said we should take the time alone and I am glad we did. I felt bad including Aunt Dora in that, but I messaged her, and I think she understands. I am to resume my sitting with Eve on Saturdays, so I will catch up – or repress more – with her then.

SEVEN

At lunch I prepare to take myself for a quiet walk. Max is too far away to make it feasible to meet up today, but I really need some fresh air. Taking a deep breath, preparing to disappear into the Central Hub streets for a while, I scuttle out of the laboratory foyer hoping no one notices me. I haven't managed more than two hundred meters when I hear: "MAIA!!"

I turn back to see Kate running towards me with such speed her beautiful blond hair threatens to free itself from the bun she has woven it into. She sees that I have seen her, but she shouts my name again anyway and I laugh. Her face is flushed from running, which is no surprise, but she is more out of breath than I would expect given how physically fit she is.

Kate stops herself by flinging her arms around my shoulders and pulling me into the tightest hug she can muster – which is good because otherwise she would have knocked me over. As she steps back, blue eyes sparkling, smile radiating, I can only guess that the news she has to share is good. Kate has an ability to make light or find joy in most situations, yet somehow, I have never seen this level of excitement in her face – not even when the Genetics Committee approved her and Tim's match when we were eighteen.

"I should wait for Tim," Kate puffs. "Don't you think I should wait for him? ...So we tell you together..." Looking at Kate's eyes, she is saying one thing and asking me to say another.

"I don't know…is that necessary?" I wink. "We've always confided in each other—"

"I'M HAVING A BABY!!!" she squeals, grabbing my shoulders and bouncing simultaneously.

I stare at her, smiling, mouth half open, totally aghast. "What?!" I say doing my best to match her enthusiasm as we bounce like loons.

"I won the lottery on Saturday night – would you believe it?" she beams. "Tim and I couldn't stop smiling…laughing – crying! I nearly called you there and then, but decided to wait until we had confirmation this morning."

"Which you now have?" I ask cautiously, hoping we are not prematurely celebrating.

"Yes! We just had our meeting with the Committee – Tim has just nipped into the greenhouses to get his coat, but I spotted you and couldn't wait… I said I would, but— *Oh! Can you believe it?!*"

Unable to find the proper words to express exactly how happy I am for Kate, who is my oldest, dearest, and undeniably most loyal friend – who will unquestionably make the best mother that ever lived – I hug her, putting heart and soul into my short words that I splutter over her shoulder: "Congratulations, no one deserves it more."

I am not sure which one of us is shaking more, but as we part, with glistening eyes, I realise this is no coincidence. I applied for one of my eggs to be donated to Kate and had the application denied. Gee-Gee told me she had played no part in the Committee's decision – Mary I am sure made her displeasure known – yet here, days after I have sold my soul to the R&R (some might add 'the devil'), and Kate has won the lottery…

What are the chances of that?

Not great.

What are the chances of lottery winners regularly being rigged?

Probably high.

What are the chances that this gift to Kate is another warning to me? A sign of how things can come and go (for better and worse), when you are in the pocket of the R&R?

I'd say, it's a certainty.

For Kate and Tim's sake, I am glad. May something wholesome and good come from this.

The SurrogacyPods in the R&R lab spring to mind again…Who's baby is she going to have? Please, if possible, don't let it be mine… I know I wanted her to have mine, but that was before I had seen them. Seeing is different and I do not want to see.

"When will he or she be born?" I ask cautiously.

"Oh, well, that I have to wait to find out. Months I think, but all good things come to those who wait, right?"

"Of course." I reach out and squeeze her hand. "Undoubtedly."

Kate releases little squealing sounds as she struggles to contain her excitement. "I get to meet them soon. We've been encouraged to visit the SurrogacyPods regularly – as if I need encouragement! Oh, I best call Mum! She'll never believe it!" Kate hugs me again, makes me promise to call her later and skips off to find Tim.

I am thrilled for her.
But life really will never be the same again.

* * *

Max and I arrive late to the restaurant on Friday evening. We have no great excuse, I think it has just been a long week – well, no, longer than that. Ever since we witnessed Henry and Mary's fight and I walked into the R&R we have both looked perpetually tired and time has a habit of ticking by faster than we realise. Claire, our Match Coordinator, called in before we left and quizzed us on our 'marital duties.' This wasn't scheduled for a few more weeks, yet Claire cheerfully explained that: 'The Committee thought it best, given the unfortunate circumstances with the late Mrs Rivers, that I check you hadn't compromised your compliance.'

One or both of us might have been tempted to make a rude or inappropriate joke, so it was a good job we were both initially too tired to do anything more than smile and flush red like someone in a chilli eating competition. Max recovered before I did and assured her we remembered our duty and had paid close attention to the 'most informative emails' that she had sent. How I didn't laugh, I still don't know. Those emails might inform, but they always make me want to hide under the covers – alone. I was more than a little relieved to find our own natural instinct led us and our discoveries were made without needing to refer to government-led guidance sheets.

Thankfully Max's diplomatic answer satisfied Claire, leaving me to my blushes. "Lovely! Yes, that is lovely news.

Obviously, the Committee understands you've had a difficult start – quite tragic in fact. I know how much Director Rivers was looking forward to seeing her first grandchild… Such a waste…such a waste." Claire had a shimmer in her eye, but it was suddenly replaced as though someone had ignited a torch behind her skin as she beamed: "Ah, but she'll be proud anyway, we all will – despite everything, you are still the poster couple. They already used your wedding video in a classroom, did you know? Yes, yes, the glory of the matching system…so lovely!" She giggled. "Then when the first baby comes – oh, the joy! I'm nearly as excited as you two must be!"

I repressed a 'I doubt it' and smiled, holding Max's hand. The truth is, although we had started well with our 'compliance activities,' that has all but stopped. We hold hands, we hug…but no more. Mary's death, Henry's injury, and our enrolment in the R&R has pretty much squashed anything extra. Sleep is a mess of blame and torment, not rest after passionate embraces. It bothers me as I think it further puts our relationship in choppy waters, but at the same time I can imagine nothing I want less than to find out that I am pregnant right now. An imminent pregnancy would mean Kate and me raising our children together, which I know she'd love; however, it would also mean relinquishing everything I hold dear to bring a child into a world with morals I am struggling more than ever to balance.

"At last!" exclaims Kate as we scan into the restaurant. "We thought you'd got lost!"

Kate knows that isn't possible, we have visited this establishment more than any other in the entire Hub. The band in the corner plays so wonderfully, paying to listen to them alone is worth it. I really hope they are on form this evening as my spirits might need their help with an extra boost. Kate, Tim, and Ella enthusiastically hug and greet us both and as I step back from Ella, I see Theo eyeing me to see if I am willing to play make-believe with him. I sigh, it isn't like I really have a choice because I don't doubt for one moment that Gee-Gee has tasked her forces to watch me in public – with Theo especially. Am I capable of holding up the pretence?

Max is. He grasps Theo's hand, pulling him into a strong man-hug, so strong in fact, I think he caught Theo off guard. I smile without meaning to, but I don't attempt to wipe my grin when I hug Theo myself. I'll play your game, but never again will I trust you. Good reason or not, you lie and cheat for personal gain – just like my great grandmother. Of course, she would argue it is not for personal gain and I am missing the point if I believe that. Always for the mission…the grand plan. The Guardianship of Earth.

Why am I so sarcastic about this? I agree with the grand plan.

Just not the method.

Poisoning people is not the way.

It isn't poison. Damn, I'm arguing Gee-Gee's points for her.

Okay, it isn't poison…but it is treating the entire population like a giant lab rat.

"Maia?" Ella's voice rings in my ear next to me. She sounds concerned. "Maia, are you okay?"

"Hmm?" I say turning to look at her. Shit, I've been daydreaming, haven't I? "Oh, sorry, did I zone out?" I chuckle, trying to make light of my potential rudeness.

"Yes, honey, you did," Max is smiling, but he raises his eyebrows at me, silently telling me to wake up. I apologise and Ella sweetly dismisses my lack of manners and repeats her questioning – honestly none of which someone else couldn't have answered, yet I still feel bad for ignoring her. She has an honest charm about her and always has had. She is smart, beautiful, and generally brilliant with no hint of arrogance about her – which just makes her sickeningly perfect if you are tired and sarcastic like I am. Ella is a red-haired, slightly younger version of Kate really – both annoyingly wonderful but absolutely a blessing to be with.

Unlike Kate, however, I cannot trust Ella. Gee-Gee said 'not yet' when I asked if she was in the R&R, but they clearly plan on including her. She was collecting data on every aspect of the agricultural sector for Mary. With brains like hers, Ella has to have noticed a pattern or an area Mary was most interested in – not to mention been suspicious when greenhouses burnt and an allotment was hit by a rogue drone. Her expertise in IT and AI would tell her – long before it dawned on me – there are no rogue or malfunctioning drones. Not really anyway. Some could be human error, but more likely, everything is done for a purpose.

Just not a purpose I can voice here.

Kate and Tim's next generation, undocked plants could not thrive because they ruined test results and allowed two women to recover sufficient fertility to breed naturally. Not only does that unbalance tests, but it also opens the authorities up to questioning and gives rise to hope in the general public that a cure or new age of fertility is dawning.

Unless the R&R want it to, that dawn will never rise.

Tomorrow will be cloudy.

Get used to the fog.

"Maia! Come on, this is a celebration! I am having a baby – we are having a baby!" Kate almost sings, clutching Tim's hand. The parents any child can dream of.

I shake my shoulders, tell myself to bottle up my issues and rejoice with my friends. My inner battles will keep for another day.

EIGHT

"Hmmphh, well look what the cat's dragged in," mocks Eve as I walk into the living room. I smile and greet her with affection and she waves her hand, gesturing for me to sit in front of her. She looks tired, but I think that every time I see her now. She has gone from using only one stick to two in the last few days. At 112 you could argue it is nothing short of a miracle she is walking at all – you'd be right, but only a few months ago I thought her appearance could have passed for someone in their eighties – yet now her body as well as her mind is slowing down at an alarming pace. When Eve is lucid, she is just as sharp, witty, and unceasingly stubborn as ever; but when the cruelty of dementia grasps her, which it all too often does, she is but a shell, and it makes my heart weep every time I see the switch of intelligence flick to mute and pause. In the time it takes me to seat myself, the switch has clicked again and all I can do is exchange a sorry smile with Aunt Dora and sigh.

We walk into the hallway. We don't need to, nothing will disturb Eve while she is 'out,' yet we do it anyway as a mark of respect – or perhaps we are subconsciously deluding ourselves, behaving like we would were she just sleeping.

We briefly go over the last few days, catching up on enough to mutually satisfy our curiosities, but Aunt Dora makes it plain any future information regarding R&R visits can be reserved for Eve. It seems her prior determination to 'know' has been frightened away. She wanted to know the truth of her late husband, she said that she wanted to know what Eve had done in the past, and who the second 'they' are. She knows these things now…or rather knows enough to know when to stop.

Wise woman.

Aunt Dora tells me she had a visit from Mark Jones, Head of Security, again after Max and my induction. She doesn't recount exactly what was said, or at least I sense she is skimming over the details, but apparently his parting words were: "Your niece and her husband have joined us. Both your and Mrs Addams' existence is balanced on their service, *and your silence*. The Director has spoken for you. She will not do that again." Aunt Dora shakes and her voice wobbles as she speaks. Despite already knowing this, I suddenly feel nauseous. The continued repetition of threats is exhausting. There really is only so much fear and loathing I can muster and I want to shout at the R&R: *"I know already, quit reminding me!"*

Wanting to change the subject, Aunt Dora shows me a family portrait she has just completed for one of Dad's colleagues. I don't know them well, but she has captured them on canvas as crisply as any photograph could.

Checking the time on her watch, she slides the painting back into its protective sleeve and leaves to tend to her errands. I return into the living room to find Eve in the same position as I left her, though from the gentle puffering sound coming from her lips, I think she could have slipped from fog to sleep – but I really have no way of knowing.

Squash, her loyal ginger cat, is curled up on her lap and Smoggy, Aunt Dora's majestic grey cat, is sleeping in her chair. Smoggy is either keeping my aunt's spot warm until she returns or claiming it as her own – depending on how generous you want to be the large, immaculate ball of fluff that lords over this home. If I get stuck at home, I'm going to ask the PTB for a pet.

Not if, *when*.

I look over the mantelpiece and see the painting of me as a child sitting under the big oak by the river. My favourite place to be. I need to go there soon, it feels like forever since I sat by the bank. It's certainly an eternity since I sat there as carefree as the painting suggests. It rained heavily earlier, with any luck the river's flow will be fast enough to sweep my self-doubt and general disbelief from my mind – even better if it clears my mind sufficiently to come up with a plan. My current limbo is all-encompassing.

"They didn't ask how you got in, did they?" I jump and spin for the thousandth time as Eve returns to consciousness with no warning. She can't have missed my whole-body reaction, but she just looks at me, waiting for a straight answer to her less than complete sentence. That said, I do understand the question.

"No, they didn't," I reply. I haven't quite worked out why, but I haven't dared to ask either.

Eve chuckles. "Good…it worked then." She chuckles again. "Good to know they ain't out shined me yet."

"Pardon?" I am confused. *Again.*

"Your button camera."

"Yes, they took that, I told you—"

"Exactly. They didn't ask, coz they think they know… that thing will read like a hack. They'll think it fudged their cameras too…" She laughs louder this time, "but they'll be studying that forever looking for the *how*."

"*How* did it?"

"It didn't. It just records, like I told yer… and omits what they think will fuzz electronics, letting you past. They won't have record of the drone catching you, no code, nothin'…" Eve is grinning at her own mastery.

"So, the button was basically a ruse to hide the synthetic sleeve?"

"Yep, *that* I don't want 'em finding. They have similar tech that I left 'em, but nothin' as developed as your skin… hmmphh."

"What do I do with it now?" I say, rolling up my shirt sleeve. "I've worn it and the control pearls all this time afraid of what to do with them. If asked, I've said the pearls are from Aunt Dora as a wedding present, but—"

"Keep 'em on, Missy, keep 'em on," Eve says, waving her hands. "Safer in plain sight, under their noses now than in here, tis only a matter of time them hmmphhing bastards come lookin' again…or to get me. No, I've made me peace with that…you're on the path, you'll do right."

I try to swallow a lump in my throat and smile hesitantly. "Are you sure?" I've gotten used to the sleeve, but I'm not sure about it becoming a permanent fixture to me. "Do you think I'll need it again?" I am not sure I want to know the answer and unconsciously grimace as Eve replies:

"You might, not gonna lie…if things…well, we'll see. Ain't a place you should go…No–no, hmmphh, no—"

"What place? The R&R headquarters?" I can't say I am in a hurry to go beyond the Hub boundaries again anytime soon.

But I would love to be let loose in that laboratory.

Ugh.

"No, not the headquarters…you'll have to go there, I reckon anyway."

"Then where?" I ask Eve in earnest, but she doesn't reply. "Eve? Eve?" I gently touch her hand, but she doesn't respond and my eyes fill with tears.

Great, a new riddle.

Just what I wanted.

NINE

Henry stayed in the hospital longer than he probably needed to, but as he now lives alone and the PTB are so intent on painting him as a wounded soldier and victim of a senseless, deplorable act by a jealous and dangerous man, they chose to keep him in longer. To be fair, he is the victim of a deplorable act – just not the one the PTB are publicising.

Even to Max and me Henry is lying about what happened. I had wondered if he knew more about the R&R than I initially thought, but as Henry is continuing his charade of being attacked at home by Peter Lloyd after he stormed their house in an angry, drunken, lovestruck manner, I can only assume he is in the dark to who his real employers and benefactors are and has just been subdued under some pretence of PTB judgment. Without risking too much, I cannot ask.

Now home, Henry is eagerly talking about getting back to work and putting 'the whole ordeal' behind him. His account is actually pretty convincing and whilst still in the hospital, or when on the street talking to his neighbours, if I didn't speak to him again, I would also believe he is an aggrieved, bereaved husband. However, once at home, with no one else to listen, he is anything but 'in mourning.'

I cannot judge him wholeheartedly. His initial actions that caused this horrific catalyst of events were, without question, repugnant, but he has had to live with the consequences of those actions for twenty-four years – and I would argue, has paid heavily. However, so has his son, who will continue to do so for the rest of his life.

Ignorance, lust, and love trapped Henry Rivers. Ignorance and lust at the beginning; love for his son after that. But if he is honest with himself, which I think possibly he now is, he *wanted* the positives of what Mary brought – the quicker routes to better roles, bigger labs, bigger budget, and more research material than he could shake a stick at. Even if his silence and tolerance over the years reaped as much as it cost. I hope I never fall into such a selfish, self-defeating trap.

Max doesn't know how to cope with his father. I can see it in his eyes when he talks to him. He listens to his dad rattling away and cannot miss the difference in his father's manner. The lightness and freedom of spirit is almost tangible – it is as though he has had to carry a burden, a great weight or tumour on his back and the doctors have finally cured him, giving him a new chance and he is overjoyed. If it weren't beyond his limits of courage, I'd question if Henry didn't kill Mary himself. He seems relieved...*grateful* even. It is no wonder he has nothing to say against Peter Lloyd or who actually shot him.

If he were able to, I think he would thank him.

I shudder as another thought seeps into my mind...one I keep internally hearing, but do my best to brush aside...it is not just Henry who benefits from Mary and Peter's deaths. *I do.* I would not know anything had Mary not broken first and if Henry had not attempted to take a stand – then I would not have spoken to Eve and mentioned the AIP and

Lilith…*Lilith*. How the heck am I going to get to her when I do not know where she is? Eve wasn't surprised my rescue mission wasn't immediately executed. It would seem I need time – but how much?

"Maia? Are you quite well?" asks Henry softly.

"Hmm? Yes, quite, sorry, did you need me to—"

"No, there's nothing I need. You just seemed troubled, locked in conversation in another world almost?"

I smile at him, trying to laugh off his concern, but as I glance at Max, I see the same worry in his eyes. Maybe I am talking to myself more than normal? *Definitely*.

* * *

Despite everything else, life has resumed its normal order. We work, eat, sleep, repeat. I would like to try cooking now I am no longer stuck in my childhood home, but our DDS (drone delivered sustenance) has continued…and will apparently continue until such time I am on maternity leave and a fulltime housewife. Then I will be delivered ingredients and recipes instead. How kind.

Every time the drone finds me, demanding I release and consume its contents, I want to practice my batting abilities on it. I then feel bad because it isn't the drone's fault it delivers my undoctored food, saving the modified food for others. Then I feel extra weird because the drone is an inanimate object and cares not for either appreciation or injury. It just is.

How enviable.

Yesterday I had my first 'marital health exam.' Suffice to say, I did not enjoy that one bit. I am not saying Max did either, yet his exam was 1000% less intrusive than mine and although I am not particularly worried about discussing periods with Kate, discussing them in front of three representatives from the Genetics Committee is not my idea of amusement. "Oh, well that was to be expected I suppose, given your last donation and marriage dates," sighed the eldest of the three. I'd say their names, but they never felt the need to introduce themselves. "It would have been a real coup had you been pregnant though – the shining star of the matching system. Plus, you know, a boost after the events with the late Director of Agriculture – a positive spin on a black area, a—"

"Yes, a shame," I cut in, unable to listen to her looking for another analogy.

I was reminded of my duty and released feeling more uneasy than before. Max and I didn't talk about our exams beyond 'well, that wasn't fun,' and I am left with the mixed emotions of being glad I am not pregnant, hoping I never am, and fearing the repercussions if I never am, all at the same time. We need to talk about this, but that side of our partnership has frozen.

Our current dilemma, however, is Gee-Gee's ninetieth birthday celebrations – which also translate into the first time I have been 'home' since I married. A fact my mother misses zero time in pointing out as we walk in.

"Ah! At last, my daughter returns! I thought you'd transferred to another Hub!" she says sarcastically and loudly so the entire family can hear her. "No, no, I didn't need your help setting up or collecting goods, your sister – you know, the one who just gave birth to your new niece – she arranged for drone delivery and—"

"How good of Abby to click a few buttons on her watch app for you. However did she cope?" I retort as dryly as I can.

As usual Mum ignores my sarcasm: "Yes, it was good of her. Have you greeted your grandmother? You ignore us all terribly. I left you a message yesterday, why didn't you reply?"

"You asked if I was pregnant – for the third time this week. Do you not think that a tad excessive? Can we not just say that unless I message and say *there is* a change, then there is *no* change on that front?" Mum flaps her arms in preparation of expressing her disapproval so I cut in with: "But no, I have not seen Grandma, nor Gee-Gee, so I will say hello now."

I immediately walk away, but as I am (in her mind) acting on her rebuke, she lets me slip away to do the rounds. I do my best to feign interest in my nieces and nephews, laugh when my sister mocks me, groan when my brother parrots our mother's questions, and hug my father when he gets off the phone. Gee-Gee patiently waits for me to get to her and embraces me as I wish her happy birthday. As I sit myself beside her, she sighs saying: "Ninety years, huh?"

"And not looking a day over eighty-five," I wink.

She laughs, mock slapping me, telling me I'm too cheeky for my own good. For a moment I relax, forgetting the other side of Gee-Gee, the side that has been hidden for a lifetime. I can see why it was easier when she had Great Gramps with her. They were in different departments in the PTB, well, R&R, but even now, I do not doubt they were each other's staff and stay – partners in absolutely everything, in good times and bad.

Joking aside, Gee-Gee didn't seem to age until Great Gramps died. Now she bears the burden alone…or is this my time to share the load?

Your mission is laid before you…all you have to do is get on with it…

"I hope Max and I can be as useful as you and Gramps," I whisper.

Gee-Gee immediately looks up and straight into my eyes. Brown on brown, gazing into one another, reading for the subtext.

"So do I," she replies. "I know you have your reservations—"

"I'm sure with time and understanding those will iron out." Liar. No. *Optimist,* I must be an optimist…or at least fool myself into being one.

Gee-Gee's smile is heart-warming. I could have just given her the biggest, most expensive present in the UNE and I don't think she would be able to beam any better. It makes my heart skip, whether from guilt or genuine pleasure, I really couldn't distinguish.

Mum calls out to everyone declaring it is time for dinner. You would think it was a wedding as she has arranged where we are all to sit. Unsurprisingly, I have been stationed between my sister and sister-in-law so I have full view and opportunity to feel the glow of the children who are seated on a separate adjacent table behind us. My youngest niece is fast asleep, but I am willing to put money on my mum thrusting her into my arms by the end of the evening.

Honestly, I don't mind, I am not anti-nieces and nephews. As far as I am concerned, they should have been the tokens to appease mum and be more than enough to prove our family has 'done our bit' for population numbers. Also, I get to laugh at their antics, teach them potentially unwanted games, and then hand them back to their parents when I leave. And, most importantly of all, they are loved and wanted by their parents – as absolutely all children should be.

No child should be poked or moulded to the whims of another and even if their arrival into this world was not the most straightforward, they should not have that smeared in their face at every opportunity like I have had. Mum hasn't mentioned it today, possibly because she wants me to get pregnant, not to remind me of how we both nearly died when I was born, but even if she doesn't say it today, she will at some point soon. She doesn't need to wait for special occasions like my birthday to remind me of the debt I owe her or the future offspring I denied her. But she could save herself the trouble, because now I am perfectly capable of putting myself down before anyone else has the chance.

Wanting to shrug off my thoughts, I look over to Max. He has been dragged into conversation with Abe, my brother, but is laughing. I actually think he finds my family easier than I do. I reach for the wine and decide a glass of it might help. It isn't my usual 'go to,' but why not branch out?

"Oh, are you drinking, Maia?" says Mum reproachfully.

"I am not pregnant, Mum, it is okay to—"

"Not pregnant that you *know of*…" she retorts.

Oh, for pity's sake.

"A little R&R will do her good. A baby will come, have no doubt, Beatrice," says Gee-Gee cheerfully. "Besides, it's my birthday!" She reaches for her wine glass to toast and I smile. That bloody catchphrase of hers, the one with the weight of the world behind it, is absolutely anything *but* rest and relaxation; yet now I am on the inside of the joke, I do feel like I am part of a new, exclusive, and potentially rewarding club. A minor, but not insignificant reward being getting one over mum now, for she will not deny or defy Gee-Gee.

"To Gee-Gee!" I declare raising my glass. "May we all aspire to so much and to live as long and faithfully," I toast with a tear in my eye.

"To Gee-Gee!" we all chime.

Ironically, I think it is the happiest evening I have spent in my family home for more than a decade, maybe ever.

TEN

I am not drunk and nor is Max, but when we get home, having been delivered by a Solarbug after Dad insisted (for which I was grateful as I am struck by spine freezing chills as I step off trams these days), we are both a little gigglier and a little freer with our words than we have recently been.

Maybe that is unfair…

We have spoken every day about any and everything, including our feelings – just not regarding our lack of physical activities. I didn't think we were embarrassed about that kind of thing. It had all progressed naturally and wonderfully once we were married and the first week was truly special.

But?

But, I think his grief, being unable to process Mary, and indeed, Henry, has taken its toll. I want to say something, but I don't know how, so I briefly kiss him good night and slide under the covers, amazed and relieved today went as well as it did.

"Are we gonna talk about it?" Max asks abruptly as I turn the bedroom light out.

"What? We just did talk…all the way home!" I giggle, slightly higher pitched than I like.

"Maia, are you wilfully misunderstanding or just…?"

"*Just what?*" I say, confused. "I thought we had an okay evening?"

"We did…we did, but it isn't your family I want to talk about."

I don't answer for a moment, then whisper, "Okay?" hoping he will just get on with whatever it is.

"Why don't you want to touch me anymore?" he asks so quietly it is a wonder I heard him.

"What? I do…I just thought you didn't…since…" I stop. He knows what I mean.

"It isn't me that stopped, Maia."

I click on the light, sitting up and staring at him to see if I understand his meaning.

"You think…*I* stopped?"

"Yes."

I open my mouth, attempting to answer, but no words come to me…is it possible he is right?

Max adjusts himself, leaning back on the headboard, not taking his eyes off me. "You pull away, or avoid eye contact when I try…I wasn't sure if it was Theo—"

"NO! What…? *NO!*" I exclaim, possibly louder than necessary. Max waits quietly for me to elaborate. "I was hurt beyond measure at his double betrayal, but it cemented our past, not brought fresh…" I pause, trying to discern the thoughts running behind Max's eyes. Then it dawns on me. Maybe the lack of communication has come from me. From *my* guilt – *my* not dealing with events, not him, or at least not just him. Max struggles with everything, his past and present, but he talks about it. I briefly asked if he blamed me for his mum's death, but I didn't ask if I blamed myself…not that I think it my fault as such. Mary was what she was, but I, with my unceasing curiosity pushed for knowledge and my part in her downfall is undeniable. Have I been so wrapped in my internal conflicts – the decision of the next step, whether I agree or disagree with the grand plan of the R&R, whether I should *benefit* from that plan – that *I* have shut down, not Max?

Crunching up the duvet in my hands as a distraction, I blurt out my thoughts and Max listens without saying a word. When I finally finish rambling, he gently takes my face in both his hands, smiling with tender warmth, and I melt.

My heart races as he leans in and kisses me gently on each cheek, soothing tears I shed without knowing they were there. As he moves to kiss my lips, I wrap my arms around his neck and join my heart, body, and soul with his once more. I briefly stretch to the side to switch off the light, but as I lean away, I see his beautiful, loving grin and I forget the light and let the covers fly.

Abstinence will not be observed tonight.

ELEVEN

The only issue with Max and I totally realigning ourselves as a couple is it has expedited the inevitable. I had hoped my recent donation would have monkeyed with my hormones longer – or my body would be led by my mind and hold off the 'happy' event. Yet two weeks later I started with morning sickness, headaches, and then cramping.

So, not only am I a Golden Goose, with 'the best of the best' fertility (Gee-Gee's words, not mine), but I am also one of those super 'lucky' women who know they are pregnant super early.

Trembling, I made my way to the clinic before work. I didn't have to lie or fumble with the truth about where I was going because Max had to be in his office early today. I will tell him straight away if I am right, but I don't want to say anything until I know for sure.

"Well, well, Mrs Rivers, I am genuinely thrilled to be the one to give you this news," beams Dr Waller as she walks back into the room holding my testing stick. "I watched your wedding, you know?" How would I? I've never met her before! "I never dreamed I would be telling you, you are with child – what an honour! And, if you will forgive me, what a superb example you and Mr Rivers are for the Genetics Committee! A better match I am sure cannot be made!"

While I do not disagree with her – Max and I are an example of the system working – I refuse to give in entirely to the notion that organically developed matches cannot work just as well. I cannot accept that the petri dish outshines the joy of self-discovered partnership. I choose to believe a balance of both is the way forward…

Balance…yes, no extremes…

Good luck convincing anyone else of that!

I smile and thank the doctor, it isn't her fault she buys into the PTB propaganda. I should buy it…but my curious mind won't shut the heck up, puzzling over every detail and insisting on ruining my most peaceful (or rather *potentially* peaceful) thoughts.

At least Dr Waller isn't Dr Oldman or Dr Singh – the doctors who harvest eggs for research and development. The latter I hope not to see for a long time (preferably ever), and the former is now off with his new R&R research project called 'The Initiative' – not that anyone will give me details on that beyond Gee-Gee's initial disclosure.

Patience, I tell myself, have patience…

Opposed to *being* the patient?

If only it were an 'either/or' choice!

Still grinning, Dr Waller hands me my test stick. There is a picture of a baby on the result panel along with the control line – a valid test. No cause for doubts. They could have just used the word 'pregnant,' but no, they want to add to the joy by adding a picture of a newborn. Is it just me, or does it seem slightly unsanitary to have an infant appear because I urinated on a stick? I feel the corner of my mouth lifting into a wry smile and look up to see Dr Waller handing me a container. I look at her quizzically.

"Some like to keep the stick as a memento of this wondrous occasion – the start of your new journey," she says, smiling expectantly.

I am guessing my gut reaction of 'ewww' isn't what she wants to hear, so I nod and place the stick inside the container. Considering we have so few physical keepsakes or adornments in the UNE, I truly want to laugh – laugh *and* cry – because if I find out Mum has three pee sticks memorialised in the house somewhere and expects me to do the same…

"Okay!" Dr Waller declares whilst washing her hands, distracting me from my musings.

After drying her hands, she sits at her desk and starts tapping on her computer screen. I feel like I should make small talk, but I have nothing to say. Nothing acceptable that is.

I am relieved when she spins her chair towards me, saying: "I have pinged you a schedule of check-ups, scans, and classes for your pregnancy. We'll have an exact due date after your first scan, but the test indicates you're two weeks at the moment."

"Due mid-September." I have already worked this much out. I hadn't thought I would have an instant schedule though. No pressure then?

"Yes…you must be so excited!"

"Not as much as my mother will be," I say without thinking.

Dr Waller's eyes boggle for a moment, but she doesn't detect the truth behind my sarcasm and just chuckles saying, "I'm sure the whole family will be thrilled!"

"You won't tell them, will you?" I ask, suddenly panicking. I want to put off Mum's glee as long as possible. Once again Dr Waller looks at me in confusion, so I quickly add: "I would like to surprise them myself, that's all."

"Of course, you do!" laughs Dr Waller, nodding with approval. "Fear not, I sent your results to the Genetics Committee and Director of Fertility, but your family need not hear it until you— *Ah...!* Silly me! Director Beaufort is—"

"My great grandmother, yes," I fill in, sighing. "Never mind, Gee-Gee – the Director – she will congratulate me quietly first, I am sure." She keeps secrets better than anyone I know.

* * *

I arranged to meet Max in the Botanical Gardens after work. I messaged him asking if he could meet me by the waterfalls and he responded quickly that he'd love to, but would be a little late. The light has faded away, but the arranged solar lights have a beautiful shimmer in the darkness and I sit myself on what we now consider to be 'our bench' – the one where we once, thanks to the Architect's inscription (a double, if not triple sign of it being poignant for us), sat together and realised we could sit and find peace from life's madness together.

The water flows in a newly fed hurry after yet another night of heavy rain, and I sit contemplating what life will hold now. Soon, if I chose to sit here with Max, I will sit as a three, a family, not two, not a pair. Technically, I am already part of a three…

I am frightened.

Trapped and frightened.

Max is going to be overjoyed, I am sure of it.

Everyone is.

Just not me.

I feel the weight of the atmosphere pushing down on me and I suddenly find it hard to breathe. I knew what the doctor was going to say, I had stoically prepared for it. I know my body well enough to know something was different, even at this early stage, yet I managed to act out the charade long enough to go through the motions at the hospital – even back at work, where I had to look Theo in the eyes, discussing research I knew was as pointless as me trying to swim up this blooming waterfall. Yet now…now I am alone and my thoughts run into comprehension…to consideration of what will be. Not what *might be* or *could be*, one day *if… Will be.*

"Maia?" I turn to see Max approaching looking concerned, "Are you okay? You're not breathing quite right…?"

"I'm pregnant," I blurt out. I had planned (whilst still in my theatrical actor role), a beautiful dialog – a reveal to remember – but in my hyperventilating state, that is all I can muster. Apparently, it is enough, as Max's smile spreads further than I have ever seen before and he positively grabs me and hugs me so tight I am almost winded.

Suffice to say, he is pleased.

Into the Fog

* * *

I leave telling Mum about the baby until Christmas day. Gee-Gee gave me a bemused smile when I begged for her silence, Kate squealed with joy, and Aunt Dora, being only too happy to be 'in the know,' had a mini celebration with the four of us at her bungalow, promising not to breathe a word to anyone else. Eve, though disinclined to speak to any neighbours anyway in case her dementia betrays her (either socially or more seriously against the PTB or R&R), sadly did not require any petition for secrecy. I have visited many times over the last few weeks, but when I have she has never been 'home.' I am desperate for further conversation from her, yet every time Aunt Dora messages to say, 'Eve is lucid, come quickly,' I am not fast enough.

I wait until all the family (Henry included, as Max and I didn't want him to be alone today) are sitting around the large Woods' family dining table. I watch the plates being loaded and remind myself that reprimanding Mum for her gluttony, regardless of the festivities, is a waste of breath. She has saved up ration tokens and was always going to spend them – as well as any extras she could commandeer from the extended family.

Self-control, in her eyes, is for the infertile, not a family of such 'high status.'

I listen to the hen-like cackling that comes from my sister, sister-in-law, mother, and grandmother as they unite over the humorous and spoilt behaviour of my seven nieces and nephews, simultaneously praying I can raise my children in a less caricatured fashion.

Finally, the desserts are handed around and I shoulder my brothers' (otherwise well received) joke about it being a 'good job it's Christmas, or I'd say you look like you don't deserve a dessert.' I have never been one to body-shame anybody, it is just rude and unnecessary. That said, I am not fat, he is just a jerk.

Actually, I have always been slimmer than he is, especially now he has 'relaxed' his gym attendance as he calls it. That is, of course, just code for 'I'm lazy and get away with the minimum my Fitwatch app requires.' I simply look at him, with neither smile nor glare as he laughs at his own joke, and coolly reply: "It's a good job no one judges your body fat too closely before you breed, or you'd eternally be in fat camp."

I keep my amusement to myself as chuckles ripple around the table. Abe's eldest daughter catches onto the term 'fat camp' and her repetition of the phrase is truly music to my ears (childish as it may be). I have no doubt her singing 'daddy's going to fat camp' is going to be the anthem of his Christmas and not one bit of me is sorry. If I could teach Abby's children something similar, my consolation mirth would be complete.

"Hang on!" squeals Mum. "Are you saying you're pregnant?!" I'll give Mum her dues: she may wilfully misunderstand and ignore most of what I say, but she isn't going to be last at the table to get a clue when she wants the prize.

I nod and Mum looks to Max for confirmation – which he gives by taking my hand in his and resting both over my stomach, smiling so broadly all his teeth shine. The rest of the room erupts and for a moment, I feel the warmth of their excitement and it outweighs my fears. However, as the decibels return to normal, the warmth dispels and doubts creep in like a thief in the night.

"I cannot wait to take you shopping for the nursery – you chose 'default' from the Housing Association, I am sure if I call Claire she'll be only too thrilled to help… Oooh, this is *the* happiest of Christmases! Three children married and *with* children…who in the Hub, nay, the whole UNE can say that?!" Mum's cooing continues all evening and I doubt it will stop any time soon.

Henry leaves when we do and before we board our separate Solarbug's he takes me by the hand and gently kisses my cheek. "Merry Christmas, my dear," he says affectionately. "I knew from the moment I saw you, you'd make my son happy and bring a fresh start and previously unknown joy to both our lives." His smile fades as he pauses. "I didn't know my path would be quite as such when I moved here," he scoffs, "but I am not sorry – not for any of it. I know what that makes me – but this coming year is a change and reboot for the Rivers' family. I cannot be sorry for the joy, the peace, that is ahead."

Max hugs his father with a hint of tears in his eyes. The mix of anger, pain, loss, and acceptance still rages in him, but like his father, he looks for a new future – a future that grows in me.

My question is: what future do we want for our child?

More of the same?

Or do I risk life and limb to forge a different future? Not just for my child, but for every child to come.

What would that future even look like?

Alexia Muelle-Rushbrook

And how on Earth will I achieve it?

TWELVE

Uneasy as I am with my new condition, it would seem it has unlocked doors in the R&R. Contraceptives are as illegal as abstinence, yet they obviously expected a longer fight with me, apparently questioning if I would embrace their decree of service by 'motherhood first' before they included me in any real work. Part of me feels frustrated and ashamed I caved so quickly, though possibly that is misplaced pride. I love my husband, sex is normal, it is everything else that is not. *In my humble opinion.*

Gee-Gee appeared at my front door on the 3rd of January, 2124 with a grin and bottle of non-alcoholic wine in her hand. I greeted her with surprise and then froze in the doorway. "Well girl, let an old woman in, we have much to discuss," she said, tutting half-heartedly, walking in without waiting for me to respond. I followed her into the house, sliding the door closed behind me and offered to take her coat. "No, no thank you. I'll need it, it's cold out."

I was about to point out that she was indoors at a pleasant twenty degrees Celsius when I became distracted by Gee-Gee's decision to enter our study, not the living room.

"Oh, that's the study, come this way, I'll—"

"I know that, I'm not here for drinks," she said, leaving the bottle on the study desk, running her hand under its rim as though she was in her own home.

"Max isn't home yet," I said as a reason to delay whatever Gee-Gee was doing.

"I know," Gee-Gee stated walking towards the lift that once again magically revealed itself in the wall. "Unless Max is interested in science all of a sudden, he doesn't need to be a part of this discussion. I'll call for him when he is required. Come."

Feeling like a mindless drone, I grabbed my coat and stepped into the lift as I was told, staring at my great grandmother as she directed us once more to the tunnels below. We silently strode side by side until we were sat on a tram. Those on the tram nodded to Gee-Gee and as she returned their attention, they greeted her with a respectful, 'Evening Director,' but no one acknowledged me with more than a smile as she led me to the gallery of the R&R headquarters.

Now inside the gallery, projectors and screens fill the room with windows to the outer world and once more I attempt to take in what and where I am seeing – looking for information I can use as well as just being awestruck. I could watch these screens forever and still find something new and amazing to observe. The world is so varied and the recording drones are, it seems, literally everywhere, regardless of human life and activity.

One screen captures my attention as there seems to be a hive of robotic activity. That in itself is not particularly amazing, robotics in one shape or form assist life in the Hubs in every manner possible – plus, we are taught how essential AI is beyond the fence in detecting radiation as well as assisting restoration of Earth. Yet here, on this camera feed, the robots, androids, and drones I can see are going above and beyond any machine I have ever contemplated – they almost look like they have a settlement and are *living* amongst their research.

"What are they doing?" I ask, pointing at the screen. Gee-Gee has been absorbed by the computer on the central desk, but looks up as I speak, gently exhaling as she replies:

"They are clearing an old settlement and replanting – *rewilding*." She pauses, I can only assume deciding whether I deserve to know more. I remain silent and am rewarded. "We have left many old settlements, either due to lack of time and resources, or because that area is not yet high enough up on our restoration schedule. However, the R&R is keen to return as much land to its intended state as possible, so we have teams, both human and AI, across the world."

"I cannot see any humans there?"

"No, not on that one, the radiation is not safe for humans, yet a lot of wildlife has adapted and moved back in nearby. We need to remove our waste, reseed, replant, and replace as much as possible and connect ecosystems that were long ago divided by the abundance and selfishness of humanity. Once those teams have moved on to clear another area, if appropriate, we send other teams to continue the research and act as conservationists."

"Ambassadors of Earth," I whisper as the term comes to my mind.

"Exactly – they can be human and or robotic Guardians, but Guardians nonetheless."

"Is Lilith one?"

"In time she will be."

"Where is she?" I ask as non-confrontationally as I can.

"Where she should not be, I grant you," says Gee-Gee quietly looking at the screen.

"So why is she there?"

"Because the rules are such as they are…and she broke them."

"Falling in love is—"

"All well and good, but not the mission, Maia."

"You bent the rule to get me here…"

"*For* the mission," Gee-Gee says resolutely, "I told you before, the bigger picture outweighs the individual or selfish agenda – hard as it may be."

"So, it is okay as long as unfair rules are enforced on someone else?"

"I wouldn't say it is 'okay,' but yes, it is different – easier, if it is someone else."

Stunned by her candid, cold statement my mouth drops open a little. "Surely the mission, the rules, the point, is for a better future *for all*, not—"

"Maia, I know you understand the mission – and I think you see the necessity of the hard-line we take, even if it is hard to follow. I also know you are torn due to your affection for Eve. That is commendable. Your passion to improve and look forward for more than yourself gives me hope for the future. Truly."

"But?" Her statement is drenched in the preparation of something.

"*But*, you cannot run before you walk, nor make change until you understand everything. Today we are starting to seriously amend that. There is no quick fix. Change, challenge, progress, as well as ruling, all take dedication. The grey in which we walk takes constant readjustment to consolidate in our minds, let alone yours, but never – *never* – do we doubt the ultimate goal. I see in your eye that you, even now with your limited understanding, see the bigger picture. The Curator has asked to guide your knowledge in genetics. He, as I do, believes you will find answers to questions here you didn't fully know you needed to ask, but once found, you'll never look back with doubt again."

As if Gee-Gee knows I am replaying her words in my mind, she turns back to her screens without looking for a reaction or reply. She taps on the keyboard, doing what exactly, I honestly couldn't say. I watch the screens, I watch enormous robots dismantle buildings, recycle materials, plant trees, collect samples from rivers and observe wildlife – some of which I thought extinct and only recognise from holograms and photographs in museums and digital storybooks. I am not sure how long I am left to my thoughts, but after a while Gee-Gee slowly turns to me and says:

"Maia, the Curator, Professor Millar, is ready. I'll connect you in conference room C and then leave you for a while. Come, follow me."

THIRTEEN

"Welcome to Detroit, Maia, it is a pleasure to see you today – it's night there, right? Ha-ha, with all our technology, time zones are one thing we can never change!" Professor Millar talks to me like a long-lost friend and I find it curious. He looks more or less the same as he did a few years ago – tidy, wearing business-like clothing under his lab coat with short grey, well-kept hair and green eyes that have a mark of youth, despite his aged skin making it clear he is a well matured person. I think he is younger than Gee-Gee, perhaps late seventies, but clearly old enough to have earned himself one of the top spots in the R&R as the 'Curator.'

"Detroit?" I ask, "Where is that?"

"Sorry, Northern Hub of United North America. I just call the lab here 'Detroit' after the city that used to be here. The lab was developed long before the Fall of What Was and expanded during and after, so the name stuck."

"Presumably it had a different purpose before?"

Professor Millar wobbles his head from left to right, pulling a face. "Or not," he shrugs. "The people before discarded this area in favour of the brighter lights of commerce elsewhere. It was ideal for us because it was not deemed worthy of attack in the wars and we could work with precious little observation in their abandoned factories and—"

"And now you have one of the largest laboratories in the world with more research, knowledge and capabilities than anyone could possibly conceive," I interject.

Professor Millar chuckles. "Indeed. I knew the Director's praise of you was well founded. I actually wanted to include you earlier, though I understood Georgia's reluctance given the past."

"But the mission calls," I add looking him straight in the eye.

He smiles smugly and chuckles: "We are going to do great things, Maia. I cannot explain nor show you all in one go, but I can introduce you to a lot. Pinch the hologram to your left...yes, that globe...excellent. Here you have the basic model of our fertility project."

"I thought that was Gee-Gee's thing?" I ask looking over the endless graphs.

"In Hub, it is, but our paths inevitably cross. I work with what is collated as well as form and oversee new and existing research outside the Hubs."

"Like the Initiative project," I state.

Again, he chuckles. Something tells me Professor Millar appreciates direct, yet unemotional curiosity. If I am to play this game, I must understand the players, and not let myself be overwhelmed by emotion or show my hand before I have a trump card.

Good grief, I hope I find one.

Don't I? This information is everything I have dreamt of... Do I want to have that revoked?

Well, while I decide that, I must play on...

"Yes, precisely, the Initiative is possibly the most essential and progressive project to date – the epitome of what we are seeking – the true patent of design and order. I hope to connect you in time with Dr Oldman, my associate on that one." I shudder at the mention of his name and my skin recoils as it remembers his cold touch as I am hoisted in the hospital bed ready for egg harvest. The idea of working with him is no less distressing, but again I tell myself to keep my poker face.

Be the ideal colleague they want.

Learn before I act.

I hear Eve's words replay in my head: *"I started her on the path of enlightenment she asked for. I told you all you didn't really want to know…I told you if you are going to take them on, it has to be all or nothing. That is not done in one go. It takes time…time to understand…then time to act."*

Then it is up to me to decide if and how I act.

"…step into that darkness and pray you step back out intact." That is what Eve said.

Surely a Golden Goose can shine her way through?

Get on with it then…

FOURTEEN

The Genetics Committee has informed Max and me we are going to be on the radio on Valentine's Day. Apparently, my speedy pregnancy is exactly the story they want to promote and the Central Hub's main radio station has decided now is the optimum time to invite us in for a chat. I joked that it must be a slow month, but Claire's scowl reminded me that my kind of humour and most of the UNE's are not the same.

Max, as usual, saved me from any form of admonishment from Claire by saying, "Oh, I don't know, I think the Hub will be happy to rejoice with us." Claire positively glowed when he said that and I laughed, which she took as my agreement, and declared 'You are the loveliest couple!' and soon forgot my previous attempt at humour at her or the PTB's expense. It didn't stop me sticking my tongue out at Max behind her back though.

Aunt Dora invited us for dinner – well, for us to eat together. I am still on delivered meals which I keep unsuccessfully begging for Gee-Gee to stop. We have been together, eating as a four for about an hour, yet only three of us have spoken. Eve has mumbled the odd nonsensical word or sentence to me, but it has been weeks since I have had a meaningful conversation with her and Aunt Dora says the chats she has had have been similar to an ebbing tide – just without the predictably of when Eve will be 'in.'

As Max describes our schedule for tomorrow and I add how nervous I am, despite being glad it isn't TV again. Eve suddenly stirs, looks me straight in the eyes and says: "Pfft, video never was great for the radio star."

I laugh so hard tears come to my eyes and blur my vision as I jump up and give Eve a hug. The relief of hearing her speak again is more than I can describe. Eve puffs and splutters a few grunts, but smiles as I retake my seat.

"You been learnin', Missy?" I tell her I have. "Good, good…yes, good," Eve says, bobbing her head.

"But I still know nothing of Lilith. I am so sorry—"

"You will. Have faith." Eve's voice is quiet, but hasn't lost its strength.

"Eve," I say softly. "When we last spoke, I don't know if you remember, you said there was somewhere I might need your sleeve – somewhere I didn't want to go. Can you tell me where that is?"

Eve rubs her tongue on the inside of her cheeks, wrinkling her nose as she does it. I am so afraid her procrastination will take up so much time she'll drift into the fog again and I will be left blind.

"It ain't time for that yet," she finally says. "Dora keeps me up to date as much as possible. Don't look at me like that, I ain't gone yet. I won't see the end of your path, I know that, but I will see you to where you need… If you chose to be the change, not the puppet."

"You doubt me?" I whisper trying unsuccessfully not to feel wounded.

"'Doubt' is the wrong word. I see, hmmphh, I've always seen, the sparkle in your eye, the need for knowledge. Now I see the understanding of the sacrifices. Hmmphh-hmmphh, I've seen so many of those." Eve pauses and takes a deep breath. "No, 'doubt' is the wrong word…"

"But you think I'll be their puppet?"

"You might dance to your own tune, but if yours ultimately aligns with theirs, the dance may well be on strings." Eve is too wise, she understands my dilemma. That I see the point of the R&R, am fascinated by the lie, but am also disgusted by it. How will that reconcile in my mind – in my actions? "You're like me," she whispers. "I don't wish that on yer, but you are what you are. Keep going – you need to carry on as you are if you're to help Lilith and keep yer promise."

"Never doubt that I will do that," I say, leaning forward to hold her hands in mine.

"I don't."

"Won't you give us a tip? A clue? Dare I ask for even one of your beloved riddles!" appeals Max. "Anything that can speed up—"

"Speed will hasten a fall." Eve looks at us both with a sharp eye. "Patience…be patient. Observe everything…and remember the codes."

"Barcodes?" I ask.

"Mmm-hmm," answers Eve through her nose.

"Whose?"

"All of 'em."

I scoff. "I can't remember everyone's codes – which are the important ones?" For a long time I have had an odd obsession with reading and memorizing people's barcodes. Until I needed to remember Mary's I hadn't confessed my habit, but if someone interests me, I find myself reciting their pedigree before I realise I have read it.

"If you have to step beyond, you cannot go as you…you will need to be another. Who? Well, that's not for me to say, tis you."

"Beyond?"

"Beyond the fence where secrets live…Tom, too." A tear tumbles down Eve's cheek, landing on her trembling lips. My heart silently sighs, but my face says nothing. The fog is obviously claiming her thoughts again, making distinguishing her deliberate riddles from the accidental harder and harder. I don't know how much time Tom, Eve's late husband, spent beyond the Hub fence before he and most of their family were executed for treason, but I dare not ask now because probing at the wrong time in the past has only produced stronger outbursts of anguish or confusion, often resulting in Eve's mind clouding faster and I earnestly want her to stay lucid.

If only wishes and good intentions alone produced results.

"Hmmphh, need more than a drone to guide me to the light," Eve says, closing her eyes. "Tis the Shepherd's delight."

FIFTEEN

Dr Oldman was expecting me when I again emerged from the underground tramline and walked into the R&R headquarters. It was my first time seeing the place in daylight. The building design is in keeping with those in the Hub and is totally covered in plants, shrubs, and trees with windows poking through the flora. However, looking at the surrounding area it is not the same and there are open fields – truly open fields without a fence, barrier, or blockade in sight. Way beyond there is a thick and inviting woodland, one that could swallow me for weeks, not a few hours like the ones in the Hub. A genuine, dense woodland. I wonder if the drone footage used in the simulations in the gym were recorded in there…either way, I'd love to go and explore.

Having lingered outside for longer than I should, a drone floats up to me, scans me, and says: "The Oologist is waiting, please follow me."

I have not heard this title before, so I feel my face grimacing slightly as I consider the word. This drone obviously detects facial expressions as it repeats its message, adding my full name at the end, as though clarifying who I am is going to help. Nonetheless I follow the little silver bullet shaped drone that floats in front of me and soon find myself in a new area of the building – at a guess, I'd say I am somewhere near the back of the building, but honestly it is hard to tell. The corridors are all long, white, and have very little in the way of signage or individual adornment. The drone activates a door and it slides open revealing another laboratory, as it does so, I notice a small white plaque with 'The Oologist' etched in grey writing. The grey is so pale I have to look hard to read it. I can only presume you are just expected to know where you are going here – after all, visitors are not exactly welcome, are they?

"Ah, Maia, I have been expecting you. What a curious turn of events that we should meet in this capacity, is it not?" chuckles Dr Oldman appearing from an adjoining room.

You mean where you are not stealing my eggs and leaving me with nightmares? I retain my desired retort. Instead I take a deep breath, smile, and shake Dr Oldman's cold, bony, extended hand saying: "Indeed, very curious."

"I believe the Curator and Director have outlined my work?" I nod. "Good, I can't tell you how excited I am to have an actual Golden Goose on my team – your contributions, both previous and future, are invaluable – but to have a willing and knowledgeable participant is truly something. Such a thing has been on this little geneticist's wish list since…well, forever!" He is beaming. I don't want to stare, but if I looked closer at his hands, I fear they would be trembling with anticipation. I suppose now isn't the time to point out his daughter is a grade 3? No? Not the time for sarcastic, disapproving jokes? Lucy is a spoilt, self-important madam, but when I consider her upbringing it is no wonder really. In the past I have enjoyed mocking her 'holier-than-thou' approach to life – her recent marriage in particular. She'd boasted of her father holding off her wedding all these years until 'the right and worthy match' presented. Now I feel sorry for her, because standing in this den of lies and collection of stolen matter, I realise her father was almost certainly delaying her marriage so he could harvest her more. There is no way he was going to waste such a resource on his doorstep until he had to. I am now the replacement. The 'knowledgeable participant,' opposed to the coerced and dictated to. Lucky me.

I don't remember signing up for extra donations though…

You didn't need to. You now *'know,'* so, if you want to help, you must also be willing to donate.

I am the lab rat who knows what it is…the control substance…the test card…

For the first time, I hold my stomach and am glad (for now at least), my eggs are safely tucked behind the baby I am incubating. I shudder. There are too many conflicting emotions flowing through my increasingly hormonal body.

"So, you left the donation clinic to become an…'oologist'?" I ask, not quite sure what that is.

"If the truth be told, it was a nickname that seemed to fit. Do you know what it means?" I shrug. "Egg collector." I roll my eyes and groan. "Primarily oology is the collection and study of birds eggs, but well—"

"Yes, I understand, very clever," I chuckle politely.

Dr Oldman runs his hands through his slightly scruffy, mousy-brown, fading-to-grey hair and puffs out his cheeks.

"One other thing we best discuss before I show you more is Henry."

"My father-in-law?" I ask, narrowing my eyes in confusion.

"Yes. Henry and I consult sometimes – a little less of late since he moved here and I've been officially promoted, but I do consider him a friend." He pauses, tilts his head downwards a little, and looks at me with a strained expression like he is willing me to fill in the gap without him needing to speak.

"I am aware Henry is not privy to all the R&R findings and I am to 'tweak' what I share and discuss," I say, sighing.

"Good…good. I do actually hope to be able to change that in time, but although he doesn't know it, Henry is an asset to the R&R as he is."

I look at Dr Oldman quizzically, but he doesn't respond. Apparently, he enjoys the role of teacher, giving me the start of the sentence and waiting to see if I can decipher enough to finish it myself. This tactic could get old really quickly.

"Do you mean his research provides a smoke screen for the R&R? A worthy, viable, sometimes hopeful, show of progress to the PTB, without the actual progress – or most of it." Bingo. Whether I like it or not, I am good at this game as Dr Oldman claps his hands together with delight, praising my quick wit.

Satisfied I am on the right page, Dr Oldman walks to the doorway he came out of and gestures for me to follow. I walk into another lab which, although large, on first glance is not any different to any other I have seen. However, that all changes when Dr Oldman activates a hologram, and the entire room alters. Not only is the space in the middle of the room a giant computer, ready to display whatever data you ask for, there are also now drawers and cabinets up and down both of the left and right hand walls. Some of the holographic beams connect to the walls and finish in dots. I follow a beam to a dot, which on closer inspection is a button, and I poke it. A drawer comes out the wall and inside is a capsule with a tiny, tiny embryo. A hologram hovers above it with all the data I could possibly want about this little being's existence: Its age, pedigree, DNA sequence, its predicted grade, what its mother ate, what substances it has or will be exposed to – you name it, it is written out here.

"Welcome to the Incubator," he says with pride.

I stare at the bean sized baby and want to ask a thousand questions. I thought SurrogacyPods were used for development…though I suppose if embryos are not intended for complete development, the expense of a whole SurrogacyPod is unnecessary.

"What is all this?" I ask, looking away for a moment.

"Not all the collected eggs are here obviously, but we store a selection from all grades of women, 0-3 alike. 3, Golden Geese, eggs are obviously my specialty. My research will one day, hopefully soon, see the release of eggs into the population that are so precise and predictable, we no longer need the food controls. We will know who will be what grade. We will control the population size so efficiently – and cheaply, compared to the constant testing and manipulations of people and food."

"You'd need to do some testing to avoid suspicion."

"Quite right," Dr Oldman says, nodding his head in approval. "We need to do it in a manner that we are seen to be searching for an all-out cure and never give any inkling that we have a hand in the decision of grade…but that can still be done at less expense than it is now. This way we will use even less resources from the planet as well as cost us less. It really is a brilliant and exciting time – if I do say so myself."

"Graded before birth, not at eighteen."

"Precisely, though we won't tell them that, the education system needs to be uniform and consistent. If the population knew there was no hope and their very genes had been altered—"

"You'd cause a revolt."

"A big one. Too many, I fear, would not understand the necessity of the sacrifice – the grand plan – even if we actually haven't changed the ultimate mandate handed to us generations ago after wars, pollution, and disease truly rendered us largely infertile. We are merely trying to map the destruction and mould it more effectively. In the world that was, there was no such order or thought for the future. We are insuring the future – *all* of our futures. Humanity, fauna, flora, the Earth herself. Our burden may be great, but our mission is for everyone."

He has his speech well prepared. The Board has obviously drummed it into him that I need the mission statement imprinted on my soul. It is certainly on my mind and body…

"So, you are altering gene expression in those that the wars haven't fully left infertile?" I ask, deciding to keep reaping information.

"Yes. Some, those graded 0 and most of the 1s, are well and truly infertile. No amount of nurture is going to change that. The bulk of the 2s however can be relatively easily swayed either way through a few subtle substances that happily aid in food production – yet are entirely undetectable to the consumer (and indeed, those who don't know to look for it in the compounds they work with). There are two grades within 3. A plus and minus if you like, though they are never advertised. All 3s are highly valuable – have no doubt there – but some, yourself included, are extra gold plated… solid gold really, for they are resistant to any form of nurture. Positive or negative. We have fed different foods and trialed you over the last six years and *WOW!*' He blows his cheeks out for effect. "Truly, just wow, your eggs are fantastic! It is as though they are protected by Thor's hammer—"

"Who?"

"Oh, right, yeah, he is a character from mythology – a warrior, a god of war and fertility – not part of standard UNE teaching." He chuckles.

"Do you want everyone to be a Golden Goose then?" I am a little confused. Right now, I feel more like a guinea pig than a goose.

"Hell, no! We want precious few, but we want to preserve those that come through and maintain a healthy population. A genetically diverse, predictable popu—"

"Got it. You just want to know what is coming before it comes. Control more…"

I am so mixed on this. This ideal has potential for true greatness. I am just not sure they are aiming for it.

"Exactly. We are not 100% there yet, the predictability and tracking need work – working out how the crossbreeding and food controls all fit in – but we are on track. You join me at the best stage." Dr Oldman looks like a child who has just been handed the key to the sweetshop. "I know February is a busy month for me and you don't have many months until maternity leave starts, but I want to at least start your induction now."

My heart sinks.

I am on a timer, and it is ticking in my uterus.

"Anyhow, we can still 'chat' when you're officially off… ways and means…there's ways and means." He winks at me. "Let's see how we go first but given the glowing report from the Curator – and the Director, of course – I hope that our friendship will prove *profitable*."

I should find hope in what he just said and can see he assumes I will be happy, grateful even, despite my role as test subject (after all, what's not to love about that?!). I don't know if it is pregnancy or general revelation, but I suddenly have to choke down a mouthful of acidic bile. I keep hearing 'for the mission,' yet all they are actually saying is: 'how wonderful am I?'

And the most unsettling thing is…?

They are starting to see me as an advocate, a partner, a colleague.

An ally.

Making me…? *An accomplice.*

SIXTEEN

Gee-Gee came to find me at the end of my first day with Dr Oldman. I felt like I was back in primary school being collected from class so I could be escorted home (after mum had done the rounds with the other parents, gleaning whatever gossip she could of course). Gee-Gee has no interest in gossip, she wants facts, she wants my reaction. She wants confirmation I am friend not foe…that revealing the keys to the kingdom wasn't wrong. I give it, as best and reassuringly as I can.

Am I lying?

That question rings in my head continuously.

I haven't had anything like enough hours to decide.

Until then, I am acting my part.

"What do you think of Dr Oldman's menopause research?" Gee-Gee asks, guiding me through more new hallways.

"It is interesting, I cannot deny."

After being shown The Initiative's design on eggs, I was briefed on the R&R's work understanding the continued early onset of menopause. I think this revelation caused me more of a dilemma than the rest of Dr Oldman's research because I can see myself being finally allowed to work, to contribute, and be listened to here. Why? Because they don't have the answers. They are still trying to halt women's rapid decline in fertility, regardless of previous grade. They haven't tampered with any of that research because they do not know the answers. My unresting, curious mind could really find a home...

"Is it something you'd be happy to major in?" Gee-Gee's eyes are trying not to show emotion, yet for a brief moment, I think I glimpse her genuine hope and excitement for me joining her secret fold. My stomach churns. The pleasure of her approval has always been my goal, yet now I cannot forget the lengths she went to hide this – to lie about this. It has been a long day with very mixed emotions.

"Gee-Gee?"

"Mmm-hmm?" she replies, opening a door into a new room. I look around as I enter and am distracted from my question when I see a family portrait on the wall. Gee-Gee and Great Gramps are seated in the center with their children, grandchildren, and great grandchildren surrounding them. I vaguely remember sitting for this photograph when I was eight or nine. I don't think I have ever seen the resulting picture though. I turn to her in surprise. "Yes, this is my office," she says without waiting for the question. "What did you want to ask?"

Something that has been bothering me, yet I have been afraid to rock the boat by asking. I take a deep breath and exhale quickly, deciding to just ask and get it over with: "I thought I'd have years, decades even, before being shown a fraction of this. Why have I been shown so much in a matter of months?"

"Yes, that was the intention – a long build up. You will still have a long time before you have a more active role, but—" Gee-Gee looks up at the photograph on the wall. I cannot be sure, but I think she is focused on Great Gramps, though it could be Grandad – another victim of falling foul of the R&R rule. She inhales and exhales deeply a couple of times before continuing: "But Mary was right about one thing: the next generation of the R&R needs securing. I will not live forever. I have been granted ninety years of good health with which to serve, yet I, no more than anyone else, cannot expect Eve's longevity and I want to be sure my reins are in safe hands. Now I know your hands are open, I must see you start your journey here."

"Oh," is all I manage to answer. Does she refer to my 'safe hands' meaning I will have the wisdom to steer her work after her, or as I fear, does she mean I'll carry on exactly as I am directed?

"Your pregnancy and acceptance of the role we have given you both, has encouraged everyone no end, Maia."

As directed…

I nod, understanding what I am told, but also so glad no one can read my muddled thoughts. I cannot reconcile them…and I don't just mean the ones questioning the R&R morality, my approval, or my role. No, the thoughts questioning – even now that he or she grows within me – if I want to be a mother.

I wonder if that makes me the bigger monster?

I think even Kate, who knows me better than anyone, thought my opinion would change once I was actually pregnant. Surely then hormones, repressed desire, natural instinct, a maternal longing – whatever you want to call it or blame it on – surely then I would feel something, *anything* in the direction or description of excitement? *Of want.*

I am ashamed to say, the very most I feel is curiosity.

Scientific amazement.

Not want.

I cannot talk to anyone about this. Max is overjoyed to be a father. He kisses my stomach each night before we go to sleep. The rest of my family, in their various forms, are thrilled – the PTB and R&R are thrilled. I tried to touch on it when I originally told Kate I was pregnant, but my attempt fell at the first hurdle…and the second, when we found out her baby's due date is 31st August. Just eleven days before mine. No coincidences there then? Thanks Gee-Gee. A subtle but clear reminder that one joy comes at a price of another. Is dependent on another. My service for Kate's child.

It should help me actually. Maybe Gee-Gee sees it as such. Certainly, Kate's enthusiasm for us both having children so perfectly timed together is abundant.

I tell myself it is fear, not loathing I am feeling.

I have just been told I will not be ignored totally while I am a housewife. I'll have some research to read and consider…but not *do*. Maybe I am just ungrateful. Even if only privately, the R&R have undoubtedly compromised to include me earlier than their rule dictates. Just not enough to satisfy me. Why can they not see the balance and see mothers as valuable beyond the uterus…the nanny. Working *and* being a mother is not a sin. It is not something to hide or condemn if not everyone chooses the same path.

Maybe I am in denial…

About not wanting the baby or wanting it really?

Both.

"You're doing well, Maia." Gee-Gee's voice suddenly jolts me back into the room. I look at her quizzically, but do not respond. "I said, you're doing well, I know you have a lot to take in, but your quick wit will see you through." She looks back at the photo. "We had meant to do another, but George died before…" Gee-Gee sighs before quickly shrugging. "Maybe it is time the family united for an update. Maybe in years to come you'll be showing your great grandchild this room, inducting them as the next generation of R&R."

She looks at me with hope sparkling in her eyes, but I am sure every sentence is laced with a double meaning – a trap I could at any moment get caught in. I look up at the photograph, so many smiling faces…so many lies. I turn back to Gee-Gee with tears in my eyes and whisper, "I'd love nothing more." The tears are real. I'm working on the words.

I pass this test, at least. Gee-Gee's bottom lip wobbles and she opens her arms, beckoning me for a hug. I need one so I do not hesitate, yet I am left in want. Her hug is not reassuring any more, even though I believe her desire is true and her conviction real. Yes, I do believe that, but the voice within, the little girl who saw only refuge, now sees and understands too much to rest easy in her arms.

Our moment over, she steps back and sits at her desk. The door knocks, Gee-Gee says 'enter' and a man dressed in a bright purple lab coat walks in with a tray of tea. How civilised.

"Thank you – yes, there will do." Gee-Gee nods towards the corner of her desk. Anywhere would have done, there is nothing but her computer on the desk and that is switched off and under the surface, so a cup of tea isn't going to hurt it. Or so I think, for as soon as we are alone again, she activates the desk, and the computer lights up. "I thought I would run through some extras," she says, sipping her tea.

I just want to go home, but I say, "Okay."

"I am assuming Dr Oldman didn't detail where his latest results are coming from?"

"His egg collections or menopause?"

"Well, either, but menopause…"

"No?"

"The FARM programme."

I stare for a moment. "The AIP?" Gee-Gee nods. "Lilith? They—"

"No, Lilith hasn't had a hysterectomy yet. Her training is nowhere near complete. Hysterectomy only happens before graduation, before posting beyond the fence. There has been a recent batch declared ready for graduation, hence the latest pool of data – with more data imminent. Oldman collects eggs, but is equally studying all the women there, trying to slow the onset of menopause."

"He told me that was the aim…I didn't think to ask which women he was trying it on specifically. I suppose I shouldn't be surprised." Careful, I cannot show scorn. Interest, but not scorn. "Why are you telling me this?"

Gee-Gee looks at me with raised eyebrows… Am I supposed to answer my own question?

"Results come from all over the UNE," Gee-Gee says after sipping again from her tea. As she pauses in between sips she looks up at me, waiting for me to understand something… but what? "But Oldman pays close attention to his Golden projects. The Curator agreed long ago that United North America is too remote for the majority of people or samples to be sent to – the cost of transport alone is—"

"The FARM is in United Britain then, not too far from here?" I speak quietly, but I can feel my eyes widen.

Gee-Gee gently inclines her head. I am right…but why tell me this? Does she want me to help Lilith? How can I? Okay, I have confirmation of the State Lilith is living in – but that's not exactly a location, is it?! *It is a start though…*

Gee-Gee taps on her computer, raises her left brow at me, then wheels her chair back and looks out of the window. I am confused, but I take the hint.

I walk to her desk, standing where her chair had been. She hasn't projected anything to a 3D screen or hologram, I have to look at the desk itself… There I see a list of thirteen names. None mean anything to me, but they are all women aged 22-29 and are about to have a hysterectomy – twelve this month… and are heading to an 'Ambassador of Earth' posting together. The date, time and coordinates are all listed with precision along with their job descriptions. But not for the last girl, for Emilia. Next to her name it says: 'Service questionable. Tread with caution – *Head Overseer request pending.*'

"What is an 'Overseer'?" I ask.

"They are responsible for daily monitoring of cadets enrolled in FARM," Gee-Gee says without turning around.

"What request have they put in?" I ask with a lump in my throat.

"The removal of a troubled cadet. For now, we have denied him, but left it pending, giving her a chance for correction." She turns to me. "Not every cadet makes the grade, that unfortunately is life. But there *is* life out there, Maia – for those twelve girls, real purpose and meaning is right around the corner. Am I glad you haven't gone there? Yes, undoubtedly, but even out there, failure is not permanent in most cases. I just wanted you to know that. For Eve to remember that. The future may be different than those girls originally planned, but it is fulfilling and steadfast."

For a brief moment, I thought Gee-Gee might have been offering me a backdoor – a look through the keyhole of how to reach Lilith. She is not. She is reaffirming the purpose of the FARM. What happens if grade 3 citizens fail to follow the UNE rule. You are repurposed – and that is that. You are harvested, tested, repurposed, and released in a new, remodeled form.

That is your only option…

No, Gee-Gee just said it. Troublesome cadets are 'removed.' If you are not in a Hub…and not on a R&R posting…and Earth is full of silent, colourless, nuclear pitfalls…*then you die.*

Conform or die.

There is no plan C.

Gee-Gee is reminding me as much as educating.

Hold onto plan A and B.

Because C is silent and cold.

Cold as in the grave.

SEVENTEEN

Neither Max nor I have ever been in a radio station. I have walked in front of the entrance before, but as it is located near the government buildings, it isn't an area I normally tend to go to by choice. The building is tall, much taller than the average in the Hub, and spirals into the sky with hundreds of windows shining out of the leaves in the winter sunshine. Seemingly sprouting off the base of the building are two TV studios; they expand outwards as well as up, but the radio spire towers over them both. I chuckle as I recall Eve's comment about radio stars, but it doesn't help my nerves as we walk towards the front doors. Is it fair to blame the baby for making me nervous?

Probably not.

I got through our wedding being recorded, why is this different? Maybe because I have no script and my confused brain may say the wrong thing.

As we walk in, Max looks excited. I need to cling to his positive energy instead of second-guessing what questions we will be asked. Claire emailed a list of phrases she thinks 'would be lovely if you pop into conversation.' Most of the list is pointless, but if it keeps the PTB off our backs, so be it.

My bladder (for the fourth time this morning) betrays me and instead of taking the lift upstairs as the receptionist directs, I make a hasty dash for the first toilet I spy. Why I need to pee so much already is a mystery… Okay, that is a lie, I know I am producing more hormones to make my kidneys work harder, clearing my body of waste quicker. Fine, I understand the science – but if this is what happens when the baby is so tiny, how often am I going to pee with a seven-and-a-half-pound occupant pushing on my bladder?

That's something to look forward to.

Max patiently waits for me by the lift and smiles at me as I exit the toilets. I am concentrating so hard on reaching him, I do not see a man coming out of the adjacent room and crash into him with surprising force. I splutter and apologise as I look into his blue eyes. He has a dangerously handsome smile as he chuckles and politely blames his own absent mindedness.

"Maia, right?" he says as I turn to walk away.

"Yes. Sorry, do I know you?" Two-day beards and hair tied roughly into a man-bun isn't normally my type, but even so, he has a face most people would remember.

"No, I doubt it. I'm a producer on the show you're on today." Of course, you are. "I recognised you off the news, sorry, you probably get that a lot," he chuckles.

Enough…certainly more than I like. "Ha-ha, that's okay."

"Is Max here?"

"Yes – just there," I say, pointing to Max who is watching with interest. I wave him over and introduce him. "Max, this is…oh, sorry, what is your name?"

"Kal," he says grinning. "I'm producing your interview on Hub2Day."

It is such a stupid radio show. I normally turn it off in the lab if I get the chance. Best not mention that to Kal. They shake hands, make a few standard comments about the building, how busy it is in here, how excited we all are… Max seems at ease, but I am thankful when Kal suggests we take the lift and 'get the show on the road.'

As we walk a hand grabs my shoulder. I turn to be greeted by Claire declaring how happy she is that her schedule altered so she can personally accompany us after all. She flirts embarrassingly with Kal as we ride the lift to the twentieth floor and he looks genuinely relieved when his watch starts ringing, allowing him to retreat for a moment.

"Well, isn't he divine?" coos Claire as soon as Kal is out of earshot.

"Aren't you married?" I ask without thinking.

Claire flushes red. "Yes, happily, I—I am very lucky the match system united us—" Claire is stuttering, but emphasizing her words at the same time. She looks a little panicked at the thought of the PTB doubting her gratitude and I feel bad for my careless comment.

"He is handsome," I say lightly. "We can be appreciative of our beloved and still appreciate beauty," I finish winking.

"Indeed, indeed," says Claire, recovering herself and straightening her dress as though someone has creased her pleats (that is unlikely, I am pretty sure all her clothes are ironed into a perfection that no mortal can disrupt). "There is nothing wrong with acknowledging pictures, it doesn't mean…" Claire is still too flustered to finish her own metaphor.

"Of course, like now, I can notice a vision before me, but only ever worship my wife," remarks Max in a playful tone.

Claire melts and swoons in reply, declaring him 'the sweetest man in the world' and 'an absolute dream.' Max beams with his cheekiest, most amused grin and I struggle not to laugh. He is very good at reading people and dispelling any awkwardness. I am definitely going to let him lead in answering the deejay's questions!

We make our way through the busy corridor and I am so intent on following Claire, I miss an oncoming man and, for the second time in five minutes, I crash into a stranger. He looks as shocked as I do, but this time I am going to put the blame firmly on his shoulders. If he hadn't had his eyes so firmly set on his watch as he was walking, scrolling through whatever dull feed is on the screen, he would have seen me coming.

I can't help smiling at the difference in manner from my first crash to the second. The first was all manners and apologies, the second, with his grey-woollen jumper, zipped up coat and scarf, looks like he is ready to hibernate, not apologise. He too has a beard, but a little longer than Kal's. I think he probably spends a lot of time grooming it along with his neatly trimmed short, dark-blond hair, as he anxiously checks his hair after our impact. Why I do not know, we only bumped bodies, not heads.

His green eyes meet mine briefly, then he looks away as though the sight of me stung his eyes. Suddenly taken aback, I say, "I'm sorry." Though in truth, I do not know why.

He mutters, "No, I am," steps back and scuttles off into the throng.

Max calls to me as he and Claire stand outside a door marked 'Hub2Day,' and without further ado I join him, hoping I don't find a third person to knock into.

We are whisked through doors, all of which record our presence, and are led into a room with three yellow walls, bright yellow lamps, and two large yellow sofas which are so soft I am not sure if I'll ever be able to get up again. I try my best to follow the instructions the tech person is giving us, but after a while, I decide Max seems to be following, therefore 'winging it' is my best option. I turn my attention to people watching courtesy of the clear glass wall that looks onto the busy hallway – which simultaneously gives my eyes a welcome relief from the sea of lemon-yellows.

"How many people work here?" I ask after counting at least twenty different faces.

"Pfft, I've no idea – lots," replies Kal reappearing behind me. "There's so many floors and departments, you'd never know who everyone is. You just learn those you work with and the regulars your schedule *bumps* you into I suppose."

I blush as he emphasises the word 'bump' whilst grinning. I don't suppose he'll forget meeting me anytime soon. Kal tells us it is time and Max and I follow to a room with a large desk. On the desk itself is just a small, pretty standard looking control panel, but above is an electronic screen with hundreds of switches on it. I am very glad I haven't got to learn what to do with them.

We are seated and a woman with long, black, incredibly straight hair rushes in. "Ooh, had to pee!" she chuckles sitting down. "I'm Lei, lovely to meet you – sorry back on air!"

With that we listen to Lei introducing us, telling the Hub: "It's such an honour to have our Golden couple here with me today – a couple who I'm sure we all watched getting married not long ago – a couple who also have had some family tragedy recently, but are proving that their match is stronger than surrounding circumstances – a couple powered by the PTB themselves and who are absolutely perfect for me to interview on Valentine's Day! So, without further delay, let me introduce Mr and Mrs Rivers, Max and Maia, may I call you that?" *Please do. I'm not your mother.* We both nod and smile. "Wonderful! Just remember to talk, you're on the radio!"

Oh, this is going well...

* * *

Lei is good at her job and actually had us laughing on air before the half an hour was up. I wondered if the questions and antidotes would ever end and had to control my desire to sigh with relief when Lei finally said goodbye and switched on a song that was more than just a three-minute breather.

"Well, see you next trimester!" waves Lei as we leave. "I'm looking forward to it."

"Great, thank you," says Max, smiling and closing the door.

"Did she just wink at you?!" I say incredulously. "And what's that about next—"

"I don't think so...maybe," grins Max.

"What are you grinning for?"

"I enjoy watching you squirm," he mocks.

"Well, why don't we add that to our next broadcast?" I half-heartedly hit his arm with the back of my hand.

Max just laughs, puts his hand in the small of my back and guides me to the exit.

"How many times are they going to use us as the poster couple?" I groan when the lift doors close leaving us alone.

"Until…" Max doesn't finish and his grin drops.

"Always," I fill in. "Right? There is no 'until' is there?"

We both look at each other silently and I take Max by the hand and he squeezes.

"Maia! Max!" Our attention is suddenly arrested as our names are called before the lift doors have barely cracked open, revealing Ella's excited face. "I'd say 'what are you doing here?' but I just heard you on the radio!"

"Wasn't it lovely?" chimes in Claire stepping into the lift. She must have decided to float around the building while she waited for our interview to finish.

"It was!" exclaims Ella.

"What are you doing here?" I ask.

"Oh, tech support takes me everywhere these days. The new Director of Agriculture is in another Hub and already has a techgirl, so I wasn't needed there after – well, you know. So, I passed on my data and carried on IT support in the lab… got asked about my other tech research and development – remember I boosted signals and found glitches, anomalies, and such? I am still hoping for that to come to more, but since…yeah—" Ella is tactfully trying not to say 'your mother screwed up my plans' to Max. "So, today I am looking into the radio team. Gotta keep applying myself, right?!" Ella looks at me with such puppy-eyes, looking for approval and reassurance, that only a cold-hearted person would leave her hanging. Mary would have happily (unless it was mutually beneficial of course), but I warmly reassure her, and her happiness bubbles forth in the form of a very sweet giggle.

It is such a shame she is married to Theo.

The only time Eve met Ella, she called her an imposter because of her red hair and was generally pretty rude. Had they met earlier in Eve's life, before the dementia cruelly seeped in with its decay and confusion, Ella would have absolutely been in her element – and possibly vice versa. If you follow the ideals of nature and nurture, in particular the things that can be naturally passed through genes, then Ella coming from Eve's family is not a far cry for the imagination. By all accounts, Eve is one of, if not *the* brightest mind IT and AI engineering has seen in more than a century. I have no doubt any tech specialist or student would chew off their digital arm if they could glean knowledge or insight from the woman that founded and guided so much of today's technology.

I know through reading and following research, memory genes exist, meaning traits, interests, and abilities (way beyond what is physically seen) are inherited by offspring for many generations. This knowledge is applied in so many areas of scientific research – the R&R's beloved breeding programme and search for Golden Geese being no exception. I have personally been fascinated by the subconscious inheritance of memory of 'how to…' which is more clearly distinguished in the animal kingdom; however, the natural interest and instinct that humans also display are just as intriguing.

Ella, though not from this Hub or known to be related to Eve, still could be. It would certainly explain why she is such a child genius in engineering. *Not every genius – or indeed, red-haired person – has to be related, you know.* No, true, I mocked Kate once for thinking Ella and Lady Fairfax (the President General's wife) are related purely because they are both red-haired. Lady Fairfax's family are actually Eve's direct relations – not that they advertise or act on that anymore. She's the black sheep – the scapegoat.

Hmm…

Suddenly Eve's words come to me… *'remember the codes.'*

I look at Ella's left arm, but she has it crossed with her right so I cannot comfortably read it.

Dammit it… Do I need to know it? I don't know, that's the point…

I try signalling to Max, but he doesn't get the hint, so I declare myself in need of a cup of tea (which I will regret later when I need the bathroom for another ten times in an hour) and invite Ella to join us. She checks her watch, decides she has time, and we make our way to the nearest café where I proceed to memorise her barcode, hoping I don't look like a stalker – and that there is a point to me starting my collection of barcodes of random people.

EIGHTEEN

Although I have already been poked and prodded in the name of checking on my baby, today is my first proper scan. Ten weeks and potentially a gender reveal – though I have been told it is more likely to be later. 3D imaging techniques make it far more reliable than years ago, but even so, if he or she decides to sit away from the scanner, their modesty will remain intact a little longer. I don't know if I want to know. I think Max is hoping I will ask, but he has promised to leave the decision to me. Part of me would like to stop calling the baby, 'baby' (as the doctor insists with her annoyingly soft, slightly moist, yet excited tone) or 'it,' yet the other part of me prefers that as 'it' is impersonal... If *it* receives a gender, that is a further step to individuality – to a name – to being real.

Real...

As in *really there*...

Not just the cause of cramps, mood swings, weight gain, and fatigue.

'It' could be a disease right now.

Or an alien.

I have to be the worst person ever. Who thinks of their child, a part of them, as a disease or an alien? I continuously try to brush these thoughts aside, telling myself it is fear of the unknown, not resentment or fear of the child.

But I do fear. I listen to my mother – both in real time and throughout history – and beg myself not to have inherited her form of nurture. I will not do that to a living soul. Ever. Even if I have to act the part of another person for my whole life, I will not let any child of mine feel unloved, unwanted, or insufficient.

Nor like a broodmare.

Oh, how I hope it is a boy! Life may have come so far, society may have developed way beyond the voteless female, yet I still feel like the subject, not the equal. Condemned by my genetic excellence and complete reproductive system. Being made spiritually incomplete by others' praise and envy for something I would gladly give up.

Last night Max and I had a lovely, romantic meal and it was wonderful to laugh about our morning at the radio station and then watch a film curled up on the sofa together. Nothing fancy, just a couple in love, spending time together. I didn't forget I was pregnant, I cannot as now I crave food every five minutes – or need a wee every two – but we felt like a regular couple, a family, and it was wonderful. A little glimpse into what I have always wanted. I am stupid, it isn't a glimpse, it *is* mine. Except my brain will not rest and settle. Thoughts rattle, anxieties rage, and I wind myself up constantly.

The problem is *me*.

"Maia?" Max says, nudging me. "Honey, it's your turn."

I snap out of my daydream, realising my name is indeed being called and I jump up, regretting the speed as I feel my breakfast and full bladder crash into one another, and walk towards Dr Waller who is beckoning me with her warm, excited smile.

Max and I are shown into Dr Waller's consultation room, she briefly welcomes us, gushing over meeting Max, and asks me to lay down on the bed. As she continues to waffle sweet nothings about her joy, she produces a bottle of cold lube, applies it to my stomach and her probe, and connects the two with little warning of the bizarre sensation it evokes.

Max takes my hand and squeezes as he watches the screen, anticipating the first images of our child. It is as though his excitement produces electricity as I suddenly feel fluttering butterflies trigger under my skin and travel to my heart – almost to the point I can hear it. Then I realise I *can* hear it, but it is not my heart, it is the baby's.

A wave of emotion I couldn't describe if I had a dictionary and a thousand years hits me. Max looks away from the monitor and beams at me with decidedly moist eyes. I smile at him, feeling the overwhelming warmth of the moment and look at the image for the first time.

I feel guilty for moments earlier calling it an alien – making it sound, even if only internally, like an intruder. I hope it cannot hear my thoughts, it must sense my fear – my sense of apprehension. What the heck do I know about raising a baby?

You know what *not* to do.

I have swayed between resolute refusal, denial, and resignation long before I ever met Max. I always knew that realistically, pregnancy would come. And I have always been clear that I would not repeat past familial mistakes, but now, in this moment, a new determination hits me and my heart skips in time with the monitor. I will not be an oppressor. I will enlighten his or her path as much as they do mine. I may sway back and forth in depression, feeling woefully inadequate, but I will not let it beat me. Because of them, for them, I will find the path out of this eternal grey mist. The light is there, if only I can keep the presence of mind to focus on it...

Nope, 'it' will not do.

"Can you see the gender?" I whisper with a wobbly voice.

"Hmm?" says Dr Waller, apparently taken up in her own daydream.

"Can you see if it is a girl or boy? I know it is early for a lot of—"

"Oh, yes, indeed I can," beams Dr Waller. "Baby is being very helpful today... Do you want to know?" She looks between Max and me waiting for a response.

Max shrugs as he gazes at me. "What do you think? You know I'd like to, but only if you're happy to know?"

"Tell us, please," I say exhaling deeply.

"Okay!" Dr Waller says freezing the screen and taking a photograph. "It is my pleasure to inform you, you are having a girl."

I don't think Max would, or indeed could, smile any wider if the answer had been the other way around. He just wanted to know – girl or boy, he is happy. I, on the other hand, feel a new, or rather *renewed,* pain. My determination would have stood firm for a son, but the path would have been easier, less of a battle. A daughter...a daughter strengthens, refreshes, expedites the need for change. In 18-24 years' time I will *not* be enforcing a match, wedding, and motherhood on her.

Please, no.
Well, stop procrastinating…act.

NINETEEN

Dr Oldman told me he is too busy to work with me until March so I am not expecting to be called to the R&R headquarters for a while. Henry is back at the lab and Theo has been directing my research quietly without him noticing a thing. One thing I will say in Theo's defence (only one, mind), is he is good at his double life. He seems to seamlessly drop in glitches – little 'red herrings' – that only those who know they are coming would ever consider. I tell myself it is better to be 'in the know' and hope that justifies my aiding and abetting of this deceit.

As I stumble home, tired from a mentally, if not physically long day, I am surprised by music starting to play the second I slide the front door closed. I follow the sound to the study and there, open for all to see, is the lift.

Subtle, real subtle.

I groan, but only delay long enough to pee before making my way into the tram system below. The tram is quiet and its gentle motion rocks me to sleep faster than I care to admit. How long I would have stayed there I can only guess, but I awake with a start when a man speaks to me whilst simultaneously shaking my arm.

"Miss, is this your stop?" he says, still shaking me.

My eyes spring to life and I sit up straight as though I have been reprimanded for my slack position.

"Sorry to make you jump, but I was just getting on – the drone here seems to be waiting for you," he says pointing towards a drone floating above me.

Meals by air, no matter where.

"Thank you," I say standing up. "I better get off. Am I halting the system?"

"No, but you're in luck, this tram pauses for five minutes," he smiles.

"Which are nearly up!" retorts a mature voice as a figure darts past me. I turn to see a man, probably in his late seventies or early eighties – though he clearly wants to appear younger as his hair is dyed deep brown and styled like someone in their twenties. Unfortunately for him, his face does not continue the deceit, and he just looks a little odd. He scowls at me as he takes a seat. "You have about sixty seconds before the tram moves off, Mrs Rivers. I suggest you use them wisely!"

I stare at him incredulously. I should just take his advice in a timely fashion, but his tone and general manner irritate me so much that now I want to hold up his precious timetable. Honestly, I realise this is daft: I have no authority over the solar-powered machine. The tram will just carry on with its schedule and take me back to the Hub with it, but I don't want to give him the satisfaction of making me go. "Excuse me, do I know you?" I ask instead of moving.

"No, I should think not." He smirks. He may know who I am, but he is not even a little bit impressed. "You may one day, we'll see…if you *need* to."

I scoff. "I can but hope not." Not my wisest response, I know, but I have never been my most tolerant when tired or just woken up.

"Ha! I so nearly had to watch over you – be glad I don't and you get to correct yourself here. Not all vote so softly, Mrs Rivers."

I screw up my face in disgust and confusion.

My drone beeps at me – it sounds anxious. I suppose it is detecting the imminent departure of the tram and knows my schedule, even if I do not. I glance at the younger man who woke me up and his face is mirroring the drone's concern for my time keeping. I sigh, then exaggerate as I shake my head at the rude old man and step off the tram. As the doors close I remember my manners and turn to say 'Thank you' with a smile to the younger man. I think he heard me as he waves as the tram pulls away, once again disappearing underground, leaving me in the dusky shadows with my drone. It beeps again, flashing its green eyes at me – mechanically begging me to take my meal.

I walk towards the building and it follows. "I really should name you if you're going to follow me everywhere and feed me every day," I mutter to the cute little metal bubble. It makes me jump as it beeps again, this time using a different tone to normal. "Huh, you understand me?"

Beep.

I chuckle, maybe I have a pet after all.

"What are you laughing about?" asks Theo as I walk indoors.

My face falls at the sight of him. I have seen enough of him for one day. "Where is the cafeteria? This guy wants me to eat," I say nodding towards my artificial pet.

"Huh, you still get fed?"

"Yes. Hey, don't make me sound like an overindulged baby bird! It isn't my choice!" I groan while Theo laughs.

When he stops chuckling he says: "I haven't been fed by a drone for years, that's all."

"Well, I shouldn't need to explain why that is," I say, rolling my eyes.

Theo nods, but doesn't answer. I wonder if it is still a sore subject for him, but I have no desire to be his confidant or therapist, so don't ask if he is sorry not to be able to have children. My cruel side would struggle not to use his words against him, retorting, 'you don't need to have children to serve.' So, as I am supposed to be cutting out the sarcastic, potentially mistrusting comments, I have decided if I cannot trust myself, the best thing to do is to avoid the scenarios which produce temptation.

"Down there, second right," he says pointing through a doorway.

"What is?"

"The cafeteria."

"Oh, okay, thanks."

"Maia?" I turn to see Gee-Gee walking towards me. "Where are you going?"

"To eat before this drone malfunctions. I didn't think eating in a lab was wise…"

Gee-Gee tuts. "Fine, yes, of course." She turns to Theo, "What about you? Go eat, I'll come with you and get something, I suppose it is later than I thought."

Silently, I find a table and sit down after finally relieving the drone of its load. I mock myself as I say 'thanks' to it, but then defend myself for there being no shame in having manners…only to mock myself again for continuing to talk to myself and an inanimate object – which stretches the definition of 'inanimate' as they strictly speaking do think and operate through their own intelligent programme, even if it can be directed by us. They may not be 'alive' as in breathing, but they are…hmm, maybe I am getting too far ahead of myself?

Gee-Gee joins me with a bowl of soup and a third of a stick of bread. The soup smells wonderful and I consider asking her to swap. I don't, because whatever is in my mash, it has been specifically formulated, and I'll ruin the balance they think I am trying to achieve if I refuse to eat it.

"You look tired," Gee-Gee says after blowing on her spoon of steaming soup.

"I fell asleep on the tram – much to a rude old man's displeasure." Gee-Gee looks at me with concern, but doesn't answer. "He said he nearly had to 'watch over me' – what does that mean?"

Gee-Gee puts down her spoon, gazing at me. She raises an eyebrow, bobs her head knowingly and picks up her spoon again. "Dean," is all she says before taking another mouthful.

"Who is Dean?"

"A man who you want to keep away from."

"Is he on the Board – a Trustee? He implied he voted against me." I pause, trying to take in Gee-Gee's reaction. She has spent too many decades cloaking her reactions though, for her body gives away nothing.

"He is," she states after a moment's silent consideration.

"Huh," I say. "So, he is the second Trustee in this State… I thought it was a woman?"

"Why?" Gee-Gee seems intrigued.

"The Arbitrator was blurred, so I guessed she's here somewhere."

"The Arbitrator is blurred for anonymity. Obviously, the Board knows who she is, yet few others need to know her identity, especially so she is not lobbied for her vote should it fall to her to decide. Her location may be in this State, but the Arbitrator is the twenty-fifth, not one of the twenty-four Board Trustees, so where she is, is neither here nor there."

"So, there are three Trustees in this State? In this Hub?"

"Maia, I just said that is neither here nor there." Gee-Gee sounds slightly irritated, but I think with herself more than me…or maybe both, because I am not taking in the information as directed.

"So, who is Dean?" I ask, returning to the original point.

"Remember the Head Overseer?" I nod. "That is Dean."

I stare at her. That grumpy old man is in charge of watching over Lilith…that man who by self-confession, does not 'vote softly.' What was his request? *To remove a cadet.* His request is pending. Not denied. *Pending.* He will not easily be dismissed because of his doubly high position in the R&R…

"How many vote like him?" I ask without explaining my thought pattern. I don't need to, Gee-Gee understands the question.

"Enough to make second chances rare, third almost unheard of," she says sadly. "But normally with good reason," she suddenly adds, defending her life's work and the hard choices in one quick phrase. Always for the mission. The grand mission – which if sung long enough, drowns any doubts you may be harbouring.

"Dean's cadets do, almost without fail, make excellent Ambassadors of Earth…I can't truly knock the results."

What about the methods?

I stay quiet, remembering my position. I must bide my time and space out my comments. This time I am rewarded as Gee-Gee continues without me prompting: "I won't lie and say his attitude is always in line with mine, but he is under the Curator's jurisdiction, not mine. I have little to do with him." I am sure she silently adds 'thankfully.'

"So, his office is here… I might bump into him sometimes?" My roundabout way of asking if a direct link to the FARM is here.

"No, no, he only comes for certain meetings. Today's timing was unfortunate. It may repeat, but only sporadically."

I nod.

Hmm, so that would suggest he lives and works in the Hub. The controls to the FARM must be in the Hub…but how do I find out where? Where exactly is the FARM? Or does he travel the tram to somewhere else?

Too many questions!

"Ask."

"Excuse me?"

"Your eyebrows were dancing so fast I thought they were going to jump off your face, so ask whatever your question is," states Gee-Gee trying not to sound mildly amused.

Which question do I confess to?

"Where does the tram go? I mean, had I not been woken up, where would I have gone?" I know the answer is 'back to the Hub' on this occasion, but the tram doesn't always return the way it came…I want Gee-Gee to tell me what is North on the track, not South.

"Without a pass, it will not take you anywhere North."

"A pass? The tram didn't—"

"The tram, like every other doorway, logs you passing through it, but unless a restricted destination, it will not notably do anything about you passing by. To go North, your barcode needs to have a 'pass' registered to it. No pass, no travel. The tram will freeze and call security."

"Okay, fine, but for example, were you to travel North, with what I presume are all the passes you can shake a stick at – where would it take *you*?"

Gee-Gee chuckles. "The train goes to the next Hub."

I sigh in exasperation. "Everyone knows where the trains go. You know I am asking about trams…your *secret* trams." I pause to let Gee-Gee answer, but she doesn't. She only looks at me, at first sternly, then I see the corners of her lips curve into a smile. She will not tell me…she will not voice it. I can only assume, that means Lilith – the FARM – is found out yonder. How far I do not know, but she *is* at the other end of that line.

"Okay! Where's Theo?" declares Gee-Gee. "I brought you two in for a consultation with the Curator – we only have twenty minutes, shall we go?" I stand and follow as I am bid. Dancing like the proverbial monkey when my great grandmother hits her drum. I think of Eve, as she not long ago questioned my strings…I certainly feel like a puppet at the moment and glancing over to Theo as he trails behind me, he most certainly has strings attached.

TWENTY

After a long week, I am honestly glad to sit opposite Eve and just snooze. Aunt Dora and I chatted over a cup of tea before she left, but since then, I haven't heard more than a gentle purr from the cats. It is wonderful. I don't even have the guilt of 'I should be exercising.' I had only jogged, or rather power-walked, for fifteen minutes along the riverbank earlier when my Fitwatch app told me it was satisfied with my stats this week and I had done enough. I wasn't going to argue anyway, but as it started raining as I read the message, I put up my hood and casually meandered to Aunt Dora's, arriving thirty minutes before I was due. Eve has been asleep the whole time I have been here, I will wake her at dinner time, but until then…

* * *

I blink awake, taking a moment to remember where I am before glancing over to Eve, only to find an empty chair – how did I not hear her get up? I look at my watch, it has just gone 1 p.m…dammit, I am an hour late with Eve's dinner and my drone will be here in a minute.

"Eve?" I say into the room, looking around, "Eve?"

"Hmmphh, sleepin' beauty is awake," Eve chuckles. I turn to see her sitting in the window seat, peeking around the curtains. "Good, it's about time you sang to me."

I laugh, it has been a while since she has tried to persuade me to sing for her and it is nice to have the real Eve in the room, even if I am not sure I want to sing.

"Are you hungry or thirsty? I should get you something." I don't wait for a response, I lift myself off the sofa, my muscles groaning at the effort.

"The watchman is back," mutters Eve, ignoring my question. "I see you little man, I see you!"

"Who?" I ask glancing out of the window. "There isn't anyone there?"

"Look." Eve points to a set of trees.

I follow the direction of her finger, but cannot see anyone, and I am about to step away, deciding it is her imagination when I spot a figure shift position amongst the greenery. "Isn't he a gardener? He looks like—"

"Hmmphh, you think I don't know the difference? You think he knows anything about hmmphhing plants? Of course not, he is a watchman…a crappy one, coz I see him… but he is one nonetheless."

I am not sure she is right, but I decide to play along. "How often do you see him?" I am impressed she can, he is pretty well hidden, and I certainly couldn't identify him from here.

"Varies, two, maybe three times a week," Eve tuts. "Maybe you should go see him…"

Or not! "If he is an R&R spy, it is best I don't."

"That ain't the R&R!"

"Pardon?"

"If he was R&R, he'd be a guard of some sort, or they'd use a drone – pretty much anything other than that guy in a bush."

I stare at him, weighing up Eve's words…I think she is right. This method of surveillance is antiquated…neither PTB nor R&R would monitor like this…*if* he is monitoring.

"Has Aunt Dora seen him?"

"No, I told her, but she went out and he was gone. Dora's convinced herself he is just my imagination. She's still freaked out since the last R&R visit."

"Have they been back?" Aunt Dora has avoided any direct conversations about them lately, only asking things like 'Are you learning?' 'Are things on track?' or 'Are you safe?' No details. She wants to help, she is as dedicated to Eve as ever, but she is no spy. She is a protector of secrets – of Eve. And she has decided she can protect without knowing all. Unlike me, who will not rest until I know everything.

"Hmmphh, they never leave, Missy, never leave," groans Eve.

"Have they bugged in here?" A sweat suddenly comes over me as I consider my words past and present.

"No, I scanned for that after they left…cocky shits scanning me," she chuckles. "They still didn't find Pandora's box, you know. The bracelets have to live in there now – that's the only safe way – the R&R will sniff them out otherwise. Dora nearly had a heart attack gettin' the bracelets and box outside quick enough – she threw 'em next to the bins. They went right past like it was nothing…nothin' at all…"

"Is there something else in there?"

"Photos…memories…you have the important bit," she nods at me, and I run my fingers over the pearls around my neck. "Ooh, off he goes!"

I look back to see the man turn and walk away. I wish I could see his face clearly. He is average height, bearded, wearing a green winter coat, blue jeans…nothing remarkable or unique from this distance. I dart to the door, suddenly determined to identify him, but as I slide open the door I startle as a drone is hovering, ready to scan the security system. I wait, anticipating its voice as it beeps and flashes my name. I sigh as I see the man disappear around the corner. I won't catch him now. Even if I could run after him, I don't want the drone to follow me and potentially record our exchange. Accepting the lost opportunity, I lift my left arm allowing the drone easy access to my barcode, it releases my food and I walk indoors, saying 'thank you' as I shut the door. Eve mutters, but I don't wait for a more coherent sentence, instead I go into the kitchen, prepare her food, and then call her for lunch.

"Hmmphhing sticks are slowing me down," she groans as she sits down. I smile but know better than to correct her. "You collecting codes?"

The question came from nowhere, but I understand. "Yes, slowly, I am trying to…though if you told me what I need them for, I'd—"

"Until you have a plan…a clear one, it is better to learn many. Then, when you know which you do need, hopefully you'll know it."

"You must have an idea of the plan you want…?"

"Ain't my plan, it's yours."

"My plan?" I am confused. "I haven't one, you—"

"You're looking around. Observing…seeking beyond."

"Yes, yes…well, there I may have a little something, though—"

"Spit it out, my time is dodgy," Eve says with a grin – a grin I would normally take heart seeing, yet I also see a worried cloud shadowing the twinkle. A shadow that I am sure mimics my own.

"Gee-Gee told me…or more truthfully, allowed me to surmise, that the tram leads to the FARM if I stay on the track rather than get off at the headquarters—"

"You need a code for that."

"That's what she said…she also said the Head Overseer goes to meetings in the headquarters but doesn't work there. So, the FARM controls, the observation tower or whatever form it is in, must be in the Hub somewhere."

"You cannot go there without power, or you'll just get electrocuted," mutters Eve solemnly whilst fiddling with her plate.

A cold chill travels down my spine.

"Do you know where it is?"

"No, they moved it…the controls and the FARM were being renovated when I left. The old FARM is further out, that was being downgraded to a Grade 1 and 2 retraining centre – you might say prison, but they—" Eve shakes her head. "Anyway, the controls moved as they were upgraded. My upgrade, just not my location, that was the Architect's jurisdiction. You need a tech to tell yer."

"Hmm, I now know what the Head Overseer looks like. I could stalk him…follow and see where he works? Dean sticks out with his overdyed hair so it wouldn't be hard to spot him, I'm sure—"

"Who?"

"Dean, the Head Overseers is called—"

"Oh, for hmmphh's sake!" exclaims Eve, almost wailing. "Why the hell would they promote him? Why? *Why!?*"

"You know him?" A stupid question, but I am trying to ground Eve before she is dragged away into the depths of her mind.

"It makes sense, his father was as strict as him, he raised his son in his image – worse really. I warned he was not to be put to the top of the Overseers. Always keep someone between him and the Trustee Board…*idiots*. Too many extremists…fanatics…"

I struggle for the right words. I could (easily) argue anyone in the R&R is an extremist (I'll ignore that that includes me for a moment). If Eve considers this guy to be an extremist, exactly how extreme are we talking? I open my mouth to ask, but Eve starts to sob again, her frail shoulders convulsing with each breath as she mutters Lilith's name again and again.

"Track and trace," Eve says eventually. "But no, that ain't enough…too dangerous if caught, you'll ruin all you have learnt. He'll happily vote you out and gain support from others if they doubt you more. Pfft, his suggestions decades ago were distressing – too much. He believes in black and white, Missy, black and white…no room for grey. He'll tell you the grey is where they work, where the change is – the hard choices to save all. That's what the R&R believe, what I believe – you too I think – but he *is* the black…the purist. You fail, you are out. No questions."

"You serve or are rejected?"

"Exactly. Lilith, to him, is the dirt on your shoe. At best a discarded hen to be repurposed or rejected – by any means and with no remorse. We were consulting on tech once, long ago. I asked him why he was so hard...you know what he said?" I shake my head. "'I make the hard choices the weak cannot. I am their salvation.' I'll never forget his grin. He enjoys it...he hates the cadets and believes he drives them to a better, more purposeful-self."

I shudder. I instinctively knew that even in different circumstances I wouldn't like Dean...but to think of him lording over anyone is enough to chill my whole body. The potential for what he could be like beyond the fence, where few eyes watch, where he can act with very little reprimand, thinking he is righteous – no, I cannot bear it!

"Lilith," Eve whispers, "I'm sorry." A tear makes its way down her cheek.

"Don't give up," I say, kneeling in front of her, taking her by the hand.

"I never forgot her... I never turned me back...you have to tell her I am sorry for it..." Eve wipes her cheeks. "I only hope she has accepted the mission, then she'll be freed from him...her heart may find purpose." She is silent for a few minutes, and I see her eyebrows wobble, not unlike mine when I am deep in thought.

I watch them rise and fall and decide not to interrupt, hoping her mind stays in the room, on track.

"Tom, oh, how I—" The tears flow again as she utters her late husband's name; the pain of his loss, along with their sons and grandchildren, grips her eyes and floods them.

"Tom, too, you'll have to see him – no good sittin' here regrettin'…you'll learn, you are learnin', but no, no, I won't have the R&R lose so much of its past good to zealots and evil, self-righteous crusaders."

Eve has real determination and anger in her voice and her resolve gives me courage – if only I understood all her words! She mutters and curses in her grunts. I am desperate for her to say something clear, something like real instructions, but none come before sleep takes over her. Aunt Dora comes home mid-afternoon, and when Eve rouses again in the evening, it is as though she remembers none of our conversation earlier in the day.

Having finished his 'boys' day' playing rugby, Max picks me up in the evening. He takes one look at my weary, crestfallen face and escorts me home to bed without a word of complaint from me.

TWENTY-ONE

President General Fairfax's 75th birthday celebrations are all over the Central Hub and craft and food stalls have popped up everywhere along with music for every taste. We attended the main event on the Plaza long enough to satisfy my parents – watching the government sanctioned performances and listened to various dedications for our President General, who sat regally in his box with his wife, Lady Fairfax, smiling and laughing with heart in all the right places. To be fair, some of the acts were funny, but I was still glad to leave the general throng behind for a moment as Max and I slipped away in the direction of the Botanical Gardens who have put on their own concerts. The atmosphere is immediately inviting despite the cold, grey weather, and all around are smiling faces and dancing couples.

Kate and Tim made us promise to come, and although Max was concerned I looked tired despite a full night's sleep, we are welcomed with such enthusiasm I instantly feel happier for having made the effort. The music and lighting are wonderful, and for a change the PTB are being generous with food rations – and I have no DDS for the first time in months!

I am not going to miss the opportunity to pick my own flavours, so munch into the various snacks that are available. We all have a dessert each and I find myself craving for more chocolate mousse the second I have finished mine. I know Max is gentlemanly enough to give up his if I ask, but the voice within tells me not to take advantage of his generous nature.

Unfortunately, it doesn't stop me from lusting after the pot as it sits on the table in front of us – nor Kate laughing at me as I sigh when it is returned to the table empty.

"It's okay for you, you get to have your baby stork delivered! I have to eat for the both of us!" I retort when she continues mocking me.

"Hey! I'd be honoured to eat for two…nature just didn't smile on me that far," Kate replies in jest, but I can see the regret in her eyes, and I instantly wish I had chosen my words more wisely. I stop laughing, feeling my all-too-familiar notion of guilt, but Kate sees my expression and understands – she always does. Suddenly, she smiles, taps on her watch, and brings up a picture that I cannot quite see. She gazes at the image and her lips widen further before she turns the image into a hologram saying: "But my blessings are numerous, and our son is perfect."

I look her straight in the eyes and realise what she is saying, "You're having a boy?" Kate nods, glowing with such pride I almost need sunglasses to look at her.

She proceeds to tell me how they met him this morning for the first time, and I become caught up in her warmth – we all do. For the first time we sit and chat as a four about our son and daughter to come, Max shares our scan picture, comparing it to their SurrogacyPod image. The difference in arrival is not lost on any of us, but the wonder is undoubtedly equal.

In this moment, I feel guilty in two directions: One for concealing so much from my best friend, (something I never thought I would do, even if I know it is for her safety), and two, for knowing that so many women are out there having their chance of a natural birth revoked – their gene expression altered without them even knowing it is possible. I gaze at the empty containers on the table and see the remains of the rare occasion we eat without direction. The one-off variation that will not influence genetic outcome…but if enough ate the modified plants Kate and Tim grow – the ones they have no idea quite how revolutionary they are – then the UNE population could look very different. For the global better? Or for general worse?

The grey question.

Another grey question.

* * *

After a while we bump into some other friends, including Bruce, Tim's Uncle from SubHub 3. I haven't seen Bruce since he was tackling the various greenhouse issues that he was having in SH3 (the majority of which I now know were due to him having unsanctioned plants that would ruin the R&R research – a fact I will have to eternally keep to myself). He looks well and has lost the anxious lines he had around his eyes, which is more than I can say for his companion, Jay.

I know Kate has tried to take Jay under her wing. I think it is a mixture of her good nature, her natural mothering ability and just not being able to leave someone who is so sad, alone. She knows he had trouble, or more specifically, caused trouble, at the Matching Ceremony last September…he and Lilith. Eve's Lilith. If this is how miserable Jay looks, I dread to think of her face. I can barely remember what she looks like except she has beautiful red hair. I just saw her being dragged away when she didn't accept the match that she was given. The fertile man to match her genetics – opposed to the infertile love her heart had chosen in the form of Jay.

"We have the right to love unhindered," I say to no one in particular and instantly regret my words as several eyes turn to me. I honestly hadn't meant to say anything aloud and Max's eyes tell me all I need to know. *Ssshhh.* He is right, castaway comments that disregard the PTB, let alone the R&R rule, are not, under any circumstances, intelligent right now. Panicking, I rub my belly and pretend I was talking to my baby. My alibi is weak, really weak, but with Max's assistance, everyone chuckles and talks babies all over again.

Phew.

I avoid even glancing at Jay for some time after that, but when I do, I see him watching me, almost like he is trying to communicate without speaking. After a while he steps away from the group, and I watch him go. I could follow him, but I am really uncertain how wise that would be. I honestly don't know what I would say if I did.

Also, Kate told me he was surveilled 24/7. That was months ago, but I have no idea if that surveillance has continued – not to mention the fact *I* am probably watched more now than ever. I have been expecting a third degree about my visits to Eve being unreadable. That is probably why the R&R swept Aunt Dora's house again – either that, or they are just very nervous about what that old lady knows.

I am not sure, but I cannot ask Gee-Gee without it looking suspicious, and if her decree is saving Eve from R&R wrath, I cannot risk further rocking the boat. I know algorithms pick up key words. I know they can access our watches for audio, yet Eve also says she has countered that with her bracelets and even now, they are unlikely to do more than set alerts for keywords because it is easier and more efficient for an android to detect words than to have a human listen to a transcript.

Regardless, the bracelets are only safe indoors away from drones and there are only so many conversations Max and I can have in the shower or next to the river when it is particularly strong… Heck, we don't even know if that still works! We need an IT engineer who is currently employed by the R&R…but as I don't see any of those lining up for the revolution against the Real Revolution…

Ugh.

I don't follow Jay. Sense tells me not to risk it. My head says to stick with caution…my heart tells me to walk. I suddenly feel the familiar comfort of Max's fingers curling around mine and I turn to him smiling.

"What or who are you watching?" he whispers into my ear.

"Jay. I was considering speaking to him," I say keeping my mouth as close to his ear as possible.

"Why? Because of what you said?" Max seems concerned.

"Maybe? I just can't stand seeing him look so hollow. I didn't mean to say anything out loud just now though…I thought I was talking internally to myself."

"Yeah, I got that from your expression. Telling you to be careful I suppose is null and void?" He raises his eyebrows – the closest thing to him telling me off. I bob my head in recognition. "Who is he talking to?" Following Max's line of vision, I see Jay has reappeared. He is with a man, standing semi-hidden to the right of a rock band. The drumbeat is particularly heavy and I have no idea how they can talk at all, let alone coherently standing there.

Or is that the point? Is our water equal to their drumbeat?

We stand and watch without moving for a few minutes before Jay walks away looking dejected. His companion suddenly turns, glancing in my direction, and my heart skips as I recognise him – or at least think I do.

"Is that the guy from the radio station?" Max asks.

"Who?"

"The one you bumped into?"

"Kal? No, Kal is—"

"Not Kal, the other one – remember you were collecting bumps that day?"

"Huh, you're right…he *did* have a beard like that… Hang on, no…that's too much, plenty of people have beards—"

"What are you on about, honey?" I can't help laughing at Max adding 'honey' as though that is going to soften the blow, and I won't notice the rest of the sentence sounds like he is weighing up if I have lost my mind.

"The watchman, he looks like Eve's watchman," I say walking towards the bandstand, pulling Max with me rather than waiting for him to catch on. As I stride the unknown man catches my eye and pulls at his sleeve nervously but doesn't walk away. I can only hope that means he wants to talk to us.

No one attempts to speak until we are huddled so close we might be about to play in one of Max's rugby matches. "Who are you?" I say abruptly into the watchman's ear. I possibly need to work on my people skills.

"You're Maia and Max Rivers?" he says, ignoring my question.

"Yes, but who are you? And how do you know Jay?"

"I cannot talk to Jay."

"Why?" I ask, confused at his response.

"I found him first…I wanted to talk to him, but he is caught up in too much."

"Such as?"

"Well, for starters, he openly revolted against the Genetics Committee, trying to marry way above his grade. That alone put him under a level of scrutiny that any sane person would shrink from. Afterwards he had three options: death, prison, or conform – and had unlimited threats laid against his family and ex-girlfriend." He pauses, watching our reaction, testing to see if we are going to deny our knowledge or understanding of what he is saying. We both remain silent and nod, which satisfies him as he continues: "The second, more immediate issue is he was trying to meet *The Silence*."

Max and I look at him blankly…*too* blankly to be confused for acting.

"Pfft, I suppose SH1 life means you don't hear of such things…or want them. Not everyone loves the hierarchy you know. The Silence was a support group."

"A rebellion?" I ask.

"Sshh." He grimaces. "No, not exactly…it was a place to talk…maybe to commune and organise to lobby local politicians for a change—"

"A union," Max says. "Yes, I can see why the PTB wouldn't be thrilled about that."

"Well, they got them, so there is no need to worry," he says matter-of-factly. "Jay got reprimanded for being on the street nearby, but thankfully having met me earlier, he was late arriving, and the security personnel couldn't prove his involvement…but he is high on their watch list again. They won't tolerate him if he—" The man fidgets with his sleeves and shuffles his feet anxiously. "I told him I can't talk to him again. He is just too risky."

"This isn't exactly encouraging us to talk to you now," says Max reaching for my hand. I think he is readying to make a hasty exit.

"Please, I—I think we have, or you might know…I need your help…maybe I can help you too."

"Oh?" Max squeezes my hand tighter.

"Jay is a hot target to the PTB, and I think, maybe you are, too." He speaks so shyly yet his words have unbelievable force. Certainly enough to make me shiver.

"I barely know Jay – his business is his own. Why are you telling us this?" asks Max, trying to sound cool over the deafening sound of the drummer.

"No, no, Jay is different… You are the Golden couple… though you are also attached to those who are anything but."

I am lost for words and the three of us stand silently weighing each other up. Around his dark-blonde beard his face is pale, yet he has a light – no, a glimmer, not a full light, but some sense of passion in his green eyes.

"I don't know what you are talking about," I say defensively.

"I found Jay looking for assistance for Lilith." He stops, waiting to see our reaction to that name. I try not to change my expression, but I can feel my eyes widen at the mention of her name and Max's grip on my hand increases again. If he holds me any tighter it is going to hurt. "You know who she is, don't you?"

I nod.

"What do you want?" Max says impatiently.

"Eve."

"Eve? Why?"

"I know who she is, her relevance… I didn't until Lilith's Shepherd mentioned her ancestry. Afterwards I looked at her pedigree and found Eve." I shrug, still trying my hardest not to get dragged into a conversation I cannot back out of. This guy's cryptic speech so far is not inspiring trust. "I am hoping Eve has answers to help the farm – to help Lily – and will want to help me to connect the dots." His voice cracks saying her name. I cannot help noticing the abbreviation – the signaling of familiarity? He pulls his sleeve down, wiping his face from the beads of sweat that have been building up despite the cold air.

"Why are you following me if you want Eve? Why not knock on her door? It *was* you outside her house last week, right?"

"I can't, she never goes outside, and I cannot log into the same buildings as any of you."

"You understand the tech?" I feel my cogs ticking. "Who are you?"

"I can't give my name," he says, sucking in his top lip.

"I've heard enough. You say Jay is a liability, but all I'm hearing is crap that is going to get my family arrested." Max tugs on my arm and motions we should leave.

"Please! Don't go!" The stranger grabs my other arm, stopping Max and I in unison.

"Tell us your name – something, anything other than just hiding in the shadows. You could be a test and we will not fail it, thank you all the same," I say sarcastically. I turn to Max, checking we are on the same page. He silently nods. I look back to the mystery man, deciding to appeal to his skittish nature one more time, though I am simultaneously questioning why we are doing the digging if he has been watching us, not the other way around: "You saw me at Eve's…you bumped into me at the radio station…"

"Yes, but Dean was the one who made me decide to reach out…to test the waters to see if he is right." A lump comes to my throat as I fear what is coming next. If this guy is of the same ilk as Dean, saying anything at all is potentially very dangerous. My heart races, but as I look at him, I cannot see a single part of his demeanour that matches the attitude or aura of that arrogant beast. This guy is nervous and fidgety. Dean was all airs and graces from the second I saw him (no matter how brief our encounter). "His disapproval of you and your *inclusion* gave me hope…hope to seek you out, to find you in the open air…where the—"

"AI systems won't pay any attention to you," I finish for him. I exhale and relax, albeit only slightly, as the pebble drops. "You're an Overseer…to know Dean and Lilith, that is the only logical explanation." His face freezes and his eyes widen. Cruel as it might sound, I want to laugh. His expression suddenly reminds me of my own fear, how inadequate, and totally unqualified I felt walking into that lift and finding the R&R for the first time. I am not a natural spy and nor is this guy. He is just a person who sees injustice and conscience compels him to act. He has to be an engineer or IT technician – a man with knowledge and unique access to exactly what I have been waiting for.

The mountain has come to me.

TWENTY-TWO

The weather is glorious today and I have decided it is a sign from the heavens that today will go to plan. I have spent weeks stressing about this. The fourth attempt *will* be the lucky one… Eve *will* be awake, and I *will* take her to the riverbank – with Pandora's box tucked under her wheelchair. I watch Aunt Dora make her way down the front path and turn left in the direction of the tram station and instantly turn to Eve, hoping against all hope she is lucid and remains that way for the next hour.

"What is it Missy, you look anxious?" Eve says as I bop in front of her. "You ain't far enough along to give birth yet, but you're sweatin' like you're foalin'."

I laugh. If anyone else said that to me I would probably be offended, but right now Eve's humour is a welcome distraction. "Eve, I have someone who wants to meet you… an Overseer. He says he is a friend of our cause – he watches Lilith."

Eve's neck angles forward as I speak, and her eyes focus more clearly than I have seen for some time. "Where is he?" she whispers.

"He won't meet us here – he'll only meet outside because—"

"Signal…aye, yes, the signals. Good, he ain't stupid…" Eve nods in approval. "Well, what you waitin' for? Push me, Missy, push me to wherever it is you're taking me."

"Are you sure? I don't want to do anything you're—"

"PUSH ME," she almost shouts, but keeps a smile on her face.

I chuckle and bow, acknowledging her authority in a playful, yet respectful way. I am also attempting to distract my nerves. Eve wasn't wrong about me sweating profusely.

"I think I should take the bracelets, but only wear them once there… What do you think?"

Eve considers for a moment, screws up her face and says: "It is worth the risk, yes, take 'em."

The walk to the riverbank only takes a few minutes, but I feel like I have run a marathon when we arrive. As planned, Max is there, ready and waiting – and thankful not to be receiving a fourth text cancelling our plans.

The text would have read 'I've run out of sugar. Can you get some later?' No algorithm would have bothered about something so boring, and our mystery friend would have scuttled off into his shadows again if Max was not there.

Instead, the three of us stand silently contemplating whether all is well with him. We haven't spoken to him since our initial meeting, deeming it only worthwhile if Eve is compliant. I didn't want to tell him how ill Eve is, so simply said it could be difficult to organise and could take more than one attempt. He said he had complications on his side, too, so we agreed to meet at 10 a.m. each Saturday until we are successful; however, with each passing week my fears of failure have multiplied.

"Huh, the watchman," Eve says as he approaches, while I sigh with relief. "I told you he wasn't a gardener," she smirks as he gets closer. "Bracelets, Missy, don't forget." I silently do as I am bid. The man, dressed in the same green coat as when I saw him standing outside the house, takes a bracelet as I hand him one, raises an eyebrow, and puts it on without voicing as much as a 'hello.'

"So, who are you?" Eve demands the moment we all have our bracelets on.

"You're Eve Addams?" he asks, avoiding her question.

"Hmmphh, who else is this old and this grumpy?" she retorts. "Your name boy, give it *now*."

"E—Ezra," he stammers, "my name is Ezra. It is an honour to meet you, Madam, you are a heroine of mine…I never thought I'd meet you, especially under such circumstances."

Eve looks touched, embarrassed even, by his address, but being true to form, she masks her feelings and ploughs forward. "Thank you, but what do you know?"

"Dean is my grandfather—"

"Hmmphh, Missy, this is not a conversation to have with *that* family!"

"Please, Madam, please. I am here *because* of him, not *for* him. He makes a mockery of what your Shepherds were designed for. I have read all of your reports and studies. Not once did I think you meant your AI to instill pain and suffering. Am I wrong?"

Eve narrows her eyes, staring at Ezra and I am sure she is replaying his words in her mind, weighing up the truth of every word.

"No lad, you ain't wrong," Eve says, still holding his gaze. "I can't say all was fluffy bunnies though…I created for all eventualities…but if you mean the Shepherds, no, they were not meant to be cruel. They are to guide…maybe they correct too, but correction need not be painful."

"They guide, but they have evolved beyond our wildest dreams, maybe even yours," Ezra says with awe in his voice. "I had the privilege of coding some, but I now watch over them – data analysis mostly. They, the Shepherds, have become their own individuals – guiding, understanding, and feeling way beyond my previous AI comprehension." As Ezra pauses I turn to Eve, and her face crumples as she attempts to control the desire to sob. I think I understand. I am no engineer, yet I understand the joy of seeing your work come to something – so far, my triumphs have been somewhat moderate (without considering R&R intervention), but I can imagine the pride in seeing the fruit of my labours. Eve has seen numerous inventions of hers work, but I see the delight in success does not get old. "The potential for trouble is in the original code though…if the coder—"

"Tries to replicate their own ideals, not sticking to the mandate," cuts in Eve. Ezra nods. "I warned of that. I told 'em not to let one person code. Do a base, I said, give individual characteristics to fit personalities, tasks, whatever, but always cross code with at least two technicians…*always.*"

"My grandfather disagrees. 113, his avatar Shepherd, mirrors his ideals and people suffer as a result…more than necessary—"

"Including my Lilith?" Eve asks with a trembling lip. She shakes her head and tears flow when Ezra nods and I fear sorrow will end this interview, just like it has so many times before.

"Grandfather says she missed her calling, falls short of her worth, and needs to quickly find her purpose. All cadets are no more than egg producers and scientific specimens to him. In short he is a bully."

"I can hear Dean's words," says Eve. "We didn't get on, your grandad and me. He called cadets failures back then, so I cannot imagine he has improved with age. Hmmphh, I know the line of study and what Dean wanted when he was in your position – he should never have got to Head. *Never!*" Eve sinks into her own thoughts, muttering expletives, and grunts before looking up at me, then back to Ezra. "You must remove him."

Ezra bops in front of Eve's chair, resting a hand on the edge of her armrest. "That is why I need your help."

"You have read my reports? My journals?" Ezra confirms he has. "The best stuff isn't in any reports," grins Eve.

Ezra's face lights up. "I was counting on it."

"We can get Lilith out then?" asks Max.

"Out?" Ezra looks up in surprise. "No—"

"Then what is this about?" I am suddenly questioning the point of this meeting if rescue is not the goal.

"Say we did…" says Ezra. "What then? For her to live unhindered here, in the Hub, we would have to change more than the Shepherds, Maia. She ultimately did break the rules…rules that I, along with the work – despite this conversation – do believe in."

"Then what are we doing here?" snaps Max.

"Lily has started to find some peace, just like most of the other cadets as they progress forward, but that peace hangs on a thread." Ezra rubs his face before continuing. "There are more than cadets in the world that have lost their path. I want to correct that – actually do what the mission says – without cruel dictators."

"You want to rewrite 113?"

"You can't," Eve interrupts. "The Shepherds are individual. If they have all become 'themselves,' you cannot rewrite that. They *are*. Just as you are."

"Then again, Ezra, what *do* you want?" I ask.

"To reset the path the Creator – you, Eve – set a long, long time ago…and clear the path of hatred and shadows. I–I hope I can because I cannot continue to watch anyone treated as they are now. But I cannot do it without the master… without you."

TWENTY-THREE

We left our new friend with nervous excitement. I've no doubt we're all petrified of the consequences if our plans fail, but Eve has given Ezra a backdoor and glitch codes to search for in the system and in the meantime, she is also trying to construct or remember an alternative code. Nothing is guaranteed, yet we have hope…*I* have hope…hope that I am not going to become the blind puppet, dancing to the beat of a drum I end up hating myself for. We are looking for a future for all, one that's worth forging – and worth risking failure for.

This initial plan doesn't answer all these issues, but it sets us off on a track that has no brakes. It propels me into a double – no, triple life that will probably keep me on the verge of a heart attack for a very long time. But my path has always been muddy. I've never been able to keep to the given route and have mentally beaten myself for it my whole life. Now, instead of trudging that ditch alone, my husband walks besides me, not because I have dragged him down, but because we have chosen to wade together. Any doubts I had about that have been squashed because every night we talk – openly, honestly, lovingly – we talk and decide, we share and lament, we rejoice and worry.

Together.

It feels weird waiting for Max to shower every night so we can have 'our' time with some degree of confidence, but it has kept me sane while we have tried to connect Ezra and Eve. Now my issue again is waiting. Waiting for either of them to report back is stressful, but especially Eve. My optimism wobbles here. I must have faith. Her failing health has not taken her mind, the fog has not swallowed her. If anything her resolve was strengthened at the weekend, giving her renewed cause to hold tighter to reality.

Have faith.

Walking to the tram from work, my watch flashes and I see I have a message from Gee-Gee asking me to meet her for tea in half an hour. My heart sinks as I desperately want to go home and moan to Max about how irritating I found Theo and his endless corrections this afternoon. Not to mention my bladder is currently on a strict schedule – one that an extra stop and drink will not take kindly to. The baby is certainly making me pay for my reservations…or maybe she just likes to constantly remind me of her presence – as if I could forget as my waistline increases by the hour!

Trotting from bathroom to bathroom while people tell me how wonderful pregnancy is, coming out with phrases such as 'oh, Mrs Rivers, you're positively glowing today!' is probably my biggest pet peeve. My hairdresser declared that yesterday, and I had to sit on my hands and pinch my legs to stop myself from asking if vomiting at 5 a.m. and running back and forth from the toilet since that was the kind of 'glow' she found attractive. I know the comments are kindly meant. I know I am lucky. I just want to be allowed to groan without feeling guilty. Or at the very least not force a smile when I am actually doing my best not to regurgitate my breakfast.

Sighing, I turn away from my homeward journey and follow my watch as it directs me to the café that Gee-Gee has chosen. I pass the main entrance to the greenhouses where Kate and Tim work and make my way towards a little side café that I haven't been in before. It doesn't surprise me Gee-Gee knows all the quiet, out of the way places.

"Maia!" I turn to see Kate flying towards me, her face wet with freshly shed tears and my gut twists as I suddenly worry what is wrong. Surely the R&R haven't found out about Ezra? Did he betray us?

"Kate? What is it?" I ask into her hair as she hugs me without any further greeting. "Are you okay? The baby, is he—?"

Kate steps back to answer. "I'm okay, the baby is fine, praise be, he is fine. Tim and I saw him at lunch. We read him a story actually, I know he is too young for that, but—"

"That's great, but why are you crying?" My heart is racing erratically now.

"Jay is dead," she mutters and bursts into tears again.

I stare at her and a lump blocks my throat, stopping me from speaking or crying. It is like my head has frozen, but the rest of me has icy bolts firing up and down my body.

"Jay is dead," Kate says again. "I can't believe it…dead!"

"How?" I eventually ask, though I speak so quietly I am not sure how Kate heard me.

"Apparently he has been part of a terrorist cell – can you believe it?"

"*No?*" No, I cannot.

"He somehow joined after…Bruce is devastated, he thought Jay was moving on after his mismatch…thought he was focusing on work…had friends…"

The only word I really hear from Kate's disjointed sentence is 'mismatch.' That is quite a term for falling in love despite fertility status. If anyone else said that, I would tell them off, but not Kate. I cannot bring myself to reprimand her. I must remember that is what the PTB want us to think of those who rebel or who don't fit their rules. Would Kate have called me 'mismatch' to my face had I carried on trying to marry Theo? Did she? Even if only to herself?

It is too easy to call others out for what we do not fully understand. Kate is normally the most empathic person I know. She still is, but she hasn't personally lived the pain of forbidden love –

she fell in love with the 'right' grade. So did I in the end. Theo and I were not right. But neither are the PTB.

"You cannot help who you love," I whisper.

Kate instantly understands. "Oh, honey, no, sorry, that wasn't—"

Kate's blue eyes fill with tears again and I cannot cope. "It is okay, I know you didn't mean it like that, you're not capable of being…"

I don't finish my sentence. 'Cruel,' 'nasty,' 'insensitive' are all words I could use, but all imply I am offended, and honestly, I feel more of a traitorous friend to her than she'll ever be to me, no matter how good my intentions are. We hug instead and I recentre our conversation by asking what she knows.

"Not much. Bruce rang Tim in such a state saying Sal, from the Vertical Farm, had come screaming into his office saying, 'he is dead, he is dead, they shot him, he is dead!' Bruce calmed her enough to get basic info, ran and found Jay with a single shot to the head. A drone had come in and left without a care in the world."

"Just him? No one else was hurt?"

"No, not there, but apparently some others have been pulled in. They called themselves 'The Silence' or something like it. Have you heard of them?"

Kate is looking at me expectantly and my heart sinks as I again have to lie: "No, never."

"No, me neither. Apparently, some got taken out a few weeks ago, now the PTB have cleared up the dregs. Poor Jay! What did they do to him?"

"Who?"

"The terrorists. He was too shy and sorry to have acted alone. They must have preyed on his distress…don't you think?"

"I didn't know him," I say flatly.

"No, I suppose you didn't."

"But if he loved strong and true enough, believed in the cause enough, then maybe, maybe he thought his actions were for the greater good—"

Kate tilts her head at me and furrows her brows. Her face asks a question, though her lips do not move. I hold my expression. If ever I doubted the necessity to keep my thoughts, plans, and doubts to myself, that time has well and truly passed. I have been blessed with a husband to lean on, together we risk all, but we chose that. Talking now, here, despite her loyalty and overwhelming kindness, would only break down and endanger. Let Kate be one of the innocents I fight for, not condemn.

"I'm so sorry about Jay. A terrible, terrible waste." I look at my watch. "I have to go see Gee-Gee, she's waiting for me, will you be okay?"

Kate takes my hand and squeezes it. "Yes, we'll be okay." The look in her eye worries me. She knows me too well.

I deflect her the only way I know how. I transfer her hand to my stomach, beam, and say, "We'll see you soon, maybe I had better start reading stories to her, or your son will be better educated before he is even born!"

My plan works: Kate is distracted, cooing over my extending girth, laughing as she confesses the library worth of reading she has prepared for baby Benjamin. Yes, he has a name already. And yes, Max has a list of names he likes for our baby...none of which I do...or can cope with choosing. I acknowledge her, that is enough right now.

I leave Kate just in time to see Gee-Gee walk into the café ahead of me. She turns to me as she stands at the counter, nods to a table, and I take the hint and sit down. I can see why Gee-Gee likes it here. The room is small compared to most cafés in the Hub, but there is a quiet, respectful hum of activity mixed with music. Anyone wishing to talk can do so without being listened to, and anyone wishing to sit and silently contemplate the world can do that without being disturbed by anyone else. The plants inside are almost as numerous as they are up the exterior of the building and, sitting in the far corner, I struggle to see Gee-Gee approaching until she is three strides from her chair.

"This place looks like it is designed for rest and relaxation," I quip as she sits down, placing two mugs on the table.

Gee-Gee immediately understands my R&R reference and chuckles: "Indeed, it is."

I do not dare ask why I have been summoned here. I was curious before I met Kate, a little concerned even, but as I hadn't been called to the headquarters I was hoping my recent meeting with Ezra had gone unnoticed. I am still hoping that. If someone could just tell my insides to stop twisting and turning, that would be wonderful.

Gee-Gee's face turns serious as she reaches for her tea. "We had to act."

"Okay…?" I try to mimic her expression, giving no fear or comprehension away.

"I think you knew him – Jay, Lilith's Jay?"

"Barely. I have met him a couple of times by chance. Why?"

"We'd tried to give him a reprieve, for his family's sake. That's the trouble with blood relations, you try to protect them, even if it means blurring the edge of the rule a little." Gee-Gee pauses, looking to see if I am going to react. I don't. "Well, we can only blur so much and he…well, that's *that.* I wanted you to hear it from me."

"As a courtesy or warning?"

Gee-Gee raises her eyebrows, sipping her tea again: "Both."

Shit.

Does she know?

Or is this a general reminder? A 'friendly' nudge…or 'I know what you're doing'?

"Well, I appreciate the gesture, but like I said, I barely knew him. I am sorry for his...*loss.*"

Gee-Gee sighs. "The Board wanted him removed from the get-go, but he was good with plants and we had no immediate role...or enough resources *beyond* for his grade."

"Well, he wasn't a 3, was he?" Cold, to the point...no sarcasm...be the model pupil.

"Exactly."

"I have a message to visit Dr Oldman," I say. Changing the subject seems wise. "I am keen to study there."

"Yes, he is pooling his data – exciting times are ahead." I never thought I would hate her smile, but I am beginning to because I realise what makes her smile, makes me cringe. When I was in the dark I thought her smile was a light to the future, to the development of real earth-breaking change. I cringe at who I am becoming and fear that I could be looking in the mirror at my older self...

Act the part, not be it.

I have to survive first...

And not get condemned for thinking outside the box. I cannot let myself become labelled a terrorist like Jay. How ironic is that? That pale, shy man was shot for being a terrorist. What terror did he instil?

The horror is before me. Alive and very much kicking.

TWENTY-FOUR

Ezra has gone cold. No, more accurately, completely silent. It has been weeks and I feel sick. I am thinking of calling my baby 'Alias' because she is my cover for my constant heart palpitations, sticky, sweaty skin, and almost continuous desire to vomit. I don't need to question if Ezra knows about Jay, of course, he does, it was splashed across the news so thoroughly that even Aunt Dora couldn't avoid hearing about it. Part of me is glad Ezra hasn't reappeared with a plan to disable 113. Gee-Gee successfully scared me and even Eve's reaction made me gulp – so much so that Aunt Dora clocks we have a secret and demands to be included if it causes such a physical response. I really wish my mind and body would agree on one method, one resolve…but they don't. I swing from new age spy to newborn pup in a matter of seconds and this time I have to run to the toilet before I can answer Aunt Dora properly. Once I have explained, to say she is 'uneasy' is an understatement.

"Have you lost your mind? You took Eve to meet this guy when you'd met him once and he wouldn't even tell you his name? And now, he has disappeared… Did you not think to ask for a backup meeting point – anyway to contact him?"

She has a point.

"We thought the risk—"

"Ugh, it is done," Aunt Dora groans. "I am glad I didn't know."

"It is worth it, Dora," chips in Eve. "If it makes the FARM a happier place…if it starts a better way. Them bastards shouldn't have let the mission slide…shouldn't have lost their humanity in the name of mission, or correction – or whatever hmmphhing idealistic excuse they wanna spout. They kill, maim, repress, and destroy too easily."

"Forgive me Eve, but have you not confessed to having been an enormous part of that cog?" Aunt Dora almost sounds bitter. "You only got out when the death toll piled against you beyond any sane person's reckoning. Hell, you only survived *that* because you are seen as some sort of queen amongst thieves! It is respect and long, loyal service beyond your own family's grave that kept you alive – and now me!"

"You chose to join with me. I've said it before, I make no apology for my past. The alternative would have been far, far worse."

Aunt Dora only nods in response.

"I lost everything for that belief, nay, understanding…" says Eve. "You know my true heart, my sorrow. Pfft, I won't keep defending meself, tis done."

"I didn't ask you to."

"Your face did."

"You're helping to mould a revolution now Eve, Aunt Dora knows that," I say, taking Eve by the hand.

"Which one?" My aunt sighs. "I fear if you carry on Maia, you'll end up another casualty. Another unnamed grave in the fight against a force hardly anyone knows exists."

She fiddles with her wedding ring. Of course, she is thinking of her Ray who was killed at the R&R's bidding.

"Ray should not have died: he fell foul by accident. If I am lost, at least I will know why – but let's stop thinking of doom!" I plead.

"Quite right, Missy, quite right." Eve sounds oddly chirpy. "You need to find Ezra though…or look into recruiting us a new tech…both wouldn't be the worst idea."

Aunt Dora's eyes boggle and I can see she has an opposing opinion. She doesn't say anything though, instead she leaves the room to make tea, probably hoping I will have changed the subject when she returns.

Max appears in the interim and looks pretty frozen as he walks in. Ezra had previously only agreed to meet us on a Saturday, but any time Max or I have spare since Jay's death, one or both of us walk along the riverbank, hoping Ezra will appear. Max just shakes his head, so I do not ask. Our only other connection is the radio station, where I bumped into Ezra the first time. We have our second interview there tomorrow and I will keep an eye out for him; however, something tells me Ezra will only be found if he wants to be. Someone that skittish is not going to be easily caught out.

* * *

"Welcome back!" declares Lei as Max and I walk into her studio. "Oh, wow! You are blooming so beautifully, Maia!"

Is that not just code for 'damn, you're huge!'? My bump does seem to be particularly ample for eighteen weeks. In addition to my doctor insisting on putting 'baby' in front of every sentence and being told I 'glow' repeatedly, my most recent pregnancy-related aggravation is people grabbing my stomach. Lei does it as she greets me, and she has the doubly annoying ability to make *me* feel bad when I don't enjoy it. Her face is full of sincere wonder as she twirls her flawless black hair with enthusiasm…so much so, I worry I am going to run out of fake warmth or zeal before we go on air.

The song finishes and Lei turns her mic on, addressing the airwaves with animation, repeating her previous introduction of Max and me as 'the Golden Couple.' I cringe, but outwardly keep smiling and answer all her questions as I am supposed to. Claire didn't come with us this time, but she did email a list of 'to mention' points. I was surprised to see her standard 'not to mention' list had disappeared. Perhaps it is now assumed I know how not to get myself in trouble… or at least should.

I can see why Lei has hosted this radio show for so many years. She radiates happiness to her listeners – *she* is the true definition of glowing, not me. Not only does her beautiful skin have a deep tone only a fool would not envy, but she also has an aura of everything good – everything the PTB or R&R want to promote. Yes, she is well chosen, and I can see her holding this chair for a very long time. When she lays her left arm on her desk, waving the right as she speaks, I feel bad making a mental note of her barcode. I tell myself it is silly; I have no need of it. Yet as my plans chop and change constantly, I rationalize there is no harm in knowing it… no more than any of the others I have gone to bed repeating lately…and hopefully I won't get any of them in trouble if one day I do use them.

Hopefully.

Lei has another hour of her show when we finish, but Kal, the producer, finds Max and me as we leave the studio. He still has the appearance of casual comfort, embodying a kind of handsome, rugged look, and I can see many of the women here have noticed as heads follow him everywhere. He notices too as he winks at a young girl who is propped in a doorway and her face flushes red. Yes, this guy definitely knows he is handsome – and how to use it. Max is just as good looking, just in a tidier, less arrogant way and I can see he is watching Kal's following with amusement – so much so he nearly walks into Ella as she springs out of a lift.

"Ooh, sorry, Ella," Max gushes when she mocks him for ignoring her initial greeting.

Ella just laughs. "How funny I see you again today… it must be our thing now! You go on air; I bump into you afterwards!"

"Well, if you want to make it a 'thing,' you need to meet us in June as well because we have our next interview then!" I am not really serious, but Ella is so overwhelmingly keen to befriend and be-friends, she takes my jest as a genuine offer. I am not rude enough to correct her and frankly her company is easy, so I have no particular desire to wiggle out of such a meeting – especially if it doesn't involve her husband.

"Other than planning our social calendar and listening almost at-source to our interview, what brings you here again anyway?" I ask.

"Ah, well, exciting news there, I have a new full-time placing! It starts in July…which is handy today so Kal cannot dob me in for taking time off to go out with you." She winks and nudges Kal as she speaks, making him blush, though I doubt it is out of real embarrassment.

"Congratulations!" Max says seconds before me. My brain is too busy calculating if this new job could be helpful to me in any way. Max reminds me he has to go back to work, so he shakes Kal's hand, makes his apologies to Ella, and kisses me goodbye. Kal takes his cue to go back to work, leaving Ella and me to make our way out into the now grey, wet day and dash for the nearest, most warm looking café.

Conversation flows from nothing to everything and before I know it, two hours have passed.

"Oops were you supposed to be at work?" I say, feeling guilty. One advantage of being a Golden Goose, pregnant, and working for my father-in-law is no one reprimands my time keeping. Actually, today Henry specifically told me to take the day off.

"Oh, no, it is okay. I'm still pretty freelance and I do such odd hours these days that I am owed a lot of time off."

"Oh? Have there been that many cyber issues?"

"Some, but it's my design projects too. My new job will have me centering on that fully come the summer, I just have to train a couple of graduate students before I leave." Wow, she is barely out of school herself – having graduated early I might remember – yet here she is training others and climbing the ranks, despite the setback of my mother-in-law.

I look up and see something I have never seen in Ella's bright eyes before – worry. At first, I think I am mistaken, only moments before she was full of enthusiasm, zeal, and her normal optimistic bubbliness. The only time I have seen her sparkle dim is when she first arrived, and she was so desperately looking for friends and feared she had none or would be rejected, but denying her friendship or affection is like spanking a puppy as it begs for biscuits – no one worth oxygen could ever do it. I look again, doubting myself, but the shadow is still there.

"Is everything okay?" I ask.

"Yes, yes," Ella beams, "of course. I've finally been given clearance to the next step. I am a very lucky girl…thrilled!"

I look at her and say, "Fantastic," in a slightly higher tone that I would naturally, all the while holding her gaze. It probably should have hit me earlier, but I suddenly realise what she has been promoted to – or rather, *who by.* Is it shock, disgust, fear, or something else clouding the twinkle in her eye? Could she be testing me? Had she lived, Mary would have taken great pleasure in turning Ella into her spy, challenging the loyalty and decisions of those she doubted. I would definitely have been on top of that list. Have the R&R ruined a sweet soul by enlightening her? Or is she actually thrilled to now have access and abilities way beyond her previous level? I still have that daily debate with myself – every single time I walk into a laboratory, especially Dr Oldman's. The man makes my skin shift and freeze, his research stretches the boundaries of right and wrong, but the freedom my mind has to roam when I am there is…

Inspiring…

Confusing…

Fulfilling…

Addictive.

Ella watches a group of girls as they enter the café. They are all around sixteen or seventeen – pre-grade, still studying, and full of tender excitement. Behind them are three middle-aged women, probably friends of my mother as they have the distinctive appearance of housewives who have no time constraints. Their children will be teenage plus, so they now have time to pamper themselves while their partners make the money – they could work, they probably just prefer not to. My eyes continue around the room, and I spot an elderly couple chuckling together and drinking tea in the corner. They may just have retired and have family at home, or they could have dedicated their lives to work and have (unlike Gee-Gee), decided they have done their bit for humanity and Earth. All of them are perfectly justified, perfectly valued members of society…all deserving of peace and tranquility.

I look back to Ella who is still watching the room in silent contemplation and tell her I had better go home. She smiles sweetly but looks like her thoughts are conflicted. I wave my arm over the scanner in the centre of the table, paying the bill for us both.

"Ooh, thank you, but you shouldn't have—"

"My treat, you can get the June bill," I wink. I'll see her before that anyway I am sure, but knowing she has a date to reciprocate the gesture seems to satisfy her. I stand, again looking around the room, and decide to take a risk by quietly saying: "I envy the innocence of *before*, don't you?"

Ella looks at me, the sparkle in her eye freezing in time as she weighs up my words, trying to decipher if I am a trap. I keep a cool, non-judgemental look on my face and wait.

"I am honoured and excited to go forward. The possibilities are now endless," she says with confidence.

"Indeed, of course," I say, walking away with a kind smile, inwardly lamenting our exchange.

I extend my left arm to the exit scanner and the door slides open. Stepping out into the damp afternoon I turn as I hear Ella's parting whisper: "But yes, I also envy the innocence."

TWENTY-FIVE

If I doubted my pregnancy – but honestly, how could I? – now I have no chance of denial as my recent odd abdominal feeling of a swimming fish or fluttering butterfly has turned into a drummer. A little drummer girl. I was relieved Max was home when I felt the first ripples of her tapping away because he had tried to feel her lighter movements, and then mocked me in his disappointment, telling me I had gas because he couldn't feel anything. But now there is no denying someone gave her drumsticks – and she is going to use them! If there were visiting hours in there, I'd say the donor was my mum as she has been waiting for me to start holding my back, groaning as I straighten up, or clutching my stomach after a big kick purely so she can say 'see, see what you did to me!' I heard similar banter with Abby when she was pregnant, yet the tone is different now, for with me it is extra personal. I was the baby that stopped her breeding career and she wants – *needs* – me to take her baton and feel its full effects. Her success in life rests on me understanding what she went through, replicating it, and then parading the streets with said child for all her friends to ooh and aah over.

The pride of the Hub.

Or I would be if I hadn't been avoiding my mum and making a point of waiting at least two hours before I respond to her messages…which then results in another angry one.

Christmas may have been nice, but I don't even visit Gee-Gee at home if I can help it. The house holds too many ghosts, both while growing up and since joining the R&R. Mary may not have died there, but I still get a chill stepping onto the pavement outside. My mind triggers the scene of me getting out of Mark's car – a proper car, not a Solarbug – and asking what the hell had just happened. That night I witnessed a double murder and almost everything came crashing down around me. Crashing down, but immediately rebuilt…rebuilt by those who are well versed in coverups, using defences that have long been in place. They are a well-oiled machine of power and deceit. One I was hoping to chip away at…but my ally has gone quiet, gone to ground, and I cannot sniff him out. I have a new ally, or could, if I dared to talk candidly to her – if only I was certain she is truly horrified, or at least firmly rattled, and wasn't just initially shocked by her R&R upgrade. Max isn't sure which she is either. We have spent a few weeks contemplating whether to approach Ella, trying to guess what level of information she is truly party to. I work with her husband almost daily, but have zero confidence in him, so I cannot risk attempting to glean anything from Theo. This evening we went for a meal and movie with them, along with Kate and Tim, but as Max and I sit in bed now, we have nothing more than 'hmms' and 'maybes' to conclude on. Our little drummer breaks our indecisive cycle by whacking me in the stomach. Max launches both his large hands across my stomach, smiling broadly as he waits for her to strike again.

"Talk to her," I say smiling, "she seems to like it."

* * *

I fell asleep to the sound of Max's voice as he gently waffled on, waking up hours later to find us curled into each other with my head on Max's chest, while his right hand still rests on my stomach. Only the incessant need to pee makes me uncurl myself and I walk past the landing window without a care in the world. It isn't until I make the return trip that I realise a light is wobbling in the dark and I squint as I try to make out what is causing the (now annoying) reflection in my eyes. Suddenly the light changes angle and I gasp as I see a face. I run into the bedroom and shake Max awake, he grumbles, but sits up quickly, fear striking him as he asks if the baby is okay.

"Yes, fine! Outside, he, E – the watchman – is outside, come!" I ramble trying not to use Ezra's name in my haste as paranoia for algorithms kicks in.

I don't wait for Max to put on his shoes and simply grab a coat and dash as fast as my belly will allow. I open the front door and Ezra has gone. I mutter 'Really?!' under my breath and then the shrubs around the corner rustle. I follow the noise to see the shape of Ezra standing in the dark without any light hitting him whatsoever.

Ezra puts a finger to his lips and hands me a napkin. I take the folded cloth and turn to gesture to Max as he bundles himself half naked out the front door. I turn back to Ezra, but he has already disappeared into the night. Maybe he is better suited to being a spy than I thought.

I shrug my shoulders and nod towards the house to Max and we silently return into the warm. I unfold the white napkin. The irony of receiving another note-napkin isn't lost on me, though I very much doubt this one is going to contain the same sentiment as Theo's did. 'I love you, but left you to unknown servitude,' is hardly applicable now – and quite frankly, I am very much hoping this note has a longer lasting sentiment attached to it.

Preferably *hope* …even better, *hope with action.*

I understand why paper is such a limited resource and why it is not readily available, but on occasions such as these, when digital communication is strictly off limits, a note on paper, not cloth, would be much more desirable. Once opened out, Ezra's handwriting is blotched and hurried, but I can read it, though I dare not read it aloud. Max understands and leans over my shoulder, putting his left arm around my waist, acting as the silent, unwavering support I absolutely need as my hands tremble in anticipation. As I read the words before me, my whole-body shakes:

Sorry, I was scared. I still am, but I cannot leave it. Things are worse on the farm. 113 worse. Dean worse. This cannot be the future. Meet me Sunday 2 p.m. The Botanical Gardens have a fair.

* * *

Max and I arrive early to the Botanical Gardens, hoping it will be obvious what part of the extensive grounds that Ezra has in mind to meet up. The waterfalls have been a significant spot for us as a couple several times now, so that sector of the gardens will always be our go-to area. Does Ezra know that is our special place? Or is he drawn to it because of the sound of the rushing water? Possibly. That is why we used the river to meet Eve. Yet there are gardens, greenhouses, and displays in homage to all kinds of landscapes from across the globe and Ezra could be waiting in any one of them. The central park area seems the most logical place to start even if it is the busiest. There is a children's playground, a range of snack stalls, and a band playing most weekends, but at the moment there is also a fair and extra gathering of games left over from the Mayday celebrations.

"Where do we go now?" I ask, looking at the multiple signposts.

"I don't think we should go anywhere. Hopefully he'll find us," says Max, watching a group of children rush around the climbing equipment. My little drummer kicks me…I wonder if she detected the lump I swallowed in my throat when I considered if I would fit in with the group of mums who are standing on the side-lines. Nothing about the scenario in front of me makes me easy.

I watch a little girl, probably aged nine or ten, leap off the climbing frame, her long black braids flowing behind her as she throws her arms out towards her mother who has just entered the fenced play area. The woman, who is maybe ten years older than me, with blonde, short hair beams as her daughter giggles in her ear and she turns smiling to a man, presumably her husband, who has his back to me. She kisses his cheek and then turns again to her daughter who looks like she is retelling a tale of her accomplishments on the playground. In that moment, the man turns and a familiar dark-blonde beard catches my eye.

I tug on Max's arm and he instantly turns to me: "What honey, what is it?"

"Don't stare, but he is over there, with his family," I nod without looking.

Max casually glances around until he clocks Ezra and simply says, "Ah." We sit on a bench facing Ezra, but make no attempt to communicate with him.

After a while, our patience is outweighed by our nerves and Max decides to go to the ice cream stand. I remain seated, eagerly awaiting the mint chocolate chip cone I ordered, though equally wondering if I can stomach it when I suddenly spot Ezra register Max's position. His eyes follow Max's direction until his eyes lock with mine. I am not sure if it is wise to hold his gaze, so I smile at Max, exaggerating the curve of my lips as I reach out to receive my treat. I silently hope my little drummer doesn't get a brain freeze as my body jolts from shock from the first bite – only to have to chuckle softly when she responds by kicking me.

Max and I have nearly finished our ice cream when Ezra moves away from his wife, hugs his daughter who has returned to the climbing frame, and walks in the direction of the exit. My heart sinks; surely, he hasn't lost his nerve again? We cannot follow and risk meeting in the Central Hub streets, it is just too dangerous.

Ezra abruptly turns left just before he looks set to leave, and I sigh with relief. The supposed path was for his family, not us. He catches our eye, jerks his head and we take our cue to follow at a distance through the tropical house, meandering through the spicy fields, wandering past the entrance to the hedge maze, finally stopping next to the largest, loudest part of the waterfalls. Ezra is holding onto a safety rail, staring out across the speeding water when Max and I rest on the rail next to him. I lean into Max as he keeps one hand across my back, gently cupping his fingertips into my side. I am glad of the comfort as no one says a word.

Ezra suddenly exhales deeply and starts talking without looking away from the flowing water: "Two things happened to me this week." Out of the corner of my eye I see him twist his lips as he pauses. "My daughter was sent home in tears…floods of them, not unlike this waterfall. She has had the odd 'incident' with her teachers, mostly normal kid-stuff, nothing too dramatic, but she thinks, she questions, she wants to understand more, challenge more. That should be encouraged, the next generation should be encouraged. It is *they* that should shape the future, how society, the world – all of it – how all of it functions and progresses. *Progress.* Isn't that what this is all for? The progress of humanity, the saving and respecting of Earth, of Mother Nature…understanding past mistakes, remembering, learning, not covering up. Live and learn. *Do better.*" Ezra stops and rubs his eyes as his voice cracks and wobbles. "Such control, such inhumanity – it is not supporting our youth, it is stifling them. Making bitter, miserable people…mindless dancers, too afraid to even ask for the toilet…

"She, my beautiful, independent, bright little girl, needed the toilet and was denied it. She was told: 'Your education is more important than your dignity. Learn self-control, learn to respect your elders, and take heed of the essential lessons and values you are being given. The life and death of the planet depends on it.'" Ezra scoffs. "*Values?* What values are we advocating? How does her using the bathroom affect respect for elders or the life of Earth?" Ezra's voice remains quiet, but the strength of feeling in his words brings tears to my eyes that now tumble down my cheeks. "She just wanted the toilet for heaven's sake…" he whispers.

Over the rush of the water, I hear Ezra swallow before he continues: "And then the next day I go to work, wondering what on earth I can honestly do to make anyone's life better. I sit there, listening to my grandfather talking about cadets like they are nothing, less than a flock of hens – a swarm of locusts to be tested and used, then discarded if noncompliant. He has no remorse for what he has just done. He couldn't care less if one is dead…or others feel lost. He left me feeling hollow inside, hollow and useless… And then I turned on my monitors to see 257 and Lily. Two totally different beings, and there they are, forming a bond, a friendship that fascinates me every day – crossing boundaries we didn't even know we knew could exist. Their discussions challenged my cowardice and I snapped. I snapped into place. I wrote on my napkin and found you before I could lose my resolve. Intelligent little girls and boys should not have their joy snuffed out or be made to fight against themselves. Not for any rule, not for anything other than truth and freedom. To guard Earth by choice, not repression…not being told 'you fail' at every faltering step. Whether I fear or not, something must change. *My small corner needs light…*and I hope it can spread further. Will you help me lift the lid?"

Max's grip of my side tightens in silent agreement as I reach out and cover Ezra's white knuckles with my right hand. Ezra releases his grip of the rail enough to let the blood flow back into his fingers as I quietly, but firmly say: "We will."

"Good," Ezra sighs deeply, "because I told Lily I had a plan – and I need Eve to find it."

TWENTY-SIX

A week of work and perceived normalcy has dragged hideously. The evenings are bright and warm, yet I know trying to persuade Aunt Dora to let me take Eve out after work is a waste of breath. It didn't stop me visiting twice this week to see if I could at least prepare Eve for Saturday's rendezvous with Ezra, but part of me wishes I hadn't tried. On Tuesday Eve was not at all well, and on Thursday she was communicative, but her mind was far from clear:

"You're pregnant, Missy," Eve said as I sat down.

"I am."

"Huh, that was quick." I had wished there was humour in her voice, but she was halfway between herself and the white noise that takes her. I desperately wanted for her to switch to the current day, but I told myself it was a blessing she knew me at all. Aunt Dora had called me in tears earlier to say Eve didn't remember who she was – I don't think she called because she expected me to be able to do anything, but I am hoping sharing helped somewhat.

"They'll be pleased," Eve muttered after a moment's reflection.

"Indeed, they are." I didn't need to know which 'they' she was referring to. The answer was the same.

"You caught down river?"

"Not if you give me a paddle." I decided to play along as sometimes in the past these odd conversations have left me with real-time riddles…although more commonly I don't know which is which until after the event!

"Swimming is overrated."

"What about sailing?"

"Depends on if you have wind."

"Do you?"

"Hmmphh."

I still don't know if that conversation has relevance.

It is Saturday morning and Eve is singing to the cats when I arrive. I smile to myself as I know it is likely she will ask me to join in. I am not disappointed – and nor is she.

"Hmmphh, you should sing more often, it suits me ears." I immediately laugh. This is possibly one of the weirdest compliments I have ever received. Undeterred, Eve continues talking, but suddenly falls silent, and I look up with sorrow as I see her frozen features. Aunt Dora pops her head in the door smiling, but the corners of her mouth instantly drop as she takes in my watery eyes and understands the reason.

"It happens too much," she says, stepping into the room. "I don't know how much long—" She cannot finish her sentence. We both know how that sentence ends…how it ends. "If you must… if you have unfinished…*lessons*, best not wait. If—" Again, Aunt Dora cannot finish, but I understand and nod. My throat feels like a brick has been cemented in the middle. A really dry, painful one.

Fear of losing Eve, coupled with fear of not being able to fulfil my promises leaves me sitting numbly on the edge of the sofa long after Aunt Dora leaves for the day. Time is ticking by, and I am sure I am going to miss the meeting with Ezra. The codes will go undeciphered and I will be sucked into the black hole of the R&R, telling myself all is well, that humanity is better off being coerced into infertility and herded throughout every step of life and love – reprimanded for the betterment of all – for the deliverance and restoration of Earth.

I want the last bit.

If the monitors across the globe show a fraction of the beauty that Earth houses, I want to protect and preserve, to replenish what was lost.

Maybe the R&R *is* the better way?

The ethos and the method…or just the ethos?

Why are my thoughts so muddled…the path so messed up?

The fear of failure is possibly naturally installed in everyone – a kind of backup to self-preservation. Do not harm yourself or set yourself up for disappointment or injury. The problem is humanity, or more specifically those in charge, have learnt to prey on this natural instinct. Most people want the approval, reassurance, love, and respect of others and they certainly do not want to embarrass, disappoint, or fail.

Fail.

Failed.

Failure.

Three words that are regularly floated in our education as the absolute to avoid. *Do not fail.* For those on the FARM, they have failed. Failed to be defined by society, so they are hidden from them…yet still repurposed by them. Made anew.

Sounds good, right?

A new beginning.

Except it isn't truly new. If what Ezra says is true, the education beyond the fence embeds the feeling of past failure again and again to push cadets forward – but that just means the new beginning is hampered by the tar of the past. How is that right or fair?

Failure.

To fail…

Those terms should be wiped from the PTB and R&R vocabulary.

Benevolence is not a weakness.

I laid awake most of the night, replaying so many conversations. Gee-Gee's words weigh on me as much as anyone's. She is such a mixture of support and encouragement coupled with tests and threats – the lines of which are as blurred as the image of the Arbitrator in Board meetings. The constant testing is exhausting, as is the constant display of enthusiasm I have forced myself to produce. The expectant mother, the enlightened student, the faithful great granddaughter.

Never has just 'me' been enough. Not as daughter, wife, friend, scientist – whatever title you want to tag me to – I am not enough as just *me*. I go round and round the thought that I could take everything Gee-Gee says as if it is for my renewal, my repurposing. *To make me enough*. For months I have doubted why I was told so much, so easily. I want to believe it was just relief on Gee-Gee's part to finally be able to tell, to share, and possibly to build. She clearly states her desire for her dynasty to continue, even if the R&R all preach how it is not about the individual. Eve told me that months ago too – that she believed, still believes, in the grand plan, the mission before family. Eve followed that belief to the point that most would have crumbled long-long before, but she still crumbled for family. Not mission: *family*.

Everyone has their limits.

But that isn't the only reason why the Board suddenly revealed their trade secrets despite my impending maternity leave, nor the reason for the repetition of my thoughts. The R&R are fulfilling their 'all or nothing' ethos: Tell me all, prime me for greatness, and see if I am worthy. Set me up for the top of the tree…or an almighty fall – for which they will have no qualms killing me for. If I waste such an opportunity, I will (in their opinion) deserve it.

For the fallen and the failure have no place in their world.

So, everything is a test. The information, the hugs, the glances, the turning of one's back, the probing question – the questions I ask, the questions I don't ask. They are gleaning as much information from me as I am them. I suppose you don't remain a secret organisation by trusting easily.

"Being told you fail alone is not enough," I mutter to Smoggy as I lean back on Aunt Dora's sofa. She purrs gently as I stroke her, but somehow, I doubt she cares much for my twisted thoughts.

"What is?" asks Eve looking straight into my eyes. It's good to see she hasn't lost her ability to startle – though she isn't wearing the amused grin she sometimes does when she knows she has made me jump. This time I think her awareness has surprised her as much as it has me – maybe she wonders if we were already in full conversation, and she just missed the rest. Though, to be fair, few people would guess I was attempting a telepathic conversation with the cat! If I hadn't absent-mindedly put voice to my frustrated musings, I would have spared us both a surprise. "What *is* enough?" Eve asks again as I lose myself in further thought.

I turn to her, sharing my thoughts: "Telling anyone they are a failure is cruel and unnecessary – and only breaks, it does not build anything. Instead, why not show the way to build – build up, not demoralise and destroy the soul. For the soul is what drives the hands, the mind, the heart – with none of those, *they* fail…"

"Cast only shadows and shame, you'll just live amongst the damned," says Eve thoughtfully. "Hmmphh, don't I know it! But you forget they, damned or not, already believe they are *the* way."

"Guardians need to guide, not condemn," I scoff. "No one is perfect and all need to consider change for growth to be possible."

"Said the future to the past. Get to it Missy, get to it." Eve's words come with quiet conviction – with pride even. "You must lead the path, forge it, fight for it."

"I am not a leader, I just want better for my small corner," I say, shaking my head.

"Small corners are fine for many – important for all, but the best leaders do not seek to lead. They take the reins with fear and trepidation when they are thrust upon them, seeking what is right, questioning what is right and wrong – determining why one says one thing and does another. Progress doesn't stop. The future is lookin' me in the face…"

Eve trails off, exhausted from speaking, but her words ring and sing in my ears.

Ezra spoke of his small corner. It isn't the first time I have considered the concept, but I suppose it is why the phrase has stuck with me the last few days. Make what you can better. Maybe the small leads to the big? I am not surprised Ezra lost his nerve, not now I know what he has witnessed recently. I didn't think I could feel worse about Jay's death or angrier at the needless loss of life –

or more disgusted to how easily the R&R dispose of those who annoy them. But I was wrong. I can feel worse. It is possible to feel sicker, and that revulsion is summed up by the image of Dean. A man who cheerfully applied for permission to hit the kill switch – while Lily was watching. Watching, but powerless to act. How her heart must have crumbled! The mere inkling of watching Max being killed makes my insides weep.

Then Lily had to watch her friend be pushed out and murdered – and for what? For not adapting fast enough to FARM life. Who would when they stole everything, including her unborn child?! I hug my stomach at the thought. The conflict of emotions rattles and tortures me every moment.

"How do you battle them? Jay was apparently trying to join a union before he was killed. If a group cannot succeed, how will I?"

Eve considers my words for a moment, too long, and I fear I have lost her again when she suddenly says: "He joined a union?"

"Yes, 'The Silence' apparently."

"Ah, my old friend," Eve says with a wry smile.

"They were no friend to him."

"Only the brave dare disturb the sound of silence." Eve's words hang in the room like a ghost, and I do not know what to say. I need to be brave and take her to Ezra…I need to disturb the silence. "Whispers echo. Beware of them. Tom knew that but forgot when it mattered most…Tom too could help…if you can find him."

I feel she is wise, yet I do not understand…I do however know I have ten minutes until I am supposed to be by the riverbank and my heart sinks. I need to stick to my convictions.

"Eve," I say, kneeling in front of her, "I don't think it is the right time today, but the watchman wants to see you again." I look into her eyes and see them fire with interest.

"There is no right or wrong day, Missy, only when I am awake and meself – which is less and less. My thoughts are there, then they are not. I am like a song without a chorus, a joke with no punchline. It is exhausting. I feel like I am watching my own heart monitor, waiting for the blip. I know it is coming, but I cannot prepare for it, nor stop it. That blip steals me words 'n' robs me thought patterns. What I know one minute – the sentence I have been busy constructing, can be entirely gone the next – stolen in the blip. It starts with one, then two…but how long until it calls time?"

"What do you want me to do? I hate feeling like I am pushing you."

"Take me out – give me a chance to dance to my own tune one last time. I am ready, my time is yours, use it."

* * *

"Hmmphh, no pressure then!" mocks Eve after she hears Ezra's story. "That is all well and good my boy, but if Dean has found all my codes, then the backdoors are closed."

"Are you sure he found them all?" I ask hopefully.

Ezra nods. "Yes, he has always been paranoid about glitches and swept for them regularly, but since my cousin tried dropping one in he has looked harder. I'm still not sure if he realises Robert made that glitch or if he thinks he missed a genuine error. I kind of think he knows, but he doesn't care enough about cadets to defend them. He does hate not being in control though, so he leaves very little room for errors now."

"Bloody idiot," declares Eve. "That was a stupid attempt at getting a girl out, it could have been done if your Robert had used his brain a bit longer instead of—"

"He isn't the brightest in the family."

"Clearly not."

"I thought about using the avatar capabilities to test codes from within…"

"And?" I ask, looking at Ezra hopefully.

"It isn't safe, I could trap myself and set off alarms if Dean has left them in places I don't spot quick enough. The cadets and Shepherds cannot even say his name without setting off an alarm!"

"What about the Shepherds?" I ask, not really understanding what they are – some sort of super android if I get the gist of Eve and Ezra's conversation.

"They have limits on coding within," replies Eve.

"Why?"

"Because they have capabilities way beyond any other android or AI system you can imagine. I wanted, hoped, they would advance themselves further…but if without restraints, they could—"

"They wouldn't—" cuts in Ezra. "They respect their mission; they live for it – even 113 with his warped view."

"You're defending them as…? Individual entities?" Max asks, blowing out his cheeks.

"Yes, I know it sounds weird, if you haven't watched and conversed with one, it would, but they are truly unique. World domination doesn't interest them, just restoration. 257 is kind and considerate…and I believe genuinely cares for Lily beyond any programming."

"Are they capable of world domination?" I ask, matching Max's confounded expression.

"Robotics outnumber man 1000-1, maybe more," says Eve. "Most are drones or machines for production, but there are those that could lead all." She scoffs. "In some ways I think they would do a better job. We certainly need one now. Only Shepherds can walk beyond freely…but it is the signal that controls the world—"

"World domination isn't really my thing," I say, trying to make light of her words even though I have not forgotten our earlier conversation about leading.

"World liberation and domination is arguably the same thing," Eve replies dryly.

"Said every dictator in history probably."

Eve chuckles but turns to Ezra when she speaks again. "You know you must take out man and machine to liberate the cadets of tyranny?"

"Yes, I had concluded that," says Ezra.

"What? What do you mean 'take out'?" I can feel my eyes widening to their fullest as the hair on the back of my neck raises. "You cannot mean—"

"I can and do," says Eve.

"I am not a mur…" I cannot say it.

"No good person is by choice. A peaceful, non-life-threatening revolution is the first choice, of course, it is." Eve bobs her head. "Yet to wage a war, even a silent one, you cannot roll over and play dead. Stop wavering."

I look around me. Eve, Max, and Ezra stare back in wordless resolution. I have been onboard with the idea of starting a path of sly revolution, but what they are talking about sounds like killing one person to stop a narcissistic bully, but ultimately keep everything else the same.

"Okay…but say we find a way to improve life on the FARM, do you think that is enough? Can we really not rescue Lilith? From what you have both told me, it is not enough. Would we not just be chopping off a finger when the body is still diseased?"

"Walk before you run," replies Eve. "Everything needs steps. You crawled to the R&R, you must walk to Lilith's rescue. Running is for after, when the gates are open, and you hold the keys."

I have no answer. For someone who spends a lot of time saying nothing, Eve is annoyingly good at her speeches.

"Hmm," says Eve, narrowing her eyes at Ezra. "What did you say about 257 and Lily? They have a bond?"

"Yes."

"One you trust?"

"I believe so. Why?"

"Ah," Eve chuckles. "Then we have our answer. The loophole maybe even I did not foresee!"

"What is that?" I ask.

"The power of affinity…love and respect crossing borders. It is time to open up our horizons and see if machine has taught man a new trick."

TWENTY-SEVEN

I wanted to act immediately while the fire of conviction flowed fervently through all our veins. I am committed to acting, I have no doubts about that now, it is only nerves that now rattle my thoughts and sleep. We have a plan. I just want to get on with it.

Ezra has explained the loophole to Lilith and 257. In a nutshell, the system is designed against solitary takeovers. No Overseer can alter significant programmes or shut down a Shepherd without the Curator's assistance or three Overseers agreeing. Likewise, no Shepherd or any other android can access all of their coding to take control from within. The mission is therefore safeguarded and no personal vendettas or overzealous reboots can happen. What no one considered, including Eve until now, was the possibility of a Shepherd evolving beyond their original code to the point of real, independent thought and friendship. True, reciprocated friendship with a human.

Lily and 257 have bridged that inconceivable void.

I am amazed by this, but I do not envy Lily's task. First, she has to access a forbidden area. This is made possible thanks to Ezra unlocking it and masking his actions with an apparent glitch. That will trigger an alarm, after which Ezra has to encourage Dean into his avatar. Ezra says that won't take much as Dean already believes he is the lord and master of the FARM and cannot abide 'wayward' cadets – so, a cadet in a forbidden location should sufficiently boil his blood! Once 113 and Dean are joined Lily needs to race to the lift, activate the control panel, press in the code 72637 (a reoccurring number in Eve's world) and say: 'The road of real reckoning requires rogue robotics to be restrained' (again, Eve does love her tongue twisters!). This sequence will effectively turn the lift into an android microwave, so 113 has to be inside for the decommission code to be applied to him… and Lily has to manage all that without getting captured or knocked out by 113 – while 257 has to ensure no other cadets or Shepherds realise what is going on.

So, yeah, I really don't envy her.

But if she does it – no, *when* she has done it – then part one of our mission is accomplished. There is a lot about this plan I do not fully understand, but I do know I had another napkin left on my doorstep two days ago, one with the simple, non-assuming message of *'Happy Unification Day'* written on it.

That is all I need to know.

The plan has been explained to all, the date set. My little drummer now has an orchestra accompanying her as my stomach has knots and butterflies taking their turns to mash up my insides. If they could just get in an orderly queue and play something peaceful until today is over I would be most grateful.

Unification Day is actually a weeklong event all centred around the establishment of the United New Earth – commemorating decades of PTB order, Hub structure, and peace for all of humanity. The equal amount of repression and control of humanity is obviously not mentioned: not by anyone that wants to see the next Unification Day anyway.

Art exhibitions, craft fairs, music, plays, and performances line the streets from Saturday to Saturday in the first full week of June. TV and radio shows are all themed around the horror of 'Before the Fall of What Was,' coupled with the 'joy' of society today. Max and I's next radio appearance has been timed perfectly with the festivities. The PTB are not going to waste an opportunity as good as this one to promote their matching capabilities and Claire has emailed us both with an extra-long list entitled: 'It would be sooo lovely if you mention all these pointers.' The list is so extensive I don't know why they haven't given Max and me a script to read. I would prefer it to be honest as last time Claire emailed me within an hour of our interview telling me: 'You did well, but you missed out…' I wonder if teachers or broadcasters are recorded and given similar 'reminders' if they miss a propaganda point of the day? Probably.

"Have you read this?" I half squark to Max as I read Claire's email. "They want me to say I am hoping Little Drummer is a 3 and, I quote, 'that she'll continue the UNE mandate and hard work for many generations to come as a housewife'…I may scream!"

Max sits next to me and takes me by the hands. "Honey, that is nothing new, you know that. We can spout whatever they want for an hour, it doesn't make it true."

"You're right." I take a deep breath. "I know you are… I'm just being hormonal." I am telling myself that as much as him. "We have a plan for her, for everyone."

"She may not even be a 3." Max remarks brightly, but takes one look at me and says: "What?"

"I – *we* – can only have grade 3 babies. It is genetically impossible for us to have anything else. Any doubt I had about that was shattered when I read Dr Oldman's research this week. I had hoped I was wrong, but I am not. My eggs are golden – solid gold, not just gold plated. Our children, our children's children, for every generation, will be a 3. There is no off switch for their genes. Nurture will alter nothing, that element of their nature *is* sealed."

"Good," says Max, standing up.

"Good?"

"Yes, *good*. For it just hones the focus…if it needed honing!" He bends down and kisses my cheek. "Happy Unification Day, Honey – shall we go?"

* * *

I knew the Central Hub would be busy today, but I didn't think it would be *this* busy. President General Fairfax is giving a speech on the main Plaza and presenting awards to whatever PTB minion has done their bidding best this year. I smile ironically as I walk past, wondering how many of those awardees are actually R&R lackies…and how many awards they would still want to give out if they knew the truth. Then I shrug to myself, maybe they do know the truth. Either way the 'prestige' of winning their favour means a lot less to me now than it used to.

Inside the radio station is as bustling as it is outside. I wonder why the security personnel has more than doubled until I realise in the centre of a group of armed guards is Lady Fairfax herself. It hadn't occurred to me she wasn't on the Plaza. She is standing laughing regally as a few people suck up and simper towards her.

I have no interest in joining the crowd, yet all attention is suddenly drawn to Max and me as our names are called out. I stop and see Kal walking towards us, beaming as he introduces us to Lady Fairfax, whether any of us like it or not. Max greets her first, leaving me to smile sweetly while I take her in. Lady Fairfax is in her early seventies and is a well-dressed, elegant woman. She has grey-hair, but still has a hint of the ginger that shone brightly for most of her life, and she has certainly retained her presence of power much the same as her husband – possibly more so.

"Ah, the Rivers, yes indeed, I have heard a lot about you," Lady Fairfax says politely. "I believe you are also on Lei's show today? I never thought of myself as a deejay, but here I am, learning a new skill at my age." Max and I laugh as courteously as expected, but since she doesn't seem to be waiting for a reply, I do not give one. "My husband prefers to be in front of a camera, I on the other hand find ways to shine in whatever medium I am given."

"Surely that is the best way?" I ask without considering how many people are listening to me.

"Quite my dear, quite. The UNE thrives on that very notion. Every member playing their part, *remembering* the importance of their role, no matter the position – don't you agree?" Lady Fairfax holds my gaze without narrowing her eyes, yet I have absolutely no doubt, if we had less observers her eyes *would* be narrowed.

"Undoubtedly Lady Fairfax, undoubtedly," I reply, matching her tone. I suddenly remember I don't want to cause unnecessary attention to myself today so mentally bow the knee as I continue: "I look forward to talking to the Hub shortly, further sharing Max's and my story on that very point. Our position is blessed and it is an honour to share our journey." Even Claire couldn't find fault in that statement.

Lady Fairfax nods her head, holding an amused smile as she glances over me and Max before she responds to Kal – who is anxiously trying to recapture her attention. Kal has obviously been tasked with entertaining her until she goes on air and it is the first time I have seen him flustered in any way, shape, or form. Something tells me Lady Fairfax enjoys unnerving people, so when a new group of admirers come scuttling up, Max and I take the opportunity to slip away.

"Pfft!" says Max, chuckling as we make a retreat.

"There is a family resemblance with Eve, don't you think?" I say as we step into the lift.

"Yes, I suppose so, but let's not attempt a reunion." Max winks.

As the lift doors close my stomach starts flipping again and my hands tremble. I cannot decide if this interview is a blessing or curse today. It has Max and me placed in the right building. The choice of day ensures the necessary people are distributed as required. But it also means I have to stay on point, not become distracted thinking about what could be occurring downstairs – or what will happen if it goes wrong.

Max and I are guided around by one of the station runners, only being shown into the studio moments ahead of our interview. Lei waves as we silently sit down and watch as she prepares to introduce us. She has styled her hair with hundreds of tiny braids and then wrapped them up onto the top of her head with flowers and pins which match the floral pattern of her dress. Her dress is nicer than mine, or perhaps it just suits her better, but today I am wearing a floral dress, too, because Max pointed out jeans and an informal shirt wouldn't work for either of us today. I grumbled at the time, but in truth anything less than the smart attire we are currently adorned in would have been out of place. Not to mention the fact I haven't worn jeans for weeks thanks to Little Drummer expanding my waistline out of recognition – dresses and flexi-pants are my best friends for the time being.

I feel increasingly sweaty as our interview goes on – sweaty and guilty. Not because the questions are difficult or I cannot remember what I am supposed to be saying in response, but because of the deceit I am about to undertake the moment this interview is over. The persona I am going to assume as I finally pull down my synthetic sleeve again and twist the pearls into position.

Ezra is aiming to time his assault with Lily on 113 perfectly with the end of this interview. His cousin is out of the office on holiday meaning his grandfather should be *in* the office covering for his absence. Ezra seemed sure of this as Dean apparently also likes to be in position to quickly head off to his Board meetings – one of which is booked for later today – which he will hopefully be unable to attend.

A cold chill hits me.

How can I, in any kind of decency, say 'hopefully' about a man's demise?

I try to shake off that notion. It isn't me. I wish no one dead or brain-dead. I tell myself it is his own doing, he would not – *does not* – think twice when he makes such calls. Thankfully I am not him. I do care. But I also care enough about others to not stop this happening to him.

As Lei's happy-go-lucky chatter wraps up our interview, my heartbeat increases tenfold. The concentration required in looking nonplussed is immense and I fear I am going to vomit, especially as I anticipate making my way downstairs using her barcode to go to a level I have zero reason to be on. I look over to Max who looks cool as a cucumber and I want to laugh. Why the hell am I going downstairs when he is the chilled one?

Because you want to speak to Lily.

Yes, I do.

"Okay! Well, it has been wonderful to catch up with you both again. I am really looking forward to seeing you next time – which will be the last time before we get to meet your daughter in the flesh!"

"Yes, I think I'll be the size of a house by then!"

"Ha-ha, indeed, but what a joy, what a joy for us all to follow your journey. Speaking of which, following in the next hour is a new joy and treat as our very own First Lady comes in and takes over! Yes, that is right, for one hour each day this week Lady Fairfax is taking over the airwaves with her own celebratory show, talking about what she loves most about our Hub, the work of the UNE – and well, whatever she feels like! So, without further ado, Max, Maia, and I will all sign off. They'll see you in August, I'll see you again bright and early tomorrow morning, but in the meantime, let's give a warm welcome to Lady Fairfax! Happy Unification Day one and all!"

Max takes my hand and I squeeze harder and harder as Lei wraps up. I don't dare look at Max or risk my masked smile slipping from my face. A song begins as Lei switches her controls and then hops up, beaming at us both just as the door slides open, revealing Lady Fairfax. She obviously knew the order of events, even if I didn't. Possibly if I listened to this radio show on a normal day I would have heard the announcement of a guest deejay…and I would have been prepared for the almighty spanner that now lies in the works.

"Ah, we meet again." Lady Fairfax chuckles at Max and me as she takes Lei's seat. "Good show, Lei – excellent in fact – I hope I can follow it with gusto!"

"Of course, you can My Lady, of course, you can! The whole Hub is eager to hear from you!" gushes Lei.

"I hope you don't mind me taking an hour of your show?"

"Not at all, there is no one I'd rather relinquish my time to, it is a real honour." Kal walks in from the adjoining room as Lei speaks and the studio suddenly feels very small. "Right, we best get out of here. Kal will help if you need any technical help."

Max and I don't need any further encouragement and we head straight for the lift, exchanging worried faces as we wait for the doors to open. I turn to see Lei slip into one of the offices and I pray she'll stay there; however, as we step into the lift, a hand appears around the edge of the door and Lei positively skips to Max's side.

"What are you doing with your time off?" Max asks lightly.

"Oh, I am going to listen to the show, of course, just from the comfort of a sofa in the lounge next-door! How about you? You're welcome to join me, there should be a decent crowd as the TV and radio stations have banded together to make a real celebration of our programmes this week –there's cake as well!"

"Ha-ha, thank you, unfortunately we've arranged to meet a few friends – but we'll catch the show on repeat later." Max sounds genuinely remorseful, and Lei looks sufficiently convinced.

The lift opens on the ground floor and Lei darts off with no more than a 'see you later!' leaving Max and me staring at each other. I cannot use Lei's barcode now – not only is she not stationary in her studio, but she also isn't in the same bloody building. Ezra was going to be able to overwrite an anomaly of a double entry, but that only works if Lei doesn't move around – and even better, has an undeniable alibi to where she truly was.

My heart sinks. I was feeling bad about assuming Lei's identity for a few minutes, but now I feel worse, because without it I will not know if Ezra's plan has worked and I will not meet Lily. Not unless I go for my dodgier plan B…and for that I require a certain redhead to turn up on time for our coffee shop date.

I look around the foyer and sigh.

"Ella isn't here yet, she did say we might have to meet her at the café. I think she is hoping Theo will come," says Max, interpreting my frustration.

"That makes one of us."

"Maia—"

"I know, I know." I roll my eyes. I know Max has his reservations, but he hasn't entirely forsaken his friendship with Theo and earlier wisely pointed out it is in our favour to move past our grievances. Max is right, but it is easier for him as he didn't have his heart stomped on by Theo (twice). That, and Max is just better natured than me I suppose.

Suddenly the lights dim for a millisecond and Max and I look at each other with wide eyes.

"Was that…? Do you think…?" I gulp and try to steady my breathing.

"Maybe," says Max gravely.

"Woo-hoo, look at the radio stars!" declares Ella as she seemingly floats up to us both. I turn and greet her with no small amount of relief as she continues: "Will you celebrities lower yourself to eat with me? I found a few extra volunteers on my travels – I hope you approve?" Ella doesn't wait for my smile to be accompanied by words. "Yes! I went looking for Theo, who so rudely ignored my messages until I was almost in the lab, but I found Kate and Tim! They have the week off – along with most people by the look of things!" she exclaims, waving her arms.

"Where are they?" I ask.

"I left them all in the market, we thought we'd find a place to eat once I had herded you two! Shall we go?" Ella takes a step back and gestures to the door.

My stomach knots and Little Drummer kicks in unison. I want to laugh, mostly out of despair, but it would seem even my baby wants me to complete my mission. Maybe she knows this is the first step to making her future brighter? I cannot fail or chicken out now.

"Do you mind giving me a minute? I just need to go to the loo – Max, you'll wait here with Ella, right?" I hold Max's gaze, praying he understands.

"Sure," he says, smiling.

"I'll just be a few minutes, bear with me," I say, backing away holding my stomach.

Ella suddenly looks sympathetic. "Ah, of course, my sister had the same *issues* when she was pregnant. Do you need anything?"

"No, thank you, just Little Drummer to keep off my bladder," I chuckle as I turn and scuttle towards the toilets.

I hear Ella question Max and he laughs, explaining: "That's our pet name for the baby until she arrives – it has proven apt so far." As I semi-slide the door behind me, Ella's sweet laughter makes me grimace and I silently say 'sorry.' I immediately slide the door again, stepping out of the toilets, checking that I am not seen. I fidget with my left arm, then my necklace nonchalantly as I press for the lift. I anxiously wait for it to open and make no eye contact with anyone around me, but immediately want to scream when a couple stops next to me. I quickly pretend to respond to a message on my watch as the couple board the lift and I wave them politely on.

I take the opportunity to message Max: *'Make my apologies, I'll need a few mins, please both of you wait xx.'* At least that should help him hold Ella in the foyer and firmly away from any doorway scanners.

Finally, alone in the queue, I step into the next lift. The control panel is like that of any other and it is only because I know 'B2' is off-limits that I feel bad for pressing it. Anyone can press that button, yet only those approved on the system will actually be taken there. I check my hair, not out of conceit, but out of experience. I am not risking another drone scanning my neck instead of my arm like one did on my first, unsolicited R&R visit; so, rather than twisting my hair into a standard bun this morning, I spent an abnormally long time arranging it into wavy curls that bounce and hang down my back. Posing as Ella – newly upgraded into the R&R world of tech, Ella – the lift does not hesitate taking me to B2 and the doors spring open.

A double layer of deceit lies before me. Should the lift by some freak accident (say an extra rider in the lift) deliver the wrong person to this floor, all they are greeted with is what looks like a storage department. In fact, it might partially *be* a storage department. Only partially because Kal happened to mention once level 'B1' is the main storage ground for the TV studio as well as the radio – acting as a convenient treasure trove of props for both medians.

I walk through the mass of boxes and set pieces, following the path to the left as Ezra told me, finding a door which looks like a boring cupboard, not an entrance into anything special. The door is locked and I knock on it, praying the flicker of lights was the signal of a successful mission – praying that Ezra, not Dean, is going to open this door.

I hear movement ever so slightly before the door slides with a quiet 'whoosh' and there is Ezra, wide eyed and smiling – not with glee nor satisfaction, but overwhelming relief. In fact, I would go as far as to say his whole body is *buzzing* with relief.

"Come, quickly, I need to get Lily out of the lift," he says, stepping back to allow me inside.

"I came as fast as I could," I whisper. "I had to come as option B."

Ezra gives me a sideways glance. "Okay, I'll wipe the movement once you're gone, if she is still you won't have triggered an alarm." I send a silent hope Max is managing to keep Ella stationary.

The room is no more than a semi-circle of carpet and nothing else. The far wall has three archways and I can see directly into the left-hand room. There is a large desk with screens, projectors, and holographs spread on, over, and around, but no one is sitting on the large swivel chair which has been left facing the exit. Next to the desk is a pod – similar to a walk-in cupboard, but it has padded walls and a headset hanging down.

"Follow me, please."

I immediately turn to join Ezra who has walked to the far-right room and I double step to catch up to him, intending to rush straight to him; however, despite my haste I catch sight of a person slumped on the pod floor in the middle room and I gasp. Although I cannot see his face properly thanks to a visor, I instantly recognise the overly bright, solid-dyed-brown hair that belongs to Dean.

I look up at the holograms: Dean's desk is full of them, but every single one is a grey fuzz of white noise.

"Is he…?" I ask in a hushed voice.

"No…not quite, erm, the smell is—" Ezra can't bring himself to finish, but I don't need him to, I know what the overheated smell is…where it is coming from. "He'll be cared for in a home until…"

We both shudder. I am glad neither of us are comfortable with frying a man's mind, no matter how despicable he is.

"Here, please." Ezra tugs on my arm, and I let him lead me to the right-hand room. In here, the monitors are all in full colour and for the first time I see the farm in real time, not just my imagination. Ezra fiddles in the corner as I watch the screens when my attention suddenly fixes on live feed of a lift with two enormous grey figures and—

"Is that Lilith?" I ask as I look at the central screen. "Shit, is she okay?"

"Yes, come quickly if you want to speak to her – she did it, but she must get back to normal routine before other Shepherds notice. I cannot keep a delay on the lift for much longer before they detect something is wrong, plus the other cadets will finish their class and start moving. I'll fill you in, but you *must* speak to her first."

The urgency in Ezra's voice numbs my desire to ask questions and I let him herd me into his pod – simultaneously gulping, trying not to focus on the fact that it is an identical version of what has reduced Dean to a vegetable.

I have thought of this moment for so long and now I have no idea what to say – nor what I am doing. Thankfully Ezra does, and he grabs my hands and tells me to put on a bizarre pair of gloves which look like a modern version of medieval gauntlets. As I pull them on, he puts a headset on my head and pulls a visor over my eyes.

"All will change once the avatar activates. You'll be in 257's head, you can control him, your hands are his, your voice is his. Say what you need to, be quick, question me after." Before I can respond Ezra touches the control panel, steps out of the pod, slides the door and dashes to his desk. I watch him push a button and hear him say "257, Maia is incoming," and then my world completely changes.

No longer am I in the grass-green pod: I am in a lift, and before me is a beautiful, if not exhausted, red-haired young woman and I am holding her hand. She instantly detects my presence as she stares at me in trepidation and whispers: "Who are you?"

I swallow the lump in my throat as my voice suddenly remembers the words I have promised to say: "Hello Lilith— Lily, it is a pleasure to finally meet you. My name is Maia. I have been sent by your great-great grandmother. You are not forgotten. Hold on a little longer, I am coming to get you."

Lily's lips start to tremble and her nostrils gently flare as she listens. She drops my hand and wipes her flushed cheeks. I can only imagine how overwhelming all this is for her – only adrenaline is powering my ability to speak – but remaining conscience of my limited time, I continue:

"I have a vision, Lily. One where we are not declared 'failures' for daring to think outside the narrow box that we are handed. No one deserves to be dictated to on the basis of fertility. Motherhood should be a choice, and those that choose it should be able to continue work or not as they see fit – either option does not make them less of a mother or person. The fertile should not be imprisoned for loving the infertile. Love is not a crime. The guardianship of Earth should not mean the loss of humanity or compassion – it should be the framework on which we build up, not destroy.

Love should be our greatest strength, not the weakness by which we are condemned. I have a vision of guidance and choice – respect for all of Mother Nature, not just part. We must reform our antiquated rules and reboot more than just how the FARM is run. All of the Real Revolution needs revision."

Lily nods and sighs. "I share your dream, I just don't see how it can be done?"

"I'm working on it, but I wanted you to know you are not forgotten out here. There are those in the Hub who want to fight for a brighter bigger picture – one where we all thrive and the path does not become so dark we lose hope in ourselves."

"Then get to it," Lily says with conviction. "You know where I am…where 257 is, should you need us."

I look down at my hands – no, 257's hands. They are huge and I suddenly realise I can feel a strength and power that I could not begin to describe. I turn and see 113 on the floor and startle as I, for the first time, take in what a 'Shepherd' looks like. The decommissioned android, even propped up against the wall, is massive and more like a giant bodybuilder in a grey, featureless skinsuit than a machine. I could describe it as an immense shadow, yet it is too complex for such a simple term, and certainly more imposing than any shadow monster I imagined as a child.

"They take some getting used to – even the good ones," says Lily watching my reaction. "257 and I have shown each other change is possible – a partnership so unexpected that even now it confounds me, yet he is as wise and kind as any creature you'll ever meet. He hasn't forgotten his mission of guardianship of Earth, nor has he compromised it because he has chosen not to be a tyrant. If this change can happen here, maybe you can do it in the Hub…for the whole UNE?"

"I am certainly going to try."

I suddenly hear Ezra tapping on the pod, I turn, but of course, I cannot see him. My consciousness is split, but my vision is not currently with my body. I love science and the codes and patterns within. AI is another level of science, one I may ask Ezra or Eve to explain one day, but for now I must just marvel at the mystery – and hurry up, because if Ezra is tapping it means I need to go.

Reaching out, I take Lily's hands, gently squeezing: "Get some rest and take care of yourselves. I hope to one day soon meet in person – preferably when I rip down that fence."

Lily smiles. "May we all dare to look and dream beyond the fence."

TWENTY-EIGHT

Stepping out of the pod and mentally back into the Hub is disorientating. Ezra is smiling at me, but it hasn't reached his eyes and he looks anxious.

"Is everything okay?" I ask nervously.

"Yes, my programmes are working as planned. To anyone else it looks like my grandfather didn't see a glitch and triggered it as he accessed his 113 avatar for a routine assessment. The glitch caused the avatar to lock, overload, and irreversibly destroy both parties' neurons as they merged. No one investigating will have any room for doubt."

"And Lily?"

"Video feed shows Lily was never upstairs or in the lift. She is logged as ill with 257 attending in her bedroom."

"So, we're okay, the plan worked?"

"Yes," Ezra says, still looking on edge.

"But?"

"But…I will be less anxious once you're upstairs."

"Me too. I have so many questions about here, but not now." Ezra's shoulders relax an inch when he realises I want out as much as him. "Max is probably having kittens by now too."

Without waiting for instruction I leave the gauntlets in the pod and walk towards the exit when a voice calls out saying: "Maia, thank you." I immediately stop as my ears adjust to the tone – it sounds like Ezra, just very slightly different.

I turn to Ezra who just nods to my silent question. I am talking to 257 – he has *chosen* to speak.

"You're welcome, 257." I pause as I am totally in awe of what Eve has achieved…no, *created*. "I know an old lady who would be very proud to meet you."

"And I her," 257 replies. "It is my honour to watch over her legacy."

My eyes fill with tears. "I'll tell her."

I nod at Ezra once more and step to leave.

"Maia?" says 257 from somewhere in the ethernet.

"Yes?"

"The sleeve you are wearing…would having more than one help your mission?"

I rub my arm, considering the possibilities. "It might. We're still working on what is next. Eve has mentioned going beyond – the point and logistics I have no idea of, but if another sleeve meant not walking alone, yes, another would be good. But Eve said this is the only one."

"I scanned you when we were connected. Your synthetic sleeve is the same as my skin, and I understand the coding. I would need a control similar to the necklace, but I have access to storage materials here…I could try to replicate the sleeve."

Even Ezra looks amazed by 257's offer. I don't have time to question 'how,' so dart for the door saying: "Please do! Goodbye 257 – until we meet again!"

Into the Fog

* * *

By the time I step out of the lift onto the ground floor foyer again I am in desperate need of the toilet. Little Drummer may have resisted squeezing my bladder like a broken bagpipe for the last few minutes, but now she and my adrenaline have worked me into a perfect storm of desperation. I wiggle my necklace to display my own barcode as fast and covertly as I can while I fiddle with my watch, pretending one action is a mindless distraction while I perform the other, then dart into the toilets and collapse into a stall.

When I walk out into the foyer, Max looks utterly relieved and Ella expresses sweet sympathy for my extended stay in the toilets. I apologise profusely for delaying them, which just propels Ella into another declaration of empathy and understanding – which in turn makes me flush red with guilt.

"Are you okay to come out?" finishes Ella. "It would be such a shame, but I—"

"Thank you, but yes, I am fine…starving actually."

"Oh, wonderful!" declares Ella linking her arm around mine. I reach for Max with my free hand and the three of us are propelled by Ella's innocent enthusiasm to meet the others. I hope she never finds out I pretended to be her…or if she does, she understands.

* * *

An hour later, I am sitting around a table outside a beautifully adorned restaurant listening to a folk band who has set up across the street as part of the Unification Day celebrations. I am thankful for their jovial melody as it distracts everyone and I can sit without forcing myself into conversation beyond 'what a lovely day,' 'this food is delicious,' or 'doesn't she sing beautifully?'

I thought Theo looked a little shifty when we arrived, particularly when Ella taunted him for not answering her calls until the last minute. I watched his face as he apologised, brushing it off with 'I didn't hear my watch,' yet I detected a glance at me. Paranoia makes me question if he was up to something I need to know about, but the other part of me says to leave it alone. How Theo and Ella manage their double existences with each other is up to them.

My concern is Ella. We may have achieved our initial goal without physically involving her, but Max was right last night when he told me we may need to keep our options open with her in the future. Especially if Ezra wants to lay low for a while. I was disappointed when he dropped that bombshell, but as I quietly sit here, I see his point. I would like to keep going immediately, but letting the dust settle on all sides means less eyes looking through the dirt for clues – or more importantly, stops them suspecting in the first place and therefore prevents them from looking for future 'hiccups.'

"Don't we risk detection if we leave it too long?" I had asked.

"No, they will just rejig Dean's job and carry on. If you try something immediately I could get replaced...or worse.

The R&R need to think this is a complete freak accident – not the start of the edges crumbling."

Even Eve had agreed with him, although afterwards I saw her talking to herself – reasoning with herself that patience is the right way forward.

I am so lost in thought I don't notice the band have paused and Kate has started talking about baby Benjamin. The only reason I answer when questioned about Little Drummer is because Max kicks me under the table.

"Ha-ha," says Ella, "I can't believe you call your baby that! Kate, maybe yours should be 'Baby Ben'?"

"Like the clock?" asks Kate. "I can't call my baby after an ancient monument!"

"I don't know, it has a certain ring to it," laughs Tim – and we all groan.

"If you felt her whacking me, you'd understand why I call her that – she could easily play for that band over there!" I laugh whilst rubbing my stomach.

"Okay, but you must have a real name in mind?" Ella says, expectantly. "Even if you want to surprise us once she arrives, you have a name in mind, right?"

I don't know how Ella has the ability to look like a lost kitten and make me feel guilty at the same time. I don't like Max's name suggestions very much and I cannot bring myself to name her. 'Little Drummer' seems like a happy medium…

"We've months to decide," I say uncomfortably.

Dammit, I cannot be the first mum to not immediately think of a name, but these four are looking at me like I am speaking in another language. I look to Max for backup and he takes my hand and says, 'of course,' but I can see he more than semi-agrees with them.

"I'm surprised you didn't give Benjamin a flower-based name," I say trying to divert the attention from me, "Basil or—"

"We want him to choose his own path. If he loves plants like us, wonderful, but we chose the name because we love it…nothing more." Kate smiles dreamily.

Lily's last words sing in my head… *May we all dare to look and dream beyond the fence.*

Dare to dream.

Kate and Tim did. Hopefully they will never know what I have become to achieve their dream of parenthood. They work hard and absolutely deserve every happiness – yet this dream took more than hard work and luck to achieve fruition. How many couples are out there in the same limbo? How many couples (love matched or by science) are out there that are in the same situation and shouldn't be?

Thousands…hundreds of thousands.

But what would our population be like if they weren't? If there were no food controls? If we spread over the Earth like ravenous ants again?

Dare to dream.

Dream there is a balance…

A better one than this.

But right now I am exhausted. I take one weary look at Max and he understands. "Right, bed for sleepy Mumma Drummer," he declares standing up. "See you guys another day!"

Into the Fog

* * *

"I love you," I mutter into Max's shoulder as he tucks me up in bed within minutes of getting home, "but never call me 'Mumma Drummer' again."

Max laughs, "I don't know, it has a certain *beat* to it."

TWENTY-NINE

I wake up from my nap feeling much better, even if sleeping in the afternoon does make me feel very old. In no rush, I drift off again until Max wakes me up. He apologises, but his face is sorrowful, not apologetic, and I sit up worrying what news he has. Is it possible the R&R have rumbled me...?

"Has something happened? Did I get cau—"

"Dora has called," Max says hesitantly. "Eve isn't well."

I don't need to hear any more details. I get up, dress, and head to the edge of SH1 to see Eve for myself. As I walk I reprimand myself, maybe I should have planned to go there first. Eve knew we were not going to visit until tomorrow, yet it is not impossible the anticipation was too much. I express my fears to Aunt Dora as I walk inside, slipping on my bracelet as I do.

"No, no, I don't think so," Aunt Dora replies, "Eve was the one who said to wait. She had a bad morning though, and before she'd rest, she made me promise to get you to visit as soon as possible."

I walk into the living room, but Eve is not there, I turn and am directed into Eve's bedroom. This change in itself is telling and my heart aches with the realisation. Smoggy and Squash are the only ones not concerned by the alteration. A sofa or a bed is just the same to them – as long as it is warm and cosy, they are happily on guard, keeping one eye on those in the room, but making no attempt to move.

"Ah, Missy, good, you are come," Eve says weakly as I sit on the corner of her bed.

"Of course, can I get you anything?"

"No, no. I need to tell you things now while I can. I wanted to wait until a little later, but my 'little later' is very little and I've no guarantees of mind beyond the now."

"Don't say that, you—"

"Pfft, it is true… Never mind that, did all go to plan?"

"Yes, yes it did. The farm will be a happier place for it. I spoke to Lily and 257…only briefly, but I told her what you wanted me to."

"She knows I never forgot her?"

"Yes."

Eve's eyes glisten. "Thank you," she whispers.

"257 is beyond my understanding. Ezra said, you said… but pfft!!" Eve chuckles at me. "He said it was his honour to protect your legacy."

For a moment Eve's face sparkles and I feel privileged to have seen it.

"You must protect it too…not for me though," Eve says after a moment. "You must stand by your own decisions, difficult as they might be. You must stick to your convictions—"

"Dare to dream of a better grand plan," I say smiling.

"Yes. Yet to hold the reins you'll have to go see Tom too…but you cannot just walk to him."

The lump that so frequently blocks my throat returns. I had dared to hope this conversation – whatever it was supposed to contain or reveal – would go smoothly with no input or interruption from the fog. Eve is looking at me as though I am supposed to reply, but I cannot find any words and I can feel my face dropping under the weight of a torrent of withheld tears.

"There is no point cryin' about it now, Missy," Eve continues when I don't speak. "You started a ball rollin' and you can't just stop...you told me you didn't want to stop. You promised in fact. Hmmphh, apathy combined with procrastination is a cocktail you should have thrown away by now."

I raise an eyebrow and then feel both brows in action as I replay what Eve just said to me. I am so confused. She sounds more like 'present Eve,' than 'fog Eve,' but I still do not understand what she is saying.

"The world had to act back then, the R&R acted, I acted. The results were worth it, even if the path was hard. The hard reality now is that action is needed again, but we only act when forced – we meander and delay and falter if given half the chance. Change must come. You must have the codes... all of them."

"Do you have them here?"

"No, Tom, too, does."

I reach out and take Eve's hand, squeezing gently as I say, "Eve—Eve, I'm so sorry, but Tom is gone."

She looks at me with narrowed eyes, grumbles a little and then laughs...yes, *laughs* at me and I feel the surprise hit me in the face.

"Do you know why they didn't kill me?"

"Because of your status, loyalty, and years of service," I reply. "Out of respect."

"Hmmphh, that is only partly true. Maybe then, but now they have not killed me because they think I have done my worst and ultimately Gee-Gee is happy about it. She wanted you in, she just didn't have the balls to open the door herself. Me cracking the door for her was the perfect solution to her moral dilemma. That is why she spoke for me. The others largely agreed because they think I'm as good as dead. Killin' me now only raises eyebrows on the Board and leaves others asking questions they cannot be bothered to tackle... not now I'm so near me end.

"But they are wrong, I ain't done. I left a backdoor – plural actually – but one major. At the time I did it out of amusement, covering myself should things go amiss, but also just because I like the challenge. I always wanted to be the challeng*er*, not the challeng*ed*. When Tom died I saw the need oh, so brightly...I saw it through blood and tears that I will regret way beyond the grave – even if, as I repeatedly say to myself, the results on the whole were worth the morally grey ground.

"But when Tom and near-all of my family were wiped out by R&R fear and dictatorship, knowing in me heart my beliefs were shaken, but that I couldn't do nothin' about it yet, I decided I must protect those of mine that were left, even if they didn't want me. The next generation must go on. Decisions of reform were, *are*, for a younger, less embittered generation.

"So, I left a backdoor should that generation rise, and I retired. I left my tech behind and retired into peaceful silence to protect mine and hope the world would see a true path – *stay* on the true path – but not be afraid to refresh the revolution. Tom too guards the power to that revolution. He is the Guardian of this world. He observes in silence. Now you must wake him up."

I don't know when I covered my mouth with my hand, but I lower it now, scrunching up my face as I try to take in what she is saying. "Are you saying Tom is alive? Why would you leave him if he is—"

"Tom, too, not Tom," says Eve, narrowing her brows in frustration.

I feel like I am going in circles.

Max enters. I hadn't told him not to come in, but he had chosen to stay in the hallway and speak to Aunt Dora before joining me. Looking at his face, he has been listening, waiting for a good moment to come in. I turn to him, hoping he understands.

"Is Tom an android?" Max asks cautiously.

"Yes! Tom, too, that's what I bloody-well just said!"

A lightbulb moment hits me. "Tom two? As in the number two?"

Eve waves her arm in relief and exasperation. "That's what I've been saying all this hmmphhing time! TOM TWO. The original Shepherd."

"You possibly should have led with that detail." Max chuckles.

"For pity's sake, it ain't my fault you TWO weren't listenin'."

I groan and laugh simultaneously. "Okay, now we understand…what does Tom*2* know that can help?"

"Everything. He holds the key to the internet...every drop of data and electricity. The PTB wanted one worldwide network – communication and control with no 'extras.' Well, the R&R wanted that, too, just they wanted to be able to skip undetected by those in the PTB that are in the dark. It was all the same to me. There was no one left beyond the Hubs, so as one nation, it made sense to unify the power network. They think there is no 'off' switch. Just a control centre. Well, the control centre has a control centre – and Tom2 guards it. He collects all data that was and will be. He is the ultimate Guardian. He can give you the code for a blackout. For the Fall of What *IS*...to force the hand for what should be, to become reality."

"And what do you think 'should be'?" I say with trepidation.

"That, my dear, is for you to decide. I give the code, the key, not the demands." We all look at each other in silent contemplation for a moment. Eve looks tired, but she continues: "My last challenge is to get you there."

"If the signal is everywhere, can I not access him from here?"

"He has the key to the signal, but he will not control it. His mission is of observation – if you like, he is the history keeper and accounts manager. He will not act without a direct order. It was a failsafe, so no hacker could bump into him. He is the silent whisper in the wind that you do not see – that you do not even know exists. If you do not know, you cannot control. Only they who seek will find."

"Okay, well how do I seek?"

"Carefully."

"That's helpful."

"You're welcome."

"Eve," I say in an amused, yet frustrated voice. I enjoy her dry humour, but I worry that she'll leave me riddles beyond any normal method of deciphering.

"Pfft, you need to go to no-man's-land…off any track the R&R use and find me cave of wonders."

"How can I do that? I'll walk into radiation. I've no gadget to detect it."

"I know, that's why for so long I held off tellin' you!" Eve exclaims. "But then I heard of 257 and Lilith, and I felt the plan was possible. Friendship beyond comprehension. A revolution of species surpassing ourselves. Let 257 be your Shepherd…your guide."

THIRTY

Although we wanted to carry on talking, Eve was too tired to form a proper sentence so we had to let her rest for several hours. With each passing hour I prayed she would wake up herself, remember our previous conversation, and continue where she left off. I understand why she felt the need to pace out the information she has given me until now. I realise that I possibly wasn't ready to hear it all at once. I even acknowledge her wisdom in testing me first and in her patient observations to see if her plans could work. Only fools rush in after all. Yet all of Eve's patience only pays off if she is granted life and health long enough to reveal all. I do not want to face that potential blow. Eve has become family and I want, no *need*, her to guide the tide *and* see it turn.

Aunt Dora is pale and her eyes have dark circles around them. No one has given more to Eve's care. Her actions have kept the R&R at bay and kept Eve out of a nursing home – which I naively thought would 'care.' In some cases, it might, but not in Eve's. Dementia or not, the R&R would not risk exposure, they would have pushed Eve off this mortal coil and I, and potentially all the UNE, would have been the worse off for it.

Aunt Dora tried offering Eve an evening meal but she could not rouse her from her slumber. Max and I stayed, and all three of us only managed to pick at our meals. If it wasn't for Little Drummer demanding nourishment, I don't think I would have been able to swallow half of what I did eat.

We chatted about recent events and Eve's new revelation. I can see Aunt Dora is too tired to resist knowing, but also too tired to express anything other than astonishment. She deserves the peaceful existence of an artist, but even through her fear, I can see the spark of outrage still remains. I will not ask her to act on it; however, seeing it there gives me courage. That may sound strange, but to me at least it proves that even the weary fight on, they play their part – and hers as a support and comforter is just as relevant and essential as any more obvious role of activism.

Eve didn't wake up until 3 a.m. and when she did, my fears were answered. She didn't know me, nor did she know where she was. Tom2 was Tom, alive and missing. Her sons were not dead and she had no time for reason. She tried to move faster than her body was capable and I strained my back stopping her falling to the ground. Thankfully Max, who was asleep in the spare room, heard my cry and helped me get her back into bed.

Afterwards we sit back panting. All three of us have wet cheeks from tears of frustration and sorrow, but slowly our breathing eases and silence resumes. The peace is only fleeting though as the confusion grasps Eve again. I didn't plan it, nor does she ask for it, but something inside reminds me of Eve's love of song, so I sing. Over the ten or so months I have known her, I have come to learn some of her favourites, although she also seems to like the odd 'wild card' tune thrown in. I start with an old, tried, and tested song – one my mother taught me oddly enough. It is better with accompaniment, but its simple tune and sweet lyrics of love and home are easy to drift into. So easy that Max joins in. Our first duet.

We carry on singing until Eve is lulled into sleep once more. Max gently kisses my temple as a sign to stop and I force myself to smile despite the tears that threaten to roll down my cheeks.

Little Drummer kicks me and I silently place Max's hand on my stomach. "How will we change – truly change the future for her?" I whisper.

"By daring to push beyond together," he replies. "Always together."

* * *

The Unification Day events beyond Monday were lost on Aunt Dora, Max, and me. We took it in turns to sit with Eve for three days: watching her sleep, appeasing her confusion, attempting to feed her, and internally begging for a few moments of clarity that would not come.

No one has left the house for more than a few intakes of fresh air for days. Taking a brief break, I wander into the living room and see the painting of me by the river. Suddenly, I feel a pang for the melody of water, yet I dare not take the short walk to it. I chuckle to myself when I consider if I have always subconsciously known I would become a 'Mrs Rivers'…maybe that is why the river has always been my place of peace? The thought stays with me as I sit next to Max and tuck myself under his arm.

He is my river now.

I doze off, but am awoken by Eve's voice ringing out. I waste no time in investigating, fearing what display I am going to see; however, I release the longest sigh of relief when I see Eve's countenance is peaceful.

"Hmmphh, mornin'," she says as I take her hand. I ask if I can get her anything, but Aunt Dora is already halfway out the door to fetch her something to eat and drink.

"Looks like I'm bedbound, or near enough," Eve says, gesturing to her legs. She can stand, but her body is withering fast and there is no point saying otherwise. "I want to go out dancin' but my legs and mind forget the steps. You must break the neck of the dancer and tell her not all dancers need rhythm."

I shudder at the thought, but as Eve looks like she is waiting for an answer, I smile and say, "Let someone else do the dancing, Eve."

"I've danced to their tune long enough, when me call comes, I'll know I did right. Remember about the rhythm." I gaze at her quizzically and she sighs. "Not all dancers need rhythm."

I am about to question her but Aunt Dora returns with porridge, jelly, and a cup of tea for Eve. She manages one mouthful of porridge before giving up, eats less than half the jelly, but does eventually drink the tea. It takes her such a level of concentration I dare not speak until she has declared herself finished, and then my heart sinks as Eve lays back in bed and seems set to doze off again. I know there is no more than palliative care to be done, yet I cannot help wishing Eve would see a doctor. However, long ago we were all sworn into complying with Eve's wishes: she wants to die at home, in her natural time. The first the R&R or PTB will know of her true state of health is when she is gone. Her last 'huzzah' to those who tried to control her. I envy her strength of spirit.

"The bumblebee flies against the odds." I suddenly sit up, eyes wide, as Eve speaks. "And so can you."

"Eve?"

"Fly, like the bumblebee, fly," she says with passion. "This old woman passes the baton of knowledge, I am sorry for the burden, but I will rest in peace knowing you'll make this world the better for having walked it. I'm sorry not to have seen Lilith, to have apologised to her face, but I send one great-great granddaughter with love to save the other. Even if not by blood, your lives are paralleled in many ways, two sides of a coin…it's time to flip the coin and place your bet together…to save all." Eve smiles peacefully: "Don't cry Missy, my time is up, I'm done."

"You're not done yet. You'll see your birthday, my daughter…" Wishful thinking.

"No, no, I won't. One hundred and thirteen is an unlucky number anyway." Eve grins, then looks serious. "I'm afraid I won't see your little 'un. Pick a good name when you're ready…maybe I could suggest a middle name?" The grin returns.

"We've already decided it's Eve," says Max from behind me. I turn to see him smiling. We had discussed that briefly yesterday. It definitely feels right.

"Ah, then I'm honoured…best you make her first name unique to make up for being linked to this old bird," Eve says with a wobble in her voice.

We are all silent for a moment and I realise Eve's breathing has changed. The rhythm has been slower and deeper the last few days, yet now it is raspy as well. I lean forward and take Eve by the hand, it is lukewarm at best, despite all the blankets. Max wordlessly approaches the other side of the bed and I look at him. He understands and nods, but neither wants to say anything.

Eve opens her eyes, the sparkle has gone, but the peace has not, and she smiles. "My soul awakens, I was made to meet my maker and my soul awakens now it is time. I sent you into the darkness, you'll walk in the fog, but I finally see the light of dawn…step to it. I've never been prouder."

A single tear rolls down my cheek as Eve closes her eyes and I gently squeeze her hand as I whisper, "I will." I am sure I feel the slightest squeeze as I speak, but Eve also lets out one deep breath and I know that she is gone.

THIRTY-ONE

The future cannot be in the hands of the Deans or Marys of this world. Their paths are selfish, hateful, and ultimately destructive. That reign must fall. Yet at the moment, it is *I* who have fallen. The knot in my throat has choked my tears and voice alike. I sobbed silently by Eve's side, only stepping away when the paramedics arrived. Max had wrapped me in his arms and Aunt Dora had joined us in a trio of sorrow as we watched the most stubborn, the most mysterious, yet equally wise and wonderful woman I have ever met wheeled away. I told myself it was only her shell. Her spirit will not be wheeled anywhere, by anyone. I hope she is with her lost family now and all are at peace.

Her funeral was brief, but I don't think Eve would have wanted it any other way. My dad and Henry came out of respect and sympathy for us and I was surprised to see Gee-Gee with a few of her colleagues sitting quietly at the back. I nodded, but didn't speak to them. A reporter asked for a statement as Eve had been the eldest State resident, dying just four weeks short of her 113th birthday. Aunt Dora answered her questions as best she could and her conclusion was perfect: "Eve touched my heart beyond description and my time with her will eternally be remembered as precious."

Her legacy will live on.

I will make sure of it…just at the moment I do not know *how*. Ezra is still in hiding. I know where he works, but I cannot risk contacting him directly and I have nowhere to leave a napkin note for him – because he has always contacted me, not the other way around. My stomach grows larger and Little Drummer now feels like she is the size of a Solarbug. I sense her impending arrival as a countdown to my reclusion. Certainly, maternity leave is knocking – Dr Oldman has hinted at it, Gee-Gee has suggested it, my mum has declared it. My time to be tied and unable to do anything of universal note or merit beyond my immediate family dynasty is chasing me into the nursery and all I can do is dream of the horizon and how the heck I can get there in time.

Tom2 *is* out there somewhere.

If only Eve had told me where! She said 'let 257 be your guide'…well, even he needs directions!

I am sitting on a bench in the bright summer sunshine waiting for Kate and Ella. Today we have arranged a girls' and boys' day. The boys are off playing rugby and although we considered joining them, the girls decided a more pampered day was in order. Someone rubbing my feet with essential oils sounds pretty nice at the moment – although I may have to tip them extra to compensate!

"Hey!" calls Ella when she is still several feet away from me. I attempt to stand to greet her, but Ella skips forward before I manage, so I just sink back into the solid frame and allow her to half hug, half contain me. We chat about the weather, passers-by, and our impending indulgence with ease until Ella suddenly goes quiet. I have looked over recent weeks, but haven't seen any hint of the sadness I saw in her eyes after her initiation into the R&R – yet now, Ella does have a similarly troubled expression.

I ask her what is wrong and am unsure if I should push when she replies: "Oh, no, nothing, nothing." She smiles, attempting to convince me, but she isn't fooling herself as her eyes refuse to mimic the happiness her mouth is trying to convey.

"If you're not able to *say*, I get it," I coax, softly holding her gaze, "but if you do want a friendly, non-judgemental ear, I will always listen."

Ella watches the words coming out of my lips and I am sure she is weighing up the meaning or potential double meaning in them all. I hope so anyway. With Ezra missing in action, I am very much on the lookout for a tech-savvy friend and confidante – one who is not wholly swallowed by R&R ideology. Something tells me Ella still comes up for air…I just need to find a way of asking without actually asking.

"I am so sorry about your friend," Ella says.

I was not expecting her to say that, so I stare with surprise as much as sorrow before I finally say: "Thank you."

Ella fidgets with her fingernails and her mouth opens twice without saying anything. My skin is crawling in anticipation (and because I hate to hear nails clicking like that), so I grab her hands and hold her line of vision with my stare as I say: "What is it?"

Ella gulps and her knee starts to jig. "I was reading a report…catching up with the Hub news really as it was a few days old."

"Oh?"

"I didn't realise who Eve was…"

Crap, what news has she been reading? PTB or R&R? I haven't seen either. "I didn't see the article on her." I admit I had figured any article would be the standard 'this old person died…' and I didn't want to wind myself up reading an underwhelming obituary.

"I knew she was old, but it didn't occur to me what she did before retirement…I should have, I have read a lot of articles written by Mr and Mrs Addams."

Suddenly, I understand. Like Ezra, Ella has regarded Eve as a mentor, an inspiration. A little bit like me reading Gee-Gee's reports – only now they are tinged with deceit and lies because my hero turned out to be wearing an extra cape that I hadn't considered. I wonder if Ezra or Ella would or do feel the same about Eve…or does the genius of engineering not taint as easily as the geneticist or biologist that causes as much as she cures?

I hope so.

I am not blind to Eve's 'greyer' choices. She knew what she was doing, what the R&R were doing, just the same as Gee-Gee – yet somehow, I forgive Eve. I understand both… but forgive only one.

Is that fair?

I don't know…

One wanted reform, the other wants continuation.

"I would have loved to have talked to her…to learn from her," Ella says, grounding my thoughts.

"Had her health been different, I might have suggested a meeting, but—"

"Oh, no, I understand! It was just a surprise to realise I was so close to her." Ella stops talking, but I am sure she is continuing the sentence internally. Suddenly, she looks up and says thoughtfully: "It has been a surprising year, really."

We hold each other's gaze and our eyes flicker back and forth as though they are searching, communicating on another level…daring us to both say something new… something *else*.

"It has," I say, still holding her gaze. "Ella, I—"

"Sorry I am late!!" declares Kate grabbing me into a hug before I have had a chance to turn to see her. "I got distracted in the hospital visiting Benjamin, forgive me!"

I watch Ella's face flash with disappointment at our broken conversation. Until this second, I have never lamented Kate's presence. However, the moment is lost and Kate's warmth washes over all of us, so all I can do is throw myself into the day, enjoy some real R&R – not the secret organisation – and simultaneously plan how on earth I am going to replicate that moment with Ella.

* * *

I read the article on Eve when I got home that evening and was amazed at how much credit was attributed to her and Tom. I had assumed she would be passed off as an elderly lady of no wider note than having lived an exceptionally long time. Aunt Dora's statement was included, but also the PTB's thanks for 'Mrs Addams' long and dedicated service to the UNE, without which, a large portion of today's technology would either not exist or be significantly impaired.' I was even more surprised when I read who the reporter has quoted. Gee-Gee and Lady Fairfax. I am not sure whose name I expected least. Eve was Lady Fairfax's great aunt – that fact has not been included, yet Lady Fairfax repeats and reaffirms Gee-Gee's respect and recognition of unparalleled service.

I cannot resist questioning Gee-Gee about it when I am called to her office two days later.

"I thought it only right," Gee-Gee replies. "We may have had our differences towards the end, but only a fool would deny she and Tom achieved a new level of AI – and inspired many, many engineers and technicians after them. No, the UNE – all sides of it – has a lot to thank them for." She pauses and smiles at me. "I—I, have a lot to thank Eve for."

I want to retort that the R&R should have perhaps remembered that in life, and not murdered most of her family or threatened her into silence to the point her mental health had to be repressed and hidden like it was an infectious disease. Celebrating the dead seems like shutting the gate after the horse has bolted. No one benefits, except perhaps the living's conscience…but I also doubt whether that can or should be appeased.

Instead, I bite my tongue.

"I called you in to talk about your maternity leave," Gee-Gee says seriously.

"Okay," I reply, shifting in my seat.

"We think it should be August 1st. Travelling about and standing so much towards the end is not wise…it sends the wrong message."

"Pregnancy isn't a disease, exercise is good."

"True, but you don't need to overdo it, it sends—"

"The wrong message. Got you," I reply dryly.

"Dr Oldman and the Curator have been following you with interest – as have I," Gee-Gee says, trying to sound encouraging. "The Board met this morning. We'd like you to return next year if you're not pregnant again." I gulp. "It would be as a very low-key consultant until, well…*later*, but it keeps you in the loop and your position under me, firm."

"How much later?"

Gee-Gee looks uncomfortable and I know I am not going to like the answer.

"How much later?" I repeat.

"When your children are in high school."

I nervously scratch my head and rub my face. This is supposed to be an improvement… This *is* an improvement, but damn, it doesn't feel like it!

Little Drummer kicks me. I think she is apologising.

It's not your fault little one…and if I have my way, neither of us will be tied to the kitchen for long – unless we want to be.

THIRTY-TWO

Aunt Dora has never been one for a crowd or even sorry for multiple days of solitude, but she has asked Max and me to come over for dinner at least four nights a week since Eve died. We are all mourning Eve's loss, including Smoggy and Squash, but I am thankful she has their company when Max and I are away. Although I knew both paintings existed, I was surprised to see the living room now has a second painting of me adorning its walls. This time I am asleep in a chair with Eve and the cats, with crisp autumn sunshine flooding through the window. Aunt Dora has captured the moment perfectly and each brush stroke expresses warmth and love, but at the moment I cannot view it without welling up. That said, I wouldn't have her hide it away for anything because sorrow and pain do not have to be lonely feelings – they just mean the heart has been touched. I refuse to see that as a bad thing.

That love spurs me on.

"I packed Eve's clothes today," Aunt Dora says after we have eaten.

"Oh, okay," I say, unsure how I feel about this announcement.

"The PTB want to recycle anything that is still good."

"Ah, yes. No clutter, right." I scoff.

Aunt Dora exhales deeply. "It is better not to hold onto unnecessary extras…the memories don't change." I nod in recognition. "But there are some things that are right to keep. Mementos are not clutter. There is one—" She pauses. "There is one item that Eve wanted you to have."

Before I can ask, Aunt Dora gets up and leaves the room. I am not sure if I am supposed to follow, neither is Max, so we wait. After a minute Aunt Dora returns carrying Pandora, Eve's secret storage box.

"I would be grateful if you would take it with you. Eve said it might be helpful and to keep it safe. It is too dangerous to just throw it out, even if I wanted to," she says, presenting me with the box.

I have never seen another box like it. Carved wooden boxes are not common, but they are not unheard of either, yet this one is excessively heavy for its relatively small size and has a figurine of woman curled in the centre by the handle – a figurine that, if lifted, reveals a keypad and dances to music if you press five. Waiting until the end of the music rewards you if you then key in 7-2-6-3-7 as the box then opens, exposing a metallic, unscannable lining as well as the trinkets that are hidden inside.

I have already explored the contents and now wear the necklace and synthetic sleeve that used to live there. Inside now are old photographs of Eve and her family, the four bracelets that block signals, and a few other items which, as far as I know, are just precious to Eve, not necessarily engineered tools.

Eve had worn her wedding ring until she passed, and now Aunt Dora wears it on her right hand. The only other jewel is Eve's engagement ring which is tucked away in one of the compartments inside its own compact, velvet lined box. The ring is simple in comparison to other jewels, but the little diamonds are so beautifully arranged amongst the white gold, I cannot see why anyone would want anything else. When I am not swollen from pregnancy, I will wear it.

Then there are two tiny sets of screwdrivers, each one with the most precise, minute laser engraving on the metal. The red set has 'T. Addams' and the other, with purple handles has 'E. Addams.' I chuckle as I turn them over in my hands, trying to imagine a younger Eve with her husband, partners in everything, so perfectly matched they even have his and hers screwdrivers.

I sigh.

Eve obviously thought I had the tools I need to carry on down the right path without her. I just wish that I felt that was true. I have mused on that repeatedly. I see a goal far, far away, but with no location of Tom2 nor any tech support or link to 257 to discuss anything, I feel like her loss has blown up the path, not left it laid out ready for me to tread.

The box is useful, or at least it could be. Having somewhere to keep the sleeve and bracelets when not in use is essential. Aunt Dora asking me to take the box is possibly her way of saying she is done with R&R intrigue – I cannot blame her, but I also cannot join her. That would be a dishonour to everything I know and to those who deserve better. So, even if currently unclear, Eve's mission is not dead, not while I am alive…

In my moments of reflection, I almost hear Eve's 'hmmphh' – her mock from beyond. She loved a riddle. Even in her final moments, she spoke in riddles, one that almost certainly made sense to her. Possibly she thought she was being clear, but her mind was so challenged by illness it was a miracle, sheer testament of her spirit, that she said anything at all in those final days that made sense.

But she rests in peace knowing I will work it out.

Somehow.

I close the lid, deciding I will look again once I have taken Pandora home. I think the box will have to live under our bed, waiting until it has a purpose – and until I can work out what I am supposed to do! If nothing else, it is a keepsake now.

Max and Aunt Dora are chatting about her latest commission, apparently Max knows the recipient from work and isn't surprised he wants a painting of his dog as he dotes on it like a surrogate child and his wife walks it to work with him every morning without fail. As they talk, I rub my hand over the box with it perched on my lap. The carvings are exquisite and the little dancer is beautiful, she almost looks alive – even more so when the music plays. The way the box is put together, hiding the seams of the lid with ornamentation until it opens is fascinating. I cannot help wondering how many attempts it took to get it right, then chuckle to myself – knowing Eve it was done the first time! I turn the box and suddenly my eye catches the most minuscule detail on the dancer's neck. It could just be how her hair is tied, with the impression of waves and a few curls falling down her neck… but it could be…no—

"What is it?" asks Max, suddenly spotting the degree of scrutiny I am giving the little figure. I glance at him, but turn back to the dancer, putting pressure on her neck as Max asks, "Is something wro—*shit!*"

We sit wide-eyed, staring between the dancer and each other. I have snapped her neck backwards, revealing it is fixed with the tiniest hinge I have ever seen. It must also be incredibly strong as the head didn't move without significant force from me. There, hidden at the base of the neck, is a miniature metal piece – not dissimilar looking to a fly's eye. I believe it is a microphone or possibly a hologram projector. Suddenly Eve's words come to me: *"I want to go out dancin' but my legs and mind forget the steps. You must break the neck of the dancer and tell her not all dancers need rhythm."*

Panicking I will lose the moment, I say: "Not all dancers need rhythm."

Max opens his mouth to question my choice of words, but abruptly closes it when the dancer's head suddenly flicks back into position and she twirls three times. It is possibly one of the freakiest things I have ever witnessed.

Then a voice sounds from the little figure and my eyes instantly blur, so much so I couldn't say if Max or Aunt Dora have the same reaction. However, given their ghost-white expressions and wet cheeks after the voice has silenced, and I have wiped my eyes, I would say so:

"Missy, I'm leaving this message in a moment I remember meself, a moment that I now have too few of. I've always been fond of the humble bumblebee. They fly despite engineering rules sayin' they should not…they prove that by doing things their way, flight is possible…but they also, along with all bees, perform such almighty tasks that they actually sustain life on Earth. We nearly lost them, not caring to realise we'd soon follow without them. Well, me code for beyond has always been in humble appreciation of them. It seems extra fitting now, when goin' against the R&R could be considered as goin' against the odds, and attempting to achieve what others say should, or cannot be.

"Record 'The Flight of the Bumblebee' in two parts. One in the original key, as first written, and play it on the piano. The second part must be played simultaneously with the first, but play the first four notes of every bar up a key. So, A is now B, B is C, etc. Play it in unison and on repeat as you step beyond until you are three miles out. No drone will follow you, nor track you and the directions you seek will be delivered like sweet nectar.

"Tell Tom2—Tell Tom2, I think Tom is a fool, but love him always. He'll know the rest. Tread carefully, have faith, as I have every faith in you. Hmmphh, forgive an old woman her stubborn ways. My sorrow and trepidation held me tongue too long. Real revolution requires regular regeneration, the Earth deserves her rightful restoration. Now and always. Yours always, Eve."

THIRTY-THREE

Finding Ezra is now essential as it is imperative that I get to 257. I am not particularly patient at the best of times, but it is already July, Gee-Gee wants me on maternity leave on 1st August, and I want whatever is to be done, done, before Little Drummer makes her grand entrance. This world *needs* to be on a new path by September. That path never ends, I know that, but I feel like I am at a crossroads with my backpack, screaming out for a ride.

"Can you play the piano?" Max asks.

"Not well enough to play 'The Flight of the Bumblebee'— you?"

"No, I learnt guitar when we had to pick an instrument."

"I chose violin – though I majored in singing." Like my Mum…for all the good that is now!

"Mum—Mary." Max shakes his head, he still struggles to name his adoptive mother. "*She* wanted me to learn at least two instruments 'properly,' but I just couldn't get into it. I love music, but listening is more my thing."

"Fair enough. Do you know any pianists? I don't think I do – certainly not at the level of expertise we need. It isn't like we can explain why we want the piece played so specifically either!" I exclaim, sighing.

"It is likely 257 can do it," Max says optimistically.

"I hope so. Pfft, why couldn't Eve leave us easier codes?!"

"I suppose that would leave them too open for hackers." Max scoffs. "Certainly no one is going to stumble into any of the ones we know!"

I rock my head in agreement. Absolutely no one is going to 'just' trigger anything Eve left behind. Even if by some miracle a glitch code was found, every action has more than one stage to unlock it. It is no wonder so many of her codes were lost in her fog – only an exceptional mind would remember them in the first place!

"Could we go to the radio station?" I ask.

"And say we're there for what? We aren't booked in again until mid-August," reasons Max. "What about Ella? Do you think it is time to risk asking her for help?"

"Maybe…she did want to say something to me. I just worry it is wishful thinking that she is already on the same track as us. She is unsettled, I see that, but—"

"She's also married to Theo who seems wholly taken in," Max finishes for me.

"He does…unapologetically so." I roll my eyes. "I have to go to the Headquarters with him tomorrow."

"Why? I thought you went there to see Dr Oldman?"

"I do normally. Theo and I usually only cross paths in your dad's lab. I think Oldman wants a joint report."

"Huh."

"What?"

"I have a meeting there tomorrow with the Architect."

"Have you met him before?"

"No. I don't even know his name, everyone just says 'the Architect.' Apparently, he likes the plans I submitted for more efficient housing structures. I was inspired by Eve's old photos actually, it made me think about how we can use even more old material, but arrange it with an extra plant layer – with newer breeds and native plants combined to improve air quality as well as make beautiful, ornate structures – I'm just expanding on what we are already doing."

"Don't sell yourself short," I say, curling my fingers around his.

Max smiles, making a 'hmm' sound before leaning over to kiss me.

We sit in silence for some time. I can only assume we are both trying to come up with a plan. I yawn as tiredness hits me, sparkling Max to yawn in unison.

"I can't think anymore today. I will try to find you in the canteen at lunch," says Max. "Our drones will deliver to us, but we can sit and eat together."

"Okay," I whisper, half awake, half asleep, "it's a date."

* * *

After a morning of nonstop chatter, graphs, and spreadsheets I am glad to sit down and not think about anything other than eating the butternut salad and yoghurt my drone just delivered. I want to kick the chair away when I see Theo making his way towards me, but instead, I mimic the smile friends give one another. As much as I struggle with his past betrayal, I also struggle with how easily we work together – how true a friendship we could have. It is such a shame that real trust has been eroded, even if I do not now lament our romantic separation.

I hope Max arrives soon. He will fill in with conversation where I now just want to fade into background noise. I look up from my plate and see Theo staring at me thoughtfully. I think he almost looks embarrassed as we watch each other. Having studied every inch of his face when we were together, I used to understand his every look. Some of that instinct has remained, but I feel guilty for it, it isn't my job to know his expressions so well, it is Ella's. Let her interpret his pain and confusion, as well as his joy.

I don't ask if he is okay, instead I turn back to my salad, but when I do look up, I am sure Theo is looking at my stomach. "What?" I ask. "Have I got food on me?" I stretch my top to see if I have splattered myself and Theo laughs coyly.

"What then?"

Theo clears his throat and grimaces. "I was just thinking *that*," he nods at my pregnant stomach, "wouldn't have happened with us…not ever."

"No…" I wasn't expecting him to say that and don't know how to reply. "Nor will it with Ella," I say softly, unsure if I am being tactless. "I'm sorry." I decide now isn't the time to remind him I categorically didn't want this to happen. I suppose he, like every other person I know, assumes I changed my mind. *Like that matters.*

"No, no it won't."

"Are you sorry?" I don't know why I am asking.

"Sometimes…but the work is so important, it is an honour," he quickly adds as though he is talking to the Board of Trustees, not me.

"No one doubts your dedication to the work," I say a little drier than I should.

Theo fiddles with his knife and fork and I just watch, waiting to see if he has a point, or if he just has regrets. I suppose he is only human after all.

"Right," he mutters.

"What is wrong?"

Theo sighs as he looks at me, then again at my stomach, and I feel sorry for him – possibly for the first time in nearly seven years. The love of the job and the understanding of the mission does not remove the basic human desire to have a family or at least to have the option of one. We are well indoctrinated on the making of a replacement family if fertility or lottery doesn't smile on us – focusing on the wonder of work, friendship, and extended family – but even in the converted, it doesn't always come easily. Not every day anyway. I think I am witnessing a down day for Theo. I am sorry, but surely this is a conversation for him to have with Ella or maybe the Board: not me.

Definitely not me.

I look beyond Theo's head and see Max approaching, smiling with such satisfaction his whole face lights up. I send a cheeky smile back to him and Theo follows my gaze as Max reaches the table, greets me with a kiss, and sits opposite me. I have seen Max's dark eyes sparkle with love, joy, and happiness before, and every time it simultaneously melts my heart and fills it, resulting in a warm, fuzzy, girly-giddiness that makes me weak at the knees…but this twinkle in his eyes is different. It is…smug? Jubilant? Victorious??

"Good meeting?" I ask.

"Very," Max beams.

"Was it in person or—"

"The Architect was by hologram, from goodness knows where," Max shrugs, "but yes, I am excited to see where *that* goes. The architectural team here, in this Hub, are really good actually. We discuss and listen, unlike my m—" Max cuts himself short. I know he means Mary. Her ghost will haunt us both in different ways, but Mary had no intention of encouraging architecture as a long-term career for Max. Whether she disliked those behind the R&R team, or just wanted Max to follow her path more precisely, we'll never know. What I do know is Max should be able to follow the career that makes his face light up like it is right now. He wants to help build a better world for all – you'd like to think that is the ethos any mother (adoptive or otherwise) would be unequivocally proud of.

Theo must understand Max's meaning too as he takes the lead, talking about Max's plans with genuine gusto. I listen, smiling and encouraging when prompted, but not attempting to distract from their line or tone of conversation. As our break time concludes, Theo takes my plate to the cleaning station and I get up to leave. Max tuts, taps his cheek with his finger and grins saying, "Have you forgotten something?" Taking the hint, I giggle and kiss him goodbye. As I motion to step away, Max holds my hand, stopping me from retreating and whispers, "I've had two wonderful meetings today, wait and see!"

He winks as he lets go of my hand and gently strokes my left arm.

My eyes boggle. "Do you mean…?"

"I do," Max says with a grin, casually reaching for his drink. "See you at home, my love."

It's going to be a *long* afternoon.

THIRTY-FOUR

My heart skips a beat every time my mind wanders in the direction of Max and I hardly dare to hope that I understand what he was alluding to at lunchtime. I am so distracted I almost missed my summons to the fertility board meeting, but at 2:45 p.m., Theo gently grasped my elbow and reminded me we had to get going.

In Conference Room A, Dr Oldman is presenting his work to the Curator, the Director, and other geneticists and biologists who are linked in via holograms from across the globe. Dr Oldman greeted Gee-Gee and Professor Millar by name; however, despite there being a dozen people physically present, no one (physical or pixelated) has bothered introducing themselves unless directly asking a question or sharing their findings.

The general consensus is fertility is still declining and the controlled downwards arch is not as controlled as they would like. Uncertain results between most matched couples (despite nutritional 'influences') and a reduction in naturally resistant grade 3s being born are blamed.

I silently gulp at this, but I gulp again as Dr Oldman launches into data from his Initiative project and how it is showing real promise at being 'the answer.'

"The future is bright with more carefully planted Golden Geese and Ganders," he beams. "Even now, with my relatively short study, I have proven the effectiveness of placing them and breeding them with selected key subjects – other Goldens, but also lesser 3's and even 2's – the results are fascinating. Accurate grade predictions in the unborn is no longer a pipe dream."

"Are you saying a future without food controls is really around the corner?" a familiar female voice asks from across the room. I try identifying her, only to realise she is blurred out. Ah, the (elusive) Arbitrator is here.

"It is…I'd like to trial it in one Hub first. Not without *any* food controls, they have served us extremely well to date after all. Instead, I propose a variation – an upgrade if you will – to what we're already doing. The results I have to date, coupled with material from the FARM programme are invaluable, but I do need to test more theories in a whole population, not just sectors as we have to date. I have plenty of donations gathered and ready to go. My proposals will be with you all in writing immediately after this meeting has concluded."

"And what about halting early menopause?" asks the Arbitrator. "You haven't mentioned that."

"Indeed, we are further away with that one unfortunately – though very much working on it. We are still able to collect from the majority of 3s until 28-30, so their samples and contributions to the gene pool are significant…but yes, such early decline is a concern—"

"'A concern,' Dr Oldman? Is that what you call it? Only yesterday I met a woman with the hot flushes of menopause at twenty-one, last week one was sixteen…*sixteen!* I would call that more than 'a concern.' That pattern is potentially catastrophic!"

"I assure you, I will have an update report on that soon. My recent cadet samples have been most interesting…but if I may, Arbitrator, I want to discuss the roll out of the Initiative today…" Dr Oldman pauses, looking straight at her. As no sound comes from the blur, he continues: "Time is of the essence, especially with Match Day around the corner again. If at all possible, I'd like the next tests to be live for the upcoming batch of newlyweds."

It is nine months since I found out the entire UNE population is actually made up of blissfully unaware guinea pigs: I haven't gotten used to it nor the ease in which we sit here discussing further in-population trials, whilst likening grade 3s to mere poultry. We reduce Lily and all her friends to no more than hens – hens who are waiting to donate their eggs until such time they are too old and then are simply relieved of all their reproductive parts. I remind myself that is exactly how I am supposed to view it. This is 'just' the genetics and science of breeding. I see the point, of course, I do, but they are still talking about me, about Lily, Little Drummer, and every other person, like pins on a board, not people.

Theo and I are here purely on observational grounds. *Whose* observation, I am still only too conscious of. I am learning their proceedings, while they scrutinise my every fidget, sneeze, or sniff. So I smile and nod as people talk…or remain straight faced – but not hard.

Showing emotion will not help me now.

I don't dare risk it.

I *do* think I am passing though because Gee-Gee's smile is warm and encouraging.

Dr Oldman, to his credit, doesn't take all the 'glory' for himself. If someone else has given him data or an idea, he names them. He names Theo and me twice – which results in another proud smile from Gee-Gee.

The Director's prodigies are proving themselves.

Yes, *both* of them.

Like it or not, Gee-Gee is priming Theo as well as me. I have actually observed she has a string of minions under her direct guidance and I can see why Mary disapproved of this. Leaving too many potential chiefs leaves the hierarchy open to dispute should the head fall – but assuming not everyone is out for blood and glory like Mary, I'd hope a natural successor would be peacefully named. Mary's replacement is located in the Northern Hub. Maybe the PTB and R&R decided a quieter, less controversial Director of Agriculture was necessary. It was certainly a surprise to my mother when they named Mary's replacement out of the bounds of the Southern Hub. I tried pointing out it was only fair to spread responsibility out over the State. Mum told me 'I know nothing' and turned to a more sympathetic listener with her thoughts of disapproval.

Once upon a time I might have agreed with her – I didn't *know*.

But now I know I am supposed to be Gee-Gee's successor.

Whether I like it or not.

Will Gee-Gee really hold on to her position until I am deemed ready – not to mention, deemed fully trustworthy?

Or will I manage to break my way to the top of the tree sooner without them seeing the axe in my hand? I only hope I have the courage to swing it when the time comes. I sit and listen to their reports and even now, part of me is sad to betray it. I have yearned to be included, to be given the key to the kingdom…to be part of the team that works for humanity and Earth. I cannot shut off the voice that says this *is* what is happening in this room. It niggles at me, asking *'Are you sure you can't see the good here?'*

But no, the other voice, which increasingly sounds like Eve, screams at me to not get lost in the darkness. This room *has* crossed the line of what is acceptable for the greater good – and I now have a different key to the kingdom. One that says 'reboot'…not 'repress'…

And I cannot wait to get to it.

THIRTY-FIVE

"Honey, I'm home!" I call as I slide the front door closed. I wanted to get off the tram and use the lift into our study, but, as Theo annoyingly reminded me, we have to go home the same way we came. The PTB system thinks I went into the lab this morning – the Central Hub lab – so I had to complete the ruse by returning via that route. Max is already home, out of his work clothes, and smiling as he lays spread out across the sofa when I walk in.

I drop my bag on the floor inside the doorway. The PTB would disapprove of such 'uncaring' treatment of property, especially as my sketzpad and laptop are both in there, but I am too distracted to care. Max shifts his position as I squeeze next to him on the sofa and casually say: "So, you had a good day?"

Turning his body to face me, grinning widely, Max takes my hands in his, inviting me to feel his skin. I run my fingers gently up and down his arms and over hands, but cannot feel anything different. I glance up at Max's face, but he just nods back to his hands.

His skin is the same beautiful olive brown as always, just the same texture as always, but I know what he is saying... something 'other' is there. Just as it is on my left arm. I check his barcode – it is his, but mine is too unless I pull my sleeve down and twist the pearls on my necklace. I reach for his neckline and pull at the collar of his t-shirt.

No necklace.

I furrow my brows… Am I wrong?

I am going to have to ask in a moment. Max senses my frustration and answers my confusion with an amused smile. He is enjoying this. Suddenly, he moves his hands away from my searching fingers and fists his left hand, squeezing all five digits into his palm and quickly releases his palm like a flower reacting to light – for light is exactly what he has produced.

I gasp as Max giggles.

It takes all my willpower not to speak. Damn these watches that I cannot remove and algorithms of which I do not know the triggers!

The light turns into a globe – a green and blue globe. Earth.

Max fists his hand again, shutting off the hologram, pulls out a napkin from his pocket and hands it to me.

"20:43. Pinch it."

I look at my watch. We have just over an hour to wait. "Fancy a shower?" I ask, smiling.

"I thought you'd never ask." Max winks, leading me upstairs. "I know you can't keep your hands off me."

I just laugh and shut the bathroom door, stripping off and turning on the shower. Max sweetly scrubs my back – something that is increasingly difficult for me to do myself – and kisses my neck. I struggle to focus on the point at hand until I run my hand down his right arm and lace my fingers through his.

"How?" I whisper.

Max chuckles. "I went to the toilet just before I found you at dinner. I came out of the cubicle and there, on the sink was a napkin wrapped around a long, fingerless glove. Not wanting to be obvious, I looked around the room using the mirror and there was Ezra, staring at me from another cubicle, pretending to be working on his watch – he scared the shit of me to be honest!" Max laughs. "I picked up the napkin and slid on the glove. I watched it mould to my hand and lower arm, simultaneously turning from magnolia to my colour in seconds. Ezra smiled, nodded, and then fisted his hand tight, just like I did downstairs…I copied him and the globe appeared."

"Then what?" I ask, too enthralled to say more.

"Then Ezra left."

"He didn't say anything?"

"No, he just smiled and left. It would have been daft to do all that, then speak, especially given our location."

"The toilet?"

"The headquarters." Max looks at me a little bewildered.

"Sorry…of course not…I wonder why he was there?"

"I'm guessing he got upgraded after Dean's 'accident.' I don't think his cousin sounded too likely to get the job."

"Hmm, true…"

Max stretches his fingers as he turns his hand back and forth. I think he is still fascinated by his invisible glove. I am not surprised, I am still amazed by mine.

"Do you think you'll trigger it by accident?"

"No, I don't think so. I have to squeeze pretty hard to activate it – plus the light comes first and it is warm, so I have a good chance of realising before I release my grip and unwittingly reveal the globe."

"Good," I sigh. "So now we just need to wait to be called!"

THIRTY-SIX

Max and I cuddle up under the duvet like children hiding from their parents just before the time Ezra scribbled on the napkin. The final minutes drag terribly and I wonder if 20:43 will ever come. Suddenly Max's left hand produces a globe and I tremble as a new jolt of energy races through me as the previously stationary globe starts turning. Max shrugs, takes a deep breath, and pinches the globe with his right hand.

"Hello? Max?" says a voice.

"Hi, yes. Who's this?" Max asks.

"257. Max, Maia, this is a tester call – we have twenty seconds. Do you have anything to communicate?"

"We do…" Max says. "Eve left code to access beyond, to find the original Shepherd."

"Then we will hear it, three days, two hours, and seven minutes from now. 257 out."

* * *

We were deflated, but perhaps unjustifiably so by 257's speed call. An android is hardly going to procrastinate and spuffle like a human, is he? Also, it made sense he would keep his transmission brief, especially the initial one. Either way we can only trust he knows how to scramble signals without causing detectable waves and so (semi) patiently wait until our next meeting, doing our best not to think about it or its importance in the meantime.

Work, dinner with my mother, and antenatal classes filled our time. One worried me, one frustrated me, and the other freaked me out. So, by the time three days are up, I am very happy to hide under the duvet again, even if it is probably unnecessary for the task at hand.

"Good evening," says 257 the moment we are connected. "Forgive the lack of image, it is just easier to hide audio than it is video."

"That's okay," I reply. "How long do we have?"

"One minute, thirteen seconds," he replies. I shake my head. Memories of that number will follow us everywhere. "Eve left code for beyond the fence?"

"She did. It stops drones following or tracking us."

"And what would you be looking for?" Lily's voice whispers through the airwaves. "You said something about the original Shepherd?"

I startle hearing her voice, but conscious of time, I just answer the question: "Yes, apparently he is hiding out there, observing all. He holds the master code to all AI – to all power across the UNE."

"And what would you do with that?" asks 257 sceptically.

"Hopefully make a fairer world for everyone!" I say passionately. "We are very much hoping you'll both help with that."

The pause is brief, but it feels like an enormous chasm in time.

"What do you need?" Lily suddenly says.

I feel my shoulders relax with relief, but waste no time by sighing. "First, I need someone to record 'The Flight of the Bumblebee' in a very specific way… then get us beyond the fence so coordinates appear. 257, can you play the piano?"

"We both can," 257 replies. "Quick, time is short, give us the details."

"Play and record the original transcript, then record it again with the first four notes played up one key on each bar. Once beyond they must be played simultaneously on a loop until three miles out."

"Okay…I'll call again when it is done."

THIRTY-SEVEN

As Max and I have been left waiting for 257 to give us the go ahead with the code, we have turned our attention to getting to the fence…because, after all, what good is it having a scramble code for *beyond* the fence, if we are both firmly locked *behind* it?

Max suggested we leave the next phase to 257…let him and Lily find Tom2. It would be safer, but Eve entrusted me with the burden of leading a revolution and the R&R – the UNE – will not be altered by machine alone. A human, one *inside* the Hub, has to step outside of their comfort zone and lead the way. Part of me would like to leave the responsibility at someone else's feet, but inaction will not be my cause of rot or decay. Lily is exiled and I am Gee-Gee's blood.

It has to be me.

It has to be *us*.

Max suggested one last alternative – that he goes alone. I know he only said that out of concern for me and Little Drummer, his family, but we are doing this *for* family. For all families and their right to live without the noose of failure swaying over their heads. I told him I love him all the more for wavering for us, but we made a pact to go together and, heavily pregnant or not, I will not back out of this for anything.

Max relaxed afterwards. I think he just needed to voice his concern before jumping to the next plan...the one I am hoping to finally attempt now.

To recruit Ella.

We need her expertise – we cannot think of another way around it. Ezra has the knowhow, and in many ways, the access, but we cannot rely on him alone...we need another angle to get us down that tram line to the FARM.

We need to know whose codes I can mimic – and how to operate Max's sleeve. He has no necklace to alter his barcode. At the moment his barcode somehow displays through the glove, like the synthetic skin has absorbed his tattoo – or perhaps it is simply mimicking that too? I don't know, but if Max removes the long, fingerless glove, his arm looks the same as ever and the glove returns to a magnolia, wobbly sleeve.

I invited Ella to lunch in the park and she readily agreed, my only slight hiccup was she also invited Kate. It makes sense, we always meet as a three these days, only meeting in a pair if it is by chance. On any other day, I am glad, but today I was relieved when I found out Kate has an appointment at the hospital with Benjamin later. So, I just have to be patient, enjoy my friends' company and be patient...

"I've been reading Benjamin a story about a mouse that wants adventure," Kate says, reaching for her laptop. I resist the urge to say, 'so do I.' Instead, I chuckle at the front cover of the book which has a brown mouse in a bright purple coat, wearing a backpack, standing like he is a superhero preparing to fly. "It's quite sweet actually. I'll send you the link to download it if you like?" I nod in silent thanks. "We've met some lovely couples in the maternity ward. We take it in turns to read to the babies, some of us act out the parts… I got quite emotional yesterday as Pete and Louis' baby had been born and they were just taking him home – I can't wait until that's Tim and I! – Oh, and Pete reads so beautifully!"

"I'm sure you'll keep in touch," I say, trying not to feel deficient for not having bought lots of baby books yet. The only things I've read Little Drummer are technically classed as research reports, not novellas.

"Oh, we will, for sure – we'll be joining the same nursery as them. You are booked in there, too. I saw your name on the year list, so I can introduce you!"

"I look forward to it." *Ish.*

"What about your antenatal classes? Any nice couples there?"

I cringe. The people there are nice, they just have the ability to make me feel woefully inadequate as an expectant mother. They huff and pant when prompted – Max does, too, actually, but he does it with a smile. They're all so serious, like there's a PTB test at the end of the session…ugh, technically they're right, there is.

Labour.

Best not dwell on that right now…

Kate reads my expression and seems concerned. I know she'll understand if I explain, but I'd feel less guilty if she didn't have a baby countdown, too. She loves every element of parenthood –

the lead up and actual – *all of it.* So, I feel bad for even slightly groaning about any of it.

"There are nice couples. Max is better at introducing himself than I am…you know me, I just feel a little awkward…and the breathing exercises are—" Kate laughs at me and Ella quickly joins in, so I don't feel the need to finish. Let them mock me.

I'm glad I can still laugh at myself and I am thankful for friends to laugh with. Kate's friendship has been the one thing that is constant in my twenty-four, nearly twenty-five, years of life. When she gets up to go, I hug her for a second longer than possibly I should. When she steps back she looks worried and asks if I am all right. Little Drummer comes to the rescue again as I blame her for monkeying with my hormones, making me soppy and emotional for no apparent reason. This earns me an extra hug and I nearly cry, though Kate saves my tears when she startles me by squealing with delight as Little Drummer kicks me hard enough that she also feels it – which results in more giggles and exclamations of baby joy.

Left alone with Ella, I steel myself to spit out a question, telling myself to just start the ball rolling and take it from there. As I open my mouth I am stopped short as Ella mirrors my sharp intake of air, only she exhales faster, and with it, she knocks out my breath and steals my thunder:

"Would I have been able to have babies? If they had *left* me?"

I look around for passers-by and above for drones. All is clear, but my heart is pounding, nonetheless.

"Don't worry, we're alone," says Ella, watching me intensely. "I can't get the question out of my head. I need to know. So…*would I?*"

I chew on my cheek and wobble my tongue. Why am I delaying? I wanted to start an awkward conversation – a leading conversation. Here it is on a silver platter.

"Honestly?" Ella nods. "I don't know…I've not seen your specific records."

"Here," Ella says, pulling out her sketzpad. "I saved it on here."

Reaching out, I take her sketzpad, doubting what record she has found and feel my pupils expand as I realise she really has somehow copied her fertility record without an alarm blaring. I glance down her info, at her feed schedule, at the graphs and groups she has been placed in. Ella is a genius in code and algorithm – a technical whiz kid – she must have a fair idea what this says, but she is not a geneticist, so some of these figures would mean nothing to her, but to me, especially since my R&R initiation…

I shake my head.

"I would, wouldn't I?" Ella asks sadly.

"Yes, I'm so sorry. You were in the 'decrease' group, so not a definite 'fertile,' but with the right treatment, you might have been."

Ella's already watery eyes overflow and I pull her into a hug and don't let go. It was bad enough learning the entire population is tested on, but I am resistant – prized even. To learn you were *made* 'defective,' to have something removed from you on a whim, as an experiment – it has to be crushing. Especially when I can see it is potentially the one thing she wants the most. Ella has been wonderful about mine and Kate's forthcoming babies. No one doubts her joy for us, but now I understand the shadow in her eye. Not only does she lament what nature has not blessed her with, she now understands it is nurture – the lack of proper nurture – that has destroyed her chance of motherhood. Maybe the R&R will grant her a lottery baby like Ezra or Kate, but if they consider her the asset to engineering that I think they do, somehow, I doubt it. Why put an infertile genius out to pasture while she raises a family when she can work throughout?

Losing me is neither here nor there. I am propaganda at its best. A Golden Goose, directly from the Director of Fertility, married to a handsome, fertile man that they matched me with – *and* we fell in love. If I can be useful behind the scenes or at a later date, great, but I am the poster girl for the PTB rule. For the majority of those in power, that *is* my most useful purpose.

Ella is just Ella: a mastermind to use behind the scenes to hide and watch over their shadows. Well, I want to bring her to the light where she belongs. Or at least show her my misty twilight and hope she sees the path to dawn.

"Ella?" I say into her shoulder as we continue to embrace.

"Mmm?"

"Do you remember the day you met Eve and me by the river?"

"Of course…she wasn't well."

"True, but do you remember what you had with you? What you were searching for?"

"Yes…?" Ella leans back, looking at me quizzically.

"Do you still have it?"

"I do."

"Excellent. Would you and it like to come to ours for lunch at the weekend?"

Ella blinks repeatedly, but doesn't look away from me. I grin at her and slowly she returns it with an enormous grin of her own and says: "Yes…yes, I'd love that."

THIRTY-EIGHT

Max thinks I have gone into labour when I wake him at 2 a.m. He jumps out of bed in a dazed panic and starts fretting about a hospital bag in such a way that, if it wasn't for the urgency and excitement of 257's call, I would stop and laugh at him longer. Instead, I control my mirth and channel my nerves into pointing out his left hand has an illuminated, spinning globe coming from it. Max's mind clicks into place and he answers the call:

"257?"

"Hello, my apologies for the time, but I have to make the timing random and I cannot risk calling when you might be in company."

"It's okay," Max says. "Do you have news?"

"I do. Lilith and I have recorded our pieces, which we are curious and anxious to hear played together."

"As are we. When?" I ask.

"August. I suggest the 10th."

My heart sinks.

"Can it not be sooner?" Max asks, reading my face. "Maia is on something of a *timer* here."

"I appreciate that, but in order to give us a potential two-day excursion window, it has to be when Lilith would potentially be off in the Hatchery for her donation. She is normally back within a day, but a two-day absence is not unheard of. We orchestrated a longer stay this time so our absence should not be seen as suspicious to other cadets when we are gone – that is important otherwise they could spark unwanted concern from the other Shepherds. Ezra is to watch and cover as best he can, but there is no need to make life harder than necessary. August works as Lilith is not booked for an actual donation then."

"Does Lily have to come?" Max says. "I don't mean that rudely, but—"

"I understand your concerns, but we do this as a four, or not at all," 257 says firmly. "We all have our reasons to need to see beyond the fence. Lilith's are as justified as Maia's. I agree Maia is uniquely placed within the hierarchy of the UNE, making her essential for implementing change, but—"

"We are *all* essential," I cut in. "That is the point, 257."

"I couldn't have put it better myself." I can hear the smile on 257's face through the airways. If such a thing is possible? "We have time before the baby arrives."

Max looks at me and I shrug.

So be it, if the 10th of August is the date, that is that.

"Can you get here?" Lily asks.

"We know the tramline that takes us to you. We just don't know how to pass security. We are hoping to get help with that on Saturday."

"The tram north of the headquarters has three lines. Left and central go to the male FARM stead and other correctional facilities. You *must* take the right-hand track. Find out who are authorised personnel and use their barcodes. If they move their location while you are logged as them, the alarm will trigger. We want to avoid that. If you get to me, I am confident we can play Eve's bumblebee variation and still get to Tom2 but getting back safely could be much, much harder."

"So, we need to try and not trigger alarms," I scoff nervously.

"Ideally," 257 replies. "We will be waiting for you at the tram station below here just after midnight. We will wait until 1 a.m. If you don't arrive, we will abort the mission and reconvene when or if it is safe to do so. Okay, until—"

"Hang on! How do I change the barcode on my sleeve?" Max asks. "It isn't the same as Eve's?"

"Ah, right. I copied Eve's, but upgraded it a little as I didn't have a necklace to command it." I smile and raise my eyebrows. I am not sure how Eve would feel about her tech being 'upgraded' – probably proud and pissed at the same time knowing her! "Both sleeves read your skin code and fingerprint from the underside. That is why only the wearer can operate or remove either one, but Max, yours has voice activation. First, make a fist to get the globe to appear and then say: '257 is the best.'"

"Seriously?!" laughs Lily.

257 chuckles. "I didn't have time to ask what passcode Max wanted and thought this was applicable!" Lily groans and giggles as 257 continues: "Say the passcode out loud and the globe will turn purple. Dictate the barcode you want and it will appear on your arm instead of yours until you say: '257 is the best, but I would like to be me again.'"

"That's it?" Max asks.

"That's it. Okay, we must hang up. Until the 10th. Safe journey – we look forward to meeting you both."

"As we do you," I say with an unexpected wobble to my voice.

The globe switches off and we are left in silence. It isn't until Max pulls me into a hug that I realise how badly I am trembling.

It is going to be a long three weeks.

THIRTY-NINE

I have to force myself to stop pacing and sit down as I wait for Ella to arrive because greeting her red-faced, sweating, and resembling a beached whale is possibly not the most awe-inspiring look. I badly need this meeting to go well. We started on the right footing: I felt we were on the same page, but to recruit her, I have to trust her...and she has to trust me.

The only way to achieve this is through honesty.

Some wise person may have said 'honesty is the best policy' but my sceptical side says that's just because it happens to rhyme. However, even if it's true, I doubt they had this much to lose.

As Ella walks into my home, I scan her face for an indication of mood. The shadow that she has recently tried so hard to hide is now quite obvious and it makes me nervous. Encouraged by how our last meeting had ended and reassured by her complicit smile, I have been telling myself I will just show her Eve's bracelets and take it from there. But now? Now she looks like she's unsure and weepy and I don't know how to interpret her.

We make small talk with the usual 'how are you?' 'what a lovely day!' and 'wow, it's hot!' as I guide us into the kitchen.

"So," Ella says, sitting down while I make tea, "what can I do?"

I turn to her and tilt my head. She clearly isn't referring to the making of beverages and I obviously didn't invite her here for tea and cakes. Maybe I shouldn't have sent Max out? I didn't want Ella to feel ambushed, but I also didn't consider the fact I could be ambushing myself.

I don't answer directly, instead I make more annoying small talk until I have placed two steaming mugs of tea on the kitchen island next to sandwiches, four buttered cheese scones, and two chocolate muffins – all of which I bought from the bakery this morning and have been craving ever since.

We sit opposite each other, neither smiling nor grimacing. Ella sighs and rests her right arm on the counter, exposing her bracelet. The memory of discovering that bracelet exists still gives me heart palpitations. Eve had left Aunt Dora's bungalow in a confused daze and went on a jolly around the river still wearing her illegal, tech-scrambling bracelet. That was stressful enough, but Ella had simultaneously been tasked by the PTB to test her own, anomaly-detecting bracelet and I found her actively searching for the source of a signal blip that was upsetting drones in the area. It was only because Eve had been unwittingly rude that Ella didn't notice her device worked perfectly and its target was around Eve's wrist.

I nod and rest my right arm on the counter, mimicking Ella, showing off my watch and Eve's bracelet. Ella stares at my arm. There is nothing remarkable about the outward appearance of either bracelet, and anyone 'not in the know' would think them simple items of jewellery – yet I have no doubt Ella understands. She clicks on an app on her watch and scrolls on it for a moment before suddenly looking up at me boggle eyed.

"It works, right?" I ask.

"Which?" Ella whispers.

"Both. I'm guessing both." I raise my left arm, showing another, identical bracelet. I take it off and slide it across the counter to Ella.

She picks it up and turns it over, smiling. "The old woman still had some tricks."

"She did," I reply, trying not to cry. I miss that 'old woman' more than I can say. "She had her reasons to love and hate the Powers That Be – *all* levels of them."

"She and her husband led the way with engineering more than I thought possible. My upgraded clearance has shown me that—"

"And most of her family paid the ultimate price when they tried to set a new, less restrictive path. They found out more than their pay grade allowed and wanted to expose the level of lies and control the people are subject to – and dragged Tom into their attempt at reform. Despite her losses, Eve remained loyal, believing in the mission she and her husband dedicated everything to. She was tested again when her great grandson was killed over a misunderstanding and as a result, she lost faith with the PTB and R&R alike and retired in silence on the grounds of keeping her remaining family safe. Eve kept that silence until the R&R broke their promise and sent Lilith, her only great-great granddaughter, to the FARM programme – what we knew simply as the AIP before. Eve believed the mission is still as essential as ever, for humanity and Earth, but the mission also needs fresh eyes and ideas –

and to turn from its current oppressive, totalitarian path. *I* believe in that mission. My question is, Ella: *do you?*"

Ella's smile neutralised, then turned upside down as I spoke, and now both our lips tremble as we watch each other. I don't think I can make my warning any clearer. What I am suggesting could undoubtedly get us imprisoned or killed. Any agreed action is firmly under the 'all or nothing' umbrella.

I wait.

Ella has to make the next move. I am in her hands.

She has three options: Join me, walk away from me, or betray me. I pray for the first, hope I can find another way if it is the second, and I hope Little Drummer forgives me if it is the third.

"I have been afraid and exhilarated since our last conversation," Ella says after what seems like an eternity. "I woke up today and part of me actually didn't want to come. I cried on and off all morning before I left the house. Theo thought it was because we argued about his knowledge of the fertility 'treatment.' I let him think that – it was easier to get away alone that way, but part of it *is* because of that – what they do to innocent people…what they push good people into doing. I don't believe Theo agrees with it all, he is caught by the love of science and he doesn't see the possibility of another way. For months, I have felt the weight of that hopelessness." She pauses, looking me straight in the eyes. "Until now. Until I stepped out of the house and put one foot in front of the other and arrived here. And though each step was heavy, I have hope."

A single tear rolls down my left cheek at the same time as one rolls down her right and our smiles spread from ear to ear.

"What do you need?" Ella asks.

"To get on a tram heading north of the headquarters. I need to know if your anomaly bracelet picks up on false codes…if I can board a tram that is heavily alarm coded and pose as someone else – someone authorised for that journey – and not trigger any kind of security alert."

"I can set it to fragment your readings, not just scramble, so tracking on the tram is nigh-on-impossible, but the sensor you have to go through…that is designed to detect codes on androids and humans. You cannot bypass that. How—"

I wave my left arm at her and suck in my bottom lip.

"What?" Ella looks confused.

"Does your bracelet read anything odd now?"

Ella gets up and scans me.

"Only your right arm, the bracelet is stopping me from recording or listening, but my bracelet sees it now that it is close up."

"And what about my left arm…how about if I remove the bracelet?"

"What is the difference?"

I hold my left arm in front of Ella so she can read my barcode. She swears as she looks back and forth from her arm to mine, realising she is seeing double. I then fiddle with my necklace with my right hand: it reads my fingertips and the underside immediately displays letters and numbers, allowing me to scramble them all. One by one, I return the pearls to blank and simultaneously remove Ella's barcode, allowing my arm to display my own again.

Ella's mouth drops open.

The hairs on the back of my neck stand up and electrify, sending shock waves all over my body as anticipation and fear grasps me. I have just admitted to identity theft and crossed the line of no return.

Ella giggles.

It somehow seems inappropriate to laugh at such a tense moment, but as her shoulders shake with each increasing chuckle and chortle, I join in. Call it a stress relief, or moment of collective madness, I don't know, but it helps.

No longer do I see Ella as the cutesy little girl who married my childhood sweetheart. Nor do I see her as the tag-along friend who was thrust upon me…or even the annoyingly intelligent woman who gets to do everything I cannot with ease. She is a true friend. I've known that for a while, but now she is also a comrade and key member of the *next* revolution.

Looking at the smile that has rested on her face, and the sparkle that now shines in her eye – the one I am sure matches mine as it balances sorrow and hope on a precarious, but unfaltering thread – she is not only moved, but she is equally captured by the need for change and will not let me down.

FORTY

I tried to act as normal as possible as I waited for time to tick to the 10th August. I tried to behave like the average expectant mother – the kind the PTB want to see. Openly lamenting my maternity leave was therefore not acceptable. On my last day, after Henry had given me an affectionate hug as I signed out of his lab, I was called in front of Dr Oldman and made to hand over all my research. This was a particularly pointless act as he is copied into everything I do in the lab anyway: as is Theo, whom I seem to have been eternally lumbered with if I want to have any kind of career. Dr Oldman has nonchalantly informed me, until such time as I am called in again, any thoughts I have regarding our research is to be communicated *through* Theo. I am sure some genius in the R&R had a good laugh to themselves when they suggested that as a test of my loyalty – and positively howled when the Board voted it in. I know it was voted on as Gee-Gee told me. She almost looked apologetic…almost.

Only the hope that I would soon be sticking a firm spanner in their stupid works stopped me from showing how annoyed I felt. I was careful not to seem totally indifferent though as I think Gee-Gee would have found that suspicious. Too much emotion and I could be disloyal…too little and I could be up to something.

Never has my Goldilocks impression been so important.

Everything has to be *just right.*

With that in mind I have spent my nine days of maternity leave being unremarkable. I have met with Kate in her lunch break, sat with Aunt Dora while she painted, taken evening strolls with Max, suffered my mother's fussing, and even had Kate, Tim, Ella, and Theo around for dinner one evening. Yesterday I meandered along the riverbank, resting every now and again, but I wanted to feel the calm from the ever-flowing waters – whilst doing my best not to dwell on the possibility I might never see it again if my plan goes pear-shaped. I have also been trying to keep up my fitness levels as much as possible. Dr Waller told me not to overdo it, but praised my interest in staying active. I know she was referring to the benefits of having stamina and muscle tone for labour – she has a point – but truthfully, I am more focused on the immediate possibility of needing to run away from a drone or guard. I obviously didn't mention that to her, especially not when she had me semi strapped to the chair to examine me and Little Drummer.

There is now nothing left to do but act on the plan I have spent so much time dreaming of. It is time to go beyond and see if I can fulfil Eve's dying wish to free Lily and reset the R&R…

Ella assured me that Max and me arriving at the R&R headquarters late at night would not set any alarms off. I have to believe that because, frankly, I have no way of testing if she is right. So, when the tram pulls up by our stop, Max and I get on, just as we would have had we been summoned.

In theory we are planning on being back in a day, but are prepared to be gone for two. 257 and Lily have a two-day window and Max has the week off 'so we can enjoy a little time alone before the baby arrives.' No one even suggested that time would be more useful to me (the wife and tired new mum), once the baby has arrived – you know, to actually help with the baby? I had to remind myself that their ignorance is currently useful to me and therefore I must refrain from rolling my eyes or voicing dissent.

Since starting maternity leave, I have had food items and ingredients delivered, not cooked meals. Food rations are normally pretty tight and although the PTB are still picky about my nutrition, ensuring I have the right balance for my combined needs, pregnancy does have the perk of extra rations and more or less unlimited options. "A happy baby starts in the womb – and that doesn't include starving," Dr Waller had gushed at me during one of my scans. Good, because I have been squirrelling supplies for three adults and have now stuffed them in a backpack. Would you believe the backpack was harder to come by? Max had to sign up to 'The Tent Appreciation Society' to get one. We didn't even know they existed, but apparently, they are excited to see us camping when Little Drummer is born. I'm excited to see if we're still free citizens when Little Drummer is born – so I guess we all have things to look forward to.

The tram stops outside the R&R headquarters. Max and I remain seated, firmly grasping each other's clammy hands. I am wearing a jacket over my t-shirt because I thought I may need it at night; however, at the moment I wish I had found a way to shove that in the backpack that Max is now carrying. We both opted for trainers, shorts, and a t-shirt – items to run in if need be. I did manage to pack a light summer dress though in case the stretchy waistline of my shorts fails to stretch enough. Max joked that my t-shirt is long enough that I could just wear that and no one would mind if I was half naked. I told him with a few expletives that I disagreed.

Ella said this tram would sit for five minutes before it leaves the R&R headquarters. As we wait for movement, doubt creeps in, yet I cling to Ella's confidence that she hacked into the correct manifesto, and it indeed states this tram is logged to transport goods north on the right-hand track. In a carriage further up, we hear what sounds like boxes being moved around. I am desperate to look, but we are both frozen in our seats. We must not draw attention to ourselves, so can only assume, hope, and pray that whatever the FARM has ordered is being loaded by either man or machine. It matters not which, just as long as neither spots us.

All goes silent and the light above the tram door turns from green to red. We are locked in. My heart races and I think I can hear Max's too as we sit in statuesque fear. The tram starts moving and I turn my head for a second as I attempt to confirm my united hopes and fears.

We are travelling north.

The lights of the headquarters are snuffed out as we head underground, leaving us with the dim tram and tunnel wall lighting. Max leers through the window and says: "Now. Change your code, now."

Without another word we scramble our sleeve barcodes via our different methods. I become Gee-Gee and Max, Dr Oldman – which is a frightening concept that I do not want to consider further.

Instead of speeding up, the tram slows to a crawl and as we edge forward a bright yellow light approaches – just like the line of light I watch on the 3D scanner at work. The light passes up the tram carriage, to the next behind us and then back to the front again, all the while examining who and what are within each section.

I can feel myself trembling and Max squeezes my hand tighter as we again pass through the scanning light. Suddenly the tram speeds up and hurries along its darkened track. We both gasp and pant for air as though we have just been pulled out of water.

I didn't even realise we were holding our breaths.

I say a silent prayer of thanks to Ella.

Her hacks got us through stage one.

FORTY-ONE

As the tram pulls to a halt, Max and I eagerly head for an exit, quickly realising unless we want to walk into a wall, the right-hand side is our only option. As we step onto the platform Max suddenly grabs my shoulders and I barely stifle a scream. Silently, he nods to a huge figure stepping into the first carriage and I am sure my blood curdles. Max and I stare at each other, trying to read each other's minds. Do we get back on the tram? Hide? Run? Run where?

We are both starting to panic. We didn't plan for there being anyone other than Lily or 257 on the platform and I cannot see anyone waiting to greet us.

Get back on the tram…that seems to be what we are saying to each other…

"Maia?" a voice calls as we take a step backwards. I turn to see a female figure stepping out of the shadows almost exactly where we were watching. She edges closer and as the dim light hits her glorious red hair I let out the biggest sigh of relief and smile.

"Lily?" I say walking towards her, extending my right hand.

Lily comes forward, takes my hand, and pulls me into a hug. It should feel weird, yet somehow, I feel like I am greeting an old friend.

As we step back from one another, I turn to Max and introduce him. Lily is slightly more hesitant for a moment, but Max's smile is enough to win over most people, and Lily is no exception. Max's grin drops however when the figure from the tram reappears in the doorway holding three large boxes – far more than any human could.

Lily follows our gaze and calls out: "257, have you got all the boxes? Come, come meet Maia and Max!"

"My apologies," 257 replies. "I must ensure the tram is emptied of goods before it departs. I can organise the contents later, but I cannot leave anything uncollected – not unless we want to deal with an extra security sweep anyway."

He puts the boxes down by a doorway – which on closer inspection is a door to a lift – and walks towards us, extending his hand just the same as I did to Lily. I hesitate for a moment, but instinct takes over and I offer my hand to the giant android. His shake is surprisingly light, his skin… his skin feels just like mine, except it is grey, steely grey, as is his entire body – or was, because as he holds me I watch his hand and arm absorb my slightly sun-tanned white skin tone.

I jump back.

Lily laughs…*properly* laughs.

"Weird, right? I screamed the first time…and the second."

"And the third I think," mocks 257.

I know I had a glimpse of the reality of a Shepherd when Lily took out 113 and I merged with 257's avatar, but now, seeing him in the 'flesh,' seeing exactly how big he is, talking to him as an individual being, even though he has no defining features…

I watch Max as he greets 257. His eyes are wide and his cheeks a little pale. If I, with my brief encounter, am underprepared to meet a Shepherd, Max is definitely justified in looking overwhelmed. He actually looks a little small. I think it is the first time I have ever thought that. Max is 6 foot 1 and although slim, has the natural physique of a sportsman. He does work out fairly regularly and plays sport for fun which has added to his strength and muscles, but even without this he is not 'small,' and never will be.

Today, however, he could be the equivalent of a cat meeting a tiger.

"It is a pleasure to finally meet you both in person," 257 says calmly. "Lilith and I have been anxious for today."

"Us too," I say, recovering from my shock sufficiently to answer.

"I suggest we get going. We can become acquainted on route, but I would feel happier if we were on our way."

"As would I," I reply.

Max and I are both wearing one of Eve's bracelets. I brought an extra one for Lily, so slip it off my wrist and pass it to her. Silently, she turns it over in her hand, nods, and places it on her right arm next to her watch – which, I notice with sadness, is not the same Hub citizen issue. The PTB really do remove all previous marks of identity when discarding people from society.

The tram suddenly comes to life and returns south. It is only now that I realise that the tram had no alternative. This is the end of the track. As that thought sinks in, I also realise that I have no option but to carry on as well. Without the tram, Max and I are at the mercy of 257's direction. There is no going back nor any point freaking out now.

"Where now? Does the lift take us out?" I ask.

"No, the lift travels into the farm, into the Dorm. We do not want to go there," 257 replies.

"But there are no other exits?" I say, looking all around me.

"What you can see and what is there, are two different things."

"Huh?"

"He says that a lot…or variations of it. I'd get used to it or it becomes really annoying," chuckles Lily. 257 turns his head to her and I am sure I hear him give a mock 'tut' in reply. How is that possible? He has no lungs, no mouth – no features at all! He is an almighty shadow – an amplified outline of man filled with code and electronics – natural laughter and tutting should not be possible, yet they do not sound recorded.

Ezra said the Shepherds have become more than anyone ever imagined possible and said they have responses, thoughts, and feelings beyond any programme or pure machinery. Something tells me I have only glimpsed what is possible and only scratched the surface of understanding Eve's greatest creations. I am sure Eve understood the Shepherd's potential for change, yet I am still sorry she didn't see it in person.

For seeing *is* believing.

Without another word 257 walks up to the wall at the end of the platform and puts his left hand flat against what I think is plaster.

The wall melts away.

Melts…

Lily steps forward first and without more than half a second's hesitation, she strides into the new walkway. She takes six or seven long steps before she glances left and right, spins round and laughs: "See! I told you there were more exits!"

"You did," replies 257 coolly.

"Just like I worked out this station was down here before you finally admitted it!"

"True. Although I didn't directly deny either, I just said neither were for you."

Lily looks triumphant regardless of 257's words. He shakes his head and turns to Max and me: "Shall we?"

I can only assume lifts are hidden in walls using the same technology as this secret doorway. As I walk past 257, I brush my fingers across the wall and find myself stroking my left arm to compare textures. 257 watches me and nods. "Yes, it is the same design. Synthetic skin can be trained and used in many, many ways. Hidden exits are just one of them."

I make an 'ah-ha' noise, but fail to construct any words in reply. With Max and me through, 257 removes his left hand and the wall encloses, once again, resembling any other boring, blank wall that I have ever seen. I doubt I will ever look at any walls the same again. This revelation certainly gives new meaning to the phrase 'the walls have ears.'

The corridor splits left and right. Right has a door with 'Q' on it. 257 turns left without hesitation.

"What is Q?" I ask following him.

"Quarantine," 257 says without stopping. "All new cadets spend two weeks in quarantine. Technically we're ruining that right now. Let's not dwell on that."

"We're aiming to build more than destroy," Lily says, taking 257's hand. He bobs his head in acknowledgement and they carry on walking hand in hand. The action is not missed by Max who raises his eyebrows quizzically as he squeezes my hand. "Huh," Lily continues after a moment's silence, "that explains why the pod arrives from underground...so I *was* trying to escape through an invisible door to the tram...*I was so close!*"

"Yet so very, very far," mocks 257.

"I'd hit you if I thought you'd feel it," Lily groans quietly. 257 chuckles.

The corridor ends and 257 again touches the wall with his left hand, causing a staircase to appear. A silent hush comes over us all as we climb the darkened stairs and my heart rate increases with every rising step. I am certain being eight months pregnant is not helping my speed, but neither is the trembling in my legs that I am struggling to control – which makes me extra grateful for Max's steady hand in the small of my back as he gently guides me forward.

When we reach the top of the staircase I look down and see nothing but darkness. Only minimal, dusky lighting triggered as we moved in the first place, but as each sensor times out, the light flicks off as though it is herding us upwards. 257 stretches his arm into the shadows towards a wall and then pauses.

"What is it?" whispers Lily, suddenly losing the lightness in her voice. For a moment I had thought her unbelievably relaxed. Now I realise it was a combination of adrenaline and trust in 257 that was cheering her tone. 257 pausing makes her uneasy – which instantly makes me petrified.

"Ezra wants a quick word," 257 says. "He'll be brief."

"Okay," Lily says, stepping back one stride.

"Hi." The voice comes from 257 but the tone is different: Ezra. We all say hello in unison. "Wow, well, there's no going back now. I just wanted to say good luck and reassure you that I'll watch secure news lines and deflect any security triggers around the farm as much as I can. I've already scrubbed you off the tram and platform feeds. Lily and 257 will be logged as arriving in the Hatchery first thing so the other Shepherds will not react to your absence. Maia, Max, your sleeves didn't trip the alarm on arrival…excellent."

"Indeed, we had help though. We'll tell you another time – when we get back, hopefully," Max says, shifting his weight on his feet. I think he wants to keep moving.

"Right…well, I cannot follow you beyond where you are now…not without leaving a trail for others to find. Once you start your music, all tracking should become impossible anyway. Thank you for giving me hope. May you find the key to change – we all desperately need it. Safe travels."

We all mutter our thanks as we watch 257's hands twitch slightly. I imagine Ezra pulling off the gauntlets in his avatar pod, allowing 257 full control of himself again. I remember how disorientated I was as I switched consciousness and consider asking 257 if it feels similar for him. Does he 'feel'? I felt touch when I was joined to him…but how do you define what it is to truly feel? Ezra once said Shepherds are sentient. The extent and depth of that seems incomprehensible, but so does swapping consciousness with an android – and yet I *have* done that. The very reason we are here, attempting this coup, is because 257 thinks and feels for himself. He perceives the need for a new, less repressive way…all because he has learnt to care for one beyond code and mission.

I look at Lily and she smiles reassuringly. She is nervous, there is no doubt of that, but as she re-steps towards her AI friend, I see undeniable confidence and trust. How long did that take to establish? I do not believe for a moment that came easily…that life as an exile came easily. She has the look of one whose youth and blossom was accelerated and squashed and has had to rebuild and reaffirm herself in a way that no one should. It is no wonder Eve howled the moment she realised her great-great granddaughter's fate.

257 places his left hand on the wall and more darkness opens up before us. But this darkness is not that of an unlit room, it is from nature's undocked glory. The air smells cleaner and fresher than anything I have ever smelt and it is silent. No drones – delivery, security, or transport – float by with their familiar hum and no floodlights illuminate the way. Everything is absolutely still and I am afraid to disturb it.

257 takes Lily by the hand and turns to Max and me: "Walking out of this door *will* trigger security. If I interfere it will cause more alarms than Ezra or even I can hide fast enough. We must trust Eve's code and just keep walking."

I gulp.

"Ready?" Max says, turning to me.

I nod and turn to Lily; her face is just visible in the last dregs of the stairway lighting. "Yes," she says, sucking her bottom lip as she motions towards the door. "I've spent a long time waiting to step beyond this fence, I'm not turning back now."

Without further hesitation Lily steps past 257 and Max and I follow. 257 waits until we are outside, removes his hand, and the doorway reverts to its disguise of a mere wall. In this light I cannot see what the structure is exactly, but it looks like a small, moss-covered hut of some description. Simultaneously music starts playing and I instantly recognise the piece despite the new variation that is being played in unison with the original.

"I call this 'Eve's Symphony, The Flight of the Revolution,'" 257 says with pride as he leads the way into the night.

FORTY-TWO

The only thing I hear as we walk is 257's music, but I can also see he wasn't wrong about security triggers as almost immediately we are flanked by two armed drones. I don't know where they were perched, but they waste no time in locating us, and their red eyes shine on us like angry, wingless birds waiting for the order to rain wrath down on us.

I gasp as the drones fly straight towards us. 257 simply repeats his earlier instruction to keep walking, but my legs threaten to fight against the order as instinct tells me to at least attempt to run. Just as my confidence is about to fail, the approaching drones turn from fiery red to mellow green and fly past like they were on a simple training mission.

Nothing to see here.

I shouldn't have doubted. I know that. I internally mock myself for not trusting in Eve's codes. They have never let me down before – fine, her answers and methods haven't always been straight forward, but she has always come through.

All of us release a long, deep breath, but no one speaks. Lily walks by 257's left-hand side, with Max and me to his right. We neither truly walk nor run, instead pacing out a quick step across unkempt grass. For now, I can keep up this speed, but my stomach feels increasingly tight and I am starting to doubt how many miles I can honestly maintain this rhythm.

"More drones are coming," whispers 257. "Continue as before."

I am about to ask how he knows when the darkness is broken by red streaks of light. These drones seem faster than the previous ones, yet as they come within range of our piano concert they also disarm and peacefully return to from whence they came. I really don't want to see what happens if someone meets one of these drones without paying homage to the bumblebee.

257 offers a torch, but also suggests it is better without one. Not wanting to risk being tracked by anything near or far, we choose without. The Hub is lit by solar lighting and although it is quite possible to find a genuinely dark spot, this kind of extended darkness does not really exist. I begin our journey by relying on the huge shadow of 257 to guide my every step, but the further we go the easier it is to walk without light. The darkness isn't truly pitch-black, even with patchy clouds, increasing trees, and no clear moonlight. Instead the world is a mix of husky, smoky greys, almost with colour, yet not quite.

I am so curious to see everything in full, splendid colour and yearn for the morning light to reveal the true beauty of being in the wilds beyond the fence. I feel like this entire expedition is a metaphor for my life. I now, for better and worse, know the wonders of the world are all around me, and although they are currently cloaked in a grey blanket, the darkness has lifted, fog challenges, but now my night has an end.

Dawn *is* coming.

That thought powers my steps and focuses my mind despite physical fatigue threatening my competence. "Do we have to keep up such a pace if the drones are not threatening us?" I pant after what I think is two miles.

"I don't know how far we have to travel," responds 257 without stopping. "If Tom2 is a long way off we need to go as fast as we possibly can or we'll not get back in two days."

"When will you know where we are going?"

"Eve said to play the music for three miles, right?"

"Yes."

"Drone security forces cover a three-mile radius from every Hub or R&R fence line, so it makes sense if Eve has left a trigger hidden beyond that distance. While within the bounds, her music scrambles surveillance, but once outside, it reveals a map."

257 sounds like he is enjoying this…like a detective who is waiting for the clues to unfold in front of him – or perhaps even like a child hunting for chocolate eggs. Either way, he sounds nothing like an inanimate calculator waiting for data to be keyed in. Unfortunately for my legs, he also doesn't sound like he is going to fatigue anytime soon either.

"Okay, but I cannot keep up this kind of speed for two days." I grimace. I hate admitting weakness. "Eight, or even six months ago, I might have easily run alongside you, but now—"

"Oh, my apologies," 257 says, stopping immediately. "I had calculated your fitness from your records and tried to adjust it to your condition now, but that is a difficult prediction to get right."

"You've seen my records?"

"Yes, I—"

"257 can access a lot more than you'd imagine," explains Lily. "The signal is but one after all."

"I see," I say, narrowing my eyes as I think. "Does the R&R know this?"

"No," says 257 shyly.

I chuckle. "Excellent. I'd suggest you keep it that way."

"My sentiments exactly," he replies warmly.

I wish Eve could hear this conversation.

"Would you like me to carry you?" 257 asks.

"Err…no, it's okay," I say, trying not to retreat a step when he steps towards me. Little Drummer kicks me hard and I grab my stomach. *Fine, I get the point.* "Not yet, anyway. I might have to take you up on that at some point though." Little Drummer kicks me again. *This child is going to be trouble.* Mum will be pleased.

"Just ask," 257 says, starting to walk again.

"Thank you." I turn to Max. "I don't hear you offering your services, my love?"

Max laughs.

"Why is that funny?"

"Because as much as I like the romantic, manly image of carrying my wife across the unknown wilds, I am not stupid," he says chuckling, "and I can happily see when one is better qualified for the task!"

I mock kick him (which takes more effort than I'd like to admit) as everyone laughs. Our mirth is cut short when a third round of drones suddenly whizz past us. This pair loop around for a second pass as though they didn't quite believe what they heard the first time. They hover over us for maybe thirty seconds — while we keep walking, looking forward, like we are just out for a stroll. I keep reminding myself that security drones react to running and their systems fire with the equivalent of human adrenaline. In their world, flight equals fight, and the results are simple.

The drones *will* win.

The music plays on and the drones keep listening. I look at Max out of the corner of my eye and see his face turn paler and paler. I think mine is red — both from retained breath and exercise.

Finally, it would seem the drones have heard enough as they make a sharp left and then disappear into the trees.

"What was that?!" asks Lily in a hushed, but relieved voice.

257 doesn't answer for a moment and I begin to wonder if he is going to. However, he suddenly tilts his head like a human does when they are considering something they are reading and says: "It makes sense, I suppose."

"What does?"

"Added security protocol on the extremities."

"Why?"

"It stops anything or anyone unwanted coming into the PTB's boundaries."

"But there isn't anyone left outside the Hubs?" Max says.

"Not now, there isn't. Immediately after the Fall of What Was, there would have been pockets of resistance…people who fell in between the cracks."

"Would have been or were?" Lily asks suspiciously.

"Were. I can see it in the records…hidden deep, but protocol for 'the unwanted' was written. They died out eventually…with a little help."

"The PTB killed them?" I ask.

"Depends on who they were, where they were. Some were left to live out their natural lives…others, in unsustainable or intoxicated places were 'put down' as a mercy – or so it says. Anyone who was deemed a threat were outright eliminated."

My stomach churns. "I suppose I shouldn't be shocked?"

"War is war. It is never pretty or pleasant. For either side. I should remind you that neither the PTB nor R&R started the world wars."

"But they did steer the course of the world afterwards. They still do."

"They made a path in an already heinous mess," says 257, "and forged a future to make amends for the global mistakes, horrors, and destruction."

"If you believe in *their* future, why are *we* here?" I ask, flapping my arms, suddenly doubting 257's motives.

"Because every plan needs review – and in its goal for restoration of Earth, humankind has forgotten its humanity. That is what we are here for, is it not? A kinder future?"

"A kinder future *for all*, yes."

"Now is not the time to doubt each other. Understanding the past is important, but getting to our goal would be nice, right?" says Max, looking eager to keep moving.

"Yes," says 257, "and we have nearly reached three miles, see?" 257 extends his right hand and a globe appears. Although he doesn't move, the globe spins, flattens, and zooms in to display an aerial map of where we are. Or at least

I am assuming it is where we are because I have never seen this area either by map or by eye before.

"Huh," says Lily, pointing her index finger at a break in the depicted woodland, "so that's the farm…"

"Yes," says 257, starting to walk again, "even then Eve and the Architect honoured the bee, laying all out like a honeycomb."

"Yes my sisters all saw that design – plus when we played laser quest we saw it on our maps."

"You played laser quest?!" Max says, failing to hide his amazement.

"Calm down, it's the one farm-wide game we play in a whole year. If you consider that outweighs everything else we go through – losing everyone and everything we knew; being enforced to donate eggs until we are given hysterectomies; to being told you're a failure; to having to forget all hopes and dreams for love, life, and family; to watching friends lose the will to live…to watch loved ones murdered—"

"No!" exclaims Max as Lily's voice falters. "My apologies, I was just surprised you had *anything* resembling fun."

"No more than I was to be fair," she replies, half smiling, trying to hide her tears.

"Ah-ha!" declares 257 as his map spins and golden sparkles flicker from left to right, round and round. We all watch as the map stops moving and suddenly a golden dot shines with a glowing and fading ring around it.

"Eve's cave of wonders?" I ask.

"Eve's cave of wonders," repeats 257.

"Is it really a cave?" Max asks.

"I doubt it. That isn't really the right location for a cave. We've a lot of fen and woodland to go through to get there. You must only walk where I do. We cannot take a direct path as here and here," 257 says pointing to his map, "there is still high radiation levels and that was a minefield…"

"So, it's pretty safe then?" I scoff.

"We're safe if you stay with me. Just remember I can see dangers you cannot."

"What we see and what is there is not the same thing," Lily smirks.

257 turns to her and chuckles, "Precisely. I told you you'd learn eventually."

"How *do* you see?" asks Max peering at 257.

"I have eyes, you just cannot see them."

"I wonder why Eve didn't give you features? Even my little food delivery drone has eyes…well, little cute lights," I say thoughtfully.

"I do not need them, they would be mere distractions for you. My eyes, my sensors – all my functions – are for me, for my collection and processing of data. I, and my siblings, have found other ways to communicate with other species. Given time, I think any boundaries built due to our differences can be broken and bridged by mutual regard and appreciation."

Lily nods at him and smiles.

"Okay," says Max as we walk, "so, what do you see now?" I can see curiosity is taking over Max's earlier trepidation.

"Other than three humans, trees, grass, shrubs, etc?"

"Yes."

"I see a map, coordinates…I see distance, I see all forms of topography. I see air, water, and soil reports. Where appropriate, I see contamination and levels of it. Normally I see other androids and robotics. I detect animals – of which there are several nearby now, none are harmful to you. I see the weather, both current and ahead. If I desire, I can access and see information and history on every object – including plans and projects to preserve, replant, or renovate each area."

"Even now without the data stream close?"

"The data stream is everywhere. It boosts everywhere. Encrypted or not, I see it, understand it. Only Tom2 I do not see. I see his location now, but not him. He is the grid, yet is off it. That is truly unique for any AI."

"Do all Shepherds see what you do?" Max asks.

"Mostly. We have the same code of capabilities, though we do not all evolve the same any more than humans do. I believe I have exceeded many of my siblings, but we all choose to reduce our 'reach' to stay in line with the calling of our kind."

"And your battery?"

"Is eternal. Not all have the Shep-X series battery, some need solar charging."

"So, you're like…an android god?"

257 chuckles.

"You could take over the world…"

"Humans," scoffs 257. "You're all so worried about being taken over, yet all you want to do is dominate each other. Judge as you wish to be judged. Live by example. Shepherds only want their place in the world – in a happy, harmonious, flourishing world. Our place is as Guardians of Earth, not leaders. We—*I*, wish to support not suppress. All species have the right to live here in peace and respect—"

"Being Guardians of the Earth, we have no greater right to be here than any other species," I say pensively remembering the words on Gee-Gee's painting.

"No greater truth can be said or lived by," says 257 with emotion. "The right to *just be* – to love, live, and die in peace – belongs to all. As does the responsibility of maintaining Earth in all her intended glory. The burden of ensuring that balance rests on every one of us, human and Shepherd alike."

Max and I look back and forth from one another. Even in the darkness I can see the white of his eyes as they boggle trying to fully comprehend what 257 is saying. Again, I look at Lily wondering how long it took to find the peace and familiarity that she now displays with him. How long it took for her eyes to no longer boggle upon hearing such a statement as 257 just delivered…for she *has* heard it before. Her face reads like a well-versed book – she knows the words and rests in their comfort and reassurance. She stepped beyond that fence in total confidence that he would not lead her astray or betray her.

I suddenly question why *I* didn't doubt him and just followed him into the night. I am afraid of his form and beyond baffled by the capabilities he claims…yet he is not frightening. Is that because Eve designed him and told me to make him my guide? Am I led by Lily's response? Is it blind faith that is disguised as ignorance? Or have I just heard enough of him to instantly know he is what he says he is?

He says he doesn't want to lead, but maybe Eve created the very thing we all need?

"Eve once told me the greatest leaders are not the ones who seek to lead…that makes you, 257, the perfect candidate."

257 stops and turns to me, softly chuckling. "I am honoured, but this is not my role nor my desire. I guide, not lead. There is a subtle, but essential difference. Humans must not leave their woes at the feet of others. We must all own the responsibility laid in front of us and step forward."

"Rise to every challenge?" I ask.

"As sure as the light of dawn is coming," says 257 as he starts walking again.

"Do you ever worry about the challenges though…the degree of burden? Does what an individual can cope with come into your consideration?" I ask, wondering the depth of a Shepherd's thoughts as well as questioning my own abilities.

"Of course," he replies instantly. "But Eve believed in our capacity to cope with the task – in *your* ability, or she would not have revealed what she did to you. No, I am sure, had it been any other way, had she thought the system perfect or justified, she would have taken her secrets to her grave."

257 is right. I know he is, but I am thankful he has the wisdom to inspire action when doubt knocks at my door – even if it's hard to breathe with the weight of so much repression on my shoulders. Eve's voice suddenly rings in my ears. I don't think she's ever said the words before, but I hear them in her voice anyway: *'Together we will shake it off.'*

I hope her steel and grit – her determination and passion – never leave me.

In the peace of the moment 257 stops playing The Flight of the Bumblebee, explaining it should no longer be necessary. I nod in reply and bask in the silence. As we walk I hear the odd scuffle in the trees as birds and creatures alike are surprised by our presence. The flash of white catches my eyes as rabbits retreat to their warrens and the hairs on the back of my neck tingle when an owl hoots in the distance and another replies. Having only previously seen and heard them in recordings, I cannot help marvelling at the sound of nature in its freest form.

It isn't cold, yet a gentle mist has started to fall and it adds to the wonder of what is around me as well as giving everything a slightly haunted haze. Tears for the hundredth, thousandth, time rise in my eyes as I am touched by so many emotions and I long for the peace of just being able to stand unhampered by anyone or anything and just listen.

"I've stood in the Hub woods, but never have I felt such a peace," I whisper reverently.

"Nor I," says Max.

"The farm woods come close, despite the fence," says Lily thoughtfully. "The bridge to nature is shorter, more obtainable. However ironic that might be."

"That appreciation of nature is what we strive for," says 257.

"I know." Lily replies. "We just shouldn't be dumped there like criminals – and those of us who technically are criminals are pushed to that point by power-hungry control freaks. R&R correction is not correction: it is utilisation. They need 'failures' to test on." She turns to me. "We are the mice for your laboratories."

I shudder. "Treatment of cadets in particular has been a great source of concern to me," I reply with feeling. "No one should be forced into the life you have been subjected to."

"No, they should not."

"For so long I stupidly thought we were a progressive society – that *I* was the odd one out. I didn't have the courage to look beyond my shell to see if others felt like me."

"That is the point," adds 257 coldly. "Never is the minority rule more efficient than when the many follow without daring to think outside their narrow bounds. Give enough freedom of self-expression so people do not rebel, make them think the path is laid with green and gold, and that any needs or issues – fertility for example – are at the forefront of governments 'to-do' list. Gay or straight, trans or non-binary, black or white, man or woman, old or young, the PTB appear to support and care for all. The rule is strict, but the people thrive. That way, when a few fall between the cracks or do not follow blindly and threaten the equilibrium, the masses thank the PTB for their removal, accepting whatever methods they deem necessary to maintain peace and prosperity. What happens to them is brushed over and life goes on."

"And the likes of Dean take pleasure in overseeing what happens next." I wince saying his name and Lily trembles. "The system plays into the hands of those with bitter and unsympathetic hearts…the hardened, selfish wannabe; the narcissist; the zealot; the one who 'needs to know', no matter the cost; the dictator. They all take centre stage."

"Do you think ethnicity or sexuality comes into selection or rejection?" Max asks 257.

"Are you asking if they are racist?" says 257.

"Yes. Are they?"

"No, I don't think so, not within the Hub system – not unless an individual does not walk the line, then I would describe the PTB and R&R thinking as 'disregarding' or 'intolerant' rather than outright racist. It becomes about fertility and re-trainability. Are they useful elsewhere? If yes, then the 'who,' 'what,' or 'whys' matter not. It is what *they* want the individual to contribute and how."

"It is a miracle anyone walks out of the FARM programme with a shred of sanity or self-worth," scoffs Max.

"I have hope for a better future now," says Lily. "My sisters and I, despite past methods and pain, we have hope." She pauses and I am not sure whether she wants to smile or cry. "Somehow joy and peace is possible. It is a sisterhood I didn't know I needed, but we get each other through. They don't know what we are doing here, but they will, one way or another. What we are doing now *has* to make a difference – a lasting difference for all."

I am glad Lily has some good memories from her time of imprisonment, but nothing is going to make up for the wrongs that she has endured. Not even if she managed to 'retire' the worst of the Shepherds. That was a dark, but necessary evil to make life less unbearable and opened up potential to the path that we now tread. I ask Lily how life has been since that day and her smile widens further, even if her eyes also well-up.

Yet more memories filled with mixed emotions. She did something bad, no, *we* did something bad, in order to spread a little goodness, but it doesn't mean we're not marked by it.

Some nights I still wake up hearing the gunshots that killed Mary and Peter. I didn't pull the trigger, or even ask for the trigger to be pulled, but I am haunted by it anyway. I knew Dean was going to be reduced to a vegetative state, but I still passed on information and facilitated Eve's meeting with Ezra.

But I do not regret it.

I didn't before. I certainly don't now. Not now that I can see Lily's face and hear how her sisters – not 'cadets' as the R&R would have them called, Lily says 'sisters,' so sisters is exactly how I shall think of them – how every single sister has felt the weight of 113's demise as a weight lifted. They still have the same mission, the remaining Shepherds have not forgotten their purpose, or what they are teaching the ladies for, but they *build-up*, not tear down.

Aim to reinvigorate, not depreciate.

Surely it is not such a difficult concept to grasp? Yet it has taken a very long time to even commence being put into practice. And it still doesn't excuse anyone being cast out there. For they are still cut off as though they have died and are made into eternal rejects of society – unworthy of human care and left to the mercy of androids.

And yet Lily smiles at her guardian, her Shepherd – she smiles at him with trust and doesn't balk at his touch. I am going to have to follow in her footsteps, for my body grows annoyingly tired and Max is looking at me with concern as my footsteps slow.

Sensing my laboured motion, 257 turns to me and tuts. I want to laugh, but fear also rumbles through me as he extends his arms to me. He waits for me to react and I nod my head. 257 steps forward and lifts me in both arms as though I weigh no more than cushion.

"I told you to ask," he says with what I'd imagine would be a grin if he had a mouth.

"She's stubborn," mocks Max. I make a mental note to remember that later when I am in position to retaliate. He catches my scowl in the dark and laughs. I'll remember that too. I laugh at myself…I really am getting grumpy and hormonal.

I cannot say I have been carried many times in my adult life, but I am not sorry Max declined the opportunity to carry me now. Even the strongest of humans would struggle to accommodate my belly and, with the best intentions, would still bounce me to such a degree I would almost certainly have to cling tight onto their neck to steady our way.

This is not the case with 257. Being in his arms is like being carried by an armchair, and as he strides through the trees it is as though he has paced our steps perfectly to reach the edge of the woods just in time to see the break of dawn over the horizon and it takes my breath away.

FORTY-THREE

The sun rose to the northeast, but we soon turned north, working our way through whatever path 257 deemed safest. Sometimes we walked in silence, sometimes we chatted. Conversation varied between farm life, the R&R projects, 257's abilities, our surroundings, and our immediate mission of finding Tom2. Two subjects in particular were noticeably avoided. The first is tucked neatly in my abdomen. I cannot hide my pregnancy, but on multiple occasions I have spotted Lily looking at my stomach sorrowfully and the guilt gnaws at me. I do not need to ask if she wanted children, it is painfully obvious she did – does. I want to tell her that our plan includes her freedom and that her family prospects can change, but a voice of caution rings in my ears. '*Wait,*' it says. '*Wait until you've met Tom2 before giving out promises and ideals. Walk before you run.*'

The second mooted subject surprises me more and I am not sure if Lily's quiet dismissal of her pre-FARM life was actually a dismissal or something else. As we walk across fields of unfettered grass and shrub land I question whether I should try again or leave it.

Feeling rested and wanting to feel the earth under my feet once more, I ask to walk again. Every so often I look back to the receding woodland that we spent so long walking through, each time being astonished at how vast an area it covers. I say woodland, but really it is a forest, and the centre seems truly ancient. The perimeter trees are still large and old compared to me, but they would appear to be part of an earlier R&R restoration project rather than pre-war specimens.

Now, with the forest out of sight, the trees are younger or sporadic and hedges line fields without restraining any passing wildlife. A herd of deer stops us in our path, and they stare at us as we stare at them. Both parties in awe of one another. They, because they are too young to remember the destruction and pain we caused their ancestors. We, because we are too young and so long restrained to have ever seen their like in anything other than a film or holographic book.

Even 257 stands to attention.

I don't know why I say 'even.' Has he not already, in a very short period of time, proven his respect and admiration for nature – for all living creatures? Surely, I should do the same? Continuously amazing as it may be, arguing he is not alive in his own way is as silly as denying the sunshine on a clear summer's day.

A day like today.

A bright day made for revelations.

All nature seems to agree as there is no fog, the mist lifted with the sunrise, and the temperature increases with each passing hour.

When we reach another cluster of trees I am grateful for the shade as well as 257's suggestion of resting. As I lean against an oak tree, I think about my favourite, mighty oak tree that stands by the river and consider the surrounding Hub flora and fauna compared to what I have seen today.

"The Hub has trees and plants everywhere, yet now I feel like we live in a display case and out here lives the nursery, the school, and the wilds all in one."

"In the time of Henry VIII, it is said that the trees were so numerous a squirrel could jump from tree to tree from south to north without touching the ground," says 257. "We still, even after a hundred years, have a way to go to restore that principle, that possibility, but that is the aim."

We sit in silence while we eat and drink some of my stashed food. Lily turns over a PTB produced energy bar, seemingly reluctant to open it, and I softly say: "I guess it has been a while since you've seen one of those?"

Lily quietly scoffs.

"What *do* you eat on the farm?"

"Home produced meals mostly. We grow what we need and have very little brought into us."

"We teach self-sufficiency," explains 257. "The idea is that once graduated as Ambassadors of Earth they sustain themselves with little or no intervention from the R&R."

"And what do Ambassadors do exactly?" asks Max.

"Preserve, conserve, observe, and restore beyond. Live free of fences and reminders of failure." Lily pauses, then adds: "And death."

"You cannot escape death," I say, not meaning to sound unkind.

Lily stares at me. "No, you cannot. It haunts me, but *beyond* is a stage further than *before*. The degree of separation can only help."

I want to ask more, but I can feel my lips and chin trembling. I do not want to cry when I have no doubt her trials have been harsher than mine. It is not a competition, I know that, but I see her pain as a living example of what mine could have been had Gee-Gee not tempted Theo away with the promise of a career, knowledge, and power and I cannot shake that notion from my mind.

Lily is my split mirror, my sliding door, and I am sorry for it.

Gee-Gee would take that as me also being grateful for her actions, but she is wrong. One action doesn't save another. One 'mercy' doesn't right a string of wrongs.

257 interrupts my thoughts, "*Before* is a difficult subject."

"It is a vetoed subject," Lily interjects.

"Vetoed?" I ask.

"Yes, moot, forbidden." Lily scoffs. "I actually disagree with that. The repression, not speaking about our lives *before* our sisterhood, is really hard to bear…we're working on that, but apparently it is a harder habit to shake than I thought."

257 reaches for Lily's hand and gently squeezes it. "Moving forward is the key to healing, but I see the importance of acknowledging the past – we all do now, largely thanks to you, Lilith. Remember that."

Her right hand still hidden in 257's giant grip, Lily chews on her bottom lip, and cups her free, left hand over the top. She looks up at his face as though she sees his eyes, holding the gaze of a trusted friend and nods, smiling for a moment before she gulps and turns to me: "Are my parents all right?" she asks with a wavering voice. "Do you know?"

Instantly I am very glad Max had thought to ask Ella about Lily's parents last week. "We asked Ella, our friend who helped us get here, to look them up. They are well, yes, they are well."

"They haven't been punished?" Lily whispers as tears flow.

Suddenly, I understand. I should have earlier. She hasn't asked because she is afraid to know. Of course, she is. Her boyfriend was killed and she was made to watch. "No, no they haven't. They miss and love you very much, I have no doubt, but they are okay. They work, they live in the same home, no one has hurt them—"

Lily bursts into a bout of sobs and it makes my heart ache. I look to 257, silently surprised he never answered this fear for her because he clearly has access to data records that the R&R don't know about.

"She wouldn't allow me to look," 257 says as though he read my mind. "I have always kept my 'intrusions' to a minimum to avoid detection, especially as 113 and Dean disapproved of my regard for cadet feelings and blocked my attempts to speak on Lilith's behalf."

"Peace reigns if the boat isn't rocked," says Max.

"Something like that," replies 257.

"Or ignorance is bliss," mutters Lily. "I killed Jay, I couldn't cope if I did it again, I—"

"*No. You. Did. Not*," cuts in 257. "We have had this conversation. Ezra told you—"

Lily nods, but shakes her head at the same time. "I know, but—"

"But nothing!" I jump in and Lily looks at me earnestly. She badly needs to believe her actions didn't kill the one she loves. "Dean and 113 just took advantage of Jay joining a union. They were called terrorists on the news, but all they wanted was a voice for the people. 113 was only granted permission to show you as it was happening anyway. I am so sorry for it all, but you did *not* kill Jay."

"But he wouldn't have been watched if it wasn't for—"

"Falling in love is *not* a crime."

"113 would disagree." Lily laughs, but without any real humour. "I failed at what he thought was my purpose in life. Even before he heard me mock him, he hated me and thought I represented humanity's greatest weaknesses. He said I needed to learn, put the past behind me, and focus on being useful. I know he was evil, but I still think my actions caused—"

"*None* of this is your fault."

"I have tried telling her that," says 257. "My life's work is guardianship and I fear it took me too long to realise the extent of damage caused by—"

"It's not your fault either," says Max. "We all need to stop looking for fault. That is the very ideal the PTB and R&R thrive on. Fault, blame, and self-loathing. A grateful, repentant population serves quietly. We are here to finally make some noise."

The twinkle in Max's eye and the twisted, cheeky smile makes me want to kiss him. Kiss him and laugh at the R&R. Their matchmaking skills are too good – only they didn't match us to march against them.

But that is exactly what we are going to do.

Are doing.

As I give in to temptation and kiss my husband, 257 leads us through the trees as they clear. Suddenly Max's eyes widen, but not through the power of my kiss (however wonderful), instead, the sight of buildings catches the attention of the architect within. As we approach the moss and bramble ridden old houses, more buildings come into view and I feel like we have truly walked into a ghost town.

There are roads, but not good ones. Grass and weeds have ripped through the once smoothly laid pathways and walls have tumbled. Houses stand in various degrees of grandeur and dilapidation depending on how kind war and time have been to them. I don't suppose this would have been a large enough place to be a target for a nuclear bomb, instead just acting as target practice for a smaller, less toxic (though no less deadly if hit), method of destruction.

The houses are made of flint – or so Max is now telling me. Garden gates have rotted away, metal signs are rusted, and plastic bins poke through in places where hedge or bramble have left a degree of light. But no rubbish blows, no clothes hang from wire lines that have remained intact, and no children swing on the frames in the gardens.

Suddenly I want to abandon the mission and explore. I can see Max is as keen as I am, if not more so. Lily looks eager and pensive simultaneously and I am about to ask if she is okay when I hear her whisper to 257: "Is this where Emilia died?"

"No," he replies. "That was west of here, a similar village, but not this one."

Lily nods and wipes a tear from her cheek.

"They poisoned her, didn't they?" 257 pauses and groans, but does not answer. Lily continues: "I have thought about it for a long time. An area of such intense radiation, that close

326

to the farm, wouldn't be safe for cadets. If we were infertile, you wouldn't care…but our physical health has always been paramount, even if our mental health suffers. Egg harvests and research is only worthwhile from the healthy. So, although Emilia walked for days, and possibly did encounter nuclear pollution, I don't think she walked far enough to die that quickly from radiation."

"She didn't," 257 says sadly.

"It was the food 113 gave her?"

"It was."

"Because cadets that rebel must be seen to die. Hope for a future without the R&R cannot be tolerated."

"It cannot not… *Until now.*"

FORTY-FOUR

We walked through the village, exiting down the remnants of a road which faded into grassland and followed 257 into another village that is in almost identical condition to the first. 257 says many settlements have been dismantled by robotic restoration teams, yet others have been left for historical value or for future projects. The two villages we have seen certainly come under the 'left' category. Whether they will ever be altered again I do not know, but part of me hopes they won't.

Late morning, we wander out of the village, heading out towards another cluster of trees. I expected to see nothing but woods and grass yet here, amongst the trees, is a cute flint cottage that could come straight from one of Eve's photographs. This cottage does not have a rotten or wasted fence. No windows are smashed and no walls crumble into ruins. The garden is as tidy as any in the Hub, roses climb the flint walls and insect houses and flowers straddle the roof as well as adorn multiple ornaments that are placed in the garden: the most impressive of which is an extensive apiary. But it is not the sound of bees that sends chills and thrills simultaneously though us all, it is the music playing.

Eve's music.

At first, I look to 257, thinking it is coming from him and he has sensed drones approaching, but then my ears adjust and I realise it is actually coming from within the cottage.

"My map has gone," 257 says, chuckling.

"Well, there is definitely a cottage in front of us," says Lily. Her tone is somewhere between sarcastic and fearful.

"Yes, I can *physically* see that, but it is not on any map," tuts 257. "A drone could fly directly over this place and it would just report unremarkable woodland."

"That is the same as when we played the Flight of the Bumblebee before, isn't it?" I ask.

"Yes, only *I* could still see everything then because I was the one playing it."

"Huh." A code hiding code still confuses me, never mind the androids. Though to be fair, 257 sounds more fascinated than confused.

Max, Lily, and I exchange anxious, excited glances as 257 walks up to the garden gate. He reaches to open it, but before he touches the metal frame an alarm blares, drowning out the music and a voice screams 'HALT' on repeat.

Motionless, 257 waits and the three of us cowardly stand behind him. Numerous bees swarm around us as the front door of the cottage opens and a jet-black Shepherd strides towards us and stops with regimental precision a metre short of the gate. I don't know what to look at first, but suddenly the dark form glows as red eyes appear on his face. This would be frightening enough, but the bees also light up, streaming red dots all over our bodies. It only takes a second for me to work out what the dots are.

Targets.

The bees contain tiny laser guns and they're quite happy to sting us should the Shepherd instruct them to – and I doubt any antihistamine will help.

We all gasp and our brains are probably telling us all to run – mine certainly is – but our feet have frozen to the spot like useless lumps of clay. 257 is totally silent and I wonder what calculations he could possibly be running. He stands square and we wordlessly wait for either him or the dark Shepherd to make their move.

"If you wish to converse with the universe, I suggest you speak the words I seek," says the Shepherd in a deep, unfriendly voice.

257 and Lily turn to me and Max squeezes my sweaty hand. Eve gave me a message, but I didn't question if the code is 'Eve says' or 'I think'… All eyes blaze through me and I feel the perspiration under my arms increasing into a flood. There is no time for questions now: "Eve thinks Tom is a fool, but loves him always," I say, closing my eyes, bracing in case I got it wrong.

The deep voice sniggers. "And don't I know it! Enter, it is a pleasure to meet you."

I open my eyes to see the Shepherd step forward and open the gate as the bees fly away into the trees. The elaborate metal frame swings open with a slight creak and he holds his left palm to 257 in a 'halt' salute. 257 doesn't hesitate in offering his hand and they wordlessly stand palm to palm. I look to Lily, and she whispers: "That's how Shepherds communicate."

I feel my eyebrows lift and eyes widen as I nod my head, but I do not move. Suddenly the Shepherds' fingers curl around each other's hands and they embrace affectionately. 257 mutters, "Brother," and I want to cry. I have heard him refer to other Shepherds as 'siblings:' I suppose that makes the original Shepherd his big brother, it just isn't a concept I have ever considered before. Lily, Max, and I respectfully watch their truly unique, yet tender meeting.

I feel a little silly, but decide it is better to be sure, so as they step back I cautiously ask: "You are Tom2, right?"

"I am," he says with an invisible smile. "I am honoured to meet you all, it has been a long time since a human has walked through this gate. I wondered if it would happen again, but if Mother Eve has sent you to me, then it is time to act. Come in, come in."

The cottage is small but tidy. Any resemblance of its past life as a home has been cleared out and been replaced by laboratory equipment – the only exception being a grand, antique chair that sits by the front window. The wood is well varnished and the red upholstery is perfectly preserved, but it also looks well used. The thought of a Shepherd sitting and literally watching the world tick by is a curious one. Though to be honest, so is a lone scientist-cum-android in the middle of a wood on the edge of an abandoned village. If I learn nothing else from this trip, I now know not to assume anything about androids, their capabilities, or interests.

"You look surprised?" Tom2 says to me. "I would think out of the three of you, you would be best qualified to recognise my work here?"

"I can see you are testing on the environment around you – soil, water, and plants?"

"Correct," he says, sounding pleased.

"But I was under the impression you, erm, had – have – a different purpose…or mission?" I am also realising I do not know the correct term for a Shepherd's life calling – or if they mind if you get it wrong.

"What you see and what else there is, are two different things." Tom2 chuckles.

Lily laughs and groans. "Are all Shepherds naturally apt at such phrases?"

"Only the important ones," mocks 257, and Tom2 laughs with him.

"Okay, but what else *is* here?" asks Max curiously.

"I have my work here in the lab. To the unsuspicious I look like a research post, to the suspicious…well, thanks to my musical bees I look like no more than trees, but if challenged, they *will* protect my secrets." 257 nods and a little chill goes through me as I remember being surrounded by their angry lasers only moments earlier. Tom2 walks to the interior wall as he continues: "However, my lab is but a hobby and the Watchtower, my cave of wonders, is…" He leans against the wall with his palm stretched out. "*Here.*"

I gasp as the wall morphs into a lift entrance. "Are there any walls that you lot don't hide lifts in?!"

"*That* would be telling," chuckles 257.

* * *

Downstairs is truly a cave of wonders. The enormous grey room has no furniture other than a matching pair of antique red chairs that are identical to the one upstairs. These chairs have no glass windows to sit next to, but it is still quite possible to sit and watch the world go by as there are more virtual screens, projectors, and holograms than I know what to do with.

Tom2 stands in the centre of the room, placing his feet into two carved-out grooves in the stone floor. His jet-black body flashes and streams colour around the room like a disco ball. Images race and reams of video, maps, graphs, and light waves around the room like forks of lightning in a storm – and Tom2 is the eye.

When Gee-Gee took me to the R&R headquarters and showed me videos from across the globe I was impressed by the enormity of it all. Live drone and camera feed from thousands, probably millions, of surveillance devices across the world all coming together to give a picture of life elsewhere is pretty impossible to take in quickly – if at all. But here Tom2 seems to have and master it all. The images slow and scenes from known places flick by like pages from a book. Suddenly, videos of Max, Lily, and me at different ages circulate us in holographic bubbles. We exchange glances of mixed astonishment and bewilderment. I am watching a film of my life, but at the moment, I desperately want to look forward, not back.

In another flash, the images change from us to the wider world. At first, I think the images are old like the ones we are made to watch at school. The archive footage of war and its aftermath is eternally etched into every child's mind, but this is not just historic footage, it is current. A drone is flying through an abandoned city, now semi-wild, but untouched by any restoration teams. A radiation count appears as if to answer my unspoken question to why nothing has been done. There is nothing *to* do. Not yet…not for a very, very long time.

Human destruction lives on. Not all scars have healed.

Our penance is not over.

The picture changes again as Tom2 flicks channels without moving. Rolling hills and unspoiled natural beauty surround us. Flowers and grasses wave in the breeze, birds fly, and animals graze without mutation, pollution, nor fear of anything greater than the natural order of Mother Nature herself. My eyes had already filled, but now they spill over. The films may be silent, but the story is loud and clear.

"Can you see everything?" asks Lily in awe.

"Everything, past and present," replies Tom2. "I am the guardian of code, the record of what was, the seer of what is. I do not intervene, I simply observe and collect data from all over Earth. All signal flows through me, yet it doesn't know I exist. You must honour and respect this principle, even if you wish to use its power. The Powers That Be and Real Revolution work with the right aim at its core. The UNE has saved and restored Earth and its inhabitants where others only destroyed. Mother Eve believed that, even when challenges raged around her. However, she also had the wisdom to build this secret backup post, always providing an alternative way should one be required. The fact you are here shows that time has come and a review is necessary—"

"Do you have any suggestions?" I ask.

"That is not my purpose. All I will say is it is not the core that needs to change, it is those wrapped around it. They are the ones who have warped the mission statement and lost what it is to truly care for others beyond selfish desire and short-sighted want. I have seen that time and again. If you are here to straighten the rule you have the greatest burden and privilege known to humanity."

"I—we, are here to try," I reply with a lump in my throat, wishing our exact plan was clearer.

"'We' is all well and noble," says Tom2, "for nothing of merit is ever done by one alone, yet all parts need a head. Eve believed that to be you."

"Why does she get to decide?"

"The Arbitrator may have retired, but she knows as well as any the qualities needed to fill those shoes. The current one is watching you closely, whether you realise it or not."

"What?!" I don't know which part of his sentence to unpick first. Tom2's only response is to tilt his head and wait for me to ask a more specific question. I may as well start at the top: "Eve was the Arbitrator?"

"I don't know why that surprises you. The Arbitrator's identity has always been hidden from the masses. Tom openly ranked above her, but they were a team in all aspects and chose to elect Eve as the Arbitrator – until Tom died that is. Then she stepped, or rather, was *pushed* down, although she stayed in her other role as Head Engineer. Eve had always developed many, many things before declaring them, but after she realised how many knives were poking her in the back she advanced this place from a mere background filter to the centre of everything – and expanded her coding system while she was at it."

"And made you?" Max says.

"And made me," replies Tom2. "When Ray was killed she lost all confidence in R&R personnel, but still hoped the mission would not falter." He turns to me. "Do you remember the R&R motto?"

I pause before answering. Not because I don't remember or understand the question, but because everything he says makes sense and it takes a moment to absorb it all. In her final message Eve said Tom2 would 'know the rest.' She really wasn't kidding. He is the final piece in this puzzle. I take a deep breath and say: "Being Guardians of the Earth gives us no greater right to be here than any other species."

"Do you agree to abide by this as long as you shall live?"

Eve's voice again sounds in my ears and her words repeat on my tongue: "Real revolution requires regular regeneration; the Earth deserves her rightful restoration. Now and always… So, yes, *I do*."

"Then I am yours to command. Maia Rivers, leader of the new world, how may I assist you?"

"To light the darkness of repression I need the power of light."

"You need to control the network of the world."

"I do."

"Do you like tongue twisters?"

I laugh. "I've been taught a few helpful ones to date."

"Excellent, I know one you'll love."

FORTY-FIVE

By mid-afternoon I am exhausted and can talk no more. Little Drummer feels like a rock in my stomach and I am glad to lean back into one of the big red chairs with Max's arms wrapped around me. Lily asks Tom2 to show her the farm and smiles when she sees her friends peacefully at work. She trembles when Tom2 switches to feed of her graduated friends, and it takes her some time to find a voice to describe their stories. As she talks about the women of the FARM programme, I am again struck by how much they have had to mentally overcome thanks to the current regime.

However, it is also impossible not to see that 257 will support Lily through anything. He stands behind her on unwavering guard. Some might call him oppressive, maybe it could feel that way, but he doesn't touch her unless it is to support and he doesn't force her to say or think anything. He is just eternally on standby, ready to catch her should fall. He really has evolved beyond machine and code.

Maybe one day that will be a commonplace realisation, but for now I will continue to marvel at it. I look over to Tom2 and wonder where he is on the Shepherd spectrum. He is the eldest and has free access to the world's data, so I can only conclude he is the most developed, but he has also stayed wholly on mission. His regard for Eve and Earth has not sent him onto his own course, or is that just his choice?

Choice…

The right to choose.

"Maia, are you listening?" Max jigs his legs and shakes me back into reality. Some things never change and my ability to lose myself in thought is definitely one of them. "I thought you'd fallen asleep on me then," he chuckles.

"Sorry, not quite. What were you saying?"

"257 says we are near the sea and if we'd like, we can make a quick detour?"

"Really?" I ask sitting up.

"I propose we rest here overnight and leave first thing," says 257. "We will still arrive back in good time and will need to wait for dark to return and start the next stage."

I have longed to see the real sea so take very little persuasion, even when Little Drummer rocks and rolls in my stomach. We walk out of the cottage into the glorious sunshine and Lily almost skips down the path. If I weren't pregnant, I might join her.

Tom2 walks us to the gate after passing directions to 257, but declines to come with us. "Surely the signal will record even when you're not here?" Lily pleads. Her peace with her Shepherd has quickly extended to his brother. I am fast losing my outright fear, but am equally happy to walk with just one robotic giant at a time.

"I am the signal…or its satellite. The signal will still arrive here, but I maintain order. I choose to stay. It is my burden and honour."

Max looks curious. "So, it isn't the cottage that streams all data? It is you?"

"It is both, and neither."

"I was imaging a giant satellite or power station—"

Tom2 chuckles. "So many look for mass when it is quality that counts. The Watchtower receiver could fit on the tip of your finger. I and the cottage just live around it. Nanotechnology is far more versatile. Even the battery that powers me is minute."

"So, you live here alone always? Are you not lonely?" asks Lily. This is another concept I have never considered. "Why didn't Eve make an Eve2?"

I softly scoff at the thought, but startle when Tom2 answers: "She did."

"Where?" I ask, looking around for signs of a second Shepherd.

Tom2 chuckles and calls, "Evie–weavie–weavie!" in a surprisingly high-pitched tone. The hedge rustles and something orange moves through the leaves. Totally forgetting what wildlife is native to the area, I am about to question if I need to grab a stick or something when a fluffy, ginger cat appears. "Eve said if – *and I quote* – 'If I'm going to live forever, it may as well be as a cat.'"

I laugh so hard I cry. These are happy tears though. Eve always said Smoggy and Squash had the right idea for life and I can picture her laughing heartily as she designed a cat-shaped companion Shepherd. Eve2, the cat, walks over and rubs herself around my legs. I crouch down and stroke her head, and she purrs. I chuckle again as the purr reaches my ears as it is not the standard purr a normal cat would give, it is a variation of Eve's 'hmmphh' – her immortal chuckle to the world. I want to pick up the cat and never let it go.

Max squeezes my shoulder and I turn to him. He smiles and I know he understands. I look over to Lily and pity her because she never got to know the woman that joined our paths and led us beyond the fence.

As we walk I ask if she wants to know about her great-great grandmother, the woman, not just the engineer, founder, arbitrator, recluse – or whatever title you want to give her. The Eve I came to know and love. The woman that sat in silence to protect those she loved, even when they turned from her, and who spoke out when the promises of others were no longer upheld.

Lily looks unsure for a moment, but whispers, "I didn't dare ask, but yes please, tell me all."

And so I do. It feels good to unreservedly talk without fear or repression, to pass on words that I know Eve herself would have wanted to say to Lily had life given the opportunity. It must be difficult to hear parts, but Lily deserves to hear the history of her family.

No longer is *before* a subject only machines can discuss. Teach the past to understand the future – that applies to all parts of life, *not* just the elements that the PTB want to indoctrinate us with.

Tom2 said it wasn't far to the sea, but I am starting to regret the extra excursion as my legs cry out to me. We walk into another village filled with flint houses and 257 tells us to stand in the street without explaining why. Max starts to follow him, but jumps back as a garage door flies open and an engine starts.

"What the hell?!" Max exclaims as 257 appears sitting on a floating device. "Is that—is that a hovercraft?"

"It is!" shouts 257 like a child with a new toy. "Get on!"

Lily and I exchange glances and shrug our shoulders. It isn't the weirdest thing I've seen today, so why not?

"Why haven't we used one of these before?!" Lily shouts into 257's unseen ear.

He laughs. "I didn't know it was here until Tom2 told me!"

"Why not keep it nearer the cottage?" I ask, rubbing my tired back.

"Protection. If one is found, the other is not. Tom2 has little use of it, but long-ago Eve used to travel with it apparently. Leaving it here meant she wouldn't leave a trail."

"I thought no one comes out here?" Max says.

"In theory, no. But why risk it? Plans and projects change. Drones roam. Humans meddle."

We sit in silence with only the gentle hum of the hovercraft in our ears and the wisp of a fresh breeze in our faces as we leave the ruined village, zip across fields and a new landscape opens up. The air suddenly smells of sweet, damp earth as we travel over marshes and past shrubs I have previously never seen. I am transfixed by the sight of hundreds, maybe thousands of birds as they wade in pools and waterways. The vision of wildlife moving in its rightful order is truly humbling and just when I think I have no untouched fibres left in my body, the horizon changes and my breath is taken away as I finally see the sea.

I stand on a beach watching seabirds circle above, seals sleep in the distance, and the rolling waves crash against the shore. The sound is possibly one of the most majestic things I have ever heard or am likely to hear. The recordings in the virtual gyms are nothing compared to this. The sand and pebbles in the Hub are but poor comparisons and the smell of fresh, salty seawater cannot be truly mimicked, no matter how brilliant or close those programmes come. I reverently walk up to the water's edge and take off my shoes. All three humans stand in awe of the immense expanse before us. I let out deep, diaphragm rattling breaths as I attempt to compose myself, but in the end, I let my salt join that of the sea.

As the tide edges closer, I startle at the touch of the water and step back. I desperately want to go in, but my fears frustrate me. The tide of life has been so long tamed, it is hard to break free – even if I know no one can truly reign the spirit any more than they can leash this water.

While I procrastinate, Lily steps forward and so does Max. Once in, they keep walking until they stand up to their waists in water and turn, calling to me to join them. 257 stands on the shore with me and I look to him, chewing my lip.

"I will not let harm come to any of you," he whispers and holds out a hand. Without thinking I take his hand and grip it like someone sealing a bond. Not the bond he has with Lily, that is unique, I know that, but as a friend, ally, protector. Someone to trust in all circumstances. Not some*thing*, some*one*. I could have argued I knew that before this moment, but I would have been wrong, a part of me would have doubted it was real. But here, beyond any kind of human fence or computer programme, he is real…the sea is real…and I choose to trust him as an equal.

We step forward and keep walking until we reach the others. When the euphoria quells I may attempt to describe my feelings in this moment, but it is not just the thrill of the sea and its combined power and freedom that invigorates me...it is the liberation of my soul. I have spent my entire existence being told life is set a certain way, that there are certain things I'll never do, and everything I can do is restricted, unwavering, and predetermined. Standing here, I finally push the last of these doubts aside and see the way is anything *but* predetermined – that the possibilities are in fact endless, and we can all be as free as these rolling, unfaltering waves.

FORTY-SIX

Unable to sleep any longer, I wake up before dawn. Little Drummer is in full swing and my bladder is so squeezed I wonder how I'll hold anything in on our journey home, even if I visit nature's bathroom regularly. I tell myself Little Drummer is just reacting to all my activity, but I also know everything feels 'different' today.

Today I implement a future into which I want my baby born.

The world is not a petri dish for the R&R, no matter how noble they think they are.

I happily dreamt of the nature reserve, in particular the seals that we saw yesterday. 257 said they breed on those beaches in the winter and I would love to see that, but he also told me seals, like so many species, were previously pushed out by human activity so they only had a few safe places where they could live. The thought of history ever repeating itself is depressing and clouds the warm haze I feel from having had a sweet dream. Showing humans the wider world cannot be at the expense of any other species. We have no greater rights, only greater responsibility. After all, we are *all* Guardians of Earth. Call us civilian, leader, cadet, Shepherd, Ambassador of Earth, Guardian – whatever you like, the name is immaterial. It is the point that counts.

257 remains on the top floor with Lily and Max as they sleep and I make my way downstairs via the lift. As I curl up in one of the red chairs Tom2 gives me a synthetic fingerless glove. Slipping it on, it seamlessly wraps around my hand in a fashion similar to Max's, only without the length up my arm – leaving a separation between it and my sleeve. With so much synthetic material moulded to my left arm I wonder if my skin will remember what it feels like to be open to the air ever again. Tom2 watches me put on the glove and then says: "I call it 'The Hand of the Shepherd.' It will translate your spoken code into mechanical law. If you do not activate the glove first, the code will be simple words. But together, the codes will join and all data driven machinery will switch off and remain so, waiting for your command."

I chuckle quietly. Eve was nothing if not cautious. I must collect *every*thing in order to do *any*thing. I need all the help I can get. I need humans and androids on my side, not just answering my commands, but guiding and supporting me. I will not be a lone dictator.

"What about the Shepherds? What about you?"

"Ah," says Tom2, "no, I am separate. Shep-X series batteries run themselves. You'll control the system Shepherds link to, but not me, I have protection against any and all external intervention."

"Good… And 257?"

"He connects to the R&R network, so yes, you'll control him too."

"Can you disconnect him from their network?"

"Why?" Tom2 bobs his head when I don't answer immediately. "You wish to give 257 his complete freedom?"

I hesitate for a second, but I know in my heart he deserves to be separate from anything I do. He has the freedom of thought, let him have the complete freedom of choice too.

"Yes, I do. I don't believe it will change his dedication, but it seems right to let him decide for himself. From what I understand he reduces his capacity to hide Shepherd development from any engineer who may comprehend and fear their abilities. I don't think he should have to do that. The fact he can do more, but has chosen not to is testament enough of his character. Can you unclip his wings or not?"

"I can."

"Excellent." I hold out my right hand and Tom2 shakes it with a firm grip whilst making a 'mmm' sound – a sound of approval I believe.

Tom2 runs through the two codes once more, making sure I have committed the words to memory, and concludes his lesson by giving me a pep talk, reminding me of my point, my purpose. I absorb his words, but he need not worry, my purpose is now firmly embedded in my soul.

I will not forget it.

"Just be careful when you say both codes though," Tom2 says, reaching out to me in earnest.

"What do you mean?" Suddenly, I am wondering if there was a point to him giving me the pep talk after all.

"Be sure you're ready for the consequences of claiming all – of blacking out *all*."

"Okay, but that is what I want, right?"

"Yes, you do. All I mean, all I ask is you time it right, not that you do not do it – only that you remember the consequences of a total blackout. Computers will freeze everywhere—"

"I know that, that is the point." I can feel myself getting irritated.

"Yes, but with them *all* generators will fail, all security will cease, and all systems freeze – all hospitals, all storage of samples, operation rooms, pods… *All.*"

I slowly close my eyes as a cold chill rises through my body and I feel physically sick. I understand what he is saying. The mission is important, but to achieve success I have to be willing to potentially kill…to maim and kill. Young and old, sick and incubating…shit…shit…shit… Kate's baby. Will he survive a sudden pod power cut? He is nearly ready to be born, but will the pod release him so he has oxygen quick enough – or will he be brain damaged or suffocated in the very contraption that has sustained him?

"You understand what I am saying?" Tom2 says softly.

"Yes…" I pause and shake my head. "I have to be willing to stake everything and everyone."

"You do."

"But doesn't that make me another monster? The very thing I am trying to step away from? Testing on humans, using people on every level in the name of gain or progress…" I run out of words. This is not the revolution I had in mind.

"Have faith," whispers Tom2.

I crumble into a blubbering mess.

I either plough forward and risk it all in the name of change and progress…or I revert. I cancel all action and Lily returns to her exile, I play the dutiful R&R trophy and submissive mother, and Little Drummer and every subsequent baby is tested and tracked, eternally following the R&R's bidding. I cradle my stomach and rock myself until the lift doors open and Max steps out. He runs to me and wraps himself around me before he even asks what is wrong. Tom2 respectfully steps away and links to the Watchtower, allowing me time to collect myself. Through my sobs I tell Max the status of our dilemma and he kisses my forehead before pulling me back into a hug. He doesn't speak. There are no words. Certainly no answers. Only questions. Questions and consequences – none of which seem right.

FORTY-SEVEN

Lily and 257 join us just after dawn. We eat quickly and prepare to leave, but as I step outside into the picturesque garden I suddenly feel a longing to stay here. I imagine Max and me living in a little flint cottage with a garden filled with our own veg, growing old together in quiet harmony, far from the madding crowd and not looking back. How easy that option seems. Except I wouldn't truly be able to forget. Trash mountains are still being dealt with, nuclear waste still pollutes, species are still on the brink of destruction, and humans are still being tested on and dictated to. My mind cannot shut this out, not forever anyway. In my moment of musing, the end of the R&R mission statement comes to me. They made Max and me pledge ourselves to it months ago. I believe the words are correct, just not their current interpretation: *'…Our mission, an honour, outshines any sorrow that we might know. Our service is forever, lifelong, and without end. To Mother Nature, our hands, we lend.'* The past has made me – for richer or poorer – who I am. I want to be better, do better, so my future cannot be selfishly spent tucked away in a forgotten corner of the world – no matter how beautiful it might be.

As we reach the garden gate, Tom2 pauses. 257 watches him with a tense posture, but doesn't speak.

"What is it?" says Lily as she studies both Shepherds' body language. "Is something wrong?"

"Have you checked your private line since you left?" Tom2 asks 257.

"No, I didn't want to risk the signal tracking to me. Why?" 257 replies.

Tom2 opens his left palm, forming a globe hologram and Ezra's strained voice comes out: "257, I hope you get this. Lady Fairfax is here, at my door, beware, she—"

The message ends and I half squeal: "*She what?!*"

"It cuts off there. I have footage, do you—"

"YES!" We all call in unison. Tom2 nods and the hologram flicks into a video.

I instantly recognise the room as Ezra's Overseer booth under the radio station. Ezra is at his desk, he starts to speak to 257 as a woman storms in, flanked by two men. They grab Ezra, put a bag on his head, and drag him away.

Tom2 flicks the feed showing Ezra being dragged into the lift where a fourth person is waiting. Her hair isn't as tidy as normal, but it is unmistakably red...unmistakably Ella. Her face is blotchy and tired. I cannot decide if she is afraid, but she doesn't run, offer help, nor look surprised as Ezra is dragged kicking and screaming into the lift.

None of the three kidnappers seem bothered by her presence either. Ella taps something on her watch as the lift doors close and the realisation that she may have double-crossed us hits me like a brick and makes me want to vomit. I try to focus on the men's faces, but I do not know them, yet the woman I can clearly identify, even if my heart doesn't understand it. Lady Fairfax stands proud amongst the men, directing them and the lift as it travels south into the ground – to the R&R tunnels.

So many questions rage through me and I hear myself shouting louder as each one comes out: "What is Ella doing? What the hell does Lady Fairfax want with Ezra? And since when does she do her own dirty work? Or know about the Overseers?"

"The Arbitrator knows everything," replies Tom2 calmly.

"The Arb—what?" I feel my face screw up as I understand. "Lady Fairfax is the Arbitrator?!"

"She is."

"Why did you not mention this earlier? Why just call her by title? Surely her identity could have been helpful for me to know earlier?"

"You didn't ask."

I flap my arms in exasperation.

"Shepherds always name people by their title, that is why 257 always calls me *Lilith*," says Lily rolling her eyes whilst half smiling. "No matter how often I ask him to call me *Lily*."

"You could call it being respectful," 257 says dryly.

"I *could*…"

"Family dynasties are a messy business it would seem," Tom2 says, ignoring 257 and Lily. "I told you the Arbitrator was watching you. As you didn't ask, I assumed you knew who she was. From my observations *Lady Fairfax* has – at least in part – protected Eve over time: possibly out of guilt, but I think genuine familial loyalty comes into it as she owes much to her great aunt. Now Lady Fairfax sees the Director promoting her line – you. Most seem supportive of this and the vote obviously passed to include you and Max.

The Arbitrator voted 'for' but I wonder if she is not wholly convinced of your loyalty."

I suddenly remember standing in the lobby of the radio station, meeting Lady Fairfax in person. I knew then she was sizing me up, I just had no idea how important that calculation was. '*The UNE thrives on that very notion…every member playing their part…remembering the importance of their role,*' she said.

I must remember the importance of my role.

Never have truer words been said.

* * *

As we make our way through fields filled with the song of birds mixed with chirping crickets, we talk quietly about everything we have seen and heard – and what might be waiting for us on our return. Tom2 had tried to find us something specific, but meetings in our absence were apparently mundane and irrelevant so we are left guessing – which is rarely a good thing as my mind has the unhelpful tendency to slip to the worst-case options. Thankfully Max's demeanour is eternally more grounded and his methodical logic calms me enough to keep me from turning into a completely neurotic mess.

Lily is anxious for her fellow farm residents, fearing her sisters will be punished for our actions. To begin with I leave 257 to reassure her. He cannot show her live video until he fully switches his receiver back on, but his words do seem to settle her as she stops objecting to his answers of sense and reason. Suddenly Lily sighs and says: "I just don't want us to fail now and ruin the equilibrium we have fought so hard for."

"I understand," I almost whisper as my own doubts throttle my voice, "but we cannot doubt ourselves now. We do this for your sisters – for anyone wrongly pushed aside or imprisoned – for anyone who has been told or made to feel they are not enough, both now and in the future. The preservation out here…" I say spreading my arms wide and distracting myself as I startle a little bird that flies straight up in the air making a curious alarm call, "…the preservation out here is unquestionably right, but we also need to preserve our own humanity, which includes our sanity and sense of others as well as self. You and your sisters have every right to return and start the lives you should have been given in the first place – only better. That will—"

"Not happen," Lily cuts me off.

"What?"

"I'll not return to the Hub."

"You will. Eve sent me to rescue you, I must—"

Lily smiles seriously. "You have, you really have, but I—"

"Don't be defeated yet, I know we have an unknown hurdle ahead, but—"

"It's not that, Maia," Lily says, taking me by the hand. "I trust in our mission. I believe we will somehow pull this off. We've already come so far and we know that there are others in the UNE that are silently suffering. When they see we have broken the seal, I trust they will come forward and join us, just as Jay and 'The Silence,' his union, would have." Lily wipes a tear away. "*If* that union has been wiped out – we cannot know yet. Call it a wish, sixth-sense, or whatever, but the suppressed *will* rise."

"Then why do you doubt you'll be able to return to the Hub?" I ask.

"I don't doubt I will be *able*: I just won't do it," she says with determination, and even 257 stops and stares.

I furrow my brows quizzically, but it is Max that asks the question: "Why?"

"Because, despite whatever future you manage to carve out of the R&R's crappy cornerstone, no matter how bright and new it is, I no longer want to live there. The ghosts of Hub life will stay with me forever, for better and worse. My Jay is gone and can never come back. He is the only man I ever want. No—" she waves her hand at me as I open my mouth. "Don't tell me I am young and might change my mind. I won't. I miss my parents, but maybe future video calls to beyond can bridge that gap, uniting all citizens as they should be. But my parents are safe and that is all I need to know. My life is not with them any longer. And I am done hiding like I have dirty secrets – which even in a reformed Hub, I would have to do. I will not hide nor be the victim. Life must go forwards."

"Then what do you want?" I ask with a quivering voice.

Lily scoffs. "Would you believe I want to learn and graduate?" She chuckles while scuffing her foot in the grass. "Yeah, I know, who'd have thought it? But despite how monumentally shitty the path to where I am now was, I do see the point of the work beyond the fence as Ambassadors of Earth. I see why humans cannot, both in terms of personal and natural safety, just roam freely outside of Hubs, but I also see why some need to. I see why we are trained and pushed. Others need to continue to see the point and want to work beyond too, just without the pain my sisters and I have endured. I want—I want an open, honest, fulfilling, *free* life with my sisters, with nature…with 257."

Lily takes a deep breath as she waits for me to react. Max squeezes my hand – a simple, yet unmeasurably supportive and communicative action – and I understand. Finding a family, in whatever form it comes, is something to hold onto. I smile, letting the corner of my mouth curl upwards and my eyes soften with empathy as I say, "Okay then."

I look to 257 and think he has frozen. Lily nervously follows my gaze. "Are you sure?" 257 whispers with emotion. Something tells me he hadn't dared hope for this conclusion, even if it is what he wants the most.

"I am," Lily says with confidence.

257 closes the gap and silently hugs Lily. She wraps her little arms around his massive back and rests her face on his chest while he leans his chin on the top of her head.

Max tugs on my hand and we carry on walking, happy to give them a moment to take in what they have just decided is their 'next.' I cannot say I would make the same choice were I her, but that is the point. I am not Lily. Each person should have the framework to find their own path without condemnation and judgement. 257 and Lily, with their unique bond and friendship, whatever it is exactly, will not find anything other than love and friendship from us.

* * *

257 continues to guide us homeward, but isn't taking an identical path to the one we previously took. Instead we visited a new village – or maybe a small town, it was hard to say as very little is still intact in the area we walked into. Amongst the rubble and weeds 257 found and opened a garage, revealing another hovercraft. We promised Tom2 we would only take it as far as its standard jurisdiction and would then set it to autopilot to return to its base. Although I would like to use it for the whole journey, any assistance getting back faster is fine by me. I am increasingly impatient to get answers and to start actions that can only come once we return; however, my more immediate concern for speed is related to Little Drummer.

What I think are contractions have started to ripple through me and I really don't want to give birth out here. When I complained of cramps earlier, 257 tried to tell me I was experiencing 'Braxton hicks' – which he then proceeded to explain to me are false labour signs. I cut him short, telling him in no uncertain terms I know what Braxton hicks are… and silently hoped he was right.

That was a few hours ago and the pains have increased. Max keeps looking at me, almost audibly praying I don't go into labour as he clutches my sweaty palms, but now, as we all stand on the edge of the forest, watching the hovercraft return to its hideaway alone, I turn to Max and say: "You know I packed a summer dress in your bag?"

"Yes?" he replies curiously.

"I am going to need it."

"Why?"

"Because my waters just broke and I can't give birth in shorts."

FORTY-EIGHT

I knew labour wouldn't be a walk in the park, I just didn't realise it would happen while I walked through the woods. Each clump of trees seems to take longer and longer to get to and Max's face grows whiter with worry by the minute. I began by declaring I could manage, the contractions were sporadic and far apart, but as they became more regular, I grew less heroic and asked 257 to carry me. If nothing else, I am hoping the misdirected gravity will keep Little Drummer inside me and delay the demand of her beat to be obeyed.

I keep looking at Lily as we stride through the woods and wonder what she is thinking. She has tried to offer reassurance that all will be well, that 257 will get us home in time, but I can see the doubt in her face as well as Max's. My contractions are now less than every ten minutes and I remember enough from my birthing classes to know that when I get to five and under, no amount of positive energy is going to keep Little Drummer contained.

"Do you have 'how to be a midwife' on your system?" I ask 257 trying to sound flippant.

"I have everything on my system, but I have never put such information into practice," he replies.

"I've seen goats and sheep give birth… I'm guessing it is, erm, *similar*," Lily says coyly. "I know you're not a goat, but—"

"Close enough," I laugh and grimace at the same time as pain from a contraction hits me. "Do you all learn animal midwifery on the farm?"

"No, only those who want to major in livestock…which, I'm afraid, is not me."

"Well, it's not like you thought this would happen!" I snort.

"No, I didn't think babies were on my horizon in any form," Lily says, trying to hide her sadness.

"Did—" I stop myself, unsure if I should ask what I'm sure I already know, but Lily's eyes invite me to finish. "Did you want children?"

"Very much."

"That could still—"

"No," Lily cuts me off. "The possibility of being a mother is no longer on my path any more than you can choose *not* to be one. We must make our difference to this world from the roles we have been given. We can work together as a team – you and Max in your corner, 257 and I in ours."

I am again struck by the wisdom of Lily, young as she is. Eve would have been proud of her, even if she, as I do, laments the road to her wisdom. Neither the PTB nor R&R can or should take credit, but our pasts have made us stronger. Labour in the forest or not, we *will* revive and reset the revolution. My frustration and self-doubt come from failing to envision the shape of that reset. Every time I think I have it in my mind, something, or someone, makes me question if my ideal is the right one.

In an attempt to distract me, we chat on things to come, including Lily's hopes and studies. She asks more about my past and we compare notes on upbringing. The PTB educate all children the same, but they do not clone family nor character. That variable is key to forming the character of each child. Max describes his childhood, confiding in Lily quite how messed up his stepmother was and she listens in earnest. It is nothing short of a miracle that Max is the kind, considerate man that he is – he is the embodiment of true nature winning over nurture.

Mary would have had him out for self-gain and power, regardless of who he stepped on to get there. Her love was tainted with blood, manipulation, and lies. She would never step out to save others, not if it risked herself. No, her choices were not to be envied, and Henry – well, he may not have killed his wife, but he did align himself with her murderer to keep his son and promote his career.

Regret and misery followed…maybe they would have done anyway, even if he had been allowed to marry his childhood sweetheart…maybe Mary would have still turned sour and hateful. But maybe, had their nurture involved less dictation, then maybe they would have been better, happier people for it?

Maybe.

Of course, Max wouldn't have been born if that were the case. Henry, a 3, and Mary, a 1, would never have had children. Max's mum would have married another and he may or may not have been fertile…and so the *maybe's* carry on…

"257?" I say leaning back in his arms as he strides though the sun stroked trees.

"Yes?"

"Do you know the stats on a population not graded…or rather, not matched?"

"You mean allowed to choose their own marital partners?"

"Precisely."

"It has been a long time since that has been calculated. It is difficult to give an exact prediction due to the very lack of predictability. Without guidance and testing, there is no way of saying who will fall in love with who, who will remain fertile, who will produce fertile offspring, gender, health status, etc." 257 falls silent for a moment. "Do you mean with or without food controls?"

"Both…preferably without."

"So no food controls…no matching system…complete liberty of choice?"

"Yes. Would, in your rough calculations, the population increase, decrease, or potentially remain as it is in such a system?"

257 exhales deeply, or at least sounds like he does, even though his chest (which I am up against) doesn't move. Max and Lily stop walking, all three of us anxiously awaiting 257's opinion. "I cannot see an increase. I would not like to give a number or percentage at this point without full data access and analysis, but no, the population would not increase. Not with natural early menopause as well as those still born naturally infertile. The number of potentially fertile grade 2 citizens would increase, but they would have to choose a 3 to consistently have offspring. With intervention, a 2 and 2 would have approximately a 50:50 chance of reproduction."

"You're suggesting a different test…a *free* test, of nature and nurture?" Max asks.

"Yes," I say, smiling through a contraction. "Why not let Mother Nature rule herself?"

"Could humanity recover enough to increase population over time?" Lily asks.

"Possibly," I answer. "But not for a long, long time."

"And the odds of a significant increase are not impressive," 257 adds.

"Huh," says Lily.

"Huh, indeed," says Max.

"*Oh shit!*" I squeal through gritted teeth and all eyes turn to me in horror. "Put me down 257. *She's coming.*"

"We only have three and a half miles to the farm," 257 says, trying to sound reassuring.

"So that may be," I cry, "but the Drummer dictates my beat today and it is anything *but* little!"

FORTY-NINE

Exactly a month early, on 11th August 2124 at 14:57, shaded from the bright summer sun underneath an oak tree, with Max grasping my right hand and Lily clutching my left, 257 assisted Little Drummer into this world. I think I can safely assume that her birth is one of the most unique known to humankind, and although I wouldn't wish anyone to mimic this location, I also would not alter the identity of any of my companions.

As 257 passes Little Drummer to me, wrapped in the top I swapped for my summer dress, I see perfection. Miraculous, awe-inspiring, gut-wrenching, perfection – and I've never been more terrified. Max curls himself around me and we sit as an exhausted, sweaty, proud family of three for the first time. Little Drummer opens her dark brown eyes and wiggles her tiny fingers and toes, testing them out now that they are free of restraint. She instinctively curls her fingers around her father's finger and I feel him quake with emotion. It is a bizarre experience, way-beyond mere 'feeling,' to realise you want to protect this little creature with everything you have – especially when you thought you never wanted a child. Maybe I didn't, but life has given me this precious gift anyway and if my destiny is to work till I die to make a better life for her, then so be it.

257 suddenly grasps my wrist to take my pulse.

"What is it?" Max asks worriedly.

257 pulls off my bracelet, hands it to Lily and reaches to take Max's, too. "Lilith, once we're back, hide them outside the Hatchery somewhere. We'll deal with them later – they are no good to us now."

"What is it?" Max repeats as 257 reads my vitals on my Fitwatch app now that it is working properly.

"We need to get you to a doctor immediately," says 257 as he scoops me up. "No arguments, we must run."

I look over 257's shoulder and see Max's face drain of joy as 257 launches into a sprint. I clutch Little Drummer close to my chest, securing her from the sudden change of tempo, but I need not worry as 257 somehow manages speed and comfort simultaneously. Max grabs our bag as he and Lily chase after us.

"What is it?" I whisper to 257.

He doesn't alter his course, but he does sigh. "Your heart rate isn't right…I fear…" He doesn't attempt to finish his sentence, he doesn't need to. I understand.

"Is Little Drummer okay?" I ask.

"I believe so. It is harder for me to read her, she is only 36 weeks so a SurrogacyPod would be ideal for her protection. Hopefully she will not need one for long though."

"Is there one on the farm? I know no babies are born there—" I cut myself off, not wanting to think of possible complications if I don't get Little Drummer to a hospital and she needs one.

"There is. It gets very little use, but sometimes cadets are pregnant when they arrive so foetuses are…well, *removed* and escorted elsewhere."

Good grief! There are no words to respond politely to the implications of that sentence. I am glad of there being a SurrogacyPod nearer than the Central Hub and I nod to that piece of information. The rest I cannot cope with right now – I will just add that to the ever-growing list of 'things that must change.'

257 plays the Flight of the Bumblebee as we approach the FARM. It now seems an oddly comical soundtrack for our anxieties, but we have found something more to fear than the threat of armed drones, so only slow down momentarily as they fly immediately above us. It is possibly no surprise that even though both are physically fit, 257 is significantly faster than Max and Lily. Every now and again 257 pauses to take my pulse and check my watch. Each time he makes a tutting sound. The third time, I ask: "How bad is it?"

257 ignores me, instead he turns to Lily as she catches us up. "We're nearly there. I am sorry, we need to get to the Hatchery as fast as possible – going to the tram and up is slower…forgive me, but—"

"Do it," Lily says in earnest.

257 nods and we take a turn to the left through trees.

"Where are we going?" Max asks.

"Through the pasture, where 113 used to evict and effectively murder cadets," Lily says coldly.

"Ezra should have left it so I can access the gate from this side," 257 says. "Whatever has happened to him, he should have left this for us because we agreed this failsafe would be implemented as soon as we left."

"Should?!" Max puffs. "And if he didn't?"

"Then I either openly exceed my Shepherd jurisdiction, override code I shouldn't be able to, and deal with the results – or we go back the way we came. I calculate that the current circumstances make it worth choosing this option first."

I try not to consider the consequences he is calculating. I look down at the tiny human that has rocked everything. I focus on her little face, the shape of her nose, her chin – both of which have a miniature resemblance to her father, not me. Good. Let her inherit Max's looks and heart and none of the guilt that I have carried. For she will have nothing to feel guilty for.

Unlike my mother, I would never blame her birth on anything other than 'just because.' Her very being has powered the will for a new revolution and has given me a reason to live more fully, even if ultimately, I now die. I want to see her thrive and grow, to have the freedoms I never had, but if that isn't my path, for I am feeling increasingly weak, then I know Max will not falter and none of this will have been in vain.

Suddenly, a fence comes into view. A huge electric fence. There are two buildings, one much larger than the other, but both are adorned in flowers and shrubs, just the same as any in the Hub. The smaller one has a paddock in front of it (or behind, as we seem to be viewing it from the back) and 257 puts me down about twenty metres from the fence.

"Stay here, all of you. I need to test it."

"The fence electrocutes anyone that approaches it," Lily explains. She waves her right wrist with her watch on. "It reads this."

"Oh," Max says as he bends down to Little Drummer and me. "How are you doing, Honey?" I try to hide the desire to grimace behind a smile, but Max sees through it. "Hold on, you hear me? *Hold on*," Max's voice wobbles.

Despite feeling increasingly faint, I look up with relief as 257 opens the gate. "Max?"

"Hmm?" he says, covering my hands with his.

"You're my lighthouse through the fog," I say as tears well in my eyes. "Remember that, whatever happens. You gave me hope and love when I barely dared to look for it. Our daughter is the future: *come what may*."

Max fights back tears as he kisses me tenderly. Holding my cheeks in his hands he looks me straight in the eyes: "Come what may, together, Maia. *Always together*."

I nod and let the corner of my mouth curl upwards. Lily steps forward as 257 returns. His footsteps suddenly sound uncharacteristically heavy…or is my hearing just throbbing with his movement?

"You must go back to the Dorm," 257 says to Lily, "just like you've been released from donation."

"What?! I cannot leave you now!" Lily exclaims.

"You must. Whatever is coming next, I need minimal bodies to protect at once. If threatened, the R&R will see you, already a named convict, as the first to dispose of. I need you safe where they and their guns are not watching you. I must be the guardian of Maia and her baby first – just for now. You know I will come back for you?" He pauses, struggling, possibly for the first time, to find the words to fully convey his feelings. Despite the urgency of the moment, I cannot help noticing how human, how individual, how fundamentally *un*programmed 257 is. "Lilith—Lily, I will never—"

Lily grabs his hands: "I know, I know," she says squeezing. She turns to Max and me, hugs us affectionately and says: "This is not the end, just the beginning, stay safe, the revolution needs us all."

257 scoops me into his arms again and immediately heads towards the gate. He pauses when I call to Max, using the remnants of my energy to shout: "Take Little Drummer!"

Max looks at me anxiously as he claims and gently cradles our baby, but I feel a huge sense of relief seeing her out of my failing grip. 257 doesn't wait for further conversation, rushing us through the gates, across the grass, and through a door – by which time I am totally exhausted despite not taking a single step.

257 commands two doors, one seen and one hidden. Lily runs through the first, briefly turning for one last glance at us all before she steps out onto the farm once more. We take the second door and I sigh with relief as I perceive the aesthetics of an infirmary waiting room. Two slightly smaller, white Shepherds appear shouting questions at 257 but my adrenaline is not enough to keep me conscious. The last thing I hear is the gentle cooing sound of my daughter and Max calling my name.

FIFTY

It could be seen as funny, or at the very least ironic, that I am pleased to wake up in a hospital bed. I have always *hated* hospital beds. They are the summary of everything that is wrong with the PTB *and* R&R – the embodiment of enforced donation, testing, and general dictatorial compliance – all laid out into one clean, crisp, white bed.

Max is snoozing to my right in a chair, his face is worn with worry, but his strong, handsome features are a welcome sight for my eyes. I look in front of his chair and see a SurrogacyPod and smile. Little Drummer, like her father, is sleeping and her little chest happily rises and falls with each breath. I cannot read it, but I can see a glimmer of light from a digital monitor as it tracks her every movement. She looks safe and my heart swells with happiness. It is only for a moment, but in this moment, I forget the struggle of before and what may lie ahead. In this moment, we are all together, alive, and at peace.

Suddenly my left hand is gently lifted and I turn to see 257 and two white Shepherds. "Welcome back," says 257. "You gave us all a fright, but the Custodians—" He turns to his companions and waves his arm, encouraging them to approach. As they do, I see they have identical red symbols on their chests – the mark of the medic. "This is 365 and 247. You were bleeding internally, they saved you."

"Thank you," I whisper as overwhelming gratitude hits me.

"Our pleasure," says 365.

"Well, our duty," cuts in 247 anxiously. "The Oologist… the Curator…"

"Will *thank you* for saving one of their brightest prodigies," 257 says sternly.

"Indeed, indeed…and the baby. It is our honour to see a baby," coos 365.

"Is she okay?" I ask.

"Yes, yes, despite the premature birth, she is strong. She is fed…sorry we had to extract from you, but it was necessary. We don't even have goat colostrum at the moment. She needs 48 hours at least in her pod, maybe a week, but I do not foresee any long-term complications if she continues to do so well."

I nod in thanks as I cannot push the lump in my throat far enough to verbally reply. Max wakes up and I nearly burst into tears as he hugs me. Maybe I should cry, but what feels like an enormous knot inside me is holding everything in, possibly steeling me for what lies ahead.

"Are the R&R aware we're here?" I ask.

"They are," says 257. "The Custodians alerted them after your surgery and were instructed to notify them the moment you are conscious."

"Have you?"

365 bows her head apologetically. "We have."

I cannot run nor hide now. I cannot pretend I am the dutiful great granddaughter learning the ropes, hoping to mimic the legendary Director. In this moment, I feel more akin to the old Arbitrator, not the new, who I trust as little as everyone else in the R&R, but I want to call a vote. My aim is to cast the *deciding* vote. Which, given my current prostrate position, I'll admit is fairly arrogant, not to mention, highly improbable.

Eve seemed to have planned for everything, whether she was at the helm or not, she always had a trump card. And now I have her last one. I wiggle the fingers on my left hand, just checking it is still there, waiting for the time to be right.

"We must all play our part," I say to the room, but now turn to 257. "Whatever happens, stay with Little Drummer. You and Lily – do not let them take her from you, please, *whatever* happens."

257 watches me. His steel-grey exterior doesn't move, but I know he is looking at me. Finally tilts his head to Max, nods, and says: "Agreed." No lengthy protests or explanations. He accepts my request and I am comforted. Max laces his fingers with mine. We trust 257 with our most precious gift and even if we do not know if he can keep his promise, we know if he doesn't, it will not be from a lack of trying.

As my mind races from one idea to the next, another comes to me: "257, you must be the backup in all things. One person cannot be the only copy or key."

Max looks confused. "We will expand once we've—"

"No, in case the R&R try to erase me – in case they succeed at erasing me." Max grimaces at my words, but I know he understands. I turn to 257: "The Hand of the Shepherd is linked to me and cannot be removed by another, but can you clone or copy it?"

"Are you not worried I'll take over the world?" chuckles 257. "It has been suggested before…"

"You could have staged that coup long ago, but haven't. Some believe in guardian angels, rarely questioning whether they have any greater purpose than to protect and guide weary souls. Well, I believe you are mine – in a totally new, unexpected form, but no, I am not worried."

257 bows his head humbly. "Then I am honoured to be the backup of code. I will be the failsafe should our plan falter today." I look to Max, and he nods in agreement. "If I might make one 'extra' suggestion? For after?" says 257 quietly.

"Of course," I reply, "what is it?"

"I would like to reconsider avatar usage and the ability to wipe my siblings. No matter how necessary 113's removal was, I would like us to be spoken to through code, rather than overridden. I harbour no resentment, and Ezra is actually pretty considerate, but there is a difference between being spoken *to*, compared to *through*."

"Embrace and celebrate individually. Discuss and listen. And wherever possible, gently correct, not break those who genuinely error?" says Max thoughtfully. "What a beautiful ideal for all life."

Custodian 247 suddenly jolts and steps forward to check my monitor and intravenous bag. I am no medic, but I am eternally paranoid and do not attempt to hide my distrusting expression now. 257 notices and obviously shares my concern as he catches 247 by the arm. "What are you doing?"

"Checking her. Surely you know I would never harm a human?" 247 says defensively.

"Never," echoes 365.

"Yes, but you also follow all orders. What did you just receive?" 247 stands in silent defiance. Wasting no time, 257 pins him to the wall. "What. Order. Did. You. Just. Receive?"

My eyelids flutter and I suddenly don't need to wait for an answer.

365 cries out: "To prepare for Hub transfer! To make her sleep—"

"Did you just dope her?" 257 demands, still holding 247 against the wall with his feet swinging for purchase on the floor that is just out of reach.

"Not completely, you interrupted me," 247 grumbles.

I clench my fist under the sheets, digging my nails into my palm, trying to keep myself awake. 257 might have stopped 247 giving me a full dose, but I can definitely feel the effects. I don't want to risk leaving it any longer…I hope the Hand of the Shepherd can hear me and the first code does what Tom2 thinks it does: "When things go black, the light I lack, but I still have a vision. Of different times, when light shines, join me in my vision. So now go black, the revolution I sack, so listen to revision. The power is mine. Watch my light shine. I will not live in your contrition."

The lights flicker, but do not go off. The Custodians freeze as they absorb my words and 257 curiously watches their pacified reaction as part one of Eve's final code sinks in. I pull my left hand from under the sheets and release my grip. The underside of the glove vibrates against my skin. I have no idea how, but it does. I am guessing that means it worked… that it is primed, ready for me to complete my coup.

But first I need an audience.

"Who is coming from the R&R?" I ask.

"Only security personnel if you're not contained," 247 says calmly. "I'm sorry, I don't think we can stop them."

"Don't try," I reply smiling. "But I need the Board of Trustees, not security. How do I get them here too?"

The Custodians turn and extend their left palms to one another, 257 grabs them both and joins in a silent three-way conversation. Max and I look at each other, anxiously, excitedly, waiting. The Custodians chuckle as they step back, lowering their arms as 257 turns to me: "We will carry out the R&R order...for now."

"What? You want to knock Maia out again? She has only just come round!!" Max isn't amused.

"I know, but the Custodians have limited reach and I need to stay 'robotic'...so, if you want to maintain the element of surprise and get all the key people together – even if they think they are assembling to see you damned – you need to look captured and compliant..."

"Okay. Agreed." I say resolutely. "Our deal?" I reach out my hand to 257. He grips my left hand in his and I feel a warm glow between my fake and real skin as our pact is sealed.

"Do it," I say lying back, taking one last, long, look at my sleeping beauty.

FIFTY-ONE

I don't know what I expected to see when I woke up again. I suppose I didn't give myself long enough to think about it before I was knocked out. Wisely or not, I was very much in the mind of action, not procrastination. Now, as I awaken, I languish in that morning haze of forgetfulness a few seconds too long…not quite giving myself time to assess the contents of the room before it is plain for others to see that I am awake.

"Ah, finally," says a familiar voice. The voice of comfort and betrayal. Secrets and lies – mine, but mostly hers. Gee-Gee. As my vision sharpens I see her standing at the foot of my bed. To my surprise, I am in the same bed as before…and in the same room. Only now it simultaneously seems larger and smaller than I remembered. Larger, because it is a well-proportioned room: smaller, because of the number of people and drones that are crammed into it.

Max is being held in the far-right corner by two guards with armed drones pointing at him. He looks angry and frustrated – I am pretty sure he didn't go to that corner quietly. I want to scream, but I am not sure my voice has yet returned with my consciousness and my gut tells me to survey before I react. Analyse all the players before I roll my dice.

Little Drummer's SurrogacyPod has been pulled away from me and is now in the far-left corner with 257 motionlessly standing against the wall. I would like to say he is on guard next to her, but truthfully, I fear they have done something to him as he looks completely inanimate.

Two more guards stand in front of them, with another four-armed drones hovering above – all of which are facing me. So many guards for one man, one woman who just had surgery, and a baby. I am pretty sure the guards are just some of Gee-Gee's trusted lackies, yet by her side is Mark Jones, Head of Security. The man who months ago saved my life, and now here he is, commanding his officers, human and drone, to point their weapons at me and my loved ones. I would laugh if it wasn't so serious.

Maybe I should laugh anyway. However, all mirth vanishes when I see Dr Oldman and Lady Fairfax standing to the left of my bed. Now I want to spit and demand to know what she has done with my friends. I shudder as I recall the footage of Ezra being dragged away. I am desperate to know who betrayed who. Did she find Ella or vice versa? I will not ask now. I will not say anything. I must wait, for my timing must be right, if at all.

No, the time for the option of 'Plan A' or 'Plan B' has passed. The idea of a quiet entrance into the R&R headquarters and requesting – or even demanding – a Board meeting has well and truly gone.

Had I not gone into labour, maybe.

But I did.

And I am here, in bed, with stitches – and a baby.

So, there is no point lamenting the options I *don't* have… although I *will* fret over the one that is left to me.

Knowing I must be the monster to defeat the monster is a horrible concept. I have to calculate how long I can risk shutting off everything to make my point without killing or damaging innocent people. How will anyone rally to my cause – my so-called *liberation of society* – if I let their family members die on operating tables, or cause brain-damage or death in SurrogacyPods? How would I ever look Kate in the eye again if I snatch away her chance at motherhood? How will I live with myself if I switch off the power and my own child suffers? For there she is, sleeping, happily-oblivious to the danger around her. The threats from all corners. The threats from me, her mother. She may not die…but she might. She may not be damaged…but she might. The Custodians didn't put her in the SurrogacyPod out of amusement. They detected genuine need. And to take control, I must deny her needs.

I am a monster.

If you cannot beat them, join them. Isn't that what I once decided?

The choice of exile and the AIP wasn't attractive. I would have lost everything. Though now I know the AIP is actually FARM, and although still a breeding programme, it is also a one-way university. Unlimited education for life outside the Hub, encouragement to reach full potential, with no family expectation. No children, siblings, grandparents…no husband. A year ago, I could have taken that choice with few regrets – for a while at least. But now my heart and eyes are opened, and I hate even the fleeting thought that the ideals of the FARM programme have any benefits. It is a huge testament to Lily's character that she has been able to see anything worth salvaging, but that is for *after*, not *during*. For during the time on the farm, the point is as despicable and selfish as any other of the R&R Fertility Projects. They have made us into hamsters running in their unholy treadmills. No animal or human deserves such treatment. There is no justification for *any* of this. Earth must be saved, just not like this.

If you cannot beat them, join them…*until you can beat them*.

Gee-Gee has started giving me a speech on her disappointment, but I am so lost in my own thoughts, I have not responded to hers. In fact, I am barely registering hers.

"Maia! Are you listening to me?" Gee-Gee switches from her director voice to her angry great grandmother voice. Some might think it is the same, yet I can tell the difference. "You are a mother now. Look at her – that is your daughter! You risked her life. For what? A senseless field trip with your husband and an android you hacked?"

I try to keep a poker face. She is talking like she knows why and how I went beyond the fence. Has she come to her own conclusions or been misled by another? Could she be covering for me? Or has Max said something I have not heard? I don't dare look at him now to ask in any form of communication because Gee-Gee and her companions are watching my every movement, examining my reactions, looking for the tiniest twitch of my eyebrows or curl of my toes. Anything to suggest or expose a lie – or a truth.

"Have you nothing to say?" Gee-Gee runs her hand over the top of her pristine grey hair. "No apology, no plea?"

"I would like to address the Board," I say humbly. "For my actions affect and concern them all." I keep my head low but set my eyes on Gee-Gee. My heart feels heavy doing it, but I will tug on her heartstrings as long and loud as I can.

Gee-Gee looks between Lady Fairfax, Mark, and Dr Oldman before nodding to a man to her left – a man I have barely registered as being present until now due to him being tucked into the open doorway. As he steps forward, I see the Custodians peering in from the corridor, but I focus on the man, squinting my eyes as I try to place him. He is wearing black trousers and a grey shirt, but suddenly an image of a purple coat comes to mind…a man serving Gee-Gee drinks in her office…

"The tea boy?" I ask incredulously without thinking.

He turns to me and scowls, but doesn't speak, instead he lays a briefcase on the bed by my feet, opens it, and switches on a projector. "Jack has many talents…IT being one," snipes Gee-Gee. *Okay, not 'just' a tea boy then…*

The standard globe appears, and the Board of Trustees materialises around the foot of my bed. I fidget with my bedspread from underneath and shift my weight to appear like I am seeking a clearer view of the figures around me. They had obviously already been summoned, ready to vote on our punishment, but looking at them, only half are in their work offices – I believe some have been dragged out of bed especially for the occasion. I cannot say I am sorry.

They start talking to one another. Not one of them asks me for any details. No one seems to question where I have been. Only that Max and I are reckless, inconsiderate of their rules, and unnecessarily risked our child.

"Ladies and Gentlemen of the Board, will you not hear me first?" I ask.

379

"What do you have to say?" asks Lady Fairfax in a flat, nonchalant tone. It is the first thing she has said in my hearing today. I wonder if she is aware I know she is the Arbitrator. No one else seems surprised to see her face, though I have no idea if it is distorted for those viewing remotely. Either way, her short sentence is enough to calm the hecklers: "Proceed."

"Thank you," I say with a curt nod that she doesn't return. "I wish to discuss the revision of order within the UNE. Specifically the R&R, but not limited to. You have all made decisions you felt right over time, I am sure Earth thanks you, generations of humanity and wildlife, thank you, but the old ways must give way to the new. Little Drummer – our daughter – must see a new, revitalized, morally balanced order—"

"She is power-hungry, look at her!" declares a red-faced holographic man in a dark grey suit, waving his arms in a tantrum. "Our respect for the Director has left us open to *this* – this wanton disregard for everything we hold dear! Everything we have worked and sacrificed for! I am sorry Director, but she cannot stay now. She has proven herself unworthy and dragged her husband into the mud with her. *They must both go.*"

The room is filled with the echo of 'unworthy' as the Board agrees. Gee-Gee doesn't agree or disagree – but the lack of words from her is as damning as the abundant.

"I am not asking," I angrily state as I clench my fist again under the sheets. No one takes any notice of me as they embellish their conclusion of me being thoroughly useless and unworthy.

380

Dr Oldman addresses Professor Millar: "Curator, we could harvest them both and turn them out – they're a security risk anywhere now. They simply know too much. Best collect data and move on." How quickly I am turned into meat in his eyes! One minute I am a brilliant understudy, the future of their organisation, the next I am a cautionary tale alongside some cells in a petri dish. "We have offspring – all need not be lost."

Max loses his usual calm and swears profusely at Dr Oldman. One of the guard's thumps Max in the guts and he doubles over. "Enough," says Mark waving his hand. "Drones," he says tapping on his watch and instantly red dots appear on Max's forehead and chest.

I want to scream…or be sick…or both.

I dare to glance at Max and he mouths 'I love you.' I instantly take strength in the reminder that we are one in this fight and tell him I love him too, but then quickly force myself to turn away – for looking means observing the drone lasers and if I fail, they will shoot him first. That cannot be the last thing I see.

The meeting continues as though nothing happened. How quickly these people forget violence in the name of order and progress! As I lay here, deciding when to act, knowing I might also have to witness my baby being harmed by a lack of power, I realise all eyes are forward *on me*. I look to 257 – who hasn't moved an inch since I woke up – hoping for a sign of life.

"Your baby cannot help you," snorts a female Trustee, who looks worryingly similar to Mary Rivers – just thirty years older. "Traitor. The greatness you have been offered –

what you have given up – you make me sick. You have the audacity to sit there and tell us you want a new order when you cannot follow a rule so simple as to keep inside the Hub! The damage you could have caused is mind-blowing! Your child will be better off without you. You have failed us all miserably!"

My heart does yearn for my child – both to physically hold her and for her safety – and the Trustee's words do mentally sting and cut me, making me want to lash out with fiery venom, but I also surprisingly take comfort from her hateful speech. They are all too blind to see 257 as anything other than an object to control, so none of them consider the possibility that I am looking at him, not my child. They are no friend, but 257 is. And now I turn to that friend for his guidance, just as Eve told me to. *'Let 257 be your Shepherd,'* she said.

I hope he is still there…

He is free…his battery is self-contained…

Yet he is statuesque…

Did Jack somehow hack into him?

A hand twitches.

My soul leaps.

My stomach knots, but my voice rises to the occasion: "The rules of the righteous revolution require a review of the right to reign. I hereby challenge those in power and the power, I do claim."

R&R officials around the globe gasp as drones instantly disarm, all the artificial lighting goes out, our watches for the first time are entirely dark, and holograms disappear. Only the pre-dawn light saves the room from total darkness as it reflects through the windows. I look to the SurrogacyPod as it continues to function, as 257's guiding hand shares his strength to my newborn babe. Relief washes over me, but only for a moment as I remember there are more precious infants that do not have their own bodyguard. In the same moment I hear all the drones turn and approach me. Their normally red lasers flash to green and in the semi-darkness they join together and say: "Mother."

In one day, I have profoundly fulfilled the meaning of my name, becoming a mother to my newborn daughter *and* a nation of robotics.

An army of robotics if need be.

An army that cannot be switched off or destroyed – for while one rests, one is charged…and should one be knocked down, ten more can be rebuilt.

I am their mother, and they will obey.

Not bad for someone who never wanted to be a mother.

I wonder if this is what my mum had in mind when she named me?

Probably not.

FIFTY-TWO

"Maia, what the hell have you done?!" Gee-Gee whispers in a hushed tone that somehow combines fear, reverence, confusion, and anger.

I would like to revel in this moment, but I am unbearably conscious of time as 257 estimated I had seconds, not minutes, if I want my impact on the innocent to be minimal. "If the R&R will not listen to gentle reason, I will take charge by force. You are all as useless as a newborn rat without technology, well, now I hold the power to it all. *All of it.*" I don't even recognise my own voice, it is like someone else is speaking for me. Someone confident, someone free. A leader. Just as Eve said. The leader within I did not want to find, but with a little – no, a lot – of help from my friends, this world will spin without the weight of testing and unbridled oppression over the many by the few.

I unclench my fist and a globe spins freely in my hand. I can see Gee-Gee and her companions staring in confusion, but I do not stop to explain. I flick the globe, controls come up – far more than I know what the heck to do with, but I know the basics, I know it listens to my voice and reads my pulse and skin.

Maybe it can identify 'me' better than I can.

I simply say: "Reboot," and all power returns.

Hopefully in time to leave no one permanently damaged, but long enough to make my point.

Everyone blinks as the lights ping back on. I glance at Max, he is beaming with pride as he strides towards me. His guards simply watch him go as if they too are robotic and under my spell. However, they are just stunned humans, totally baffled by the idea that anyone might be able to alter the regime. 257 pushes Little Drummer's pod towards us, only stopping when she is back next to my bed, where she should be. As if she approves of the repositioning, Little Drummer gurgles and waves her arms. I feel overwhelmed with love and responsibility knowing I must care for this little creature, but I push that aside for a moment and look up at my audience, both physical and holographic and say: "I'd like to call a formal meeting. Are you all now ready to listen?"

"It hardly seems like we have a choice," grumbles Dr Oldman.

I want to hit him (not just for his tone now, the feeling has haunted me for a long time), but I ignore him. Instead I sit myself as straight as nature will allow in this bed, ignoring the pain in my stomach, and I address the Board of Trustees: "The efforts to restore Mother Nature to her rightful state are admirable, correct, and essential. I have only seen a tiny fraction of the damage our ancestors inflicted on this land, but I can see the scars and Earth still bleeds as a result. Our work beyond must and shall continue. We must never lose sight of the importance of the balance of life, our position in the hierarchy of life, and our great burden and responsibility to protect, respect, and preserve *all* life – not just those who appeal to us or do not get in our way. As Guardians of Earth we have no greater right than any other species, but we also have no greater responsibility than the one to continuously strive to do better. Beyond the fence, I applaud your efforts; however, in your quest to restore balance, you have also lost it. Your rule is fundamentally flawed—"

"How so?" cuts in Gee-Gee. "Neither you, nor anyone else here knows what it is to be hungry or homeless, cold or alone. That is because of *us*, what we *did*, what we continue *to do*. No child is uneducated, none have more or less, they are raised together, equally—"

"Under a dictatorship!"

"Maybe, but also in safety, with clean air and the fewest conditions and diseases ever known to humanity. Our controls are—"

"Too tight," I cut in. "Control may be essential, but not at the expense of individual spirit and choice – the right to be both responsible *and* happy. To choose a career, to choose a life partner *or* to be matched, to eat untampered food, to have children *or not*, to donate *or not*. The list goes on. You cannot so unequivocally remove choice."

"We will be swamped. If left, Earth – the planet you are so keen to respect – will be swamped again if people have choice in the way you are describing. Have you learnt nothing from your history lessons?" declares Professor Millar from behind his regal desk across the ocean.

"Have you?" I retort. "And you are wrong, the population will not explode with choice. It will *decrease* to begin with, then in time, it will settle into its own, natural, *unpredictable* rhythm." I stare at Dr Oldman as I can see he wants to protest. The joy of predictable results is what gets him up in the morning – to him variety is anything *but* the spice of life. "The R&R structure may have been necessary when the PTB formed after The Fall of What Was – I wasn't there, nor were most of you, certainly not at the beginning – but yes, I have studied the past and I know the world was a dangerous, messed up place in need of severe change in order to survive. I could still argue the line of *necessary* and *not* was crossed, but we cannot change those choices and what's important now is the choices we make *now*. For now people must be given a chance—"

"A chance to fail?" Gee-Gee grimaces.

"No, a chance to *succeed*. Stop using the word 'fail.' Give people the building blocks and guidance to do better. Set up them to succeed. Listen to the opinions and points of view of others as well as yourselves. You are not the only ones with wisdom!" I sigh. "A wise woman taught me to look for the light when standing in the fog."

My voice threatens to crackle as I think of Eve, but it is a muffled chuckle that interrupts my rhythm. I follow the sound and look straight at Lady Fairfax. She is smiling. To my amazement it is not patronising or dismissive, it is – or it certainly looks – *proud.* Her eye twinkles as she speaks: "I don't know about you all, but I have been wondering, waiting, for one to come along and challenge our way – to truly test our rule. It happens in every civilisation, sometimes the old buckles to the new, sometimes the new falls to the old, but someone always falls. War breaks out and blood is spilt…the planet we live and rely on suffers. Maia is right, our mission does need a refresh. How about we do it without covering the land in more toxins and save our souls to boot?"

Muttering and murmuring rumbles as people confer. I stare at Lady Fairfax. I had been secretly planning ways to corner her as a priority…and here she is – my first convert?

"What is there to stop us just killing you and snuffing out your tiny rebellion?" asks the Curator after a moment's pause. "Your blackout was impressive, sure, but we can gloss over that, we can gloss over you, your husband—"

"You cannot gloss over me," says 257 firmly.

"Don't be ridiculous," says Jack, Gee-Gee's tech/tea guy. "You can be overwritten easily."

"No, he cannot," says Lady Fairfax.

"Arbitrator?" says Jack, "With respect, Milady, he can—"

"No, he cannot," Lady Fairfax repeats slowly. "Our new Head Overseer and my granddaughter have just both reliably informed me he is un-wipeable. All Shepherds are actually pretty difficult to alter, but—" Jack attempts to butt in and she shuts him down with a curt wave and says: "Listen boy, for this news is quite new. You thought you'd commanded him now, but you hadn't. Our *friend* here is disconnected from the network, as well as connected."

Jack scoffs. "That is ridiculous. Not only is that not possible, but that would also make him totally independent, a sentient being, a—"

Lady Fairfax raises her eyebrows. "Yes, a species of his own, with just as many rights, and the ability to continue the blackout if you kill Maia. How do you think he kept operating when all else switched off just now?"

"A trick? Maia programmed it—"

"There is a fine line between ignorance and stupidity," spits Max. "You have crossed it."

The room falls silent.

I look to Lady Fairfax, my unexpected advocate, narrowing my eyes and she meets my gaze.

"Your friends are fine," she says smiling.

"How is that possible with a bag on your head?" Max says, sneering, but Lady Fairfax remains calm as she replies.

"You like to study genetics, Maia, well I have paid attention too. Particularly to an older study on inherited traits. Red hair isn't the only thing my family has passed on. Many a technician and engineer have been bred from my line – well, Eve and Tom's line, but also my grandfather's. Frozen eggs transplanted here and there across the globe. I looked for some and found Ella. The results are quite fascinating."

"Does she know?" I ask cautiously.

"Now she does. I was watching her as well as you. A link between Eve and the Director could not be ignored, though neither could my respect for one of our founders, my bloodline. My relationship with my great aunt may have been cut off, but I remember what I – what we – owe her."

"And so you took Ezra," Max groans.

"Yes, to assist covering your tracks when I learnt of your successful tram ride – if you'll excuse the pun."

"Arbitrator?" Dr Oldman cannot break out of habit and call her Lady Fairfax. "Are you saying you helped this… this…display of treachery?!"

"I stopped the R&R looking for more than a rogue IT guy until I saw what the result would be…*yes*."

"And now you've seen?" I ask cautiously.

"I think I am ready to vote."

"Well I am not!" shouts Professor Millar and others join him. I suppose I shouldn't be surprised they are not willing to release their grip of absolute power so easily. "This girl is proposing to doom us all and flood the world with people again...all for some misplaced ideal of nobility!"

"Said the man who has lost nothing to gain and control everything," I counter. For every demon wants his pound of flesh without paying a penny. Well I am willing to pay. I am done carrying their guilt for daring to have independent thought. I was blinded by them and believed that I was in the wrong. But now I will shake off their darkness, shut out their dismissive words and lay out my thoughts: "And before you protest again that my plan will overpopulate the world, stop being so short sighted and *think*. The fertile may not choose to marry the fertile, they may not choose to donate – or the infertile may not choose to adopt. Let a 3 marry a 0 if that is what their heart desires. Let a woman work or not. Let a young man or woman donate once, twice, or not at all. Be open to the opinions and dreams of others. That doesn't mean jetting all over a nuclear waste land, increasing waste or damaging fragile ecosystems. The choice and greed of man may have been its downfall before, but with education and care, it does not need to be again. Earth will not suffer again. Let nature be free to nurture us all – and study that instead. Nurture the minds and bodies of everyone, not the select few. Even if the population dips, options can be offered. Individual people can grow up, can wake up, and know there is a path for *them*.

"There are no misfits. No one needs to feel the way is too much or their value too low. Life is as rich and varied as they are. If people want to dedicate their lives beyond the fence, to study and be Ambassadors of Earth, let them. Celebrate them. Honour their service to the greater good. Do not exile or reject them as failed nothings or enforce celibacy – and certainly do not test on them and use their parts and children for whatever research you, the tiny, selfish, minority have declared 'of interest.'

"Let punishment fit the crime. Of course, there needs to be consequences for serious breaks of law, but for those of you who are confused, *love* is not one of them. Guilt and failure have been your pillars for education for too long. You, and you alone, should be ashamed. You live in the shadows and call yourself the light. Well not any longer, I—*we*, are going to open the doors and let real, unsheathed light in. One day I hope you will thank me."

I stop, waiting for someone to object, but no one speaks. I don't know if they are considering what I am saying and agreeing or simply thinking of ways to quash my rebellion. My heart races, but my resolve stands firm. The memory of 257's warm touch tingles in my fingers. He will finish what we started, he will support and guide. He and Lily are, and will continue to be, the ultimate ambassadors of what is possible with an open heart and eyes. Life beyond *and* within the fence is better thanks to them. Thanks to love and friendship – a vision for more than oneself.

I turn to Gee-Gee, the woman I have admired since I was the one in the cradle. I am sorry to cause her any pain, for I know, deep down, any pain she has caused me has been unwittingly – or at least reluctantly, done. But now the future must be met, no matter how scary it might be.

"I may not have seen what was, but I see what *is*. Gee-Gee, you told me you wanted me to be the next generation of the R&R, to continue your hard work, building up, not down. That is exactly what I am proposing. I cannot renounce the past without causing a riot, but neither will I blindly follow the old rule. Call it a new development, an advance in testing, scientific breakthrough, or whatever you like, but the revelation of a new revolution starts now. The opening *up* of choice within our boundaries. Not absolute freedom, but the gift of choice and freedom of expression. Let go of the reins and give chance and choice their time in the sun… A new path stretches before us and I want you all to embrace it. A new day *is* dawning. The sun will flood in and clear the fog of yesterday, bringing with it a new age for everyone, starting with my daughter."

"The daughter you haven't even named?" Gee-Gee says half mockingly. "Or are you really planning on calling your daughter of this new age 'Little Drummer'?"

"Dancing to her beat wouldn't be the worst thing," I say smiling as I see pride creeping into Gee-Gee's tearful eyes. Change never comes easily, but that doesn't mean it is entirely unwelcome. "But, actually, we have named her."

"Oh?"

I look to Max and see the sunrise reflecting in his eyes as he gently nods in unity.

"Her name is Alba."

"Alba? That's beautiful. What does that mean?"

"Dawn."

BOOKS IN ORDER OF TRILOGY:

THE MINORITY RULE

THE MINORITY RULE:
BEYOND THE FENCE

THE MINORITY RULE:
INTO THE FOG

ALEXIA MUELLE-RUSHBROOK

Alexia Muelle-Rushbrook is a sci-fi and fantasy author who was born and raised in rural Suffolk, UK. Having lived and worked with animals all of her life, she has a passion for the natural world as well as an interest in genetics. Never really fitting the 'norm' as a teen or adult, Alexia has always found solace in books as well as in her own storytelling. She enjoys a variety of genres, but has always had a firm love of all things sci-fi and fantasy. Although she had thought about writing a novel for many years, it wasn't until she was inspired to write poetry based on her love of terriers that she finally found the courage to put pen to paper for her debut novel, The Minority Rule. That standalone story quickly became a trilogy and Alexia has plans for other works in the future.

You can follow Alexia via social media or her website www. alexiamuellerushbrook.co.uk.
Sign up to her newsletter for updates on forthcoming works.

Have you read Alexia's work and want to share your thoughts? Any reviews on Amazon or Goodreads are very gratefully received.

ACKNOWLEDGEMENTS

At the risk of repeating myself for a third time, there are some consistent, but very much appreciated people that I must thank here.

My loyal beta readers, Kerry, Lucia, Roxanne, and Stephanie – your continued support, feedback, edits, and eagerness to champion my trilogy means everything to me.

Anna and Paul – I send you an enormous, heartfelt thanks for your unwavering support, reading drafts, suggesting edits, and promoting the finished works. Much love to you both.

Miguel – you have cheered me on throughout the trilogy, providing invaluable assistance and edits along the way and I am so grateful.

Belle Manuel and Jessica Netzke, my brilliant editors, thank you for polishing my manuscript with joy.

Richell, my cover designer and typesetter – I said wow before, I will have to say it again. You took my rough concept and brought it to life.

Sergio, my husband, you have undoubtedly and unfalteringly been beside me for this trilogy. Your encouragement pushed me to stop procrastinating and just write in the first place. You are and always will be the person I want to share my first draft with, who bounces ideas with me, and stands with me on my preferred side of eccentric. Thank you, my love – here's to the next book!

Printed in Great Britain
by Amazon

23105046R00229